TWO NOVELS OF THE MEXICAN REVOLUTION

TWO NOVELS OF THE MEXICAN REVOLUTION:

THE TRIALS OF A RESPECTABLE FAMILY

and

THE UNDERDOGS

by

Mariano Azuela

translated by
Frances Kellam Hendricks
and
Beatrice Berler

Principia Press of Trinity University
San Antonio, Texas
1963

CONTENTS

Typeset by Linden Print Shop, Linden, Indiana
Printed by Litho Press, Inc., San Antonio, Texas

PREFACE

The temerity of those who attempt translation is signal. Some contend that at its best a translation is an apology. Others say that to be beautiful it cannot be true; to be true it cannot be beautiful. We make no effort to challenge these or other judgments about the inadequacy of a translation. We hold, however, that the fascination of the task outweighs the possible inadequacies of the production. For us the rewards have been much greater than the frustrations. We offer our English version of two novels of the Mexican Revolution by Dr. Mariano Azuela, *The Trials of a Respectable Family* and *The Underdogs*, in the hope that it will bring to the attention of a new public the vigorous and perceptive works of that eminent figure of Mexican literary history. We have tried to convey faithfully his meaning without wholly losing the flavor of his style and the effectiveness of his presentation.

In disregard of current literary fashion in Mexico, Azuela in *The Underdogs* made use of the speech of the people of the region as his sensitive ear caught it. His use of the vernacular is vivid and expressive but poses problems in translation for which we found no entirely satisfactory solution. We decided to use the broken, elliptical, clipped style of the dialogues without attempting to put bad Spanish into bad English. We have been sparing with English colloquialisms for fear they would sound out of character. We have supplied no expletives not in the original. In the effort to convey some measure of Azuela's style we have kept wherever possible his figures of speech and unusual turns of phrase. We have chosen to use Azuela's spelling of names and to retain in Spanish various appellations for which there is no exact English equivalent and the nicknames of several of the characters. *The Trials of a Respectable Family* presented its particular problems in the intricate descriptive passages and figures of speech, the numerous *mexicanismos*, unusual use of words, and involved constructions.

Our warm and heartfelt thanks are due many who have helped us. Among them are *Lic.* Salvador Azuela and *Lic.* Enrique Azuela of México, D. F., sons of the author; also Mr. Joel Quiñones, Sr. and Mr. Rómulo Mungía, Sr. of San Antonio, Texas. Our principal obligation is to *Sr.* Enrique Ruíz F., México, D. F., who carefully read our manuscript. Through his extensive knowledge of both languages he saved us many errors and provided us with insight into

TxSar

PREFACE

the meaning of many *mexicanismos*. It goes without saying that any errors remaining are our own. That many have been willing to aid us is a tribute to the author of the works here presented.

FRANCES KELLAM HENDRICKS
BEATRICE BERLER

San Antonio, Texas
1963

PROLOGUE

Influence of Émile Zola on Mariano Azuela

by

SALVADOR AZUELA

My father, Mariano Azuela, felt profoundly the influence of Émile Zola's works. The news of the accidental death of the great French author distressed him deeply. On account of the fact that my father had formed a great admiration for the man as well as his works, Zola became a familiar figure to me from the time of my childhood. In the room in which the author of *The Underdogs* carried on his work, a picture of Zola presided over the daily tasks. It was a representation of him in his later years, showing the head of a powerful, indefatigable intellectual worker. A fringe of hair silvered by time surrounded his bald head. His beard, trimmed in the style of the times, gave him the appearance of any ordinary sort of man—notary, office worker, businessman.

Mariano Azuela did not profess Zola's doctrine of "experimental naturalism," nor did he think the novel should be treated as means for the scientific enlightenment of people. Azuela took from him, however, the lesson of vitality which overflowed his works of magnificent proportions formed like a series of great murals in which the author revealed his love of people and his repugnance for all he considered sophisticated.

Zola's influence was definitive in awakening Azuela's literary vocation. On the occasion of any reference to the French author, Azuela spoke with warmth of the one he considered his teacher and source of inspiration. In notes left by Azuela made in preparation for a lecture he expected to give at the National College on the occasion of the fiftieth anniversary of the death of that man of integrity, my father told how virulent attacks in *The Lantern of Diogenes*, a newspaper of Guadalajara where he was a student, had filled him with curiosity about him who had hurled the famous "*J'accuse.*" His first contact with Zola's works through his reading of *La Bête Humaine* filled him with aversion. But as he continued to read his books he devoured them with increasing admiration.

PROLOGUE

Azuela preserved his copies of Zola's works bound in red. They held singular emotional value for him. Although he was a student with modest resources, he made sacrifices to buy them one by one. To obtain each new volume as it appeared in Guadalajara he used a portion of the scanty monthly allowance which my grndmother sent him from Lagos de Moreno for the continuation of his studies. Even in his last days, *Germinal, Le Débâcle,* and *La Faute de l'Abbé Mouret* still aroused in him his youthful enthusiasm.

When Azuela began the practice of medicine in his native city of Lagos de Moreno, Jalisco, he often talked about Zola with his friends, especially the poet, José Becerra. The hate which the French writer aroused in Azuela's friends provoked his indignation. Also, he told me, he suffered painful distress on learning of the protest resulting from Zola's presence at the funeral of his comrade, the gentle Alphonse Daudet. Indeed the French fighter's destiny was a light for my father. Often when I was a child he recounted to me the incidents occurring in Paris following Zola's death. Though newspapers which had opposed his political and social thoughts hurled the vilest insults at his memory, a great, silent, solemn throng of working people, intellectuals, and artists followed his coffin.

At the end of 1914, my father had gone to Guadalajara at the orders of Julián Medina to become head of the education department of the State Government. In that city a group of restless and active young men formed the *"Centro Bohemio."* Among them were Manuel Martínez Valadez, Juan de Dios Robledo, José G. Zuno, and Alfredo Romo. Soon Azuela joined the group. When the members invited him to give a lecture, he began to set down a series of notes about Zola. Before he was able to complete his work, however, the city fell into the hands of the troops of Manuel M. Diéguez.

In spite of the new literary vogue appearing after Zola's death and continuing for many years, Azuela retained his admiration for Zola's works without, however, denying the defects of naturalism. Azuela had the joy of promoting the literary revival of Zola which Henri Barbusse in his work, *Le Feu,* initiated by his re-evaluation of the novel, *Le Débâcle,* the chronicle of the French people during the War of 1870.

I was sent in July, 1947, as an envoy of the *Secretaría Educación Pública* to a conference of UNESCO in Paris. I received only one directive from my father: that I visit Zola's tomb. One memorable

PROLOGUE

morning I carried out his injuction. As I walked around the Pantheon, I was delighted with the transparency and spirituality of the frescoes by Puvis and Chavanne. Then I descended into the crypt where lie the tombs of Victor Hugo and Émile Zola.

Death took Mariano Azuela as he was preparing a lecture for presentation at ceremonies commemorating the fiftieth anniversary of the great master. So intense was his fervor for him that Azuela, a few months before his death, on hearing the expression of a scornful opinion of the French author, arose vigorously to his defense. He saw Zola as a romanticist in the exuberance of his fantasy, in the epic manner of his conversion of multitudes of events and persons into narrative form, and in the creative force which transformed reality seen through the temperament of an artist who was always an exemplary citizen.

Excerpts from

MARIANO AZUELA, Life and Works

by

LUIS LEAL

Dr. Luis Leal, Professor of Hispanic-American literature at the University of Illinois, is a dedicated authority on Mexican literature who has written many articles and books. He graciously permitted Beatrice Berler to make the translation of the following excerpts from his work on Azuela, published by Ediciones de Andrea, Colección Studium, Vol. XXX, México D. F., México, 1961.

Mariano Azuela, son of Don Evaristo Azuela and Doña Paulina González, was born in Lagos de Moreno, Jalisco, Mexico, January 1, 1873, in an humble house in the San Felipe section of the town. His father was a modest merchant, owner of a grocery store in Lagos and a ranch about 20 kilometers from the little town. The first business with which the child Mariano became familiar was the store, *El Tigre,* which his father established with the help of a "rich" brother who loaned him 300 *pesos.* He had repaid the debt by the end of the first year and saved enough money to buy a small piece of property where the child Mariano "had his eyes opened to justice." There he saw the first "skirmish" between the government forces and those who opposed them.

During his early years, Mariano's mind was nourished with stories he heard from Camila Rocha [his nursemaid] and his maternal grandfather, Don José María González, whose tales of the adventures committed on the main highways [*caminos reales*] amused him very much. From Don José María, a typical example of the Jalisco muleteer, Azuela learned the customs and psychology of the Mexican *rancheros* that he later utilized in his novels.

Azuela called two significant remembrances of his youth tragedies —the execution of his grandfather who had killed a friend and the first occasion on which he [Azuela] wore a "dress-up" hat. His reaction to these two events—his feeling of injustice in the killing of man by man and his fear of being made ridiculous (for when he wore that funny looking hat, he felt the people were staring at him)— became dominant factors in the course that his life was to take.

MARIANO AZUELA

His father's ranch, the people who worked there, and even Nature herself revealed to Azuela the many raw and unpleasant episodes of which life is composed. The worldly knowledge and teachings of morality he received from his mother, Camila Rocha, his maternal uncle, and the employees of the general store, *La providencia;* the games with his numerous brothers and sisters and friends had greater influence on the formation of his character than his studies at the antiquated Convent of the Capuchines at Lagos. There he studied Latin, grammar, physics, and a few other subjects that the old village priest thought the young men who claimed to be interested in a career ought to know. In the same school, however, the intellectual of Lagos, Padre Agustín Rivera, had great influence on the immature mind and thoughts of the future author.

His parents always referred to Padre Rivera as the "wise one." The esteem they had for the Padre they did not hold for his taste in novels. Young Mariano, still a grammar school student, managed to read these in private. First he read the works of Pérez Escrich, then Dumas. "In between the boxes of soap I hid some of the novels, such as *The Count of Montecristo.* When my father took his siesta in the comfortable make-shift bed and was snoring I hid myself in the attic to enjoy the literature that my parents forbade me to read."

Thus the years passed. The primary grades and then four years in Padre Guerra's *Liceo* where Mariano failed in philosophy. At last, the time came when he had to say good-bye to the pleasant little village, to the hiding place in the store, to his favorite books, and the ranch he adored. At the age of fourteen it was not easy to leave home to go to Guadalajara to continue his studies. The memory of that first departure! His mother giving him a thousand advices, his father trying to hide his grief, his brothers and sisters excited and not understanding that scene of tenderness and sorrow!

Azuela's first year in Guadalajara was not very pleasant. "As soon as I finished the course of Morals and Religion I deserted the seminary. The sacerdotal career never interested me and my stay in that establishment was merely accidental. I enrolled in the Boy's *Liceo* of the State, revalidated the courses that I had taken in Lagos and finished my preparatory studies. When I left the seminary my father suggested that I should take a room in the home of Dr. Alvarado, where the environment was the same, as the majority of the boarders were theology students. The next year I moved to a boarding house on Belén Street very close to the Alameda, not very far from the School of Medicine and the General Hospital. Then when I began to know Guadalajara, another locale, naturally there were other men and other books—Jorge Isaac's *María*, *Gil Blas de Santillana*, the horseman D'Artagnan, and the sweet Margarita Gautier.

"If during my childhood the execution of my grandfather had made an impression on me, the assassination of Don Ramón Corona, Governor of the State, gave me a similar reaction—though now in such a manner that I could transform it into my first literary triumph. I wrote a long letter to the members of his family relating to them the details of that important event. Perhaps I added many exaggerations and even lies because I found out that the neighbors of my village passed the account from one to another."

Another aspect of the personality which revealed the future novelist was his pleasure in the solitary and in the study of the types of people in the city that later were to appear in his novels. He said of himself, "The student is shy and the solitude pleases him. Perhaps, it is unusual. He has desires that clash with each other. For example, he will follow the first outlandish type that he comes across in the street, yet he would not give him a thought in the *Liceo*." When he was sixteen years of age (1889), Azuela wrote what he considered his first attempt in the novelistic art, *Registro*, which is mostly autobiographical.

The young student spent his vacations at his father's ranch with the members of his family. "My mother and my native soil together were an invincible attraction. I did not want to waste any time in our house in the city. Canuto or Rosalío were waiting for me at the railroad station with my horse saddled and from there we went directly to the ranch." The presence of a childhood friend who later became his sweetheart did attract him to the city.

On finishing his preparatory studies in 1892, Azuela enrolled in the School of Medicine of the University of Guadalajara in order to became a medical doctor. "Why a doctor? I never knew why." [When this translator asked the author's son the same question, *Lic*. Enrique Azuela answered, "My father did not have a particular desire to be a doctor but he did *not* want to study for the priesthood."] From then on Azuela had two interests: medicine and the novels which he converted into one thread that made the design of his future life.

Days passed, then months and years. On life's road he met Honoré de Balzac, Émile Zola, the Brothers Goncourt, Alfonse Daudet, and Gustavo Flaubert, for Don Mariano had spent many hours in the public library. In 1899 Mariano Azuela wrote his doctoral thesis "The Treatment and Care of Pneumonia"—an illness which befalls many of the characters in his novels.

When Doctor Azuela returned to his native town with his medical sheepskin, he married his childhood sweetheart, Doña Carmen Rivera, niece of the famous Don Agustín Rivera. Ten children were born to them. The first years in the practice of medicine were not easy. Azuela served as general practitioner, surgeon, male midwife, gynecologist, psychiatrist, etc., without any more fortification for these roles than the knowledge of "how to use the index of the medical text books that were thrown at us. When I was not making calls or seeing patients in the office, I spent many hours reading and consulting the various medical books." Did Azuela abandon his literary efforts during those years? Absolutely not. Among his friends there was a small group dedicated to the art of letters which nourished his drive to write. When Don Mariano was certain that he wished to be a novelist, he began to write with great enthusiasm. "I found the 'bad' men for my novels in my practice of medicine in the villages and the rural districts. When they solicited my professional help, I had many occasions to observe them in their most intimate moments and in their own lairs."

The Republic began to shudder and shake when Madero's revolution started to erupt. It can be said that 1908 was a decisive year in Mexican history: Francisco I. Madero published his book, *The Presidential Succession in 1910*. Although Azuela had never participated formally in politics for fear it might brand him as cowardly or presumptuous, he immediately placed himself at the disposition of Madero and his followers. In Lagos de Moreno, with the help of some friends, they created a center for propaganda. Why did Azuela break his tradition of no political interference? "Once I determined to be a part of the revolutionary movement that Francisco I. Madero initiated, I entered it wholeheartedly. I was never interested in or had sympathy with politics by force, but in the action against the ancient regime of Porfirio Díaz my feelings dominated my reason. I do not regret it nor have I ever regretted it." In Lagos, Azuela and his friends formed the anti-Díaz nucleus.

MARIANO AZUELA

On the triumph of the Madero revolution in May, 1911, Azuela was named *Jefe político* of Lagos de Moreno. When he took possession of the post offered him by the people, not by official command, the *caciques,* psuedo-*maderistas,* blocked his path. Azuela resigned the position. These experiences, however, gave the author many ideas for the novels that were yet to be written. "It revealed to me that the revolution would be a great failure. It disillusioned me and from then on I determined to be a calm and impartial observer. First I was a witness then an actor, roles which served me as a basis for my writings."

On the 22nd of February, 1913, Madero was assassinated. Victoriano Huerta, the usurper, however, was not recognized by all the governors. In the North, Francisco Villa appeared surrounded by thousands of peons. When he took the city of Zacatecas in June, 1914, Azuela determined to write his novel, *Los caciques.* "I was finishing up the final chapter when the last group of Federals arrived in my hometown. They had all the markings of the beating Villa gave them—ragged clothes, emaciated faces, bandaged limbs. The Revolution had triumphed!"

Huerta's government fell in July, 1914. Unfortunately the conflict between Venustiano Carranza and Villa resulted in a ruthless struggle between the revolutionaries themselves. "I never thought that the irrepressible wave would lift me up and place me in the fratricidal and bloody struggle that was to come—not because of ideals but for ambitions to command."

The armies of Álvaro Obregón and Venustiano Carranza occupied Mexico city in August of that year. Carranza assumed the title of First Chief and did not recognize Villa's power. The followers of Villa and Emiliano Zapata called the Convention that met in Aguascalientes in October, 1914, where they named Eulalio Gutiérrez as Provisional President and refused to recognize Carranza as First Chief. Azuela allied himself with the conventionists "not because of sympathy, but because they represented the legal authority of the country." It was then that the author joined Villa's forces.

By the end of October, 1914, Azuela joined the staff of Julián Medina as a medical officer. When he and his chief were in Irapuato the leader enjoyed telling the physician-author about his revolutionary experiences. It was there that the novel, *The Underdogs,* first saw the light of day and its protagonist had markings of Julián Medina.

MARIANO AZUELA

Chased by Carranza's soldiers, the revolutionaries were obliged to withdraw toward Guadalajara where they arrived in December, 1914. There, the Governor of the State named Azuela to the post of Director of Public Education. He did not hold the position very long, for Julián Medina and his followers were driven out of the area in January, 1915. During this brief interval it occurred to the novelist, who was continuing his famous work, to give the protagonist of his novel the name of Demetrio Macías, as it would be safer to forge his protagonist as an anonymous character.

Villa, defeated by Obregón on the 16th of April, 1915, obliged Medina to withdraw to Lagos de Moreno. During this maneuver Azuela remained in Lagos attending to the wounded. Pushed by Carranza's forces, the author and eighty men fled to Tepatitlán and then Cuquío. "In the canyons of Juchipila a *carrancista* horde attacked us. But as all the men in our group were capable riders and accustomed to the steep slopes, we soon reached the heights of the sierra and were able to fire on the enemy. I, in the meantime, took refuge in an open cave on the edge of a cliff, taking notes for the final scene of the novel that I had hardly begun."

From there the remnant group of Villa's forces took the train to the North getting off at the last stop, Ciudad Juárez, a city opposite El Paso, Texas, where Azuela arrived "with a bunch of papers under my rough cotton shirt." Two-thirds of his masterpiece, *The Underdogs*, was completed!

What an ill-fated year Azuela had suffered! He had wandered across the sierras of Jalisco and Zacatecas "eating unsalted fresh beef roasted over coals, drinking a concoction made of toasted chick-peas that was sweetened with an extract of the mesquite." Yet, this did not compare with the spiritual suffering due to the disappointment of his ideals. "That is the reason the novels I wrote in these months of bitterness were conceived, expanded, and completed, impregnated with stinging mordacity. My defeat was twofold: I had lost economically as well—all my savings for the past two years went up in smoke and without ideals, full of disenchantment I had to face the facts and perform my immediate duty—the maintenance of my family."

In 1916 Azuela and his family moved to Mexico City where he dedicated his efforts to his profession, withdrawing entirely from the political scene. He sold a novel which gave him enough money to buy clothes suitable for his profession. It was not easy to get started in this large metropolis. The doctor from the province apprised the corner drugstore owner that he was at his disposition and soon a few patients came to his home.

"The heavens took pity on me, sending a typhoid epidemic and then the Spanish flu to Mexico City. There weren't enough doctors to attend the sick." No matter how much time Azuela gave to his professional duties he never stopped writing. His success in both fields is a matter of record.

What kind of a man was Azuela? In his physical appearance let us imagine him as a man of average height, body well-proportioned, eyes penetrating through his rounded glasses, thin lips framing his mouth. He wore a slightly graying moustache until he passed middle age. His eyebrows were heavy and his hair thin; his walk calm, without haste. Morally, Azuela's character was beyond reproach. He was withdrawn and circumspect, one who liked to be alone and who was jealous of his independence. He avoided evening social gatherings and banquets where literary men gathered. His habits were methodical and orderly. "A little before six in the morning he began to work at his typewriter. Usually he wrote a page every day that he was not correcting proofs for his editor, Andrés Botas. He was a generous man, full of kindnesses. From the very moment he started to practice medicine, he preferred the poor patient whom he never abandoned even though he did not pay his doctor bill. He also took care of the bullies and 'tough-guys' (whose patois is found in his novels). More than once these petty-gangsters would steal his handkerchief, hat, and even the money in his office," said Doña Carmen, the author's wife.

Among his distinguished friends were José Vasconcelos, José Clemente Orozco, González Martínez, and Diego Rivera. The latter gave him a book in which he inscribed: "To Doctor Mariano Azuela, the only great writer that the Mexican Revolution has given us. With my great admiration and deep respect."

INTRODUCTION

by

FRANCES KELLAM HENDRICKS

Most famous of modern Mexican novels, *The Underdogs* by Dr. Mariano Azuela (1873-1952), has appeared in more than twenty languages. The importance of the work as a landmark in Mexican literary history, as a vigorous and original novel, and as a revelation of significant aspects of the Mexican Revolution which began with the overthrow of Porfirio Díaz determined the decision to undertake a new presentation in English.

The Revolution itself in one of its most violent, brutal, and discouraging phases is the theme of *The Underdogs*. It was the first and greatest of the cycle of works on revolutionary subjects, written in the period 1915-1918, which form the principal basis of Azuela's literary fame. A medical officer in the forces of the rebel leader Gen. Julián Medina, the author observed at first hand the wild excitement, the bewilderment, the brutality, the hopes, the frustrations of the people of the sierras, of the underdogs.

Last in the cycle, *The Trials of a Respectable Family* turns from the fury of violent action to the impact of the Revolution on people of property and their conflicting responses to the moral and social issues involved. Again Azuela's observations and experiences provided him with much of the material. In 1917 he moved with his family to México, D. F., where they suffered from the disorders and confusion of the times. The insight he derived from his participation in events gives both works the impact of documentary accounts and imbues them with historical significance.

Though *The Trials of a Respectable Family* has received little critical attention outside Mexico, its irony and satire, its humor, and above all its analysis of the conflict between the obtuse who seek selfish advantage and the sensitive who summon courage in the face of disaster make it a fascinating work in its own right. It appears in this volume for the first time in an English version. Both works deal with approximately the same period in Mexican history.

Mexican literary critics generally accord *The Underdogs* the distinction of stimulating the creation of the novel of the National Revolution. The response, however, was not immediate. Appearing first

xxi

in issues from October to December, 1915, in a Spanish language newspaper, *El Paso del Norte*, published in the Texas city of that name by means of a subvention from Venustiano Carranza (Azuela, *Obras completas*, III, 1077), it aroused little notice then or in several subsequent small editions in book form. Late in 1924, the Mexican poet, Rafael López, stated in a press conference that it was the "most seriously realized" work of its sort that had appeared in the previous decade. Its wide public acceptance followed, however, upon a vigorous polemic concerning the question of the existence of a vital Mexican literature in the course of which Francisco Monterde, who has since written the prologue to Azuela's *Obra's Completas* published in three volumes under the auspices of the *Fondo de Cultura Económica* (México, D. F., 1958-1960), strongly called attention to them. (*Obras*, III, 1088.)

The Underdogs, only novel of the Revolution written in the midst of the events, stimulated others to create works which constitute the important literature of that elemental aspect of recent Mexican history. "The Revolution found in Azuela . . . its most apt and worthy chronicler," according to Pedro Manuel González, eminent critic and friend of Azuela, in his work *Trayectoria de la novela en México* (México, D. F., 1951). In his opinion, Azuela's works have exercised a decisive influence on the destiny of the Mexican novel, "pointing out new directions for it with respect to point of view and technique as well as theme." In spite of the early lack of critical notice, Azuela had given the *coup de grâce* to novels of traditional themes and techniques. His works "marked the end of one century of the Mexican novel and introduced a new era. His influence has been so deep that not even the authors still following the realist school of the previous century . . . escaped it." (*Trayectoria*, 144, 149.)

Azuela had already developed his interest in writing when he settled in his native state of Jalisco to practice medicine. There he produced several works which constitute his literary apprenticeship. Involved in the Revolution, he published nothing between 1912 and 1915. When, however, he reached El Paso after the disastrous defeat of the rebel forces and their terrible march north, he had already composed two-thirds of his masterpiece. His experiences in that "tangle of crimes, tears, blood, pain, and desolation" (*Obras*, III, 1266) and his own sensitivity to them resulted in the work which is *the* novel of the Revolution. In want, he accepted a small advance from the newspaper. Never in his life had he relished money as he did that, he recorded. (*Obras*, III, 1077, 1268.)

Vivid and realistic with flashes of poetic insight, the work is the product of a man with a trained mind, acute sensibilities, and strong moralistic bent who had rich opportunity to observe the Revolution at first hand. He has recorded that he composed the greater part of the narrative from the conversations he had with revolutionaries of different classes and backgrounds, but above all from their conversations with each other which he found of "insuperable interest on account of their authenticity and significance." (*Obras*, III, 1086.) His series of pictures, lightly bound together with a thread of fiction, form a work which "created itself." Azuela said further that his labor consisted of collecting types, gestures, landscapes, and events which his imagination aided him in presenting with the greatest embellishment and color of which he was capable. (*Obras*, III, 1078.)

Azuela's acuteness of observation is supported by his gift of characterization. Though somewhat two-dimensional, the figures come alive through his deft use of dialogue and apt though sparing detail. Each character has his function as a person, but each, too, is a type: Demetrio Macías, the natural leader of raw courage; Luis Cervantes, the time-server and opportunist—pseudo-revolutionary, Azuela labels him—who always lands right side up (*Obras*, III, 1081); Anastasio Montañés, the epitome of loyalty; and others to whom he assigns qualities or features typical of those who made up the revolutionaries.

He evidences a strong feeling of sympathetic understanding for the countrymen of Jalisco and Zacatecas "whose eyes were those of children and whose hearts were wide open" as a consequence of his having shared with them "many of their joys, many of their longings, and much of their bitterness." Years later when almost all of them had disappeared, he expressed the wish to pay homage to "each indomitable member of the indigenous race, generous and uncomprehending, who though he did smile as he killed, knew also how to smile as he died." (*Obras*, III, 1268.)

The succinct, uncluttered style so effective in *The Underdogs* in passages of violent action contrasts with the rich language of the brief, almost lyrical descriptions of the countryside. In both the works in this volume, Azuela commands an extensive and varied vocabulary which he uses with flexibility and subtlety. Some of his striking effects of style result from his use of the vernacular, a practice previously uncommon among Mexican writers.

Episodic in form, the very structure of *The Underdogs* reflects the scenes and events it relates—chaotic, horrifying, violent, disjointed. The structure proves, after all, of one piece; for his presentation follows the way of the Revolution. The movement of the story, maintained through the characters, is circular. Demetrio Macías and the last of his companions die in the canyon which saw their first victory. The episodic form conveys the destructive effects of the Revolution; the circular form its futility.

Although Azuela speculates little about revolutionary principles and plans, he conceives the movement he deals with as an irresistible force beyond the control of those caught helplessly in its course. Disillusion follows, expressed in the words of the officer Alberto Solís who reflects Azuela's own situation at the time he wrote the novel. (*Obras*, III, 1081.) When Luis Cervantes asked him why he stayed in the Revolution, Solís replied, "The revolution is a hurricane. The man who is swept up in it is no longer a man; he is a wretched dry leaf snatched away by the gale." Though the Revolution is beautiful, Solís exclaimed, its aftermath is brutality. Just before he died he thought he saw a symbol—maybe of hope—in the mingling of the columns of smoke rising from the fires of a burning town. It is interesting that Azuela, called on to select a portion of his masterpiece for inclusion in editor Whit Burnett's anthology, *The World's Best* (New York, 1950), chose the section in which Solís appears.

For many thousands, Azuela later wrote, the image of the Revolution turned out to be the "red of pain, the black of hate. We came out with what tatters of soul the assassins left us. And how may we heal our disenchantment, having grown old and mutilated in spirit? We were many thousands and for those thousands *The Underdogs*, novel of the Revolution, will be a work of truth since it is the truth." (*Obras*, III, 1266-1267.)

In spite of the disenchantment and sad picture of humanity the novel leaves with one, Prof. González holds that "it achieves merit by having penetrated the depths of the collective psychology of the Mexican people in an instant of crisis and of having revealed it to us in all its terrible brutality—neither more terrible nor more cruel than any other human group in similar circumstances. By having delved into the Mexican manifestations in this novel, Dr. Azuela reached the human universal in its worst dimensions." (*Trayectoria*, 148.)

Much less well known than *The Underdogs*, *The Trials of a Respectable Family* reveals new aspects of Azuela's literary gifts and of his ability to reflect the age in which he lived. In this novel the force and action of the Revolution are in the wings of the stage. The author centers attention on the impact of the Revolution on the people of the middle class and their reactions to their trials and tribulations. Seized with panic engendered by reports of the excesses of the revolutionaries, people of means fled to seek safety in the capital city. There through successive stages they descended to penury and hardship. Azuela undertakes to explore the ways in which the altered conditions affected the individuals concerned and how they reacted—how they revealed themselves.

His primary theme, he wrote, is as old as time but inexhaustible: that pain and suffering are the most fruitful source of noble deeds. Though many of the formerly favored class failed to meet the test imposed by the events of the Revolution, many found in it their "structure as men." Many enriched in the days of Porfirio Díaz, now ruined, regenerated themselves by undertaking humble tasks, ultimately achieving respectable positions gained by their own efforts. Such men were, he stated, in striking contrast to the crowd of grasping self-seekers suddenly in possession of power and riches "whose faces revealed their insatiable voracity." (*Obras*, III, 1097.)

The grossest error to Azuela of some of the revolutionaries consisted in their killing the best in themselves, forgetting their humble origins and simple habits formed in poverty and even in misery and "letting themselves be seduced by the mirage of power and money." In conformity with his own modest tastes and personal humility, Azuela denounced those who proposed as a "doctrine of salvation for our people the creation of wants they do not have" and held that they did more damage than "all revolutions put together." He extolled the simple life without "complexity or waste," pursuit of which he thought would solve all the worst ills of the time without "blood or tears." As long as anyone is hungry or needy, "he who wastes is a thief." In spite of the cruelty and destructiveness of suffering, when a spark of energy remained, it could revivify in man unexpected forces. (*Obras*, III, 1097-1098.)

With these ideas in mind Azuela set about writing *The Trials of a Respectable Family*. Though founded, he said, in distressing events, it ended overflowing with hope and optimism. "If I put passion in the pages, I included no lie or unfounded judgment. . . . Of all of which I may be accused, the least is having deformed the truth." He called upon the daily press as his witness. This brief novel was a presentation of what one could obtain only by "submerging oneself in a sea of printed matter." His endeavor had been a "faithful reflection of the fortitude and bitterness of those days of trouble." His animosity was directed against the men "who corrupted everything," not against ideas. The excesses of the people of the Revolution did not, however, justify those of the days of Porfirio Díaz. Azuela wrote that he "put these words which expressed his ideas in the mouth of the protagonist," Procopio. (*Obras*, III, 1098.)

The actors Azuela creates to carry out the presentation of his ideas are members of the Vásquez Prado family of Zacatecas. He takes them from their flight from Zacatecas before the threat of Pancho Villa's forces through the successive stages of their descent to bitter poverty, and finally to Procopio's victory. The mother, sons, and son-in-law are the characters by means of which he exemplifies and excoriates those who are grasping, selfish, power-hungry, and oblivious to the pain and suffering of others. In Procopio and one of the daughters of of the house, Lulú, Azuela develops his theme of regeneration through pain and suffering.

Azuela indulges freely in this work in a propensity for satire and caricature, especially in his depiction of the unsympathetic characters. Though the effect is sometimes humorous, the principal consequence is to make them hardly believable as human beings, but admirably suited to demonstrate the despicable nature of the traits and attitudes he uses them to typify. In Procopio, the protagonist, he creates a distinctive personality who is more than a conveyance for Azuela's thoughts, though he serves that purpose, too.

An interesting feature of both works, but more prominent in *The Trials of a Respectable Family*, is the way in which Azuela indicates

INTRODUCTION

his medical interests, overtly on occasion, sometimes subtly. There
is a certain wryness in the way in which he has Procopio disregard
his doctor's directions although the action is necessary to Azuela's
purpose.

The curious division of *The Trials of a Respectable Family* into
two parts with one written in the first person and the other in the
third arouses speculation. Azuela has given a faint clue to the explanation for this peculiarity of structure. He started the work to fill in
his free hours. Nothing, he said, makes bad times more tolerable
than a good dream, and writing is almost dreaming. (*Obras*, III,
1094.) Thus possibly he undertook the work without any overall plan.
Having begun with the weakling son César (ironically named) telling the story, he may have found him an inadequate means for
developing his principal theme. That Procopio's basic character is
apparent only vaguely in "The Book of Bitter Hours" supports this
view. Thus it became necessary for Azuela to provide for César's
sudden death and to change the mode of his narrative in order to
widen its scope. He shifts effectively from the mannered affectations
of César to a more straight-forward style in "Procopio's Victory."

Azuela's warmth of spirit, his affection for the simple life, and his
moral fervor are essential ingredients of *The Trials of a Respectable
Family*. The worth of the work lies not only in the force with which
he displays his indignation at outrages against human rights and the
effectiveness with which he explores his central theme, but as well
in its character as a social document of the Revolution.

THE TRIALS OF A RESPECTABLE FAMILY

BOOK I

The Book of
Bitter Hours

THE TRIALS OF A
RESPECTABLE FAMILY

I

My brother Francisco José is a poet. He has written two works: "Inescapable Agonies" and "In Praise of Anxiety." Who but Franscisco José should be entrusted with writing *The Book of Bitter Hours?* Mama, however, says I have to do it.

Well, the Vásquez Prados, like all respectable families, have been in reduced circumstances since the Madero revolution. The government of Huerta, as we say at our house, was only an ephemeral dream of restoration which was followed by the horrible nightmare of the Revolution of 1913, then by the amazing triumph of Venustiano Carranza. The final blow was the financial disaster which established the theory of transfer of property by robber-factions who acted on the principle: "It is necessary to take money where you find it."

A barrier in the way of my course of thought makes my pen hesitate; it is the necessity for considering the antecedents of my family.

I will explain once and for all: I do not know very well how to reason out things. If I ever had an aptitude, it had no chance to develop; for at home I was never permitted to take part in serious conversations. As the youngest of the family, it seems that I am condemned to be the baby the rest of my days. Mama is oblivious to the fact that it distresses me that even yet when I go out I have to wear as I did three years ago in Zacatecas, short pants, ribbed knee stockings, a flowing tie, and a flat straw hat with a blue ribbon. Even though I am twenty, Mama will not allow me to go out of the house without her or one of my sisters.

The Vásquez Prados have in their paternal line one of the framers of the Constitution of '57. In our maternal line are a number of military personages of merit. Among them who figure as stars of the first magnitude are two of opposite views: my great uncle Don Dionisio, who gathered laurels with as much valor as loyalty in the service of Emperor Maximilian of Austria until the tragic disintegration of the Empire at the Hill of Bells; and my grandfather Don Ventura, who boldly defended and never abandoned the cause of legality and progress, of the integrity of our country, and of the person of the *Benemérito de las Américas,*[1] the attorney Don Benito Juárez, and harvested not only a full measure of laurels, but bushels of money as well.

That is what my mother Agustinita says, more or less, in praising our grandfathers highly. My father Procopio observes, however, with a sly smile that has the ugly quality of striking one like the sting of a scorpion that, thanks to their political noses, the Generals Prado always fell right side up.

Pascual, my sister Berta's husband, objects, holding the view that the interests of the family are man's most sacred charge on earth. In deliberately attaching themselves to opposite factions during our internecine struggles, they revealed talent and nobility of heart. Honors, ambitions, glory, life itself in the service of the most exalted ideal: the family! Naturally, the family will gain no matter who is the victor.

Archibaldo, my sister Lulú's fiancé, a rascal without profession or property, observes that the Generals Prado were in fact typical of this home and should have a monument. If he intended to be malicious, he was disconcerted; for that very day Agustinita had provided that Canuto, a diligent and skillful brick mason from the hacienda, should come to erect a stone statue in memory of the Generals Prado in the garden in the shade of the honeysuckle.

Certainly our lineage should be above criticism, especially as it is the key itself to our domestic advantages. Papa is in the habit of forgetting that fact and sometimes causes painful scenes such as one which occurred a few months ago. We had then been installed for a brief time in a big old house in front of the Ángeles Garden. According to Francisco José, no one need envy our new home any more than one would envy the hut of our poorest sharecroppers. Eight large, battered columns, half eaten up by insects, hold up a roof so rotten that it is practically falling down on us. Back of the portico are four tiny windows which have wooden grills and a sort of a triangular-shaped cornice with red-painted plaster ornaments. In order to be absolutely truthful, I must say that on seeing the little yard of the house, Agustinita found a pretext to reminisce with pleasure about Zacatecas; and that Francisco José was enchanted by a discovery: a showy fountain of recent work in the best modern taste. He states that in this big old house there are important vestiges of colonial art. Those were exaggerations; as for me, I was satisfied, being a little lazy as well as ignorant of the arts and sciences, to run up the window curtain in the hall and contemplate the warm splendor of the garden and the red cupola of the Angeles Church which was silhouetted above the tops of the trees against the blue sky. That is when the sky *was* blue; for in September it rains from midday on; at least, there is a slight drizzle. Under a leaden sky all seems shrouded in a mantle of ashes. Those afternoons, nevertheless, have their superb quarter of an hour when, near six, the sun rips the clouds apart violently, a flash of light stretches out on the horizon, providing a deep luminescence among the tremulous arabesques of the Alameda, and expires as a shimmer of quicksilver on the paving stones and the dark green benches of the garden.

One time at that hour, as the members of the family were grouped at the window watching the death of the day in the deserted plaza, they noticed two large automobiles passing by, packed with *carrancistas* and women of ill-repute, all drunk and taking on scandalously. Papa, who had passed the week sunk in a dilapidated wicker chair, his head between his hands, without opening his lips, suddenly aroused himself and came to the window.

"There are the founders of the aristocracy of the future," he said faintly.

Agustinita, in the blackest humor in the world because she was again out of funds and had not heard from Pascual, titular angel of the family, vented her feelings by insulting the government.

"Pay no more attention to the matter than it deserves," Procopio interrupted her almost without listening, following only the thread of his own thoughts. "From the time of the Wars of Independence to the present, common people of that sort, assassins and bandits, have been the foundation of successive aristocracies of the country."

"Procopio, Procopio! Do you realize what you say? Your words exceed the bounds of the rearing you have received and of good breeding. Blaspheming the sacred memory of our elders!" (Perhaps this is the opportune moment to say that Francisco José insists that he derives his poetic talents directly from his mother.)

Procopio did not answer; he did something worse—he smiled! The members of the household are divided about the meaning of that smile. Lulú, my younger sister, agrees with the opinion of her fiancé that no smile reveals more intelligence or a more noble heart than the smile of Procopio. The uncouth impression, almost rustic, of his austere countenance with its dark eyes; his rough, very dry skin like the bark of an old oak; his unkempt beard; all are modified when one first speaks to him and an easy smile rises to his lips while his eyes open wide like the windows of a country house where no one has anything to hide.

But it seems otherwise to Agustinita, Berta, Franciso José, and my brother-in-law Pascual. Francisco José, for example, says, "When I laugh, when you laugh, when all of us laugh, no one is in doubt about why we laugh. Papa's smile, at its least, is a smile just for one; at most, a smile for two."

Pascual is of the opinion that Procopio's smile is the sort that fends off good will, loosens the sacred bonds of the family, produces conflicts, and provokes disagreeable scenes.

So then, as I said, Procopio had not answered; he had smiled! Mama, who is not well versed in national history, in fact is not very well informed, found no suitable reply but broke into a flood of tears.

Lulú's voice broke into the scene, calling to us in an ironical tone: "I've put the soup on the table."

At that time our food was no longer the sort we used to enjoy.

Francisco José and I, as always, were the first to dash to the dining room. As soon as we had quieted somewhat the insistent clamors of our appetites with a cup of hot lima bean soup, and while Lulú served in the same little plates the inevitable and despised boiled potatoes, Francisco José, patting his soft, warm stomach, rolled up his eyes, breathed audibly with satisfaction, and disposed himself to talk.

Franciso José, it might be said, is the living antithesis of Procopio. Franciso José aspires to a life of meditation. His dream is *The Art*; and the measure of his aspirations, *the eternal snows of serenity.* He wishes his voice to be but the murmuring of ferns, the sound of a rippling brook, and that his gestures indicate the ineffable grace of a statue by Praxiteles.

That day, however, Agustinita cried enough to make a glittering lake overflow.

"Where did the viceregal aristocracy come from? What was the derivation of ancient nobility of Europe? Why should we belittle anyone for evident blemishes?"

Procopio turned from his inner absorption with suprise in his eyes. He repeated Francisco José's words. A perverse smile followed his gesture of surprise.

"And—?"

As the most timid seminarian in a logic class would argue emphatically—that which proves too much, proves nothing.

"And—?"

Procopio's reply was his smile, more solemnly deceptive than ever.

"Your father, Procopio, was one of the framers of the Constitution of '57; the Generals Prado left in your country's history a shining record. As Francisco José says, neither one nor the other knew how to laugh as you do. No, they did not know how to laugh that way, but they knew something that has absolutely escaped you—"

Agustinita's voice, increasingly hoarse and muted, faded out like a rattle. In the meantime, a shadow darkened the peculiar brilliance of Procopio's glance and his smile became fixed.

"They would always know how to avoid for their children the shame of having to live in an indecent pigsty of a place and of having to eat only boiled lima beans."

Changing color suddenly, Lulú arose abruptly from the table, her plate scarcely touched, and left with a fixed expression in her staring eyes.

Procopio became very pale, raised his hand to his chest, and half closed his eyes.

"A dizziness!" Agustinita explained to us very softly. "It seems that the lima beans have caused him some distress."

II

Three years have passed since we left Zacatecas. Step by step we have come to this pass.

What a day it was that we left Zacatecas! The very remembrance torments me. While we packed trunks and valises, laughing and joking with evident pretense, Procopio, contrary to his usual custom, walked in a pensive mood back and forth from one end of the corridor to the other. When he realized how we had upset the household, he went over to Agustinita and said to her tenderly,

"My dear, remember the adage: 'Go slowly, for I am in a hurry.' "

"Bah, within one or two weeks we shall return and shall have composure and more than enough time to put it all in order."

"I fear that these weeks will be as long as that of the creation of the world."

Without paying any attention Mama proceeded with her bustle. Archibaldo said to me as though talking to himself,

"To suppose that Agustinita's mind has ears would be the same thing as supposing, dear César, that your malice has a nose."

"What does that mean, Archibaldo?"

He laughed heartily but I did not press him for an answer. Agustinita and Francisco José say that he frequently likes jokes and a play on offensive words. In consideration of everything I now ask myself, hasn't Agustinita with her recklessness been the cause of the penury which we now suffer and which it seems will never end?

What a day! At sunset we waited for the train which was supposed to leave at seven with the respectable families of the region who had hoped until the last moment for the triumph of the government's forces. The hubbub of the people became feverish. From streets, plazas, and boulevards scurried people in groups: children, men on horseback, disreputable camp followers, all rejoicing as on a day at the fair. Bumping along with harsh noises through the rough streets, enormous pieces of artillery, carts of ammunition and of provisions, and ambulances rolled heavily. From every part of the city rose a confused but incessant noise. What expressions on the faces of those men and their animals! It was like a tempest about to break loose upon my unfortunate land, the unhappy land of my heart!

Among a group of colorfully and elegantly mounted officials soon appeared General Medina Barrón with his staff. In order to call his attention to us, Mama, her eyes flashing, jumped with uncommon agility upon a pile of decayed railroad ties. Upon recognizing us, he came with his usual gallantry to greet us.

"At last you are leaving!" It was not his intention, even jokingly, to dissuade us. Nevertheless, yielding to Agustinita's importunities, he agreed our only difficulties would be those arising from the trip itself. In less than two weeks we should have the pleasure of seeing ourselves on the way home.

"That's what I've been saying all along. Did you hear that, Procopio?"

Papa, chewing on the tail end of his cigar, did not even raise his eyes. Pascual, my brother-in-law, agreed, quite convinced. But Archibaldo smiled sneeringly.

On few occasions have General Medina Barrón's words made us so happy. The esteem he had always enjoyed in our social circle, his pre-eminence as soldier and statesman, his contagious optimism, the assurance of his affirmations and promises produced such an effect that his very presence dissipated our anxiety and fears. The very accent of his voice was enough to return to us the tranquillity which crafty people would like to deny us. We felt as though tons of lead had been removed from our chests. Who is like Mama in her fervid admiration of Huerta, the hand of steel which the country truly requires; who can exceed her in praising, like an article of faith of the household, the gifts of energy and patriotism of our great president? Overflowing with enthusiasm for the brave and lowly ones who heroically spill their blood in defense of the privileges of the upper classes, her diatribes were always for the rabble followers of Villa and Carranza, rebels who could keep going solely by the grace of their unspeakable cowardice, only to hide as usual when meeting bold and loyal forces face to face.

"What about the taking of Ciudad Juárez? Of Torreón? And of the fighting at Tierra Blanca?"

"Even with your very manner, Archibaldo, you know how to promote boldly the rumors of the common people."

"As a matter of fact," said Pascual in defense of Agustinita, "the taking of Torreón by the *villistas* was nothing more than a betrayal by a Judas of a Federal."

Not crediting the exaggerated accounts of the triumphs of the rebels and powerfully influenced by Agustinita's faith, we had held out firmly and resolutely against abandoning any of our property to strange hands. But the succession of events had changed things abruptly. Agustinita, seized by an inexpressible anxiety, had demanded that Procopio go immediately to ask General Medina Barrón for a special train. It happened that *Señor* Moneda, adviser of the Bank of Zacatecas, Papa's great friend, came looking for him, much agitated. The two gentlemen had shut themselves up very mysteriously in Papa's office. Agustinita, incapable of enduring her curiosity, had flown to find out what it was all about from *Señora* Moneda. There she learned the whole truth: that General Huerta was going to relinquish his power, and that members of his cabinet and the most prominent persons of his government were taking the road to the ports, soon to leave the country. The triumph of the revolution was indisputable.

"But then, why haven't you left the city?" Agustinita had asked, with a modicum of doubt.

"We are going to an hacienda immediately. The American consul has offered us every sort of protection."

In spite of such a formidable blow, Mama's faith in General Medina

Barrón had not been extinguished. Now a few brief seconds of speaking with him brought forth anew all her hopes and energies.

Archibaldo asked us to take a cup of tea in the station restaurant. Mama, in enviable good humor, joked with Pascual and with Francisco José; scolded me for not having changed my stockings; and Lulú for wearing a hat that was out of style.

We left, talkative, contented, satisfied.   Pascual repeated with emphasis the refrain of his friends at the Casino: "With the brave veterans of Porfirio Díaz and the valiant lads of the Cadet School there are enough and more to put to flight the sheep-like followers of Francisco Villa."

"So that's why you have such a tremendous *argolla*,"[2] murmured a miserable beggar with a marked lack of respect.

I do not understand the patois of the common people, but by the tone, I presume that word had a derogatory significance. Some ragged, lousy people, with their big mouths open from ear to ear, were laughing at our flight.

III

Precisely at the time of our greatest anguish, Zacatecas was at the mercy of the soldiers and of an emboldened and insolent people who laughed at our panic.

At seven we had settled ourselves in a cattle car as well as God gave us the ability. As everyone could travel without tickets, we were forced to be surrounded by low-class people, to being piled up with fewer conveniences than cattle in a pen.

The streets were no longer visible in the night; the dark masses of El Grillo and La Bufa were scarcely discernable in the brilliant flickering lights of the fortifications. Weak lights of one or another habitation sparkled in a settlement of makeshift houses.

An hour passed; we felt the return of oppression in our breasts. Sadly and silently, we awaited the parting signal. Procopio and Archibaldo went out to see whether they could find out the reason for the delay. My sister Berta, full of distress, asked about Pascual. Finally, Procopio came back and told us that the engine was scarcely puffing. Engineer, brakeman, nor conductor had arrived. Mama then grouped us together to say the rosary. I fell asleep, because for me the murmur of prayers is a powerful soporific. At nine o'clock a terrific rupture of the silence awakened me. Double beats on the drums from the military coaches ahead sounded stridently; and notes of trumpets and bugles mingled in a tumultuous din with reverberations from the rocks of the hills and the melancholy, dull sounds from the distant troops. The orgy of noise went on for about an hour, after which everything was as quiet as a cemetery. There was not even the sound of crowing cocks or barking dogs. One by one the lights of the town went out, and the rays of a red, clear moon began to glide over the landscape. Now and then the awe-inspiring silence was broken by the hoof beats of some patrol that drew near, then receded until they could no longer be heard. From time to time a shot sounded far away; a lost cry: "Halt! Who goes there?"

About midnight the engine gave a cough and a tremulous moan. The train at last began to roll. Sighs rose from many breasts; tears rolled from many eyes; supplications ascended from many lips. Truthfully, we were not so naive as to believe that we had embarked on a pleasure trip; for, indeed, General Medina Barrón had warned us it would be difficult. We never supposed, however, that we would go from one pole to another; from one planet to another; from a world of comfort and opulence to one of miserable economies and innumerable sacrifices: first going to irritating mediocrity, ultimately to indigency.

Berta gave a cry of anguish, "Pascual! Where is he? Pascual!"

Agustinita exerted herself in vain to convince her that there was no reason for alarm. Pascual is, like us, a person of such good reputation in Zacatecas that certainly the train would not get under way without him. But Berta began to cry.

Then Francisco José took his turn. A cursed headache was tormenting him just as though it had known he had forgotten his aspirin tablets.

Our rheumatic and wheezing engine got under way with difficulty. It would run for an hour, then stop for another to get up steam. At noon we arrived at the station in Aguascalientes. In spite of the fact that the train was already full, a horde of people got on there, stepping all over us and pushing us heedlessly. We became separated— Mama and Berta at one end of the coach; Francisco José, his head covered with a large white handkerchief, abject, was in the opposite end; Archibaldo, Lulú, and I were very close to the door.

The change of altitude, the suffocating heat, the dense atmosphere nauseated Lulú. She became very pale. As though everything had turned dark to her, she held out her hands to me seeking help.

"Mama! Berta!" she exclaimed.

"Catch her in your arms," Mama shouted forcefully to me.

Less confused than I, Archibaldo had already caught her. I thanked him. What else could I do? We were packed like cigarettes in a package, unable to wiggle hand or foot. Lulú, waxen-faced, rested her head on Archibaldo's chest. The attack was, however, very short. Color began to come back into her cheeks and she opened her eyes. Evidently until then she had not realized that she was in Archibaldo's arms. Blushing, she jerked away abruptly. I smiled, pleased to see her recovered. Also, in order to calm her, I told her, with that naiveté which then characterized me,

"I shouldn't mind seeing you faint again just to see your cheeks change colors, becoming first like a lily and then like a carnation."

Archibaldo looked at Lulú and smiled slyly, while she, turning as red as before, made a vigorous gesture at me to indicate that this was neither the time nor the place for my frankness.

Procopio soon appeared. Berta asked him anxiously about Pascual. He said,

"I preferred to ride in the vestibule rather than to suffocate within."

"But didn't Pascual come with you?" moaned Berta, wringing her hands, overcome by distress.

"I don't know anything about him," Papa replied indifferently.

I saw two tongues of fire flash in Agustinita's eyes. There would have been an altercation between her and Papa if at that moment the clear, serene, and amiable countenance of my brother-in-law had not appeared at the side of the grave and disdainful Procopio.

"I bring you the news that I have secured a place in the caboose where we shall be able to continue our journey all together and with less discomfort," said Pascual before quieting the lamentations and complaints of his lovesick Berta.

We left the coach, trampling on everybody as others had taught us, and hastened by way of the platform toward the end of the string of coaches. The caboose seemed to us an enchanted palace. Then Pascual brought us some milk and bread and we lunched with keen appetite.

When Procopio started to pay for the food, his appearance suddenly altered. He searched through all his pockets, turning them inside out. His eyes opened wide in stupefaction. Thus he remained for a few seconds. Pale as death, he turned toward Mama.

"My dear, I have been robbed of my wallet, all my valuable papers, and the receipt for the strong box," he exclaimed in a broken voice.

Agustinita's serenity surprised me.

"I understand your absent-mindedness," she said, smiling lightly. She slowly drew toward herself the little satchel of Russian leather which she never relinquished when traveling. Putting a little key in the lock, she repeated,

"I am constantly aware of your absent-mindedness. In order to avoid just this eventuality, which I foresaw, I took the valuables from your wallet while you were changing clothes and—here—here—"

Mama wavered. Now she was the one who became pale and opened her eyes with amazement. Her face contracted in a violent tic, and her limbs began to jerk convulsively.

An attack! An attack! All of us leaped to her aid. Yes! Agustinita had indeed left the wallet as well as the valuables which she had taken from it on the table in the dining room.

After the seizure, she remained listless for more than two hours. Solicitous as always, Pascual did not leave her side for an instant. Procopio again became abstracted and, at a distance, smoked and smoked, lighting one cigarette with the end of the other. But when Agustinita recovered, he came over to her, animated and serene as though nothing of importance had occurred.

IV

About four in the afternoon, a white mist began to appear vaguely in the immensity of the dark green valley somewhat like a great dirty gray mass which little by little the oblique rays of the sun cleared up.

"Mexico City!" exclaimed Archibaldo.

Overcome with emotion, I climbed up to the little window of the caboose. The sublime panorama of the capital emerged from the floating mist which wrapped it in an immense festoon of thin and impalpable gauze. The enormous buildings began to be discernible individually, as well as the endless number of houses, when Agustinita made me get down. She had undertaken the orderly distribution of the baggage so that we could get off at the station without haste or disorder and without forgetting anything.

"Take care of your pockets!" Pascual, an experienced traveler, warned us as he buttoned up his smart coat. Francisco José, giving signs of life, opened his eyes and sat up. Berta took hold of Pascual's arm and did not let go of it until we arrived at the hotel.

Agustinita left to Procopio's care all the purchases she had made along the way: two little willow boxes from Salamanca, a dozen lime tree twigs from Silao, six heavy baskets of strawberries from Irapuato, twenty *cajetas* from Celaya, I don't know how many small packages of sweet potatoes from Querétaro, and a little blue-colored lariat from San Juan del Río which she insisted on buying for me to play with at the hacienda on our return. It seemed that Pascual had tried to make a good show; indeed, it was he who had paid for it all out of his own pocket, evidently to try to make Agustinita forget our disaster.

Procopio, burdened down with all those goods, was perplexed and distressed. On noticing him, Lulú resigned herself to interrupting her interminable colloquy with Archibaldo and offered to help. But the more Papa and Archibaldo puzzled with her over the distribution, the less it seemed that the three together were equal to the task.

"You are bothering yourself with a small matter, Uncle Procopio. We must begin by ridding ourselves of the nuisances and the useless things. There are no more strawberries in all six baskets than Lulú can hold in one hand. Thus we shall be able, without the least compunction, to throw out the baskets along the way. The *cajetas* of Celaya can have a like fate, for they are no longer milk but starch which no respectable person would eat."

"I have not asked your opinion, chatterbox," said Mama, stopping to listen.

A brief dispute ensued, for Archibaldo is a veritable Jesuit. First he made Agustinita angry, then he mollified her with apologies and amends.

"Aunt Agustinita, it is far from my intention to bother you, but please examine the baskets of strawberries and taste the *cajetas*."

Mama was finally convinced that under the top layer of large red strawberries, the baskets contained dry leaves mixed with dirt. If the *cajetas* of Celaya had not precisely turned to starch, at least they were of a very respectable age to judge by their color and the cracks in the crust. She herself gathered together her purchases and said dryly that she needed nobody's help; that she knew how to arrange them in order to get off with all of them and that we should attend only to the baggage. She vigorously objected when I was the first to get a suitcase.

"You should not carry anything, César! In Mexico there are plenty of urchins to do that."

From that moment, I put myself in the care of Lulú and a woman servant we had brought from Zacatecas.

How the contagion of the city did stimulate our old engine! Now it made earnest efforts to take on youthful vigor. By some miracle it had quickly recovered its agility and lustiness. It now rushed clamorously and turbulently at a great rate across the poor and melancholy little alleys, then thrust itself like the head of a snake through a red-painted wooden gate between two whitewashed walls. We were then lost in an ocean of trains, some panting, throwing out flakes of very black soot; others mute, dusty, and inert. At each change of direction, at each crossing, the train paused; now advancing through the narrow way left open by the others, now backing in order to give way to a train going in the opposite direction. We spent an hour among the shrill and dissonant ringing of bells of the widest range of timbres and tones. Finally, when we least expected it, we drew up to a platform at Buenavista Station.

What chatter and confusion! We were stupefied with it all and with Agustinita's admonitions. Pascual, the cleverest one, was useless; for Berta stuck to him like ivy to an oak. The rest were searching for everything and finding nothing; trampled by and trampling on the other passengers who had arrived as confused as we. Soon an avalanche of porters, Indians equipped with aprons to carry heavy loads, coachmen, chauffeurs, and travel agents fell upon us, snatching our baggage out of our hands, and confusing us to the point that we almost took leave of our senses.

"The Union Hotel, sir!" a well-dressed man said to me, politely checking my progress, his chest against mine.

"Take care, young man!" warned another man back of me, causing me to turn around. "It is not a suitable hotel for a respectable family. One can't even imagine where he might take you."

I was going to pay my respects and thank my unexpected friend, who could not have been other than my guardian angel; but at that very moment my attention was distracted when I felt a hand slip slyly into my jacket pocket. I tried to grab it, but unsuccessfully. Lulú and Bernabé were holding me securely by the arms. I yelled with all my might,

"Someone stole my watch!"

"A thief, a thief!" cried Pascual.

A tumult ensued. There in the exit, a policeman had just seized someone. I wanted to protest, for I wasn't able to believe that the well-set-up gentleman was the one who had robbed me of my watch. I restrained myself, nevertheless, because I recognized the respectable man who had just recommended the Union Hotel to me.

The policeman asked for a description of the watch, our names, and the place where we were going to stay. He referred us to the Police Commissioner.

As we came to the exit an employee with very courteous manners stopped us. An examination of baggage was necessary.

"We are supporters of Huerta," Francisco José said haughtily.

The guard turned a deaf ear and began examining the valise which Archibaldo, the first to comply, had opened for him.

"He may well be accustomed to these humiliations," Agustinita observed, "but no one has ever treated us this way before. In addition to being a respectable family, we are intimate friends of General Medina Barrón."

The employee raised his head to look at us with a certain disgusted curiosity. With a sarcastic smile he continued examining the luggage.

Archibaldo called attention to the fact that we were losing time and making ourselves ridiculous as well. Things being what they are, no one should raise any more obstacles.

We rested until the hour and moment when Procopio had us get into an enormous automobile which took off rapidly. Mama gave thanks to God that up to that point nothing seriously distressing had occurred. Aside from my watch, we had arrived with all in order, including Mama's purchases.

The fresh air had dissipated Francisco José's headache. With animation, he began to identify the buildings and monuments which we passed. I must confess that it seemed to me like a moving picture rapidly displayed. Except for the gigantic steel framework of the Legislative Palace, there was nothing to help me orient myself. All seemed hopelessly uniform: streets, boulevards, houses. Might that be the statue of Columbus, that the hemicircle honoring Juárez, that the Grand National Theatre? Pascual insisted on stopping the automobile at that building in order that we might look at some famous statues of Pegasus which to me seemed somewhat like sticks of wood bound together pointing toward the sky.

Vehicles crossed in every direction: electric trolleys, automobiles darting like arrows, all sorts of slowmoving vehicles pulled by teams of rearing chargers, clattering carriages pulled by old nags with scanty harness miraculously making their way in all that confusion without colliding.

"God bless my soul!" Mama exclaimed, giving such a sharp cry that the chauffeur slammed on the brakes. No, no, it was only a natural exclamation which she made on seeing a very elegant lady crossing the street among all that coming and going and disorderly commotion as though she were strolling alone through a park. Mama thought she would be smashed any moment. All of us, to tell the truth, were petrified with astonishment to see her on the opposite side unhurt. Agustinita had already prayed the *Magnificat* seven times. It would have been the simplest thing in the world for some automobile to cause us to fly into bits or that ours would dash us to pieces against some corner or an electric light pole.

There was an instant in which I became stupefied with it all. The sound of the streetcars, of the rumble of the automobiles, of tinkling bells, of deep-throated ones, of hoarse sirens, of the shouts of newspaper vendors—all ended by making me lose my sense of identity. "Who, now," I thought, "are the Vásquez Prados of Zacatecas? Where is the well-gloved hand raised to salute us cordially as we pass? Where is there a single head bared respectfully and inclined humbly on seeing us? Cold countenances—disdainful, apathetic, insolent. Nothingness! The hateful city! Yes, here we are nothing more than a tiny drop of water in the immensity of the ocean."

V

We stopped at the Gillow. Only Pascual was determined to stay at the White House near an American residence where, it is said, there are interesting things going on.

"Sheer pretext!" observed Agustinita acidly when Pascual left us.

The truth is Pascual is trying to keep at a distance from us. And it may be that he is right. A gentleman of such refinement, of such nicety of taste is easily upset by things which others scarcely notice.

Procopio acted as though he were deaf. It seems that Pascual resents the fact that Procopio always maintains a certain reserve and lack of confidence toward him, but is frankly cordial toward that drunkard of an Archibaldo. Papa's eccentricity! Pascual has been a member of the family scarcely two years, it is true; but his conduct has always been that of a polished gentleman. Berta adores him; Mama looks up to him. And what could be more eloquent of his dispatch and zeal than this trip from Aguascalientes, as the comforts we had were provided only through his efforts. The very afternoon of our arrival in Mexico City it was possible to observe the most distinct contrast between the conduct of my brother-in-law and that of Archibaldo who aspires to that status. While Pascual contrived a loan of funds necessary for our immediate heavy expenses which came as a great surprise, the other disappeared, as though through a trap door, for a period of eight days. Lulú's weeping eyes and pale cheeks made us aware of his absence. Apparently even the lack of money did not make him abandon his habits of dissipation. According to Mama, these periodic disappearances give an accurate means of evaluating the man. But that did not make any difference to Lulú; she continued to insist that *he* was the man for her.

What for us was a plausible, disinterested, and noble act was on Pascual's part, according to Procopio, officiousness with a "tail." He meant by that vulgar expression that Pascual is two-faced and that his intentions are deceitful. We weren't surprised when, instead of showing gratitude for Pascual's services, Procopio precipitated an acrimonious dispute about certain details which Agustinita thought were of slight significance. It seems that the person with whom Pascual made the loan for us demanded a provision in the note that we should repay it in hard money. Since we had received only paper money, Procopio objected to the condition.

"It is merely a formality," Pascual observed, surprised. "As a matter of fact, how can we demand silver? It has disappeared from circulation and no one takes it into account in commercial transactions!"

Agustinita made plain to Procopio the injustice of his obstinacy. Objection to the loan, already made on these conditions, would make

Pascual appear ridiculous. Anyhow, as the arrangement had already cost a good deal, it would be impossible to cancel the agreement.

"My dear," Procopio still insisted, "give me a free hand in these matters. They are not the sort you understand."

"Wouldn't any one of the houses we have in Zacatecas be worth many more thousands of *pesos* than those papers represent? What money have you provided for me to meet the urgent expenses for food and getting settled?"

Procopio, taking his pen and nervously signing the document, murmured, "I guess it is evident that I do what you wish."

In spite of all that, Pascual continued to visit us as usual. Isn't that proof of his inexhaustible good will and perfect self-control? Agustinita excused Papa: "Those are just his peculiarities."

Indeed Procopio is full of peculiarities which quite well explain his aversion for Pascual and his preference for Archibaldo. All of us recognize Pascual's merits. With respect to Archibaldo—well, no one has to tell us about his past life because we already know too much. Although Pascual's origin was humble, he had succeeded in achieving a very enviable social position. They say that when he came to Zacatecas, his baggage consisted of only the title of attorney from Tlaxcala, a half dozen collars, a pair of celluloid cuffs, and not even a shirt or any underwear to his name. So much more to his credit; for with no more weapons than his intelligence he succeeded in opening wide the offices of the banks and business houses, afterwards even the very drawing rooms of our highest society. His physical, moral, and intellectual gifts are captivating. He holds himself erect with manly self-confidence. He has white skin as firm as that of a fifteen-year-old girl and a wide, sagacious forehead under glossy black hair which he wears parted in the middle. Everything about him reveals intelligence and good will. The pure lines of his countenance, set off by black eyes and an aquiline nose, are not changed by either a dry smile or ordinary anger. Moderation distinguishes him. He knows well how to get into the center of things, gaining the admiration and regard of all who know him. It was he, speaking for high society, who talked with the bishop about matters related to the dignity of the bishopric. It was he who personally discussed with the civil authorities the affairs of the upper classes. The clergy as well as the laity singled him out for special attention.

Certainly, empty heads like Archibaldo or shameless, vacuous girls like Lulú are incapable of understanding such outstanding merits. Archibaldo sank his fangs into Pascual like a snake into an eagle: "If Pascual has earned in our drawing rooms the reputation of being learned, it is unquestionable owing to the fact that he is a solemn windbag." A double insult which for us goes in one ear and out the other.

Here, on the other hand, is a sketch of Archibaldo. All who know this dissipated youth will agree that there is no calumny nor exaggeration in the severe judgments I have passed on him and to which I continue to attest. The estimations are not only mine; they represent the common feeling of the whole family. He is a distant relative, orphaned at eighteen with a fortune of 200,000 *pesos*, who caused much talk in Zacatecas with his youthful escapades. He was, apparently the *aribiter elegantiarum* of our region. I believe that Lulú is in love with the man that he *was*. Only thus can I explain her unusual attachment for this relative. If the ardent glances which young and old turn on my sister Lulú are any evidence, then she is surely a lovely young thing.

That he threw away his fortune with both hands was of little or no concern to any of us except Lulú whom he had courted since she was a little thing. One day he disappeared from Zacatecas. After a while we learned that he was in Mexico City wasting the last of his inheritance. Then no one heard any more about him. We thought he was dead when one day he turned up at our house with the dust of the road still on him, his clothes old and ragged. He was emaciated, balding—a wreck of the Archibaldo who five years before had been the cock of the walk among the marriageable girls of Zacatecas. He had wandered through all America as a journalist, sportsman, bell-boy, soldier, etc. In sum, his body and soul were worn out as much from the consequences of the enjoyments of the flesh and the spirit as from the pains of misery and vice. Naturally he was received coldly and only with strict politeness. But Papa! That Papa! Not only did he gather him in with open arms, but he actually took him into our home with the warmest and most absurd sympathy. He gave him a hearty welcome. He arranged a party. The young people from our best society came; and there was music and dancing, and cider to drink. When the last guests were leaving, Archibaldo said solemnly,

"Uncle Procopio, now I know the true warmth of a home!" He

raised his handkerchief to his eyes, they say to wipe away a tear; and, with a break in his voice and without the frivolous tone which usually characterized it, he added,

"I have wasted my fortune and my very life. I find myself here hardly knowing why. I am fit for nothing. But in this fortuitous hour, my soul catches a glimpse of an unforeseen course; I have found a purpose in my life."

His voice was becoming more solemn with each word. Quite diverted, we were listening to him as to the blind man who tells stories at the door of the church.

"Uncle Procopio, instead of shooting myself on leaving here as I had planned to do, I ask you for Lulú's hand with all the great respect this house merits and with all the formalities of custom."

Procopio let out a big laugh; the rest of us remained stupefied by the gaffe. The color in Agustinita's face ranged the gamut from that of old marble to a deep, dark purple. Lulú was agitated. Procopio, the only one who kept his head in this wicked comedy, took Lulú's hand in one of his and with the other took a revolver out of Archibaldo's pocket.

"Dear nephew, one of your ideas appeals to me as much as the other; so much so that I am unable to make a decision. It is up to Lulú to decide."

Who could imagine this odious farce would be the beginning of relations which have hung like the sword of Damocles over the name and honor of our family?

VI

On the day after our arrival in México City, Agustinita and Procopio quarreled. Mama was praising Pascual highly for the way in which his disinterestedness and expeditiousness had resolved our difficulties. Procopio, with malign words and malicious smile, indicated his suspicion of my brother-in-law's motives.

"Why should he leave a blank space where the name of the lender should be?"

"You very well know that Pascual is poor and doesn't have even a thousand *pesos* to his name."

"I wouldn't be a bit surprised if he isn't the one lending us this money."

"All the more reason to be grateful to him."

"If he had lent it to us in gold and silver."

"What notions you have, Procopio!"

" I hope that I may be mistaken."

Daily, Procopio asked for Archibaldo; Lulú remained secluded in her bedroom. If the rest of us paid no attention to his absence, it was because we breathed easier without him.

Visiting temples and store windows in the morning, discussing what we had seen the rest of the day, the time passed insensibly. Francisco José, in his ivory tower, devoured new books.

A week passed before Archibaldo returned. He was much thinner, his clothes were disheveled, his beard unshaved, and his eyes inflamed. What shamelessness or what manly courage!

"I swear that it will be the last time, Uncle Procopio," he said to him confidentially.

Agustinita protested under her breath, feeling sorry for "the poor woman who should decide to become the wife of such a good-for-nothing."

Poor little Lulú! She is so loyal that she cried all afternoon. That evening, nevertheless, I found her kissing him as though nothing had happened.

Two weeks passed. Francisco José gave us his intellectual first-fruits achieved in this City of Palaces. With a voice sweeter than the honey of Hymetto, he recited to us his poem: "I Search Now for the Heights of Serenity." Agustinita listened enchanted. But Procopio, stretched out on the sofa, yawned, and did not stop smoking an instant. Archibaldo entered on tiptoes and waited for Francisco José to finish his poem which he was reading with a voice full of emotion and his eyes wet. Then Archibaldo said,

"The Federal troops, disbanded, are returning to the city. They have suffered great defeats in Zacatecas and Guadalajara."

Francisco José, terribly irritated by such a stupid and inopportune interruption, abruptly left the room.

"My dear," remarked Procopio getting up excitedly, "we must take a house with all the necessary conveniences as I told you from the beginning."

"Yes, dear Mama, we need a house," Lulú seconded him, as though the hotel had become too constricted a place for chatting with her sweetheart.

"Don't even consider it," asserted Agustinita. "The defection of some miserable Federal troops is of no significance. I'll just let you know, Archibaldo, that I have better news. Pascual Orozco and Pepe Pérez Castro have raised the flag of General Huerta. Just note what men they are! Pascual Orozco and Pepe Pérez Castro! It means that before a month is out we shall be back in Zacatecas!"

Francisco José, who returned to get his aspirin tablets, indicated his approval of Agustinita's views. Archibaldo, patting me on the shoulder, said in a low voice,

"That return to Zacatecas is as unlikely of achievement as the finding of 'the heights of serenity' which your brother goes about looking for."

"I appreciate your affection and consideration, Archibaldo," I answered him, "but surely you must know that my silence does not indicate agreement to what you say; just good manners."

Agustinita, noticing Archibaldo's satisfaction, exclaimed indignantly, "See, Procopio, how Archibaldo cannot conceal his happiness at the events that have caused us so much pain?"

"Archibaldo is one of those in the revolution who must come out ahead," observed Papa, distracted.

Remarkable! Archibaldo, who according to Agustinita plays deaf when he wants to, blushed to his eyes. When it was least expected, he disappeared with all his things, including his suitcase. Lulú, naturally, was very sad. In a few days she became very pale and even lost a little weight. But it was all for the good and tranquillity of our home.

Unfortunately Archibaldo's dismal forecasts became reality. One morning Berta and Pascual came with the news. By the very manner of their coming I suspected a catastrophe. She wore a cheap, sleazy shawl and a skimpy skirt that she never would have worn in Zacatecas; he had the collar of his shirt loosened and his shoes unshined.

I thought, "Are they coming to give me a fright?" I began to tremble all over.

Pascual showed us a copy of *La Tribuna*[4] which announced the arrival of Constitutionalists in the vicinity of the capital.

"All that has nothing to do with me," sharply remarked Francisco José who was pretty well knocked out with a headache.

Agustinita was speechless; her tears flowed freely. It was more than an hour before she was able to say anything.

"Procopio, it is urgent that you look for a house."

"I made arrangements for one a week ago," he answered with remarkable equanimity.

VII

We were seized with a feverish agitation. Francisco José, who foresaw the necessity of taking a fifth aspirin, came to help us pack the mattresses. Agustinita, exasperated by the repeated absences of Lulú who could not tear herself away from the balcony, said to me,

"Go see what it is outside that attracts Lulú."

"What else can it be, Mother dear, other than that immovable Don Tancredo there on the corner?"

Now at least poor Mama had an object on which to discharge her anger. If Archibaldo's ears did not burn that day, then surely they are made of asbestos.

We finally left. I was surprised when the auto stopped after turning in to a certain street. Papa got out quickly to show us the new house. The car had followed along streetcar tracks which, shining brightly in the sun, had blinded me so that I was not aware of the moment that we entered the Roma district.

We opened an iron gate embellished with ivy and bougainville; we went up an ornate marble stairway decorated with flowers and greenery. We entered the house! God pardon my spiritual poverty for the sake of my good faith! At that moment I blessed the fate which had forced us to leave our vast, gray land of Zacatecas for this delightful corner of the world called Roma. Not only I, but Lulú, too, felt the same way. Since the disappearance of her sweetheart, she had not recovered her usual appearance. Now her glance was bright and warm and on her fresh lips trembled one of our sweet songs of the tropics.

We spent the first afternoon on the terrace, contemplating with joy the warm greenness of the trees, the red brick benches, the stone façade, the simple line of the concrete cornice above the stone work, and the touches of vivid light in the deep heart of the park. We enjoyed the sounds of running water and the chirping of birds in their nests. We watched until it all faded away into indecisive lines and diffused masses among the innumerable arc lights.

Francisco José said to me very gravely,

"Notice, César, how the beauty of nature is enhanced by the hand of man. In other words it is stylized and ennobled. I will write: 'In Praise of the Arisocratic Suburb.' "

Mama, although she refused to acknowledge it, also yielded to these enchantments. Her deep frown was erased and she even permitted me to go out with Lulú to wander along some of the streets. We walked along aimlessly stopping often for trivial reasons. The façade of a modern church elicited my most fervent praises.

But Lulú, with that Voltairean spirit which she had not inherited from Mama, and of which she sometimes boasts, replied to me that the cupola looked very much like the bald, sharp-pointed head of Pepino, a clown very well known in our native region. When we saw on Orizaba Street some little lions, ferocious-looking even in their crumbled state, we laughed heartily.

The morning would have ended as one of the most pleasant in the world except for an incident that was as pleasurable for Lulú as it was disagreeable for me. Archibaldo came up to us as though he had sprung from the earth. Smiling, he greeted me, placed a letter in Lulú's hand, and continued walking by her side.

"Dear Mama is expecting us at ten o'clock sharp, Lulú, and it is now ten minutes of the hour," I said, taking out my watch.

Archibaldo smiled ironically, but my expression and the dignified tone which I gave to my voice must have convinced him; for he accompanied us only two more blocks and then said goodby. Lulú and I went on our way without talking. Naturally I again felt withdrawn from her.

Just as I do, Francisco José likes to take a comfortable seat on the balcony and to lose himself in contemplating the view. Sometimes he was so entranced that he wasn't even aware of my presence. A lady with a very distinguished bearing passed along the sidewalk in front; next came a group of four aristocratic looking young girls with very small red lips, big black eyes, and slender white necks. The apparition of such a lovely bouquet shook my brother out of his absorption, and he said,

"How enchanting a woman is from a distance. That is how we should always see her. Slender, glowing, airy like the muslin that caresses her bosom, her body, her thighs, wearing a narrow skirt which enables one to conjecture about her Venus-like nudity."

"How sensual you are, brother!" I interrupted him, blushing and seized by a most vivid alarm. "How much better it would be to return to our customary amusements with worthy gentlemen, shrewd and valiant pages, tale-bearing squires, chaperones who ignore what is going on, fat canons, elaborate cups of chocolate, and the rest of our fancies, which, if they benefit no one, at least they do no harm to soul or health."

"Shut up, stupid! What do you know about such things, César?"

"As much as you do, Francisco José, but it isn't proper to discuss them, for it offends the honor of our souls and the modesty of our bodies."

Our jubiliation was short-lived; before forty-eight hours, swarms of *carrancistas* made a sudden incursion into the city. Suddenly hordes of animals and people worse than animals darkened the streets. Those cobbled streets so clean, with their stately trees, with the clear sky above, with tall, princely houses along them, were filled with masses of big, broken-down, muddy horses and ragged soldiers dripping with mud up to their heads on which they wore straw hats adorned with red and green ribbons. Very dark people with scanty, ruddy beards, with pointed, white fangs, with idiotic, ferocious smiles on their faces that were enough to make one shudder.

"The Men of the New Régime!" said Francisco José smiling.

Agustinita fled to the bathroom to hide her alarm. In spite of our natural anxiety, Lulú and I raised the window shades.

"Horrors, what faces!" cried my sister and fled, frightened.

Not understanding, to tell the truth, why the others were so afraid, I opened the window. In the circus I had seen many wild animals of ferocious appearance that were harmless. I called to Francisco José.

"What was that you read to me last night about a famous sculptor who in his representations of animals smoothed out their features, bestowing on them the appearance of an even more refined cruelty than nature itself?"

"The sculptor Rubeck in a work by Ibsen."

He came to the window, too, with his curiosity aroused.

"This is beyond exaggeration, César! Look, the one who comes there on the right is a man-wolf, the one on the sidewalk is a man-coyote, and the one coming to the left is a man-pig."

"I admire your insight, but what I see is a combination of two animals in one person who is a man-jackal at times; at times a man-ass."

"Notice that the most interesting type is missing. There should be one who is arrogant, courageous, noble. Understand? We do not have a man-lion."

"That is a species which, I am afraid, has disappeared from our breed," responded Procopio, back of us.

After he left, Francisco José said to me,

"When Papa wishes to be clever, he can."

"Why do you say that?"

"Haven't you heard him many times justify the work of the bandits?"

Who would have imagined that our lack of awareness in the face of danger and the serenity and calm with which we were diverting ourselves at the expense of the savages would be precisely what saved us from falling into their clutches? The pillagers respected us! As a matter of fact, we noticed a little later that the mob invaded the abandoned homes or those left in the care of servants. With the blades of their knives, with hatchets, guns, and butts of rifles, they broke open doors and windows and looted everything.

Procopio said that nothing happened to us precisely because we did not show fear or distrust. But Agustinita insisted that it was the Virgin of Guadalupe in whose hands she had entrusted us who had performed a miracle for us in the time of our affliction. I remember that many years ago an employee at our place of business took me to the Norris Circus and put me on the back of an elephant. He also had me take hold of the tail of a lion. Later when they told me what could have happened to me, I had the same sort of sensation which affected me now on our being exposed to the dangers which we ran on account of these men from Avernus.

Our streets were turned into corrals for animals. When I seek for something very filthy with which to compare them, I can only think about the neighborhood of the Merced market which appears to me to be like a symbol: the actual heart of Mexico.

Automobiles with filthy, propped-up tops of canvas which took the place of the luxurious carriages were always full of horrible marauders and women with painted faces resembling decorated cakes. The cars were veritable itinerant pigsties which passed by like Furies, sowing seeds of panic in hearts, even one as steady as Procopio's.

And it must be said that it was not the nightmare of a moment, nor of an hour, nor of a day. Our eyes became accustomed to the brilliance of the powder flashes and our ears to the blasts of the shooting. What am I saying? Our own moral attitude was dulled to the point that we could listen without great emotion to stories with details of chilling cruelty of a hand-to-hand assault, of a rape, of a treacherous attack—all of which had occurred right out on the street.

One day a changed Pascual, nervous and unnatural, came to see us. It was the first time I had seen him like that.

"It was impossible to bring Berta," he told us as he dropped heavily in a chair. "It is impossible to get a cab. They are all dashing about packed with people wearing *huaraches* and carrying rifles. The common people have taken command of the streetcars and it is an adventuresome exploit to ride in one as I have just done. They took my watch from me and I almost had to thank them for doing it. There are no respectable people that they do not insult."

"That is nothing yet!" exclaimed the realistic Agustinita. "These people kill for no more reason than their pleasure in seeing blood run. Oh, mercy me!"

Pascual withdrew into profound meditation. After a while, in a bitter, muffled voice he told us about the latest occurrences: a series of assassinations perpetrated among the revolutionaries themselves.

"That's good!" exclaimed Agustinita, radiant with joy. "They are now divided? Praise God!"

Francisco José agreed that the hand of the All Powerful could be seen in that development; that never had any common people been able to survive in anarchy.

Overflowing with faith and hope, we allowed joy free entrance into our hearts. Agustinita begged Pascual not to expose Berta again to danger by leaving her alone in order to come to visit us; he should be mindful of her safety until the restoration of order and individual rights.

VIII

A week passed. We were atoms lost in this hell. The volatile imagination of Agustinita was continually at work. Like pursuing

Furies, omens raced through her mind.

One day Procopio decided to go out.

"Man of ice!" she scolded him, beside herself. "You realize that you not only risk your life but those of your wife and your own children. That is surely tempting the grace of God who with eyes of compassion has seen us through to this day."

That very morning Bernabé returned from the markets with news as well as just the daily necessities. It seemed that the bandits were hanging all the respectable men from the towers of the Cathedral.

"Pascual is lost!" cried Mama with such a scream that it surely could have been heard in Cortés' palace. "It is impossible that they have spared him. Dead! Pascual is dead! What shall I do?"

Human cruelty. It is sad to say but some people in trying to do good, do harm. Procopio replied to her laconically,

"Be calm, my dear, be calm, for Pascual is fully as well known in Mexico City as our cook, our good Bernabé."

Mama was at a loss for words. Flashing anger in her eyes was her answer.

Afterwards spasms began to alter the lines of her countenance and she began to twist like a chicken with its head cut off.

"An attack!"

I dashed to the bedroom to look for the ether and alcohol and came face to face with Lulú who came in crying out,

"Pascual is here! He just got out of an automobile full of soldiers."

Suddenly Mama's twitching body stilled.

"Prisoner!"

Then she began to talk at random,

"Prisoner! They come for the ransom! Procopio, save him! Save us all! Sell the hacienda—pawn the mine. All, all for him!"

Neither the alcohol nor the ether nor Procopio's vigorous words had the effect on Agustinita of just Pascual's presence. Calm as always, smiling as always, kind as always, handsome as always.

"Pascual, my son!"

Mama cried and laughed at the same time; the muscles of her face seemed to have gone crazy again. She ended by throwing herself in his arms.

"What is happening? Why are you crying?"

"You come here a prisoner, Pascual, don't hide it from me."

"What an idea!"

"And we not providing funds to save you! Procopio, his ransom! Quick, his ransom!"

"But where did you get this notion?"

"I know all about it; it is useless for you to persist in denying it. The bandits bring you here a prisoner."

"Bandits? Captain Covarrubias, my wonderful friend, and the other gentlemen who are waiting for me outside?"

We looked at each other, stunned. An ambiguous smile hovered on Procopio's lips.

"I have established relations with eminent personalities encharged with our new government. Some, like Captain Covarrubias, are very honorable. Anyway it is to our advantage to accept the new men. Today and tomorrow are in their hands. The Captain enjoys the confidence of Carranza. He is a sincere and loyal friend who would be able to secure all sorts of protection for the family."

Abrupt and varied changes ensued. Procopio himself who listened to all of it with a certain evidence of scorn and irony, scowled fiercely and bit his lips.

"If you will allow me," continued Pascual, failing to consider the effect of his words, "I will introduce Captain Covarrubias to you right now."

I confess that notwithstanding the respect and fondness that I have for dear Mama and the great affection and near veneration that my brother-in-law inspires in me, in this instance, in my mind, I stood aloof from them. If Pascual's astonishing about-face was inexplicable to me, Agustinita's answer left me dumbfounded.

"Procopio, what Pascual says is very reasonable. It is necessary that you meet Carranza. What talent and what insight! Have you finally come to understand Pascual?"

Papa was as surprised as a colt caught in a lasso. Lulú, as though she had not been reared by the rigid principles of the family, replied vehemently,

"And what about that famous honor?"

While Agustinita looked daggers at her, Papa, with a halo of tenderness emanating from his paternal eyes, supported Lulú firmly and proudly in her disdainful attitude.

I do not know why at this point everything came to a stop. Pascual without being disturbed, said,

"My proposals not being acceptable, I will leave. But I must not conceal from you that it is dangerous for you to stay in this part of town."

"What! What mystery is hidden in your words?" moaned Mama in consternation.

"I said it very clearly," he responded, rising to his feet. "Respectable families are the ones most exposed to abuse."

Pascual left. Agustinita, choking with anger, ordered Procopio to look for another house immediately.

"Where can we go that we shall not meet up with them?"

"In the Bolsa district or in Santa Julia," Francisco José spoke up nervously. "It is logical to suppose that now in those sections, respectable families will find the maximum security."

"All these anxieties and difficulties would be avoidable if Procopio were not so obstinate," said Agustinita.

As Procopio remained silent she insisted, "Stubborn man, talk to Carranza, talk to Obregón. Pascual will open those doors for you—"

"Yes, my dear," he responded with mellifluous voice and mordant smile, "I will go right now to Carranza, as Pascual has counseled us, and then straightway I will bring home all his new friends. What joy! Our house a den of bandits. Isn't that what you called them only yesterday?"

It is necessary to confess it—if Carranza's mob is capable of all sorts of abuses, how could we grant them the freedom of the house? How could we abandon Lulú to them? How could we entrust into their hands honor, life, and property?

I made known my thoughts and my fears to Lulú. I told her that I would be an innocent gazelle in the middle of a pack of hungry wolves, and she burst out in a disconcerting laugh.

"These people of the revolution frighten me as much as a little lap dog that goes trotting down the street."

IX

It was necessary, though, for us to change our place of residence. What a house the new one was! Through a narrow and interminable passage, in which artificial light was necessary by five o'clock in the afternoon, we came to a damp, cold patio, like the bottom of a giant well, with walls on four sides pierced by dark openings in which could be seen, indistinctly, restless feminine heads, like doves in a dovecote. They had heavily painted dark eyes like the masks in illustrated magazines, and bare arms and necks which moved among masses of chiffon and laces.

I had a suspicion and I asked myself, what sort of a place had we got ourselves into?

The woman porter, a shrewd forty-year-old, of the "worthy type of the Archpriest of Hita," on speaking to Francisco José, alleviated my fears.

"In all of Mexico City you will not find a neighborhood more respectable than this." She pointed out that for us from the interior, manners and customs are so different that for whatever pretext one wanted to hide, the shame of living in these apartment houses could never free one from the anguish of having fallen a long way down the social scale.

We went through the empty apartment that she offered us. It was the best one on the second floor: a series of rooms with only one window which opened on the street and with no view but that of an all-encompassing plastered wall of a chocolate factory. Its architecture was hatefully geometric with stupid lack of originality. I felt suffocated.

Mama, who divined my uneasiness of mind, tried to console me.

"Make believe that we are in a provincial hotel, as transient guests, only for one or two weeks."

Since we arrived in Mexico City, she had insisted that we just take one thing at a time. That will help us endure with patience our distressing exile.

We went away resolved to take the house, and that same night Procopio signed the lease. We abandoned our beautiful little palace, resigned and depressed.

The first few days Procopio did not open his lips, but at the end of the first week he began to complain of the cold and suffocating surroundings of the bare white walls. Then he took to walking from one end of the house to the other, stopping from time to time to breathe with his breast raised and his nostrils dilated. Finally one day he burst forth.

"Here one lives like a caged animal."

There was no human force capable of controlling him, and he dashed out into the street.

Like Agustinita, Pascual achieved his purpose. One afternoon he brought Captain Covarrubias to see us, a proud youth with sharp eyes, a small mouth crowned by two red, scorpion-like mustaches, and eye-teeth excessively brilliant and sharp.

"My great friend, Pepe Covarrubias," announced Pascual noticing our cold and almost hostile reception, "is a member of a wealthy frontier family. He and Carranza, who is his friend, are natives of the same region. It is true that he is only a captain, but it is because his ambitions are not along that line. He entered the revolution only to protect his family's interests."

Agustinita, whose expression changed abruptly, hurried to make excuses.

"Please be good enough to pardon us, sir; but all these people who wear leggings and Texas style hats frighten us terribly. With Pascual's explanation, I understand everything. Your motives for taking up the cause of these people are very noble and just. Consequently, you now know that you are welcome in this house."

"Señora, I consider it a great privilege to have the friendship of such a distinguished family," Covarrubias responded with the resonance of bugles in his voice.

The conversation was very animated. Pascual always charms us with his agreeable and persuasive tongue. We had forgotten the captain's presence, but after a while we noticed him seated at the side of Lulú. We had the unpleasant surprise of seeing him courting her with a manner which, although maybe very Mexican, was not customary among the respectable people of the provinces. Mama screwed up her mouth in disgust, calling Pascual's attention to the situation. Pascual explained to her in an aside,

"It is his manner of behaving, but I guarantee his gentlemanliness."

When he saw that his words did not succeed in extinguishing the fire in Agustinita's eyes, he called out to the soldier,

"Pepe, come here. I told you one time about Francisco José's literary talent, didn't I? He is a poet of promise. I want you to hear some of his latest compositions."

When the captain left Lulú, she smiled, imitating in an admirable manner Papa's sarcastic and hard-hearted expression.

He came over to sit by us and said that he was a devotee of art in all its manifestations, and that he cultivated intimate friendships with writers, painters, musicians, and eminent intellectuals.

Francisco José, standing in the middle of the living room, threw back his abundant black hair, revealing a bulging and serene forehead, dreamy eyes, aquiline nose, and a prominent, kind lower lip. As he fanned his face the ends of his flowing tie fluttered. Drawing together his eyebrows in order to collect his thoughts, he commenced with that grace so characteristic of him to recite a sonnet.

"How is that, Pepe? How is that?" exclaimed Pascual almost in ecstacy.

"Young man," replied Covarrubias emphatically, "you have indisputable talent; only I find it—how may one say it? A little out of date—I say—it lacks method—atmosphere. Meet me tomorrow at seven o'clock to go to a meeting ot writers so that I may introduce you to them. You, and Lulú too, please expect me then. It will give me much pleasure. Or if you prefer it, I will come here for you at nightfall. Will you go, Lulú?"

But Lulú could not answer him, because she had disappeared. Mama commented afterwards, "If this young man should succeed in erasing the impression which that tramp of an Archibaldo has made on the girl, it might make me a little tolerant."

But Lulú was not of the same opinion. On the two occasions that the captain came to the house, Lulú refused to come out or to greet him.

X

One day followed another with discouraging slowness. One morning Lulú called me aside,

"César, I am dying here. Without air, without light, without sun! You, who are Mama's favorite, beg her to allow us to go out at least for an hour."

"But Lulú, are you in your right mind? Would you venture to put foot out of the house, seeing that the streets are still full of people without faith and without fear of God?"

"Now you've learned that tune. Dunce! Come to the window and see how everybody goes along peacefully."

She was probably right, but I gave in because of the innate weakness of my character. Naturally, Agustinita's reply was a round "no"

for me and a solemn phillipic for Lulú. Mama is sufficiently astute
to realize that such a notion could not have been born in my head.
However, the devil who meddles everywhere made it possible for my
sister to realize her wish that very afternoon. In those days it happened that articles of primary necessity had become alarmingly
scarce—a weak delineation, it's true, of the specter of hunger which
now we know so well, of the hunger which we never suspected except
as a hypothetical existence—as the creation of the fantasy of dema-
gogues. Well then, Mama had been forced to come to the point of
acknowledging that in less than two months the last boxes of supplies
had been exhausted. There was nothing for breakfast for the following
day.

"You should have told me that before now, I will go at once to get
some money," responded Procopio without being disturbed.

"No, Pascual will obtain it more quickly. I will telephone him."
Prociopio took his hat and went out into the street without answering.

By three o'clock, we became alarmed, because Papa is remarkably
punctual. Agustinita speculated that some interruption in the traffic
had detained him; with that we all went calmly to eat. But four
o'clock came and then five, and he had not returned.

"I hope that there has not been some accident, now that the bandits
assault men even to take away their hats," said Agustinita.

"Let us talk to Pascual, Mama dear. It is possible that he knows
something," I observed.

Lulú and I ran to the telephone in the drugstore out front. But
it wasn't possible to get a connection. Lulú, who used the instrument,
said that the lines were out of order, that no one answered, and I
don't know what all. We returned to the house, and Lulú pleaded that
she and I should go personally to look for Pascual. In the final
analysis he would be the only one who could do something for us.

"If we're going, then be quick about it," I replied, "because it
is getting on toward nightfall and I should not dare to go out on the
street then."

Alarmed, Mama was perplexed in the face of having to make a
decision. Lulú demonstrated to her with much cleverness that we
should not have to walk more than twenty meters, since it was only a
matter of going up to the corner to get on the San Rafael streetcar,
getting out at the front of the hotel, and then returning in the same
safe way. Who knows why I imagined that there was something

suspicious in Lulú's attitude? I wished to voice my alarm; but I was
sorry for her and I kept silent.

Agustinita still struggled for a few moments in an effort to make
a decision.

"You take unfair advantage of my distractions, Lulú. Do you
think that my book of prayers of St. Francis can be your scratch pad?"

She snatched the prayer book on whose covers Lulú had illustrated
her plan with a map. Then she found many faults with our clothes,
assuring us that never before had we been seen dressed in such a
fashion. Finally, commending us devoutly to all the Celestial Court,
she sent us out into the street.

Then in the foyer, the poor little thing urged me to take care of
Lulú and Lulú to take care of. me.

No sooner had we put foot in the street than Lulú knocked me
speechless with inconceivable audacity.

"Streetcars! There are no streetcars! That is the last thing we
need to bother about. We leave the house numb; why should we
choose to go in a streetcar packed together as though in a box when
we have the open streets and at least two hours for roaming about?"

"In the name of the Virgin Mary, Lulú!"

"I'm not afraid of anybody as long as I am holding César's arm."

She took hold of me firmly and let out a loud, sonorous laugh.

"Oh, Lulú, how perfidious you are! How can I answer you when
you test my worthiness as a man that way?"

We went on like crazy ones along God's streets, lost among the
crowds that were moving rapidly in every direction. The tranquillity
of the people going about restored peacefulness to my spirit. I actually caught Lulu's crazy, happy spirit. When we encountered a multitude of coarse-looking men, untidy and of curious appearance, I
thought with horror: "It is they!" Actually they pushed me before them as we collided; but as I left the collision unharmed, I had
a strange sensation of mingled happiness and fright that caused me
to remember Johnson, Papa's magnificent Newfoundland who, had
he wished it could have devoured me in one bite. When I was very
young, I put my little hands in his wet maw, red as the heart of a
watermelon; and the immense dog licked them gently, making me
feel at the same time the slight rake of his sharp teeth and a singular chill.

I told Lulú what I was thinking and she replied,

"When one lives thus, between the walls of that sausage-like establishment which we call home, it is easy to give way to the worst sort of lies and fantasies. Whom have you seen that these men have harmed?"

On passing through San Fernando Street I was vexed by Lulú's effusive greeting to someone whom I did not see.

"Someone from our region, Lulú?"

"Yes," she replied to me smiling, "someone from our region."

I looked with eagerness for some familiar countenance, because Lulú's happy face was beaming.

"Can't you guess who it is?"

"No, no, I do not see anyone I know." Then I was able to discern a young man, his black beard unshaven, his clothes disheveled, who was coming in our direction, smiling and happy. "I ought to know that face, Lulú."

He burst out in a hearty laugh. Now Archibaldo was in front of us, bare-headed, radiant as the sun at midday.

"Since you were always clean-shaven, I did not recognize you," I observed dryly.

I intended to convey to him my disgust on account of our running into him; but without giving me time to begin, with unequaled impudence, he took Lulú's hand from mine, holding it himself with a very ardent manner. Then they made me go along in front of them.

I turned my anguished eyes in every direction. I thought I would die of shame. Who would be the witnesses of my humiliation? Fortunately no one paid any attention to me, nor to Archibaldo and Lulú. It seems that in Mexico City it is the vulgar custom that sweethearts go out for a walk together and that the brothers close their eyes to what is going on. Such reflections calmed me, but for a short time only; then, the tacit mission with which Agustinita had encharged me became very clear. "I will not speak to them the whole way," I thought with pride. But they, happy as sparrows that have escaped from their cage, were very much occupied with themselves and did not pay the least attention to my existence.

Burning with a justifiable rage, I was giving thought to the most adequate means for making Mama aware of the episode without injury to my pride and without avoiding my responsibilities, when a storm blew up.

XI

"Let's go down San Diego Street, then turn into Avenida Juárez," Archibaldo said to me, patting me affectionately on the shoulder, making me turn the corner.

This was not so strange but that I would have complied without protesting. If, however, I am slow-thinking, at times I am quick-acting. My sensitivity rose to a white heat. "*Now* I will make them understand," I said to myself, "that I am not precisely one with whom they can do as they please." And from that moment I was determined to make them feel the weight of the authority which Agustinita had invested in me, watching for the first propitious occasion.

We passed through the Alameda. The wind was howling. The tops of the trees were in violent motion with the furiously shaking foliage making a moaning sound. Happily for me there was no lightning or thunder which would have made me lose my proper manner. Nevertheless, when the wind blew the grass and shrubs flat and, roaring the length of the street, knocked a light post off its foundation, a reflexive movement made me fall back and put myself elbow to elbow with Archibaldo.

"Don't be frightened; it is nothing," he said to me.

I felt that my face was burning but I had sufficient strength not to make any appeal. I continued ahead maintaining my threatening attitude and my complete silence.

Dense dust extinguished the illumination from the street lights along the length of the entire avenue. Large drops of rain began to spatter on the asphalt.

"We can take refuge here under the trees," said Archibaldo.

Then I thought, "Now it's my time." It was even more the case since I was aware of the great responsibility which the events so unexpectedly had placed upon me. Resolved, I pulled together all my strength and replied authoritatively,

"Mama hasn't sent us to take refuge under some trees; Lulú and I must continue on our way; and as for you sir, you are free to choose the route which best suits you."

I believe that up to that moment they were hardly aware of my existence. They looked at me, surprised; they looked at each other and then laughed as if someone had tickled them.

Nevertheless, my triumph was undoubted; they did not dare disobey. And precisely because I was fully aware of what was in his mind it seemed to me that a cruelty still persisted in my caprice. Just then it commenced raining like water pouring out of a pitcher.

"On the sidewalk in front of us is an open entrance. Let's go there, Lulú, until this squall passes."

They followed me without saying a word; but just as we arrived at the threshold, the porter slammed the doors almost on our noses.

"Listen, you," I cried, angered, "we are the Vásquez Prados of Zacatecas!"

A more impolite people I have never seen in my life.

Perplexed, in spite of having taken the rôle which legitimately belonged to me, I meditated on new measures, while they laughed and flirted, quite contented, squeezing close together in the furious tempest as if it were the soft warm clarity of the moon.

There was a flash of lightning; the lights went out. I felt around, searching for Archibaldo and Lulú and, on finding them, held on tightly. What else could I do?

Like fugitive fireflies little white, green, and red lights rapidly moved about hither and yon to the sound of a deafening roll of trucks, carriages, and bicycles. Bulky shadows fell against the wall then instantly disappeared. Water drained off my hat as from a canal. Soon the street lights came on and the great avenue that had been deserted sprang to life again, bathed in refulgent clarity. Falling diagonally, the rain made designs that looked like arabesques of crystal. But it was the vision of an instant. A new flash of lightning threw us into obscurity again.

Then something horrible occurred. Near us a tremendous clamor arose: "¡*Viva* Francisco Villa! Death to Don Venustiano!" Immediately shooting began, and people ran in every direction. An avalanche of them came toward us and violently dashed against us. I tried to draw back to look for Lulú, but I did not know where I was; I could not determine in what direction she had gone. Such fear seized me that I began to pray and with staring eyes I cried,

"Archibaldo, Lulú, here I am!"

Just then armed men came out of a very large entrance and spread out in opposite directions. Soon a heavy hand fell on my shoulder.

"Is it you, Archibaldo?" I moaned.

They replied in a language which I could not understand; then they threw me down forcefully and practically dragging me, took me—where, I did not know.

Intense cold penetrated my bones. Shuddering, I gave a weak lament and opened my eyes. Horrors! Some big men, with faces like Aztec idols, had submerged me up to my neck in a fountain of icy water.

"Jesus Christ! Where am I?"

I could not understand the dialect of those abortions from hell. They were all around about me, talking, revealing their very white teeth with their horrible grins. One of them, as muscular and as big as one of the Green Indians of the Canal of Viga, picked me up out of the fountain and with rude pushes took me to a very dark place where he abandoned me. Without enough strength to get up on my feet, I stretched out on the ground. An acrid odor of manure struck my nose; then I sensed that I was very close to the shod hooves of an animal. I realized that they had put me in the stable of the barracks. As a consequence of my misfortune I cried bitter tears that would have moved the most impervious heart. But what could one expect of people who, as Mama says, have no souls to save?

There were various responses to my lamentations: now a silence of death in the gloomy obscurity, now the brief, sharp neigh of some colt infuriated because another robbed it of its share, now the stamping of a placid mare. I felt consoled to have companionship.

Come, Lulú, see where your caprices and giddiness have brought me. The idea came to me that my life was going to be extinguished on that dung hill. Then what an extraordinary and wonderful thing happened! In place of commending my soul to God, as victim of an attack by rebels, incomprehensibly I yelled with all my power,

"It is enough, God. You afflict me like a new shoe! Cursed be the hour!"

Frightened by such foul blasphemy, or lack of respect, I realized that it was Procopio's blood which in that instant had boiled in my veins; and, with repentance for all my sins, immediately I made an act of contrition and disposed myself to die at least reconciled with God.

They say that one who is dying lives his entire past life in a second. That which I felt in that solemn moment was an incomparable fortitude. I saw myself encompassed by all my most tender earthly loved ones. Agustinita with her fastidious love was not absent, nor

Pascual with his refined courtesy, nor Lulú herself, frivolous and the cause of my misfortune; and, what do I say! neither Procopio whose blood made me blaspheme. Nothing disturbed the spell of these tragic moments. Then I closed my eyes very tightly, disposed to render my soul to my Creator. But the clock of time had not yet struck my hour; a brutal hand, perhaps the same one who had dragged me in the street to the barracks, abruptly raised me from the ground, then forced me to go out of the corral. In obscurity I traversed an immense patio, then I had to go through a shadowy and interminable corridor. I heard a vague murmur of soft voices, almost like singing women. A nauseating odor of human effluvia which saturated the atmosphere erased my first impression of a tropical forest at the hour in which the parrots begin to go to sleep. My feet stumbled over a multitude of bulky objects. Shadows fluttered and became gigantic in size so that I found myself less frightened when I drew near the only electric light in the middle of the corridor. When my eyes became accustomed to the half-light of the surroundings, those shadows began to come alive. Some of the people were cooking, others darning old black clothes, many were getting rid of lice, and the rest, tumbled together like beasts, seemed to be sleeping soundly. I observed the remarkable sameness of them all; the same dull, olive color, the same flat cheek bones over which the skin was tightly drawn, the same expressionless eyes without eyebrows, thin beardless lips, the same long hair, straight and glossy. But since they moved, they were not idols; then, who were they? Which were the men; which were the women? A light flashed suddenly in my mind, and I began to shiver: a garrison of Yaquis![5]

They took me to the entrance. A very formidable *charro* wearing a well pressed shirt of calico, riding breeches of white drill, fitted black puttees, and a straw sombrero with a brim so wide that it touched both walls, came out to meet me.

"Do you know this guy, young fellow?"

"Archibaldo! Archibaldo, my brother-in-law!" I cried with an inexpressible happiness.

Hatless, drenched, his hair disheveled like an old scrub brush, Archibaldo, the color of a dead man, was in the middle of an escort.

"Notice, my general," he said, "that that poor boy is incapable of what you say. What I tell you is the actual truth."

By the light of the bulb in the entrance, the terrible bandit looked at me from head to foot with curiosity; and, giving me a kick in the save-it-be-what-part, thrust me out in the street quite willingly, and growled,

"He is no *villista*—nor anything else. This milksop would be better made into jerked beef."

"Blessed be God!" I said to Archibaldo as soon as he was at my side, also at liberty. "You don't know what tragic hours I have lived through."

"You still don't know the main part. They were going to shoot both of us. There was a conspiracy around the barracks and they seized you as a *villista*. When you lost us, it occurred to me to come to the barracks to ask about you and then they seized me, too. What saved us was your limited physical development and your appearance—not very masculine."

"Archibaldo, come to my arms! Come to my arms, Archibaldo! I owe you my life! I owe everything to you!"

I embraced him crying with emotion and gratitude.

"But, oh my!" I groaned, "Archibaldo, I am wounded to death!"

"You wounded? Where?"

"Blood is running down my face."

"That's not so, César. Remember that you are soaking wet and bewildered—"

"No, Archibaldo, really, I am wounded to death. The water of the fountain was icy cold and that which is dripping from my chin is warm, almost hot. Blood, Archibaldo, blood!"

"But in the barracks I got a good look at your face which you had just washed."

"Say whatever you want to, Archibaldo, but I already feel my head going round and round. Help! For pity's sake for I fear I am dying! Archibaldo, support me, for my strength is leaving me!"

XII

Much alarmed Archibaldo carried me over to the light and examined me with minute care. Then he let out a disconcerting laugh and said to me,

"Don't worry, César, it isn't blood but a secretion from your nose; abundant, certainly, on account of the bad ducking you got."

In spite of the disconcerting tone of his voice I felt my soul was returning to my body.

"Now it is necessary to go look for Lulú," he said to me, full of sudden dread.

"¡*Virgen de los Remedios!*[6] Now where did you leave Lulú? For the glory of your parents, Archibaldo, please be kind enough to tell me where the poor little thing is!"

God punish us severely for our sins! Oh sister Lulú, I had even forgotten you!

"Lulú is waiting for us in the Alameda."

"Alone in the Alameda? Is it possible that you are so irresponsible, Archibaldo?"

"Surely she is better off there than you were in the barracks."

His expostulation required no reply.

Very quickly, we went in under the trees. Archibaldo proceeded to a bench from which arose quickly on discerning us, a young gentleman in trappings of rags who threw himself into my arms, sobbing.

"Blessed be God!" I exclaimed.

It was she, Lulú, wrapped up in Archibaldo's raincoat and with his hat on her head. We kissed and cried for happiness. The poor little thing could scarcely believe in the miracle of my reappearance and her broken words revealed the sincerity of her intense joy. She caressed me with such tenderness that I, incapable of resisting these family scenes, without reflection on the consequences of my words and responding only with the voice of my grateful heart, said,

"I forgive you for everything; my life is yours. I had the intention of giving an account of everything to dear Mama; but by the venerated memory of the Generals Prado, I swear to you that my lips will be sealed."

Intoxicated with joy, they embraced above my head and it seemed to me they even kissed.

When we arrived at the San Cosme market, Archibaldo took leave of us, and I began to realize the monstrosity of my offer.

"Now that we can count on César," said Archibaldo, "we can see each other more often, Lulú."

I barely gave him my hand.

"What do you think about all this, Lulú? Look to what depth of depravity you have made me lower myself! What are we going to tell Mama now? What are we going to say to Papa?"

Don't bother yourself about such a trifling matter. At this hour
Papa should be in bed and much warmer than we are. Hurry up,
it's almost eight o'clock."

In fact, a few moments later we were deafened by the trumpets and
drums from a barracks, and a retrospective horror made me shiver.

"For God's sake, Lulú, don't make me go at this pace, for I am
breathless! What good will it do to go so fast?"

At the door of the house I stopped, perplexed, anguished. How
could I explain to dear Mama our delay in returning without failing
to tell the truth and at the same time without breaking my ill-advised
oath to Lulú and Archibaldo? It was useless to wind up my brain
like a skein of thread; my strength was exhausted. I understood
my absolute incapacity to give them a logical account of my view
of the matter. Leaving everything to be decided by chance, I took
a step forward and entered.

Mama let out a cry and began to faint. All ran to support her
in their arms.

Berta and Pascual were there, much alarmed because of our delay.

"Mama wanted to raise an alarm and start a search throughout
the city."

"What difficult hours you have given us, children!"

Francisco José kissed me on the forehead. Then Mama came to
herself, pulled me close to her breast, and our kisses and tears mingled.

How alike are the ways of Archibaldo and Lulú! With obvious
boldness my sister said,

"It's this way. We had no more than got on the streetcar and
it had gone about half the way when it began to rain. Then the lights
went out; and in the dark when it seemed to me we had reached
Isabel la Católica Street, we got out. There was a narrow alley like
the mouth of a wolf; then streets and more streets without a soul
about. 'It seems to me that we have lost ourselves,' César said to
me. I was sure of it but I kept silent. We wandered about, got
some soup, God knows where. Purely by chance we found ourselves
suddenly on the San Rafael streetcar line, and thanks to a miracle
of I don't know what saint, now we are here."

"But how could you come on the San Rafael line," observed Berta,
much surprised, "if it has been suspended since six o'clock on account
of some defect, I don't know what sort? We had to take a cab

because they assured us that it would be tomorrow before the street-cars would run again."

How are you going to deal with that, now, bold Lulú, in order to get out of this sticky spot? I raised my head in order to observe their expressions, and the first I noticed was Papa's who had a tremulous smile on his lips and an eloquence in his ironical expression which I had seen on few occasions. I felt as though I were stripped naked and I had an impulse to tell the truth, to shout it out. But in compassion for my torture, Procopio came discreetly to my side and stroking my head with his habitual benevolence, whispered in my ears,

"Poor little one! You are a true son of your mother."

Why, instead of lowering my eyes humbly, did I lift up my head in silent protest? Why did I feel hurt?

Lulú, in the meantime, got out of her entanglement with the greatest of ease.

"I am not positive that it was really a San Rafael streetcar that left us near here; the only thing of which I can assure you is that we are here together and without anything worse happening to us than getting back as wet as frogs."

"Yes, indeed, you even have begun to croak," I exclaimed, unable to restrain myself.

But she did not understand my bitter reproach.

"César, brother of my soul," she broke in with a happy laugh, "no one had noticed you! You look like a rat that has come out of the lard!"

All made merry, even dear Mama, who disregarded the question of blame for what had happened without paying any more attention to Lulú's perfidious insinuations. I thought with profound bitterness about the sad future which awaited this frivolous girl who did not care a straw about the tears and laments shed in such an honorable home, for which she only was to blame.

XIII

"God visits calamities on us, but does not hang us," is one of Agustinita's sayings. And it is so. Against all expectations, that night I slept only as I do when I have a cold, and dear Mama, before I have a vigorous general massage, makes me swallow a warm dose of milk with elderberry flowers, poppies, and prunes in it. My first thought, on awakening, was the correction of my errors. How could I go on living with the weight on my conscience of my infamous complicity by which I had compromised myself in a moment of complete lack of conscience or of absolute imbecility? I sat up, jumped out of bed, and went to the wash stand. The pitcher of cold water I dashed on the nape of my neck returned my lucidity to me. At my first opportunity, I thought, I will talk frankly to Procopio, because his smile had penetrated me like the fang of a venomous snake; afterwards I will tell it all to dear Mama in order that she may take the measures that her duty dictates to her.

But my match wasn't wasted, neither was my saliva. Events turned out in accordance with my wishes; that same morning I was able to explain with overflowing joy: *Lavabo inter inocentes manus meas.*[7] As I came out of my bedroom, I saw Papa who was talking from his window with someone in the street.

"Come on up, man, come up, Why do you hover around the house as though you were a marauder."

Sure he would come up. Just look who asked him!

Shamelessness in his monkey-like eyes, shamelessness in his insignificant rabbit-like teeth, shamelessness even in the happiness which brought color to his cheeks.

"Aunt Agustinita, it makes me happy to see you looking so well. The San Rafael district suits you better than Roma. It has brought a color to your cheeks which would make anyone think that you are Lulú's sister instead of her mother."

The big flatterer went over to greet Francisco José.

"Congratulations, Paco, on your verses in *El Radical.*[8] They were really a revelation."

Just as I am telling it, with a couple of sentences and a couple of paltry gestures of sheer mendacity, Archibaldo had put them anew in his pockets, melting the ice of an interview that for another would have been one of torture and confusion.

Naturally his return to the bosom of the family in this manner relieved me of a heavy weight. I doubt that his joy or Lulú's either could have exceeded mine.

For certain persons the use of words is unnecessary redundancy. Between Archibaldo and Procopio neither explanations nor excuses were exchanged: a light smile, a vigorous clasp of the hands; that was all.

His visit was brief. When he took leave with an obnoxious "until this afternoon," we took ourselves quickly to the dining room.

"Where are you all going? It would have been better to stay in bed. I am very sorry, my children, but we shall have to tighten our belts."

The tone was so sharp and the allusion so direct that Procopio, contrary to his habits and ways, felt himself constrained to reply,

"I recognize my fault; I lost the afternoon searching for money and I have returned without even a crumpled paper which might contain something for breakfast. The truth is that one cannot make up his mind to be the undefended victim of those thieves at the Bank, who, infected by all the precedents of our illustrious magistrates, attack one with: 'Your purse or your life.'"

"You saved your purse, there is no doubt, and now we breakfast on your gallant action," Mama exclaimed allowing a wounding smile to appear on her thin dry lips.

Papa, changing color suddenly, rose to his feet,

"If I defend any interests—it seems to me that they're yours—your—"

"Pascual will succeed in getting money without difficulty—you will see."

"On the conditions which Pascual arranges it, certainly I, too, could have brought it."

"Could have—but you haven't."

Procopio slammed his fist on the dining room table.

I was frightened. Vague recollections of my childhood came to me; and, as they became clear in memory, I became afraid. Why didn't Mama remember too? Why, instead of showing prudence, did she resort to her attacks?

"Understand," she said to him, "that on account of your aversion, no one breakfasts."

"I have confessed my faults. That's enough!"

"You should confess also that the hatred you feel for Pascual is unjust."

"I hate no one."

"Always you have doubted his skill, his talent, his—"

"In order to do business with another's purse, one does not require any talent."

"Pascual will bring us funds."

"Just as on the other occasions: a mound of paper-garbage which will have to be paid back in real money."

"Paper-garbage which will make it possible for us to eat. Anyway something which in no manner have you been able to get."

"That's enough, I said!"

Procopio's voice resounded like thunder. What grief! Surely the neighbors would be talking about this disgraceful scene. How could we face them the next day?

Francisco José, whose esthetic temperament found repulsive all manifestations of violence, took refuge in the water-closet. I shivered, drawing near to Mama's skirt.

She was as tense as though she had been wound up like a watch.

"What has happened is that Pascual's qualities have awakened the envy and hate of the impotent."

"What has happened is that Pascual is a *cheat*, worthy of veneration by silly old biddies."

A new blow of his fist made pieces of the table service roll off on the tile floor with a clatter.

As Procopio got up and left the room the doors closed behind him as though blown by a strong wind, making the whole house shudder.

A profound silence followed. Mama remained immobile and livid.

With a muffled and hoarse voice and with an incomprehensible boldness, Lulú said,

"Papa is right."

XIV

To the honor and glory of our home, scenes of this sort have been exceptional. I can assert that only on one other occasion something similar occurred. Papa had insisted that Francisco José and I should go to the United States to complete our education. When Mama's resources of affection and ingenuity were exhausted, she conceived the idea of consulting the Bishop. The results were decisive.

Mama returned from the episcopal residence full of vigor. With great audacity, she took the offensive openly and spoke in this manner to Procopio,

"I want you to show me how the North American universities are superior to our institutions such as, for example, the college of the Marist fathers of Zacatecas or that of the Jesuits at Saltillo."

Papa thought that he could respond by only disdainfully shrugging his shoulders and smiling.

"Then what you are trying to do is simply to make our sons Protestants, Masons, atheists?" Mama burst forth impetuously.

"You know very well, my dear, that I have never contended with you about the education of the family. I wished them to be prepared for the struggle of life, that is all."

"Yes, I understand; to pull up the wheat that I have planted in their tender hearts and supplant it with the nettles of these times."

"The nettles which are the ideas of the times!" he exclaimed smiling, still in good humor. "That means that you have come from the confessional."

"From consulting with his Illustrious Excellency."

"Admirable."

"I warn you that I am determined to defend myself."

"What you have said is enough."

"I warn you if my words fail to overcome your arguments, the Bishop is prepared to discuss matters with you."

"That's enough, I have already told you!" cried Papa.

"Now is the right time for you to accompany me to visit him. He has conceded to me the favor of an audience in order that we can come to a definite agreement about the education of the family."

An electric spark could not have set off a charge of dynamite any quicker. His face blackened with a wave of blood, his eyes rolled in his head, and in a hoarse and stuttering voice as if the words were molds too narrow to contain his impetuous rage, he uttered sentences without coherence or meaning. Agustinita explained later that what he wished to say was that he would never tolerate any interference in the affairs of the home. But she had her way. It seems that she reminded him that when the money does not come out of the trousers, then the trousers do not command. And, consequently, as all the capital belongs to Mama, the result of the dispute was decisive. A tremendous blow of his fist crushed the lid of the desk. Then as now, terror, agonized faces, slamming of doors, then silence.

Procopio's detachment from us dated from that time. He never again bothered about our education. It seems that all his fatherly affection was concentrated on only one being. He adored Lulú.

This will explain why the almost pitying benevolence with which he treats Francisco José and me, far from drawing us to him, keeps us always at a distance; and also excuses our decided predilection for Agustinita.

From that time Procopio's fondness for solitude and for books grew. He secluded himself in his section of the house. I remember that at one time when I entered his study, I was amazed to see so many newspapers, illustrated reviews, paper-backed books, others luxuriously bound, all tumbled together in piles on the floor. I observed, astonished, that the honor of being on the bookshelves was enjoyed by a volume as long as its pages weren't opened and that many scarcely commenced went on a pile on the floor in order to give their places to a beautiful ear of corn, or a fine spray of wheat, or to rare and exquisite fruits, all products of the hacienda. The question of the influence of Papa's reading on the management of our interests had given us much to think about. One time Pascual had Mama look over the valuable papers in the strong box and provide for a detailed examination of the ledgers. Surprisingly it revealed that the income exceeded by fifty per cent that which was normally obtained by General Prado, my grandfather. But, where was that surplus? Secret information brought to light by that same Pascual revealed that it was all paid out in general expenses. "There isn't a peon," he said, "whose debt is more than he can pay, working all of his life in the service of the house. The major-domos enjoy greater salaries than those of any of the neighboring estates; they have their own houses and more conveniences than any employee of high standing in the city. The sharecroppers possess chickens, goats, pigs, and all they want to have. Many are even owners of saddle-horses. It seems that the aims of Procopio are to make them participants, without their being aware of it, in the general profits of the estate and without prejudice to their salaries. What is the source of this river of silver? Where will these quixotic practices lead if not to the ruin of the proprietor?"

"That's so," Mama answered him, "but I can say nothing to him because the account books are always open to my disposition as well as the strong box, and never, not even in my father's time, were there such large amounts for disposal as now."

I think that, given Papa's sensitivity on this particular subject, the slightest allusion would have brought an immediate and definite rupture.

Did my parents marry for love? One time I was surprised to hear Agustinita say,

"My father was a rough man, but he had a noble heart. When on the death of his father, Don Albino, Procopio became an orphan, General Prado sent him to the United States to be educated. He subsequently put Procopio in charge of the hacienda. Within a few months he found out how to capture Papa's sympathies so that he gained entry into the house, not like an employee, but like a member of the family. He was a good young man, most attentive, always respectful, who simply ate me up with his eyes. He didn't look so bad to me either, you can depend on it. We understood each other. Then occurred a catastrophe. My father suffered a cerebral attack, paralysis ensued, and then death snatched him away from us. Before the period of mourning was over my hand was given to the young administrator of our hacienda. When I came to myself, it was all settled. Procopio revealed himself to me as a young man who did not even know how to tie his tie correctly, who liked to go out of the house in his shirt sleeves. One time he went to a formal ball in his street clothes. He wound up by embarrassing me because of his disconcerting acts, his detachment, and the fact that he was always out of harmony with society. For all of this had they sent him to St. Louis, Missouri, to be educated?"

XV

Well, after this scene, Procopio took a determined stand.

"Come with me, Lulú!"

As they went out, Pascual came in. Procopio scarcely offered him his hand.

"There goes the frantic one," Mama said in an aside to my brother-in-law and she told him in detail all that happened.

"Haven't you breakfasted yet?" he asked, shaking with indignation. He did not wait for an answer. He flew to the market and a few minutes afterwards entered with a bag full of appetizing food. Agustinita could not hold back her tears. Francisco José threw himself in his arms. I had to restrain myself in order to keep from kissing his feet as a sign of gratitude. We quieted our hunger as politely as possible. Then he took out many packages of paper money from his pockets, so much that it spilled off the dining table like a cataract. It reminded me of the way magicians take enough banners and flags from their bare arms to decorate a salon. Agustinita, surprised, observed,

"What if he refuses to sign the promissory note?"

"For me your word is the best sort of promissory note."

"You are sublime, Pascual," exclaimed Francisco José, crying. Pascual smiled lightly.

"But he will not refuse. On account of what has happened, he will be as yielding as wax."

"But you haven't seen him the way he can be."

"His rages can be no more dangerous than the little fireworks the urchins make to play with; the kind which burn their own hands but harm no one else."

As soon as he left, we threw ourselves at the food which good breeding and discipline had kept us from doing before then.

Near midday, Procopio and Lulú returned smiling and talkative, she with a big armload of flowers and he with his pocket bulging with money.

What keen insight Pascual had displayed! That same afternoon, and in his presence, Procopio signed the document for the new debt without opening his lips. When my brother-in-law left us, there was a long silence of waiting. And not until in the evening when we had finished eating supper, Procopio asked,

"What's the total of all Pascual has brought?"

Mama brought out many memoranda. After making an account of the capital and interest, Procopio commented coldly,

"By selling the chain of my watch just now in San Ángel, I obtained half as much money as we owe Pascual. Just the chain of my watch! Those who have ears, let them listen!"

"That means," responded Mama, "that with selling only one of our houses in Zacatecas—"

"If we could dispose of only one piece of property it would be more than enough to cover the debt provided we could pay it back in the same paper money we received."

"Pascual has assured me, upon his word of honor, that the clause relative to specie that we have to pay back is only a formula that all businesses employ and accept."

"On his word of honor," repeated Papa like an echo, and smiled bitterly.

Agustinita, undoubtedly fearful of a new scene, preferred to shut up.

One day we had a strange visitor. During conversation at the table after lunch, a very short, fat woman with deep-set eyes and a cat-like nose planked herself down. She came into the dining room and greeting us with an irritating familiarity, divested herself of a strange, rat-colored cloak that reached down to her heels. Then she took a seat, which no one had offered her, and said,

"Your astonishment doesn't surprise me. It is natural you don't remember me. I left Zacatecas twelve years ago after I married Payito."

She stopped a minute in order to take off her veil and hat with feathers which stuck up stiff and rigid around her head like the plume of the Eagle Knight in my *History of Our Country.*

"Now don't you remember Payito? An agreeable and likeable young man of Zacatecas in those good old days, Agustinita. The little boy that we knew when we were about fifteen years old. A young rascal! But he is no longer like that. At my side he has become meeker than a little lamb."

She crossed her legs shamelessly, took out some cigarettes and matches and calmly began to smoke.

"Payito," she continued in an even more affected voice, "is one of the most important lawyers in the legal profession in the city. He deals with the aristocracy. He is an adviser of the Jockey Club and of several banks. He doesn't have much to do now; for, as you know, millionaires have suspended operations."

(Archibaldo says that there are two epidemics in Mexico: typhoid fever and megalomania. It has been my intention to test his assertion with my own observations. I have been able to do no less than confirm it.)

"Payito has some property. We live in the Roma section and have a vacation house in Coyoacán. The hacienda *El Tecolote* in Morelos is ours and we are owners of shares in a mine in Pachuca. We have six automobiles. We are thinking about going to live in Havana or the United States because now people of means are not able to live in Mexico. Now you have recognized me, haven't you? Haven't you guessed everything?"

"She has taken us for a band of gypsies!" exclaimed Archibaldo in an undertone, provoking a half-suppressed smile from Lulú.

"Well, I am Aurora Caloca de Tabardillo," she continued with more animation. "You and I were on first-name terms in school, Agustinita."

As she continued giving us intimate details of the family, we finally became convinced of the truth of what she said.

"I have a very good memory, but as I paid little heed to your corps of servants, I do not remember whether that man (indicating Archibaldo) was with you at that time or not."

We bit our lips. "Now," I thought, "you are going to meet your match."

He started to reply immediately, but an imperious gesture and severe look from Agustinita restrained him.

Impossible to follow the thread of this good woman's conversation: Payito is a model gentleman; as a husband he has no equal. At times it seems to me that she was speaking to us seriously and that at times was pulling the wool over our eyes. Anyway her conversation made me doze off when she began to reel off facts about her family's genealogical tree which had more branches than a huisache. Little by little, my eyes closed, my muscles and joints became limp in the delightful prelude of unconsciousness. Then a glance from Mama, penetrating as an X-ray, made me wake up frightened. I didn't know whether minutes or hours had passed. I made a titanic effort to remain awake.

Still she did not stop talking.

"Heaven has not seen fit to bless our union with a single blonde cherub; our expectations have been reduced to the hope of a tranquil old age and of entering 'the grave in abundance as a heap of wheat is brought in its season,' as the Sacred Scriptures say."[9]

Surprised, Agustinita raised her eyebrows, indicating sympathy for the tears that sparkled on *Señora* de Tabardillo's thin eyelashes.

"Of course we are down on our luck now. We no longer enjoy any income from our property. Our only resources are what I get from writing the section for ladies in the daily paper."

She leaned over to speak confidentially to Mama,

"Just as in your case, Carranza's bandits have robbed us of everything."

Mama became very sweet. She reached toward her with a kindly gesture and, in an effusive manner, took hold of the hands of her old friend.

"If I tell you that Payito and I do not now have a change of clothes, you will not believe—"

"Oh, yes, ma'am, it strikes one in the eye!" Archibaldo broke in, not being able any longer to hold in his unworthy thoughts.

Agustinita, really annoyed, told him to join Procopio who was alone in the living room.

Finally, *Señora* de Tabardillo pled for a loan of fifty *pesos* which she promised to pay back the first thing the next day.

XVI

Actually, she did return the next day; not with the money, but certainly with an important piece of news.

"Carranza's bandits are on the move. They are being thrown out; they don't leave of their own accord. General Villa and the ex-Federalists are on the way."

In spite of the way she looked in that coat and hat, *Señora* de Tabardillo was wonderful.

"Yes, Agustinita, before another week, we shall be cured of this infection."

Overcome with happiness, Mama hastened into Procopio's bedroom. Yanking at him she got him into the living room.

"Oh, you rogue, how you have hidden the truth from me! Now I understand why you refused to go and pay your respects either to Carranza or to Obregón! I have quit singing that tune! I forgive you because of the soundness of your intentions; you wanted to give me the joy of a surprise."

Procopio stared at us.

"Yes, I know all about it from this little friend, our fellow countrywoman, whom I shall have the pleasure of presenting to you."

"I don't understand—"

"Oh! Don't you know that General Villa with all the Federalists are coming to throw Carranza and his followers out of Mexico City?"

"And we—what has that to do with us?"

"Just everything! When the Federalists enter the capital, then we go straightway to Zacatecas."

Just as Procopio's smile has the singular quality of striking Agustinita like an asp when she is at her quietest and most contented, so do some of Agustinita's words and gestures have the effect of provoking Procopio to hilarity when he is in a most bitter humor. Our neighborhood, sunk in ten o'clock silence, must have been shaken by Papa's stentorian laugh.

"It had never occurred to me that Villa would grab Carranza by the hair just for the pleasure of smoothing the way for our return to Zacatecas."

Mama, shrugging her shoulders scornfully, sat down beside her friend and paid no attention to Procopio. Now it was her turn to talk. She reminisced about the good old days of her youth in Zacatecas. When *Señora* de Tabardillo with tears in her eyes asked Mama for another hundred *pesos* because they did not have enough for breakfast, Mama put in her hand, not just a hundred *pesos*, but a tightly rolled bundle of bills.

"You will let me know of course, the exact day and hour that *Señor* Villa's forces enter Mexico City."

Agustinita's spirit is to mine as Procopio's is to Lulu's; nevertheless, I was quite unable to comprehend this "*Señor*" Villa" on Mama's lips.

During the night strange sounds awakened me. I was accustomed to sleeping through the calls of the nightwatchman and the shouts, laughs, and shots of drunken *carrancistas;* but that night the noises were different: the shuffling of multitudes on the march, cavalry in a deafening confusion, automobiles stopping for a moment, brief words of command, then the whirring of engines starting up again, and the roar of cars setting off at great speed.

The next day we went to visit a haunt of the *carrancistas* and found only rubbish and rough-coated dogs, their ribs sticking out, ravenously gnawing on big bones.

"The arrival of the winning forces," said *Señora* de Tabardillo on her promised visit, "will be a big affair. There is more enthusiasm than when Madero entered the capital."

"I should like to take part," said Mama, "and throw flowers as they pass, which they say is the custom in Mexico City."

"Currently some people are offering two hundred *pesos* for just a little balcony on Juárez Avenue, but for the same money I can get one for you on Plateros Street which is more elegant. I will personally buy the flowers. I will go myself to Xochimilco to get them, for you can't even buy them for gold in Mexico City."

One hundred *pesos* for flowers and two hundred for the rent of the balcony flew out of Mama's purse.

XVII

But it's God's will that in the world there is no perfect happiness, as Agustinita says. Just as *Señora* de Tabardillo left, Berta and Pascual burst in all excited.

"We come to tell you goodbye. Within half an hour we shall leave for Veracruz."

"You, to Veracruz?"

"Yes, Agustinita, we are going with the First Chief."

"Who is that?"

"*Señor* Carranza."

"*Señor* Carranza" in my brother-in-law's mouth had the same effect on me as "*Señor* Villa" in Agustinita's. I did not want to believe what I heard, but Procopio's words convinced me that I had heard correctly.

"Bah!" he exclaimed gleefully, "now equilibrium will be restored—Pascual a *carrancista* and Agustinita a *villista*. May it all redound to the good of the family!"

Pascual bit his lips and Agustinita pretended she did not hear him.

"But how is it possible, Pascual," Mama asked, "for you to make common cause with those bandits?"

Pascual said that owing to his repeated attempts to get funds for us, he had made some business contacts with many men in high places among the Constitutionalists. As he had been seen with them in Mexico City, he was exposed to being a victim of Doroteo Arango, the barbarian.

"Who is that Arango?"

"The bandit who now goes by the name of Francisco Villa."

"But I've learned that *Señor* Villa comes giving guarantees, returning confiscated property, and respecting priests and religion."

"If Villa triumphs I will be back in two weeks, as soon as they get through wreaking vengeance; but if Carranza wins we'll be back even sooner; and in every respect our influence will be favorable for the family."

He took out many packages of paper money and, on their being counted, handed them to Agustinita.

"Here is this—because if my absence is prolonged—"

"I suppose that a receipt should be made out to you immediately."

"You know that I need no document whatever from you. This money is mine and what is mine is also yours."

But Agustinita would not let him get ahead of her in magnanimity, and asked that a document be drawn up showing that twenty thousand in gold coin was due him.

"Yes," extolled Francisco José, who was moved deeply by all gracious gestures, "it will be no less than an act of fundamental justice."

Procopio's lips were pressed together in a sarcastic smile. When Pascual, astounding us with his foresight, took a written promissory note out of his pocket, Procopio said to him,

"You are a great psychologist," and signed it.

"I warn you, my dear," he said as soon as Berta and Pascual had left, "that with the documents we have made out to Pascual, and the present state of our affairs, we are on the edge of an abyss."

The next day, *Señora* de Tabardillo wrote Mama a short note saying that on her arrival in Xochimilco she had suffered an accident. After she had been attacked and robbed of everything, she had been forced to walk back to Mexico City barefooted. Then she had become seriously ill. She asked for another two hundred *pesos* "as a sacred debt which I will repay as soon as General Villa's forces begin to return our property."

Poor little thing. We have not had any more news about her. When we happen to mention her name, Mama makes us pray an "Our Father" and a "Hail Mary" for the eternal repose of her soul.

Anyhow, owing to our recent sorrow on account of the unseemly departure of Berta and Pascual, we wouldn't have been able to accept her good services. Thanks to Lulú's obstinacy and good luck Agustinita permitted us to go watch the troops parading along the Alameda. With the multitudes of people in the street no one would recognize us.

"Francisco José," instructed Mama, "all three of you hold each others' hands tightly, because there will be a lot of confusion."

Once in the street, however, how could Francisco José and César cope with Lulú's caprices?

Since very early that day people had swarmed on Chapultepec Avenue like ants. The morning was crisp and fragrant; the warm rays of the sun reddened the romantic paleness of my brother and made Lulú's cheeks as red as apples in season. Francisco José, head uncovered, allowed the foliage to caress his thinker's forehead and to lift the locks of his abundant hair. Delicately he breathed the pure air and the odor of the wet earth. The sky was blue, unbroken, and smooth as satin. In the northeast, within the limits of an immense valley, on the white summits of the mountains the snow was piled up in peaks of ermine.

From each side of the silver ribbon of the boulevard waved shaggy, dark green trees and cultivated plants; the whitened tops of houses emerged from the sea of verdure; and red brick buildings blazing in the sun made up the colors of the national ensign. Green, white, and red bunting decorated battlements, cornices, and balustrades. In long strips banners waved over silvered roofs of porticos, slate covered spires, and roofs of metal shingles. They fluttered from rigid lances and were spread with profusion from the tops of light, telegraph, and telephone poles, from the black shafts of chimneys, and among the scaffolding of buildings under construction. Like confetti raining down, the national colors were scattered over silvered eaves, friezes gilded by the sun, steel turrets, water tanks, and in the very foliage of the trees. As if infected by our crazy Mexican joyousness, the flags of foreign countries also waved over their legations and luxurious residences.

The crowds of people began to obstruct the marching troops. Those in charge of them swarmed all over the place in their autos, on their bicycles, and on their horses. There were turbulent bands of coarse soldiers as greasy, as brutal, and as repugnant as those who had just

left the plaza. On the sidewalks, intermingled among the dark clothes
of the men, were the fresh muslins, silks, laces, and flowers of the
ladies. Little girls in snowy white pinafores walked along pushing
wicker doll buggies. One could barely see the bright-eyed faces of
chubby babies in the white, blue, and pink froth of their clothes.
Numerous foreigners who watched the spectacle echoed the note of
gaiety. We remembered that Americans had paid well for choice spots
in El Paso, Texas, to witness Madero's attack on Ciudad Juárez.

"What a sad note for our country," commented Francisco José.

"And worse for those who call themselves the mentors of nations!"
responded Archibaldo who had joined us; just when, we didn't know.

XVIII

"Come, César," Francisco José called to me suddenly, stopping in
front of a ruined aqueduct.

"Viceregal ruins?" I inquired, disconsolately.

"This is excellent!"

"Archeology? I had rather follow Lulú even with Archibaldo
along."

A few days ago Francisco José had made me accompany him to
that place near the Arches of Belén. I had stood in the sun half an
hour in front of a horrible, deteriorated little stone baptismal font.
My death by sunstroke was a very near thing.

"Francisco José," I said to him disgusted, "these contorted rocks
that look like *charamuscas* of Zacatecas, these fish with slippery snouts,
and these cross-eyed and noseless matrons of your marvelous monument won't let me go to sleep tonight. I swear that I have never
seen anything so ugly in my life."

When I looked around for Lulú and Archibaldo to join them,
they had disappeared. I searched in every direction without finding
them. Then making a superlative effort, opening a way for myself
with my elbows among the agglomeration of people, it took me almost half an hour to retrace the twenty-five steps which separated me
from Francisco José. Moral responsibilities get me down.

"Lulú, Lulú has become a lost woman," I told him in a scandalized
tone.

Absorbed in the contemplation of his stones, he didn't choose to
answer.

"Lulú and Archibaldo are lost— It is evident that Lulú and Archibaldo—"

"Leave them in peace—and me too." That left me stunned—but discharged of a heavy burden. If Francisco José, my older brother, could ignore the matter, so could I.

Just then we heard the far-off sounds of trumpets and drums.

"Will you wait for me here? I want to see what is going on, too, Francisco José."

"Until the centuries have run their course."

I threw myself into the middle of that sea of people and came up against an impassable human barricade. A moving mass of hats and heads blotted things from my sight. Near me some children were perched in a tree. I remembered that one time in my childhood, instigated by the man who tended the calves, I climbed a mesquite tree to rob a pigeon's nest but nothing happened to me. Then I put to the proof my acrobatic enterprise but had bad luck, for I left half of my trousers among the brambles. I wasn't able to think about the slap on the behind that Agustinita would give me, because the martial notes of the trumpets and the sonorous beating of the drums deafened me. The vanguard of the triumphant troops at a turn in the street blotted out the beautiful greenery. Hanging by one arm to a limb like a lizard, I was able to observe the immense crowd, which like an arm of the sea inundated the road. What strange aberration of the spirit made me feel an intense desire to be one of those palm-hatted Indians, toasted brown by the sun, with their shining eyes and white teeth? Some were wholly naked, others dressed in old, cast-off clothing, and all covered with mud up to their eyes. What did all those people there have that was superior (I should like to say sublime if that would not make me sound ridiculous) which drew from me a clamorous and spontaneous "¡Viva!" which was lost in the thunderous applause and enthusiastic shouting of a multitude intoxicated with excitement.

It was a slow interminable march. Going by holding guns carelessly across the pommels of their saddles, their arms and legs limp, they were indifferent, as if unaware of their triumph. There were moments when I seemed to recognize some of them. Wasn't that Zenón, for example, riding that cinnamon colored stallion, that stallion the color of cinnamon in milk, going along half asleep at the end of a squadron? It seemed to me that I saw familiar faces among all those passing by. Bonifacio, the milker, with his face of eternal content; *Señor* Luis, the wagoner, who used to hold me on his knees when he carted in the bundles of hay in the icy days of February after the harvest; Petronilo, the old, long-legged hunchback who, in the late afternoon on returning from taking care of the cattle, would put me up on the broad rump of a cow; Uncle Crucito, the eighty-year-old, in whose arms I dozed as I listened to him tell of the enchanted mountain held up by four gold *tenamastes* which only Indian eyes could see.

It was not, surely, it was not they, but instead some people like them. How was it possible that those people of such good dispositions, so affectionate, so loyal, so simple and humble could be capable of committing the horrible crimes which Agustinita and Pascual attribute to them?

"Archibaldo, Lulú, look here, here I am!"

They passed like dry leaves carried off by a rushing torrent. They disappeared instantly. But with the hope of making myself at least heard by them, I shouted again,

"Francisco José is waiting for us by the Ermita."

Undoubtedly my words were lost in the shouting of a half million voices: "¡*Viva* Francisco Villa! ¡*Viva el general* Ángeles! ¡*Viva* Emiliano Zapata!"

XIX

Suddenly the branch which held me began to sway. I noticed that some other vagabonds were trying to climb up by swinging on it. They did not give me time to warn them how inconsiderate they were, when the tree broke and the three fell in a heap with shouts of laughter, insults, and fisticuffs. I escaped without further mischance than that of leaving the seat of my trousers on a branch.

In the Ermita I found Francisco José quite undisturbed. Together we threw ourselves into the human torrent. The enthusiasm of the people had no bounds. The most solemn and pompous yielded to the contagion: I swear that my brother Francisco José shouted many times, "¡*Viva* Franscisco Villa! ¡*Viva* Emiliano Zapata!" I am all the more convinced that he did, now that he persists in denying it. The waves of applause came like violent gusts in a storm. When from time to time the pitch of the shouting diminished, the rumble of the great column of human beings made an harmonious background to the chimes in the church, from the happy and playful tones of the bells in the little belfries to the solemn, grave, and magnificent ones of the Holy Cathedral Church; an infinite mixture of tones: the whistles of hundreds of locomotives in the station, of factories, workshops, bath houses, etc.; the strident martial sounds of bugles and the hoarse, sonorous, rhythmical beats of the drums.

The streets were filled to capacity. The buildings were crowned with people, not only on the balconies and the roofs, but on the very edges of the battlements and in the embrasures between them and on the moldings of pillars, and on the eaves of the porches. Many thousands of hands clapped without ceasing in resonant applause at the passing of the squadrons. A rain of confetti and paper streamers fell over those impassive beings who had begun to go by at midday and were still marching when the sun set.

We reached home in a sad state, suffering from exposure and hunger, for we had not had a bite to eat. Agustinita lashed out at us. Procopio took up for us, pointing out that in these tumultuous times no one can do as he pleases. As soon as we had eaten something, we gave Papa an account of what we had seen without omitting a period or a comma. He was thoughtful. Then he said, smiling,

"In *some* way, Mexico should have expressed its affection for Don Venustiano!"

Since then I have concluded that even though I had applauded along with the rest, I really don't know why I did.

A week later Agustinita said,

"It is very strange that no one brings us news about home. I have read in the newspapers that trains are coming in from Ciudad Juárez."

"I think we shall soon have reliable news," Papa replied, calming her. "I have written to the bookkeeper asking him to come here as soon as possible."

But that week passed, then two more. Mama became extremely uneasy. At that point we had a visit from Pomposita, a woman who had until a year ago been encharged with selling milk from our dairy.

"It distresses me to tell you what has happened; but you can be sure that I do not exaggerate one bit; that anything I might say would scarcely be the shadow of what did happen in Zacatecas."

I felt cold; Agustinita became the color of lead and her lips trembled.

"But it is better that you know about it. After a night of terror there wasn't even a puppet with its head on. The generals gave a grand supper in your home. The next day it made one sad to see the mass of feathers from your turkeys, herons, parakeets, parrots and other fine birds from the aviary which those men ate. It was a tapestry of a thousand colors from one sidewalk to another."

We suffered our greatest distress when we learned that the garbage collectors on their rounds picked up photographs from our family album which those monsters had disfigured with their impious pencils. Thrown out among lumps of stone were the noseless and one-eyed heads of the Generals Prado.

When that woman left, I felt that it was possible to breathe again. I do not know what strange eagerness and what infernal happiness I discerned in her eyes and on her lips indicating that she enjoyed intensifying our distress with a narration full of the most grievous details.

I cried out with all my strength,

"Pomposa's story is all lies."

Francisco José seconded my words; but poor little Mama, drowned in tears, wasn't listening.

"I remember, Mama," said Lulú, "that Pomposa had hard feelings toward us from the time that you took the milk delivery away from her."

"Who does Pomposa think she is?" said Francisco José. "In Zacatecas everybody calls her 'The Talebearer.'"

In vain. Mama began to twist in a convulsion. An attack! Papa was not at home, Lulú quite ineffective, and Francisco José almost as bad as Lulú. I became charged with energy and ran to look for a doctor. Mercy on me! Two hours I ran up and down streets; up and down stairs apparently for no other reason than to convince myself definitely that in this hateful metropolis no one takes me seriously and that our name is entirely unknown.

By the time I got back, Papa was lavishing attention on Mama. The doctor came and prescribed some medicine. When Mama had calmed down, Procopio sat down beside her and said,

"I have good reason to believe that there is some exaggeration in what the woman has told us. If there is any property that has any likelihood of being respected it is ours. It is necessary to look at the situation as it really is, my dear. This revolution is the reprisal by the peasants whose masters have robbed and exploited them. Well, then, nobody in the state paid better wages than we did. We had the best workmen, because no other estate provided its day-workers such advantages as we did ours. He, who once worked as one of our sharecroppers, remained with us. This winter, for example, everybody was very pleased because they were supplied with wool blankets without any charge against their accounts. For the past two years the hacienda has had an agreement with a doctor and a dispensary to take care of our servants without cost to them. All enjoyed suitable living quarters. Our overseer, Roque, this year received a most signal service through his father, who without the expensive operation which was performed on him in our own home and without the personal care of the family, surely would have died."

"It's very true; Lulú served as his nurse," exclaimed Mama, wiping away her tears.

"Do you think those men would turn into our enemies even though the benefits which they have received from us are their just due?"

"They would be monsters of malice!"

Thus hope and happiness followed the skepticism with which Agustinita listened to Procopio's first words. Mama asked him to tell her again in detail about the benefits made available for the poor.

XX

Agustinita, sobbing, conciliated us,

"Children, I have been unjust to your father. I ask for your pardon and God's too. May God and the good works which Procopio had sense enough to do save us from catastrophe!"

This produced an abrupt change. For many days not only were our burdens supportable but we came to regard them as a bitter dose which restores the health. Pain had purified us of our old sins. Agustinita repeated to us: "We owe to him the salvation of our property." Procopio's importance was enormously enhanced in our eyes. His acts and his ways which at other times had seemed so despicable, found a reasonable explanation even to achieving our sincere appreciation.

Procopio did not scorn the idea of conversing with us for a few minutes. Had Heaven finally taken pity on our misfortune and blessed our home with unity and peace?

I observed, nevertheless, that while Agustinita thought only about the hacienda and money, Francisco José about a new poem, and Lulú about Archibaldo, that Procopio wore a mask to mislead us about everything. Frequently I surprised him, pensive and absent-minded. I saw how each day he became paler and thinner. He was very careless about his dress. He, who had always shown a very serene spirit, now vacillated about everything.

One afternoon the spell was broken in a most brutal way. An old man, dressed in the custom of our part of the country, knocked on the door. He wore a large, ill-fitting palm sombrero and baggy old chamois-skin pants smelling strongly of huisache flowers. We went out to meet him and threw ourselves in his arms. It was Victoriano, the oldest and most privileged of our servants. We cordially grasped his sinewy, calloused hand. We made him sit down; and, with unconcealed anxiety, asked him about all our things.

The poor old man, who until that moment had been quite contented, became confused. The exceedingly white ivory of his teeth disappeared, lines congested his forehead, his eyes darkened, he became tongue-tied, he could not figure out where to begin. Papa questioned him with serenity and firmness. The old man sighed audibly, spit on the patio, and made an ominous and solemn gesture. We were all silent, waiting for the words just hanging on his lips which would not come. Again he shook his long, dusty, tousled hair, trembling and stuttering, he said,

"Nothing, master, nothing—except they broke in and took all the corn. Didn't leave enough for a hen. Filled enough wagons to make a line all the way to the station. Not a living animal left in the pasture—took them all to the United States. Cleaned us out. Couldn't break up the machines. Mad as anything, they blew them up with dynamite. There they go! Just piles of scrap left. All gone, except the land, because they could not figure out how they could take it off."

"And Roque?"

"The overseer Don Roque, same's usual. Still giving orders. Now he's the mister with an auto and pays no attention to the generals coming and going to the hacienda."

Agustinita's eyes, like a flash of fire, sought Procopio. But Procopio, depressed, did not look up at all.

As Victoriano engulfed us with more details, Papa invited him to come in and eat. Then Papa sealed himself up in his study.

"Grief will kill him," exclaimed Mama with uncommon fortitude, "but certainly not on account of the great losses we have suffered; what's important to him is the mortal blow his pride has suffered!"

Francisco José, discerning Agustinita's meaning, added,

"Sure! What will they think of him now, of 'the one who appreciates our common people and the most noble genius of the indigenous race and the laws of our social and economic development?'"

If Agustinita did not assuage her grief in tears this time, it was because she found their equivalent in words as sharp, as piercing, as lashing as the end of a whip.

It was another of the saddest days of our lives. In the anguished silence of the house nothing could be heard except the feverish scratching of Francisco José's strong and agile pen. "What could that man be writing now," I asked myself, astonished. Silently, I drew near to read over his shoulder the title of his new poem: "These, Fabian, which you see now, oh sorrow!, fields of solitude, gloomy hills—"

Francisco José's depth is matched in degree by Lulú's frivolity. At nightfall her fine, delicate voice broke the profound silence of our house intoning the *"Abandonado."*

"Who is singing?" asked Agustinita surprised and greatly disgusted.

Then she gave her head a jerk and exclaimed resignedly,

"She is the daughter of her father."

That meloncholy folk tune continued falling like a mist of sadness on our hearts.

Pain and distress refine sensibility in an extraordinary way. Never have I seen Lulú more beautiful than on that night. Her graceful silhouette appeared in the twilight. She came slowly into the living room where we were all sitting abjectly, not raising her eyes from her embroidery. In her floating, rose-flowered, sapphire-blue dressing gown, the purity and delicacy of her profile, the ivory smoothness of her neck, cheeks, and forehead, the burnished gold of her wavy hair, and her long eyelashes were all accentuated. Without taking into consideration our whispering, she occupied an easy chair in the circle; then as the light faded out in the portion of purple sky visible through the glass, she got up, pushed the button to turn on the lights, and imperturbably returned to her needlework.

Ten times I counted the figures of griffins in the carpet. Did half an hour pass or a day or a century? The silence, the close air depressed me. I got up and opened the window, but the fresh night air did not lessen the oppression in my breast. I went to the door of the bedroom and drew the curtain. There in the room at the far end of the apartment in the half light of a little oil lamp Procopio sat immovable, his face sunk between his hands, and his eyes cast down.

"Come, César, don't be so upset, it will pass."

Agustinita's fingers, smoother than ermine, fell lightly on my disarranged hair. She had divined my anguish, because my mind and my heart are like crystal to her.

"How much more worthwhile it would have been to speak to *Señor* Villa instead of being like this—no more than a ninny."

"Don't speak that way of him!" broke in Lulú, shocked.

It was almost without precedence. Agustinita excused herself,

"I did not intend to offend him child; but it is necessary to tell the truth—"

"My father is a worthy man—"

"I have made a simple observation—"

Mama's disconcerting humility was the worst punishment Lulú could have received. In fact, she began to cry.

"Dear Mama, Lulú did not intend to offend you—at the same time she is fond of Papa."

Then Agustinita, infuriated, assailed me.

"Since when do the children of this house take part in the intimate affairs of the family? What times, sir, what times! Everything is lost, even discipline."

A word, a glance, a gesture from me was sufficient to bring about the inevitable tempest which was suspended, as by a miracle, above our heads.

Silence reigned again. Archibaldo who had remained beside me without speaking, said to me in a very low voice, "Only a spirit forged to the fine temper of your father's soul could ascend from this calvary."

I replied to him,

"And are we in a bath of roses?"

XXI

"Things are incredibly rotten," said Agustinita. "Bernabé has become intimate with the janitress and that is a serious matter."

The best servants, those who come from the country, are infected when they come in contact with the clever servants of the capital and soon give themselves airs, reaching an incredible state of perversity. Agustinita, then overcoming the instinctive repugnance that the lower classes inspire in her, had me accompany her to the market where she made her purchases personally. From that test Bernabé came out poorly. The merchants were abusive beyond the very limits of decency. The Spaniard at the bakery, for example, short-changed us a five-*peso* bill in making change. "It's too bad about your color, your blood, your race! You are no better than those naked Indians that take to begging," burst forth Agustinita not being able any longer to hold in her anger. The milk vendor, after selling for a fabulous price a container of milk diluted with starch water with curds in it, left half the fluid in the bottom of the measure. In vain Mama reminded him of the awful moment when we shall have to appear before the Supreme Judge to render an account of our acts, "Listen here, don't you have a soul to save?" she scolded sharply the pork seller who instead of loin gave us some repulsive pieces of the skin.

Such justifiable complaints got only noisy hisses in reply. They called us "no-goods," "reactionaries," "*científicos,*" besides mouthing obscenities; the only language in which those wretched people could talk with each other. A bunch of dirty, lousy urchins gathered around and followed along with us, shouting and whistling, to the door of the market.

"What happened?" Archibaldo asked us, surprised at Agustinita's anger.

"That scum! Isn't it enough that they take the very shirts off our backs? Now they propose to starve us to death. I doubt God's justice!"

"Mama dear!" I let out a frightened cry.

I looked up in terror. Nothing! The sky was clear and bright with a little white cloud floating across its vault. Really, it would have been difficult to produce a thunderbolt. Consequently, full of gratitude to the Supreme Judge and Creator, and overflowing with joy, I exclaimed,

"Dear Mama, God will not forsake us! 'Not a leaf of a tree moves unless God wills it.' "

"César," she said to me, "count the money Pascual has left and make an approximation of how long it will last us."

She poured a basket full of Constitutionalist paper money on the floor. It had appreciated by weight, not by the face value. After spending the whole afternoon at the job, I was able to say,

"Presuming that prices of necessities go up 100 per cent, we shall have enough to last six months."

"By the end of six months, of course, between themselves and Señor Huerta, the bandits will be done for, and all the honorable people in Mexico will be governing us as it ought to be."

Six months? No, sir, twenty-four hours. Archibaldo, pale and slack-jawed, brought the news.

"A decree has just appeared. Carranza has repudiated his paper money."

Procopio's eyes burned somberly. The rest of us looked terrified. What words, what laments, what crying would have produced the effect of such an unexpected blow? Agustinita slipped out so quietly that we didn't even hear the rustle of her skirts. Automatically Francicso José followed her. At a sign from Procopio, Lulú left, too.

Only I, thanks to my insignificance which makes it easy to confuse me with some decorative object, was left in the room where I stayed motionless in a dark corner.

"And what now?" whispered Archibaldo.

"I don't know—I don't know—"

The two were silent with their eyes lowered. Procopio's smile had vanished. Procopio without his smile, Archibaldo without his frivolity is neither Procopio nor Archibaldo.

I had an indefinable feeling. These abrupt shifts are hard on my nerves. I was getting up courage either to speak or to leave when Archibaldo spoke,

"You must decide what to do, Uncle Procopio."

"Yes—yes—I ought to, but nothing occurs to me."

Archibaldo's lively agitation contrasted with Procopio's stupefaction.

"An immediate decision is necessary," insisted Archibaldo.

"I've lost my capacity to think—to work—my will power is gone—tell me—advise me—"

"I already have my plan. You've got to make one today."

"This very day; that's so."

A silence ensued and again each one became introspective. Then suddenly Procopio stood up.

"Archibaldo—"

His eyes burned intensely. I saw how they turned toward that which shone even more brilliantly: the diamond which scintillated on one of his fingers. Then his smile was visible again on his lips and I was at last able to breathe freely again.

"Archibaldo, do me a big favor. Go and sell this right away."

"General Venturo Prado's ring?"

They exchanged a smile, and I was glad that Agustinita was not spying on them.

"Well, we have found a solution for the moment. Now tell me, what is your plan, Archibaldo?"

"Very simple; to get money where everybody gets it nowadays."

"Soldier?"

"Why not?"

"It's not suitable for one of your standing. The barrack is the school of complete depravity."

Archibaldo shrugged his shoulders with complete indifference, grabbed his hat, and as he was leaving, said,

"The important thing now is to sell this. So long, Uncle Procopio."

When Papa was left alone, he suddenly noticed me, and quite incensed, whether on account of surprise, anger, or shame I don't know, he caught hold of my ear without saying a word and thrust me into the bedroom.

XXII

On top of everything else that day, it rained. I was mentally and physically dejected. No one, moreover, urged me to continue with my jottings. Taking up my pen again is an impulse resulting from the complete idleness in which we live.

It isn't my task to give an account of historical events or politics, but they have become so entangled with our personal affairs that I just have to. As soon as Don Pablo González expelled the *zapatistas* from the capital, our hopes in Carranza were dashed: Pascual did not arrive with the *carrancistas* as we had expected. Carranza a second time repudiated the money which he had issued, and with the same extraordinary effrontery that he had displayed in ordering the banks robbed. I regret Pascual's absence, because he would be able to explain much of what is happening. According to Procopio, this history of blood and rapacity on the part of some and of misery and suffering on the part of others defiles us all. Every one is playing a rôle either of iniquity or of misery. It goes without saying that we were not all in accord with his judgment nor with that of Archibaldo who, before going to join the *zapatistas*, said: "Carranza's followers propose by their infamies to wipe out the stains from that assassin Huerta and his crew, leaving them whiter than ermine." We don't agree because that implies an insult to *Señor* Huerta and his supporters.

This long period of revolutionary government and this very lack of orderly government which still afflicts us has been the painful road to calvary which we travel without rest, atoning a hundred, a thousand times not only for our sins but for those of all our descendants. Thanks to Mama's jewels, for which we got two baskets of the paper money most recently issued by the bandit of Cuatro Ciénegas,[10] we are still alive. Nevertheless, the fear of waking up some day to learn of a new decree and the loss it could cause us led to our decision to leave the apartment on Arquitectos Street and reduced us to living in a humble dwelling in this poor quarter of the city. As for our food, we have become so economical that I can say without the least exaggeration that the beggars who used to come to our door, in times when honorable people ruled, asking for alms in God's name, were fed better with our leavings than we are now.

After the latest quarrel between Procopio and Agustinita there is a semblance of tolerance with the appearance of cordiality. A lie is the basis; the situation is so tense that something must give way.

Now Agustinita is the principal person in the home. She bolsters our failing spirits, constantly revives our faith, and feeds our hopes with the illusion that Don Félix Díaz "would come the first of next month to take the city." He has been a year at the job and still hasn't done it.

Procopio's calmess was farcical. His stupefaction and apathy were obvious. He did nothing but smoke cigarettes and read books which he borrowed from the grocer on the corner. We all grieved to see his passive indifference in the face of our horrible descent to veritable beggary.

Lulú lost her color, became thin; in a word, ugly. Not, however, so much so on account of our penury as on account of Archibaldo's absence. We hear he's serving with Zapata. A worthy fate for such a fine person!

Yesterday, boisterous ringing of the chimes of the Ángeles parish church awakened Francisco José. With his eyes full of tears and his heart overflowing with sadness and bitterness, he said,

"César, my brother, did you hear them? The bells of home!"

"They sound very much like them," I replied, moving lazily under my blanket.

Plaintively, Francisco José told me about the mystical language of the bells: "The solemn and rich bells of the Cathedral on the three great Thursdays of the year: Corpus, Ascension, and Holy Thursday; the bells calling the people to the afternoon prayer in the tranquillity of the city surrounded by the mountains; those of the suburbs on festival days, with orchestras out of tune, dissonant fanfares of oboes; and sounds of Indian drums, firecrackers, and rattles; the panting of the eccentric dancers; and the uproar of crowds rejoicing in the simple happiness of having a part of the village life."

"Bravo, Francisco José! I bet you've forgotten that we've had nothing in our stomachs in twenty-four hours except air."

"I haven't become such an imbecile that hunger could keep me from vibrating to the voice of the magnificent bronze bells."

"How clever you are, brother. You know how to obtain an advantage from hunger. Your empty stomach has in fact freed you from two miseries: headaches and the eternal aspirins."

"Hush, you ordinary simpleton, and listen to the bells!"

"I tell you that in this never-ending tumult of the capital, in these vulgar surroundings, the chimes are meaningless and flat. The feeling for music has been extinguished in me. Moreover, having to listen to them ringing every morning and every evening in celebration of 'the triumph of the faithful' has the same effect on my enthusiasm as an icy douche."

"You are right, César. The hustle and bustle of Mexico City is overwhelming. The monster devours everything, good or bad. Only we, who have been lulled in our tender years by the sound of the village bells, really understand their celestial music. Our deepest sorrows and our most intimate joys are indissolubly associated with the sound of the bells."

This section of the city evoked many memories: from the thick, rough wall of the parish church of the Ángeles with its dusty door of mesquite wood under a rounded arch and the rose window mended with tin, musty and gray with cobwebs to the little bell towers like small forts erected in each corner of our hacienda and the prolonged and melancholy bleating of calves in the stables of the poor, peaceful quarter.

That day there wasn't any point in getting out of bed, but force of habit made us get up at the regular hour.

I said to Mama,

"Dear Mama, won't you let us go out in the street?"

"Neither now nor never. What would you look for in the street?"

"Just what we look for here, dear Mama."

"Not a month ago a *carrancista* ran over a poor little boy playing in Chapultepec Park and mashed him as flat as a tortilla."

I looked at her as if to say, "Wouldn't it be just as well to die under the wheels of an automobile as of hunger?"

But she misunderstood me.

"Oh, you doubt it?"

Quickly she went to her bedroom, got a package of newspaper clippings, and unfolding one of them, she read the detailed account of one of the savage offenses committed daily by Carranza's hordes.

"Mama, dear, I give you my word of honor; I won't go near Chapultepec Park."

"But danger is everywhere," she answered me stubbornly. "A few days ago students from the military schools were required to take part in a military exercise, and those assassins and bandits, with characteristic bestiality and cowardice, assassinated twenty of the defenseless boys."

As if she thought I might doubt her words she took out another clipping and read it.

"I will not add my name to the list of the idiotic and criminal parents who entrust the lives of their children to those monsters of iniquity."

"But now there isn't any military exercise and I am not a student of any school."

(I really should call to your attention Mama's calmness, for hunger produces profound changes in human behavior. I, for example, have lost much of my timidity and am a perfect dissembler.)

I was more than willing to argue with Agustinita, but Procopio saved us from getting into a compromising situation by coming in with a basket full of rolls and coarse bread and a pitcher full of milk. It would be useless to give the particulars of how we devoured it all without even waiting to go into the dining room.

"You must have sold what I had hoped never to touch," Agustinita murmured resignedly, "the golden reliquary containing bones of the Holy Martyrs which my uncles, the Generals Prado, brought us from the Holy Land. God's will be done!"

I was fully occupied with my hunk of bread and could not be bothered with Mama's scruples. But it did seem that Procopio had received the money in a somewhat strange and mysterious way. The fact is that he arrived in such a wonderful humor that he took my side of the argument when he found out what we were talking about.

"Yes, dear, let him go. General Pablo González has assured us of every sort of safety measure. If you read the papers, you will see as a matter of fact that now the only ones doing the killing are the generals, the colonels, the majors, and the captains and only in the prisons, in the cemeteries, in the theaters, in the restaurants, and particularly in their favorite haunts."

"Enough!" interrupted Mother, indignant. "I know what kind of houses you refer to. It is not necessary for you to designate them by name in front of your children. How lax your standard of conduct has become! Anyhow, I say and repeat that César may go for a walk because César is a well-bred child and will have nothing to do with those centers of perdition. He may go and Lulú may accompany him."

I told you, didn't I, that hunger has transformed all of us?

XXIII

At the end of the street the dark green angle of the Alameda and the square shoulders of the National Theater came together in a dark mass. We walked along holding hands in a silence that was almost religious. We were afraid of being so happy. The blood rushed through my veins. I was being restored with new vitality. My lungs expanded as I breathed the air of the streets. The sun on my pale and almost parchment-like skin felt like an ineffable caress. Ideas thronged through my mind; new and disconcerting sentiments. At the sight of the Pegasus of steel which, at the top of the theater, seemed to shoot out toward the silvery-gray clouds, I had an intuition of the meaning of life and I also burst out,

"Oh Lulú, how beautiful it is to run!"

"But where are you taking me like this?"

"How do I know! Let our feet lead us where they will. These moments of happiness are very rare!"

"It's a pity that all of us are not able to be as happy as you are."

"What's the matter now, Lulú?"

"It's Father—who suffers more than all of us put together."

"It's not your fault nor mine."

"Selfish!"

"You have your own point of view—the same as Procopio's."

"And you, the same as Agustinita—"

"Look, Lulú, I'm not in the mood for sentimentalities and sighs now."

A motley multitude walked through the streets: women crowned with ivy and roses with their damp hair hanging loose; men with flowers adorning their lapels and in the ribbons of their hats. Flowers and greenery decorated the streetcars, automobiles, and carriages. Even the filthy pulque wagons were brilliant with flowers of vivid colors and bunches of green leaves.

"It is the fiesta of Santa Anita," Lulú told me. "That is why all the church bells are chiming."

"Ringing for a religious festival? I don't believe it. The crocodiles that are in power would not allow it! Nevertheless, it may be so, these hypocritical clergy have never been embarrassed to grovel at the feet of these men they abhor, if that is the only way gratify their brute appetites. It is bad enough that some of them have a Lola in the house."

We stayed in the Alameda for half an hour listening to the water falling from a stone fountain; another half an hour in the Juárez Hemicircle. Now the elegant avenue was just a route for the automobiles of the *carrancista* pigs and their women.

"Let's go down Madero Avenue now," said Lulú.

"No it's better to go by the way of Cinco de Mayo Street. I don't want to see those ridiculous hulks they call triumphal arches which have been waiting more than a year for Don Venustiano's return. Dyed cloth and pasteboard boxes stuck together. I've seen better in the most grostesque, miserable village in our region."

We proceeded and then paused a moment to read one of the inscriptions which crowned the first triumphal arch. "Hero of Peace, your redeemed ones salute you."

We laughed spontaneously.

"Yes, may he come to see his redeemed ones along the length of the street, making a queue under the burning rays of the sun, their tongues hanging out like those of tired dogs, waiting from early in the morning to buy a liter of maize or a kilo of damp brown sugar."

I patted my stomach with satisfaction and praised God. Far from being inspired with compassion by that confused multitude of lousy, naked people, half-dead from hunger, which stretched the length of the sidewalks in the very heart of the city with barely enough strength to wait for a handout of bread, I said: "Now they have the government they wanted, the downright fools!"

"How different from the Mexico City we used to know, isn't it, César?"

We recalled our first vacation visit to the capital: the shining streets, the carriages in two lines drawn by magnificent horses, the dazzlingly beautiful and elegant women. One hardly knew where to look—whether at their arms, breasts and heads, where precious stones clustered, or at the shop windows which were like pools of gold and diamonds under cataracts of electric lights.

Our hearts were breaking with sorrow to see those enormous glass show windows shattered by stones and bullets. Some were protected by wretched patches of sheet metal and tin plate. In place of rich and artistic articles, the windows displayed piles of onions with roots like hair; mounds of watery tomatoes; barricades of potatoes; cones of brown sugar; and bread more anemic than the people outside looking at it longingly. This led me to say that misery has lost even modesty. The boldest shopkeepers, those who escape the authority of the Provost who rounds up deserters and conscripts, displayed the left-over of all left-overs: hats from the time of His Serene Highness, shoes of Leonese manufacture, which in the heat of the day exhaled a fetid odor sufficient to pass through an inch of glass. The height of mockery were the tags with fabulous prices for such worthless things.

"César," exclaimed Lulú as we entered Constitution Plaza, "the Calvary of Holy Friday!"

"Extraordinary," I responded. "Chimes, flowers, and now the altar of the Passion in the very Zócalo. I swear I don't understand it."

I took her hand and we went toward the center. The plaza had been turned into a level lot where constantly whirls of dust clouded the very Cathedral itself. The semblance to any little town plaza to be perfect needed only rows of harness near the great fires where the muleteers were warming their provision and beasts of burden wallowing in the loose dirt.

"Lulú, the author of this prodigious monument is a general without doubt; but I would judge that yesterday he was a sacristan. Observe that such a pastiche of the Passion could occur only to a technician of a sacristy. Only, instead of the symbolic ladder, the cross, the holy sheets, the nails and rooster, there is a little derailed train, some mines blown up, a burnt bridge, and telegraph poles on the ground. Very beautiful! The creator must have said: 'I prefer truth to art.'"

"Hush," whispered someone beside me, pulling on my jacket.

I turned around.

"A spy. They are listening to you."

I turned to the other side. An old, fat woman with streaked, bristly, white hair and with bulging, short-sighted eyes was engaged in a sort of panegyric about Constitutionalism and the First Chief to four or five idiots who did not know what they were doing there.

"A heroine, emulating Doña Leona Vicario or Doña Josefa Ortiz de Domínguez?" I asked the stranger.

"Yes, one of today's heroines; the ex-cook from the Rincón Gallardo[11] home and now one of Don Venus'[12] secret police."

I thanked the stranger and Lulú and I hurried away from the Sagrario. Then in front of the Cathedral the sound of horses and the sharp notes of a bugle stopped us. We stepped back just in time to keep from being crushed. An enormous automobile passed like a flash of lightning.

"It's he!" I shouted, my voice choked by emotion.

"Yes, it is he!" exclaimed Lulú.

We two had recognized him at the same instant: his enormous

black eyeglasses, his nose like a Manila mango, his beard like the brilliance of yellow hemp.

He drew near the small opening, extended his hand, saluting with his Texas sombrero. Whom? We never could tell. Immediately, at full gallop, a platoon of cavalry with an officer at its head who shouted with the accent of a fool: "Long live the First Chief!" His cry was lost in the atmosphere of glacial indifference. I looked about for the old pop-eyed, white-haired woman and was able to say without fear,

"That's just fine."

Like someone fleeing, like someone taking refuge from grave persecution, like someone escaping from imminent danger, like someone who hides furtively in a strange house, the yellow-bearded one crept through the great door of Mariana Palace.

The cathedral bells turned slowly. I, stupidly standing in the middle of the street at the risk of being mashed as flat as a tortilla by the passing cars, opened my eyes like an idiot and looked all around. Nothing: neither the huge, ancient stones of the Cathedral, nor the cold stones of Cortés' Palace aroused themselves from their somnolence; neither did the filigrees and stone lace of the Municipal Palace even blush.

That night I had a fever. I, Cagachitas, pursued by the Ogre of the Hundred League Boots—the Ogre had enormous nostrils like mangoes and ferocious black eyeglasses and a huge beard of hemp.

They awakened at my cries,

"Ay—Ay—a basilisk—"

THE TRIALS OF A RESPECTABLE FAMILY

I

Berta passed through an ornamental wrought-iron gate in front
of an imposing structure facing Chapultepec Avenue. As she ascended
the marble steps, she trailed her delicate hand negligently along a
bronze banister against which bougainville grew. The smooth stucco,
the aromatic wood veneers of walls and archways, the garishly colored
tiles, the vari-colored pieces of glass of the marquee were startling
to the eyes of the rich young woman from the provinces, lighting in
them a spark of happiness. On passing through the hall to one of
the drawing rooms, she paused in astonishment at the marble and
bronze statues, porcelain vases, exquisite carvings, luxurious tapestries
—a profusion of harmonious forms and warm colors reflected to in-
finity in the massive Venetian mirrors framed in crimson velvet and
brilliantly gilded wood.

The contrast with the immediate past was so great that, like stone
struck by steel, Berta's heart threw out a spark of protest. She had
just endured the slow and tedious pilgrimage of Carranza's retinue
in its triumphal return from Veracruz to Mexico City.

Towns and villages in a Dantesque procession: Orizaba, Jalapa,
Córdoba, Veracruz, Tampico, San Luis Potosí, Querétero, and Mexico
City—the whole country in desolation. Masses of human beings like
a dense confusion of rags stood along the sidewalks waiting since early
morning for a scrap of stale bread, a handful of beans, or some worm-
eaten corn. Wild-haired people with frightened, emaciated, dirty faces
hiding grief as though it were shameful; people anxious and distressed,
mouthing curses. Working people, pockets bursting with Carranza's
paper money, half dead with hunger; humble clerks, dressmakers,
small rentiers, orphans, the infirm: the middle class condemned to a
double torture in their intimate contact with the vile, mean rabble,
for whom nothing was ever any better or any worse and who now,
all puffed up with pride, spat insolently in their faces.

But Berta, a well-to-do Christian, reasoned to herself, "This luxury,
however, has nothing to do with the misery outside." She was unaware
that the effect of a bazaar which her drawing rooms produced was the
natural result of the procedures by which the new rich acquired things.
Consequently, she soon recovered her peace of mind.

Her small feet sank into the soft carpet. The sight of the agglomeration of furniture and objects d'art made her eyes shine. Her hands touched them as though they were old and well-known friends. After an hour of exquisite joy, she felt that everything around was asleep; that the cold atmosphere, the silence and the solitude were blowing a breath of death over her face; faint lines quivered in her forehead, two creases furrowed her sad cheeks; over her clear eyes, usually so inexpressive, fell a veil of melancholy indicative of an old grief.

Smothering a sigh, she dropped down on a divan just as the telephone began to ring.

She answered it immediately. At the first words, her expression altered completely: "Yes, Pascual, I just got here. Very beautiful! Indeed, it is a palace. No, I'd never imagined anything like it. . . .Yes, I'm more than content; it couldn't be better. . . . With whom? . . . Yes, without you, nothing has any meaning; I don't know how to explain it to you. . . . You are really coming home? . . . Of course, bring anybody you wish; but do come, for God's sake! . . . Yes, why should I refuse you? Your ministers, your generals, all those new friends of yours are to blame and that's why I despise them. . . . No, I shan't say any more; but take care not to deceive me again this time."

The heavy draperies parted and a servant ceremoniously announced *Señora* de Tabardillo.

"Who? That's no one I know. Tell her I'm not receiving anybody."

Berta, full of happiness, went to the dining room to give orders to the servants. The footman returned to say that *Señora* de Tabardillo insisted on being received, for she had brought news of Berta's family.

"Oh, a friend of the family. Then let her in right away!"

Berta, her interest aroused, went herself to receive the guest. Breathless, *Señora* de Tabardillo dropped down in an easy chair that hardly more than halfway accommodated her vast proportions and rested for a few moments. Mouth open and nostrils dilated, she drew in a tremendous breath as though she wished to take in not only air but also the furniture, tapestries, vaulted ceilings, and floors: all the riches of the magificent residence which her eyes absorbed without tiring of the sight.

The actuality surpassed the suppositions and conjectures which she had derived from reading the news in *El Demócrata*[1] that Pascual, chief of a ministry, had taken charge of the office provisionally.

In no more than three hours she had succeeded in getting in touch with her illustrious fellow-townswoman and her emotion overflowed. She thought, "With Payito one of those in Pascual's confidence, we could leave this miserable life forever."

Her mentality differed not a jot from that of the average metropolitan. The fever of getting rich was endemic. Who could escape the contagion if daily you see by the hundreds *hacendados*, industrialists, magnates, who one or two weeks before were poor devils sleeping in filthy, verminous, pasteboard dormitories? Improvising a fortune as a highwayman had passed into the realm of legend; but if Porfirio Díaz had closed the highways as a means of getting rich, he had left the barracks and public office. No knowledgeable follower of Villa, of Zapata, or of Carranza failed to discover *those* means. The secret of how to get rich under Díaz was made public by the men of the revolution to their great advantage.

"Dear mama? My brothers and sister? I am terribly distressed because I haven't seen them yet although we have been in Mexico City a week! But Pascual is overwhelmed with work and I'm so helpless."

"Pascual is one of the principal officials of the government, Berta. I've come to congratulate you on this fine, well-deserved triumph."

"He has had the good fortune to please Carranza."

"This luxury reveals everything. Your house is a palace. You can go beyond that if you wish. Pascual is young, very intelligent and lacks only a good adviser, a person who knows his way around Mexico City. You've no idea how honorable and gentlemanly my husband Payito is! If you should wish to say a favorable word to Pascual—"

"I never interfere in such matters, Madam."

"Payito's references? Banks, industry, business, petroleum, railroads. The truth is, he's had experience of every sort."

"What can you tell me about my family? I'm really impatient."

"Of course, my dear friend—only—that is to say, for the moment—I cannot—"

"Oh, what are you trying to tell me? What secret keeps you from speaking?"

"It's not that, Berta, I tell you—"

"You're hiding something from me. My God!"

"The fact is that since I stopped visiting in your house on Arquitectos—"

"That's what I want to know. What has become of them since then?"

"I truly wish I could tell you, but the truth is that—for the moment at least—"

"Something very serious has happened which you don't dare reveal to me. I understand. By the holy memory of your parents, Madam, tell it all to me at once, don't keep me in this agony."

"But I—"

"Some one of them has died, I've a presentiment—"

"Your own fear deceives you. The truth is that I have not seen them since they left the San Rafael district."

"Then what are you looking for here? Why did you come here promising news of my family?"

"Be calm, Berta, be calm. Servants always misunderstand. The doorman told me that you had not had any news of your family and I simply offered to go look for them. I am in an exceptional position to secure information within twenty-four hours about anybody whatever who is a resident of Mexico City. Don't be astonished; Payito is the head of a private investigation agency. A big North American company! One can find out anything one wishes. You don't believe it? Then I'm going to show how I, Aurora Caloca de Tabardillo, know Mexico City inside out. You see, this furniture which we are sitting on came from the drawing rooms of the rich Spanish property owner, Don Íñigo Noriega. Do you think I'm lying? Those Japanese vases, those Persian tapestries, and those pieces of Sèvres decorated the house of the minister, Limantour. Do you still think I'm lying? Oh now, don't put on such a long face! What do you take us for?"

Berta's inability to speak, her thin hands trembling below her kimono sleeves, her distressed countenance had the effect of abruptly stopping the cataloguing which had scarcely begun.

"Jesus Christ, don't think a perverse spirit guides me. In whom can we place our hope if not Pascual? Payito, for example, as a private secretary to your husband, and I—well, I would be contented with a class at the Conservatory. Listen to me and judge for yourself."

A long mouse-colored coat and a hat with an Aztec-like plume moved across the room against the background of the gold and crimson of the upholstery and draperies. The woman sat herself down at the piano and through the silent precincts of the house burst forth the first measures of the quartet from *Rigoletto*.

The color of lead, trembling with anger, Berta bit her lips. The woman quickly closed the piano and, beaming with satisfaction, went over to sit beside Berta.

"Why do you look that way, child? Come close, my dear little doll, so that I can kiss your forehead, your cheeks, your eyes, your lovely mouth. Tut, you're really a child still! You see, Pascual, an intelligent, clever man, knows his way around. Fortune has knocked on his door and he has simply opened it. You don't have to pay any attention to the rest."

"Those are the same words he has said to me many times. How did you know that?"

"Ha, ha, ha! It's just as clear as that sun shining through the window. Only an idiot wouldn't do it."

"You frighten me. You say the same things to me that he does."

Half an hour later, the Tabardillo woman had been entrusted with the mission of searching for the Vásquez Prado family. She went away with three gold coins obtained so skillfully that Berta was the one expressing thanks.

II

An automobile stopped abruptly. "It's he," thought Berta, running anxiously to the window. Two figures alighted from the vehicle and walked slowly along in the shade of the trees.

Berta quickly closed the window and turned back into the drawing room, pressing her hands tightly against her breast. The flush in her cheeks faded, the lines of her soft profile blurred, and her eyes filled to the brim with tears. It was no longer the way it used to be in Zacatecas when evening fell. Then it was he and she who got out of a carriage; just the two of them. Tightly holding hands, leaning toward each other, they would walk leisurely among the trees, while their carriage rolled along slowly behind them. One evening? No, many; all the evenings of a whole lifetime of dreams from which one awakened suddenly, surprised and anguished. When she recovered her sense of time and place, drying her tears, she spoke to the mute statues and the immobile paintings. "What am I doing here? This is not my house; nothing here was ever mine. Pascual, why are we still here? Let's go to Zacatecas; let's go to our own house. Let's go so that you can return to me the only thing I asked in exchange for my hand: your heart!"

Two musical bells rang out, their tones muffled by the thick carpets and hangings. Berta ceased crying. Her attention concentrated on the telephone receiver. She anticipated the usual excuse: "Berta, I cannot come to dinner; General B_____, Minister J_____, my distinguished colleague N_____have invited me to dinner. To refuse would be unpardonable." And always those, the same ones: the ones who wore the detestable Texas-style hats, the despised riding breeches, the puttees of crude leather; all the abominable influences which had been insiduously taking possession of Pascual since that cursed trip to Veracruz. In her excited state of mind she sensed a murmur of laughter, a breath of mockery. Like one crazed, she hurled herself at the first picture on which her eyes fell.

Fragments of gilded plaster fell on the carpet. Still intact in spite of the catastrophe, Francis I and his favorite beauties continued their amused, ironic contemplation of her. Then, feeling impelled to destroy everything within her reach, she pulled down a curtain, sinking her sharp fingernails in the fabric. Just as the massive curtain rod fell to the floor with a crash, she came to her senses and realized what she was doing. Pascual's automobile stopped in front of the house. Shortly afterward she heard masculine voices on the stairs. Then the eternal miracle: the radiant sun back of a black tempest, the frantic flight of her unpleasant thoughts, and the lifting of the shadows from her heart. As creations of a sick mind, she cast out her suspicions and doubts, her fears and recriminations—everything which had caused her to suffer acutely during her interminable hours of idleness and loneliness. She opened her arms and went to greet her husband.

"I'm so happy because we shall soon have news about Mama. Do you remember a *Señora* de Tabardillo?"

While she was giving a detailed account of the visit, Pascual's guest, General Covarrubias, took in the whole room with a cold, almost indifferent look at the rich surroundings.

"Let's go right now to the dining room," Pascual interrupted her, "the General is our only guest. Don Ulpiano will come later for coffee."

The linen shone whitely; the flowers, the china, the crystal, the silverware, even an ill-favored Negro with his back bowed and a napkin

over his arm gleamed in the soft light. Pascual and the General talked
a great deal about politics and finances. Their conversation was like
an enigma to Berta. She was satisfied, however, just to be near
Pascual, to hear his clear, sonorous voice, to look at his shining eyes,
to delight in his sober and distinguished aspect. There was, nevertheless, a moment when certain phrases attracted her attention.

"Our whole project is a house of cards without the old man's
signature," said General Covarrubias, darting a glance at her.

"We will have Don Ulpiano's signature no matter what it costs,"
answered Pascual in a metallic tone.

One phrase and then another kept going through Berta's mind with
strange obstinacy. Was it perhaps because of the prolonged silence
which ensued or because Pascual also looked at her quickly and
intently? Pascual, in contrast to Procopio, was not a man who con-
sulted his wife about everything. What, then, did she have to do with
the discussion?

If Pascual's new friends weighed down Berta like the links in a
prisoner's chain, Don Ulpiano affected her like a catapult. If only
Pascual would find out! Hadn't that insolent old idiot dared to try
to make love to her? To her, for heaven's sake, a married woman!

When Don Ulpiano Pío came in looking like a trained dog in a
circus, Berta straightened up with a haughty air. Although her face
felt as though it were burning, her reflection in the large mirror of the
sideboard revealed no flush. The effect of the light tempered by the
green, violet, and amber glasses of the chandelier on her face might
be instead the shadows of her own hidden grief. Her countenance
glimpsed through the flowers, fruits, crystals, and silver was the sad
one of a sick little bird. The mirror reflected the perfect oval of her
face marred by an elongated jaw and prominent cheek bones. Her eyes
shone feverishly. Her lips were thin and colorless; her hair rough
and disarranged; her neck and chest so thin that the tendons and bones
stood out in sharp relief.

"Punctual as usual—just as punctual as a broken watch. Ha!
Ha! Ha! Berta, I throw myself at your feet! You are somewhat pale,
but in every way divine!"

He smacked his lips and let out a burst of laughter that rang out
with solemn stupidity.

Pascual made a vehement gesture to Berta who rose to her feet immediately without responding to the ridiculous old man's gallantry.

At seventy years of age, Don Ulpiano Pío was still acting like a Jean Jacques, at least in the propagation of the species. *La Sirena, Pulques Finos,* and *Curados,* license number 3500 of the Department of Health, and his forty branch stores well located in all the districts and sections of Mexico City were the same as breeding grounds, if not harems, where anyone who would try to unravel the tangled skein of paternity of the most recent off-spring of the servants would have a difficult chore; for their children had equal rights with the legitimate children to take their father's name, or their brother's, nephew's, uncle's or even their grandfather's, that of Don Ulpiano Pío, the great progenitor of the whole herd.

Crafty to the point of improbability since the day he saw his establishments staffed without any salary by members of his numerous progeny, there appeared on his lips a smile of Buddhist beatitude, one of supreme felicity of a person living in contemplation of his well-fed stomach. Since then, Don Ulpiano Pío smiled all the time, and the secret of his smile was precisely the poem of his life.

Berta, faded by the effects of her continuous grieving, was just the sort to arouse the gallantries of the seventy-year-old satyr. When General Covarrubias had presented him to her, he had said, "He is a man who laughs." She thought, however, with the usual acuteness of her sex, "He is not a man who laughs, but a pig that grunts." Shortly afterward, she understood that she was not mistaken.

After coffee was served they engaged in a long and mysterious conference conducted in very low voices. Mysterious only to them, however: the collusion of *carrancismo* with businessmen in order to seize the contents of the few pockets not yet ravished by general looting was sheer, naked cynicism. With fields desolate, public coffers exhausted, banks robbed, safe-deposit boxes broken into, coins no longer in circulation, not even the filthiest bronze piece, the *new men* in a stroke of genius (the only one which *carrancismo* had had in the course of its glorious career) discovered Columbus' egg. The military, which had already sunk its claws into the centers of production, in the streetcar lines, in the highways and trails, and which had become master of every means of transportation, now conceived the idea of making itself into a business concern. It was not necessary to exert any new effort; having the markets in their clutches was enough. In a moment the lives and purses of sixteen million cowardly human beings, spiritless and degenerate, were at the mercy of less than a thousand bandits. A new kind of miracle: crystal water did not burst from the rocks nor did manna of all flavors rain from the sky; but the sweat of the poor, the tears and the hunger of the widow, of the orphan, of the infirm would be converted into a river of gold which would flow into Danaides' cask: the greed of the businessmen and the rapacity of the military, supreme rulers of the paper money issues.

The *carrancista* evil was slavering with stupidity in its apotheosis. The work of the revolution was shattered into a thousand pieces. The government's paper money enhanced the value of the gold in the safe-deposit boxes of the men in power. Capital, yesterday's implacable enemy of paper money, now had in its hands elements of the most formidable revenge. With paper money, the few honest transactions yet carried on in the country would be at the mercy of the military-businessman combination.

If for the working man there were some miserable grains of corn, they were just enough to keep alive the goose that laid the golden egg. The rest—the orphan, the widow, the sick, the old—had no consolation other than their rending cries of desperation and impotence, drowned out by the clamor of the merchants. Possessions from those of utmost domestic necessity to the most sacred family relics went from the homes of the unfortunate in a sorrowful procession to the market place. It seems that the curse of Luis Cabrera, the brain of *carrancismo*: "*Wretched are those who can see in a tear or a drop of blood the gold into which they can convert it,*" would be like spit which, ejected toward the sky, falls back to bathe the faces of the crowd of cheats.

III

Two days later the Tabardillo woman had herself announced. Eagerly, Berta came out to greet her.

"At last! What have you learned?"

"Look at this marvelous pair of earrings! Rubies, emeralds, and a huge diamond in the center. Take notice of the mounting. What quality! What settings! Isn't that so? Of course, there were many interested persons and they made offers, but I arranged it so that you could buy them."

"I'm not interested in that, Madam. Pascual has bought me enough jewels since we were in Veracruz."

"You haven't shown them to me. I'm just crazy about jewelry."

"What have you found out about my family?"

"I'm just about to locate them. Just be calm and I'll tell you. Perhaps tomorrow I will know all about them. But good God, Berta, don't miss this chance! Even as a simple business proposition it would pay to buy these earrings. Only five hundred *pesos*. As soon as silver money circulates, they will be worth three times as much, as sure as anything. Of course there is no urgency whatsoever about the money. As a matter of fact, if you prefer it, your personal card would · be sufficient. I would take it to Pascual and collect from him."

"I never do anything without consulting my husband."

"Berta, have you spoken to Pascual about my recommendation as we agreed?"

"I have given you a commission for which I will pay you; that is the sum of our agreement," Berta replied with spirit.

"Jesus Christ, what a nerve! Tomorrow when your dear mama is here, you will speak to me in another tone. It'll be a pity if you don't buy this jewelry, Berta. Pascual will not forgive you for letting such a chance go by—and, by the way, do show me your jewelry."

Subject to the woman's strange fascination, prisoner of an inexplicable uneasiness, Berta immediately led her to the bedroom and showed her the jewels in order to cut short the impertinent visit. The Tabardillo woman's behavior was irreproachable. She revealed exceptional knowledge of the work of gold- and silversmiths and, by the time she took leave, had succeeded in impressing Berta favorably.

The oblique rays of the sun tinged with rose the opalescent hall when the dirty woman, like a dingy little owl, traversed it. As she descended the flight of white steps and put her hand on the wrought-iron garden gate, a Ford suddenly stopped at the entrance. Through force of habit, the woman withdrew quickly and hid behind some azaleas. The newcomer was an old man wearing a long, sweat-stained frock coat frayed at the edges. The heels and soles of his unshined shoes were worn out. Under a tobacco-colored felt hat two thin locks of dyed hair stuck out stiffly. His sharp eyes instantly caught sight of the bulk of the hidden woman.

"Hey! Listen here—you who are hiding. Take my card up immediately."

"You here?" asked the woman very surprised, coming out of her hiding place.

"And you? Do we have some bait here? You're a rat who's never caught sleeping."

"We'll talk later."

In the meantime the doorman had appeared.

"The lady of the house is not in."

"I know it. Announce me anyway," said the old man insolently in a nasal tone.

The doorman withdrew into the house. For several minutes Don Ulpiano and the Tabardillo woman kept on looking at each other and smiling slyly without uttering a word. She gave no indication of going away. Ungovernable curiosity shone in her eyes. A servant called out discourteously from the entrance hall that the lady of the house would see no one.

Don Ulpiano frowned and puffed up his cheeks while the Tabardillo woman, her eyes as sharp as blades, covered her mouth with her hand to suppress laughter.

"Now you see that without me you can't do a damned thing. Ha! Ha! Ha!"

"Let's go outside."

Both went out and got in the automobile and drove off toward Chapultepec Park.

A week went by. Half sitting up in her bed, Berta summoned the maid. Immediately a young girl came in carrying the linens for the room. She put a flowered combing jacket about Berta. Brushing up her hair from forehead to neck, she arranged the abundant tresses into a thick knot. Berta let her do it, still drowsy, weighed down with an unconquerable lassitude, her eyelids swollen and reddened, her lips white and dry.

"You weren't able to sleep last night either?" Berta did not answer. A pleasant aroma was diffused throughout the warm bedroom. A vigorous massage of her limbs with eau de cologne gradually brought back her sparkle.

"Raise the Venetian blinds."

A puff of morning air impregnated with resinous aromas came in suddenly from the balcony.

"A lady is waiting to see you," said the maid as she began to dress her.

The everlasting nuisance. Unknown people at all hours asking for recommendations.

"I think she is the person that you are expecting."

Berta's confused thoughts and tangled memories began to clarify themselves and become more definite. Agustinita, Procopio, César, Francisco José and the deceiver—the Tabardillo woman who had extracted five more gold coins from her last week.

"She comes for money. Show her in, then."

Now she resolved to stop the game even if it meant sending for a police commissioner.

"Now you owe me a present in exchange for good news! I have found out everything! I have found their address and if you want to, we will go to see them at once."

The Tabardillo woman had rudely insinuated herself into the bedroom.

Berta withdrew with distrust from the arms which attempted to embrace her around the waist.

"Let's give them a surprise, Berta; they don't even suspect that you are in Mexico City."

Berta was unable to make up her mind about what course to pursue.

"But are you deceiving me again? Tell me, where do they live?"

"I myself would accompany you if I had not left my house without breakfast."

"Come to the dining room. Then we will go."

Berta took her hand and conducted her to table; at the same time she gave orders for her automobile to be brought around at once.

"Are you telling me the truth?"

"You can't imagine the work that it has taken me to find them. The janitress at the Arquitectos place refused to give me any information. The neighbors knew nothing about them. Police commissioners, policemen, secret police—closed doors, until Payito said to me, 'Take this magic wand and it will open them for you.' And it did: money here, money there, money everywhere. Just awful. But it's no matter; it was for getting what we wanted."

"I will pay you back what you spent, but for your kindness you have my gratitude."

"Hush, what are you saying! What better payment than the friendship with which you both honor us? By the way, Payito told me to bring the earrings to you. 'Make a gift to her of them,' he said to me. The kindnesses which we hope for are worth more.' He had rather you would have these precious jewels than anyone else in the world. 'You have done a wise thing in proposing that I be of service to Pascual. Our relationship will be a mutual benefit. If he finds me useful now, when he comes to know me better, he will see that I am indispensable. What's more, I'm not particular about the salary.' "

While Berta barely touched a glass of milk to her lips, the Tabardillo woman gulped down all the food put in her reach without letting a chance pass to build up Payito. When Berta left to go change her clothes, the woman cleaned off the table.

"Very good!" she belched with satisfaction. "It was a good idea for you to dress modestly. Your family isn't well off and they would feel humilitated if—"

As Berta stepped off the last step into the vivid sunlight, she became very pale and felt as though her legs were giving way. She surely would have fallen had the Tabardillo woman not supported her, practically carrying her to the car.

"Go by way of the Ángeles Garden," she ordered the chauffeur emphatically.

Berta wiped her forehead with a fine batiste handkerchief. Her transparent cheeks began to regain their color. Gradually she came to herself.

"You are unhappy, Berta. You are distressed."

"Oh, yes, much more than anyone could imagine."

"Pascual makes you unhappy."

Berta became deeply perturbed. The Tabardillo woman's owlish eyes stared into hers.

"How do you know? Who told you?"

"There are things one can figure out, Berta."

Berta secretly made the sign of the cross, thinking, "There is nothing in my mind or heart hidden from this woman."

"I'm afraid, Madam—"

"The truth is Pascual has found an enviably high place for himself. Not only has he given you all that is necessary for your social position, but the luxury and pomp of a real millionaire as well. What more can you ask of him?"

"The only thing that belongs to me: his heart."

"Ha! Ha! Ha! Do you expect a five-year honeymoon and in this revolution? How naive you are, Berta!"

"What good is money to me if it steals his spirit from me?"

"Understand, girl, that Pascual lives in a world where conventional morals are not the best recommendations for getting—"

"What?"

"Would you be capable of demanding that he disregard the fortune that has fallen in his hands simply to satisfy your childish whims?"

"I'm no child; I am his wife and I have sacred rights which obligate him."

The Tabardillo woman, laughing violently, almost fell out of the automobile.

"How can glory, honor, riches mean anything to me if I have this burden on my chest? My life is my own!" Berta moaned vehemently, shaking with a spasm of pain.

"All right. Suppose your worries haven't any real foundation? You are so nervous! You have such a vivid imagination!"

"What would I give if only that were the case! I should be born again!"

"Test it. It is in your own hands."

"I don't understand."

"Awaken his self-pride. Let us say, make him jealous."

This woman is a devil, thought Berta, crossing herself again.

"You have let yourself go a bit now; but if you wanted to—you are beautiful, elegant. Pascual has many friends and at least some of them would have—"

"That's enough!"

"Perhaps right now some old millionaire is mad about you."

"Stop it! Understand that you are speaking to an honorable woman."

"Ha! Ha! Ha! Then what do you think I was going to suggest to you, Berta? I really hit it when I said that you have a wild imagination, Berta. Horrors! No, my dear, I wasn't thinking of such a thing. Ha! Ha! Ha! It only needs to be acted out like a play, nothing more!"

"I'm not capable of such things, not even in a play. Hush up now."

"A play only to awaken Pascual from his drowsiness, my dear. If he opens his eyes, if his suspicions make him demand explanations, if he imagines something, if it comes to the point of provoking a scene, marvelous! What more assurance could you want from him?"

"You tempt me like the devil himself."

"Ha! Ha! Ha!"

"For God's sake, woman, don't laugh like that. You frighten me!"

"Poor girl. Now I understand everything. Pascual has not even known how to awaken the sleeping woman in you. If he had, you would have cast far away that burden which weighs you down so."

"Hush up!"

"I'll hush. Keep on with your doubts, your hesitations, with your willful and useless martyrdom."

As the Tabardillo woman spoke, the car turned abruptly into the little plaza of the Ángeles section and stopped.

"It's Berta, Mama dear!" cried Lulú in surprise as she stood looking through the blurred glass of the big window.

They all dashed to the door to greet her.

IV

After embracing, they separated, warm and excited.

"No one told you anything, then?" moaned Agustinita.

"How could I have heard anything, Mother dear?"

"My poor César! It happened the day that Don Venustiano, that ill-fated man, entered Mexico City. When César returned from the Zócalo, he died."

Agustinita began a detailed account of César's illness, but as the Tarbardillo woman hadn't the slightest desire to cry, nor had she included listening to such a relation in her program for the day, she interrupted,

"Extraneous matters disturb us in such solemn moments as these. My greatest sympathy and at the same time my felicitations because we are together again."

"Thank you. My chauffeur will take you home. Give me your

address so that I can send you a remembrance and the payment for the earrings."

"Don't worry about that, Berta. I'll come to see you tomorrow."

"You didn't know anything about our return to Mexico City?" asked Berta when Agustinita had finished her interminable story.

"Not a word."

"Then you did not know that Pascual occupies a high position in Carranza's government?"

"Not until this very moment."

"But in the newspapers almost every day there is a photograph of him, or an interview with him, or a statement he has issued."

"Newspapers!" sighed Francisco José.

"Some time ago that item disappeared from our budget," added Procopio smiling.

Berta cast a quick glance over the walls of the little living room and its furnishings: three chairs without backs, another with its cane seat spread out like a fan, a large plank resting on an old packing case for a table—those things which were unsaleable in the Tepito market.

"Well, then, is everything pawned? Sold? This is a shame, dear mother of my heart. We are in luxury and you in—"

The words stuck on her lips, burning her tongue.

"Let's go to my house immediately. Pascual will know what to do."

"Do you think that with his influence, our properties will be returned to us?" asked the trembling Agustinita.

"Everything. The branch of the government dealing with such matters is one of those under his direct control."

"Property that has been confiscated?"

"Yes, Papa. He can get whatever he wants. You just can't imagine—"

A tragic smile shone on Procopio's face. Lulú was on the point of crying.

"Let's not lose any more time, Mama dear. Go get dressed too, Lulú."

"I can't go, Berta; I must take care of Papa."

"The chauffeur will bring you back within an hour. I want so much to talk with you all! You will see what an elegant house it is, Lulú."

"I'd rather go some other day," replied Lulú in a muted voice.

"Go and change your clothes," ordered Agustinita sharply.

Her other clothes were no less ragged; the only difference was that they were cleaner.

When the car returned after taking the Tabardillo woman home, Agustinita and Berta were waiting impatiently. Lulled by the rocking motion as they rode rapidly over the paved streets, Agustinita soon stopped talking, her ardent imagination fired by the most fantastic schemes. The reconstruction of her estates; Pascual administrating everything and using valuable official influence for the benefit of the family. He would of course introduce modern machinery which, without having to pay freight charges or import duties, would be very cheap. He would bring in breeding cattle from the United States; he would introduce new methods of cultivation. With that vigor and skill which Pascual understood how to apply to such matters, the first harvest would certainly recompense them, and with interest, for all the hardships they had suffered on account of the revolution. Poor Procopio! His unfitness, his imprudence had for a long time kept him out of the place in the house which he should have occupied.

In the meantime the thought of her unpardonable impulsiveness was troubling Berta. Her cheeks broke out in small red spots. She thought, "Why did that woman talk to me about an old millionaire madly in love with me? Who does she think she is? I ought never to receive her in my house. A servant will count out each *peso* to her that she comes to collect, but I will forbid them even to announce her to me. She is an evil woman! The Devil himself!"

Lulú, who also appeared abstracted, was actually not thinking at all.

With her mouth dropped open in astonishment, Agustinita ascended the steps of her daughter's home. Her eyes were delighted by the sculptured adornments, the marquee of multi-colored pieces of glass enlivened by the sun shining on them, by the winter-season plants set among the small statues of marble, bronze, and precious metals.

Lulú, also seized with admiration, observed everything. Only everywhere she encountered the semblance of a delusion; the smile of one possessed, some white lips, pressed together, dry: a picture of Procopio in macabre caricature. Closing her eyes tightly to keep from crying, she thought, "They in their opulence; we in our misery."

Berta answered the telephone.

"Yes, it is I. . . . I have a wonderful piece of news. . . . We found them this morning. . . . They're here now. . . . Yes, Mama and Lulú. . . . Yes, Lulú. . . . What did you say? . . . To her, to Lulú? . . . I'll tell her. . . . Certainly, why should she refuse? . . . Leave that to me. . . . I'm so glad you're coming home. . . . Goodbye for now."

"Lulú, Pascual wants you to join us for dinner. General Covarrubias will be here."

"Oh, no!"

"He's a respectable young man," protested Agustinita.

"I had rather join you some day when you are dining alone."

"I have already promised Pascual that you would join us here."

"Lulú, you should remain. We are greatly obligated to Pascual."

"I'd rather another time, Mama dear."

Lulú moved over close to her mother and said to her ear,

"They didn't invite you. Can you put up with such a slight?"

Augustinita shrugged her shoulder and answered aloud,

"I order you to stay. I will go home to prepare dinner for Papa and Francisco José. I've more than enough time. Right now I don't want to leave this palace. Berta, don't forget to speak to Pascual about our affairs. You have no idea how anxiously I shall be waiting for Lulú to come home with the information."

"Don't worry about that, Mama. It's as good as done."

Agustinita found Procopio reading.

"Pascual holds a very high position in the government," she said with deep emotion. "His house is a palace. He has servants in full livery and an automobile standing at the front door. I suppose he did not accompany Berta to this pigsty because he did not want to humiliate you."

With supreme indifference, Procopio took his cigarette out of his mouth, stopped reading and said slowly and quietly,

"The future certainly belongs to men of Pascual's sort."

"Undoubtedly. If he doesn't deserve it on account of his intellectual gifts of the highest order, he deserves it on account of his excellent upbringing and the exquisite way in which he deals with people."

"Wonderfully acute," extolled Procopio, pushing his glasses above his eyebrows. Cuttingly, he continued, "The improvisation of a fortune today requires primitive means. The future, I repeat, belongs to men like Pascual. Because of his fine manners and excellent upbringing he found out how to open the door of our house the day he wanted to; by his excellent upbringing and exquisite manners he will know how to open any other doors necessary to him. The only difference between him and other bandits is his exquisite upbringing and his fine manners."

Agustinita drew back so enraged her hair stood on end. Even more ironically, Procopio continued,

"The perfect bandit has to begin by being the perfect gentleman."

An awkward silence ensued.

"It seems that at last, some justice will be done: the number of rascals made rich by the revolution now exceeds the number of rascals impoverished by it."

Agustinita's eyes flashed.

"Society, in other words, the moneyed class, the middle class, the intellectuals have been rather severe with the bandits. Not really because they are bandits but because their procedures disregarded traditions and customs. Today's thieves and assassins are not embarrassed when they are designated by that name in Congress, in the press, in public or private gatherings. Far from it. In fact they are even surprised that anyone would attempt to tarnish their reputations with such trivial charges. During the time of General Díaz the thieves and assassins were among the privileged classes; they wore white gloves, they shaved every day, they knew how to tie their ties correctly and to wear cutaways and high-hats, they spoke the very best Castillian and wrote flawlessly. Society, therefore, always refrained from interfering with them. Theft and assassination did not anger Society unless the theft or assassination was committed by persons of the lower classes. The *pelado* dressed in *huaraches*, white pants, and straw hats mortified them, but the ones who wore gold braid made them feel proud. Crude procedures wounded Society and made it blush with shame. Victoriano Huerta belonged to the same class as the *pelado* even though the eminent poet Díaz Mirón may have said when the troglodytic assassin of Madero visited the offices of *El Imparcial*:[2] 'General Huerta yesterday visited our editorial room leaving behind him an aroma of glory;' even though the Jockey Club would have celebrated his savage deeds with a gala celebration. Victoriano Huerta never procured for himself a gesture as satisfying

as the one which that group of ladies of our highest aristocracy bestowed when they decorated the Red Cross hospital with flowers and
welcomed with thunderous applause the two famous assassins[3] who
came with their hands dripping with blood, treason, and infamy to
visit those wounded in the affair of the Ciudadela.[4]

"That's right. Pascual is the precursor of tomorrow's magnates.
The Pascuals of tomorrow will be able to kill and rob with impunity.
The most exclusive circles of Society will not disdain them. Society
will always clamor for its privileges. The future is for such men
as he."

Agustinita's indignation contracted her jaws and paralyzed her
tongue, incapacitating her for any response. Francisco José, as usual,
took refuge in the water-closet to shelter his esthetic sensibilities from
the ensuing quarrel.

V

The ridiculous old man came in talking and shouting boisterously.
He had acquired his mannerisms in his pulque taverns from the
waiters and his boon companions. He kept repeating himself convinced
of the importance of what he said, ending each sentence of his discourse
with a burst of idiotic laughter which he believed to be most subtly
malicious. Under his crushed, dirty felt hat, greasy hanks of hair hung
down; monkey-like eyes shone like coals, and an eternal smile
wrinkled up his short nose and jutting chin.

"He has the appearance of a swineherd!" whispered Lulú in her
sister's ear with loathing in her voice.

"He was one in his youth," replied Berta without turning her eyes.

Don Ulpiano Pío who cursed the lower classes, forgetting that the
Tuxtepec Revolution[5] had taken him from the pigsty to an hacienda,
believed himself one of the true aristocracy. He did not utter the
word "bandit" when he spoke of Madero's and Carranza's revolutions.

Pascual presented the old man and the General to Lulú.

"I have had the pleasure of meeting Lulú," said the latter. "Who
could forget those eyes once having seen them?"

Lulú abruptly withdrew her fingers which the General had caught
in his big hand. She turned her eyes angrily and resentfully toward
Berta who also blushed furiously in embarrassment.

"A very attractive young lady," exclaimed Don Ulpiano, greeting Lulú and patting her on the cheek.

A septuagenarian may behave in that manner without offending society, even though he might be hiding under a paternal air the hot ashes of a senile passion. Lulú made a gesture of revulsion as though the cold, viscid stomach of a frog had been pressed against her cheek when she felt the touch of the old man's hand.

"Pepe Covarrubias was only a captain the first time you met him, Lulú, but now he is a general; not one made at a banquet, either. He earned his rank by killing many of Villa's and Zapata's men."

"I owe two bullets in my chest and this stiff arm to those who resisted us," observed the General modestly.

"Then blessed be the resistance which not only enabled you to preserve your properties but most assuredly to increase them," responded Lulú lightly.

"What a good memory!" said Pascual with an air of elation.

"I congratulate myself for having endured it all," added the highly incensed General.

"In your place, I would not have congratulated myself."

The General bit his lips. Lulú burst out laughing as though she herself had not taken account of the implication of her words.

Pascual then passed the cognac. As he came up to Lulú, he said in a low voice, "This game is not becoming to you."

Lulú stared at the General. His skin, tanned by the sun of the coastal region, his blond mustache curled and twisted more tightly than when he was a simple captain, his legs like steel springs under the tight breeches of gray corduroy and the puttees of yellow cowhide gave him a most complete martial appearance.

Disgusted, Lulú said,

"Archibaldo has also become a soldier—pst."

"Do you detest us so much?"

"Detest you? No, that is not exactly the word."

"You're just like your father, Lulú," interrupted Pascual, "always on the opposing side."

"If Lulú is on the opposing side, then I betray Carranza," exclaimed the General very pleased with his discovery.

"You'd even go that far, man," exclaimed Don Ulpiano Pío, putting his hand to his forehead, catching the phrase without understanding it.

"Yes, that is what you ought to do, abandon Carranza. I have continually thought about it, but have not screwed up the courage to tell you. You, young people of respectable families, in the den of bandits!"

Neither Pascual nor the General paid any attention to the old man, being concerned only with Lulú's sharp repartee.

"Well, what does your father think of the soldier's career?"

"I have heard him say many times that the barrack is the school of complete abjectness, and that the soldier must be a wolf or a sheep—in any case, be one of the pack."

"Let's go to the table—to the table," said Pascual suddenly as he noticed the course the conversation was taking. "You are talking about things you don't understand, Lulú."

"They don't pay any attention to me!" she answered as she hastily caught hold of Pascual's hand before the General could offer her his arm.

They all went into the dining room. Just as he finished the first glass of wine, Don Ulpiano gravely began discoursing,

"Now, ladies and gentlemen, there is the Monroe Doctrine, Carranza has his doctrine, and I have mine as well."

"We know it by heart, Don Ulpiano," General Covarrubias interrupted him discourteously. "Let us talk, rather, about Lulú's eyes."

"Ha! Ha! Ha! How angry the *carrancistas* get when one knows their secret! It is useless for you to deny it; Carranza is obligated to President Wilson to turn over the country to him denuded of its people. The Yankees want Mexico without its costing them a drop of blood. Each one of Carranza's soldiers must, then, kill ten Mexican civilians. After that hunger will kill the ones left and that will end that. That's the explanation for so much stealing, for so much killing, such high taxes, such high prices for everyday necessities so that respectable people can't obtain them. Of course, I was never taken in by all this. I was educated in the United States and I was a fellow-student of Wilson's. A medium in New York told me all that more than twenty years ago, just the way it's happened. Ha! Ha! Ha! Just look at the expressions on your faces. It makes you very angry that I have guessed your secret? I also know what they are thinking in Japan! Watch out! Ha! Ha! Ha!"

"What a wretchedly ill-bred person!" murmured Lulú in Berta's ear.

At least all that was bearable, but when dessert was served and the wine had gone to their heads, the gentlemen were inclined to express their emotions in an unmannerly fashion and the fictitious harmony came to an abrupt end. Without concealing her indignation, Lulú arose, wrath flashing in her eyes as she looked at the General who puffed up and got as red as a tomato.

Berta, very pale, got up immediately to follow Lulú on the pretext of getting a bottle of wine that Pascual had sent home that morning. The men kept laughing boisterously.

"What shall I tell Mama?" Lulú asked just as they stepped through the doorway.

"You are leaving, Lulú?"

"Right away."

"You've a right to be angry, sister. I could never have imagined that this—"

"Go on, tell me right now. Your house gives me a chill; it gave me that feeling the minute I put my foot in it."

"Lulú!"

"Consult with Pascual or I'll leave right away."

In anguish, Berta went back to the dining room and called Pascual aside. Their conversation was brief. Pascual returned in good spirits to the dining room. Berta, inconsolable, said to Lulú,

"Tell Mama it's very difficult to arrange things the way she wants them."

"I understand everything. Good-bye."

Crying bitterly, Berta tried to keep her from going.

"Oh, don't leave this way!"

"What else do you want from me?"

"Oh, Lulú, they have changed him so! He wasn't like this before!"

Suddenly moved to pity, Lulú put her arms about her sister and covered her with kisses.

"My poor little sister! You are the one who is changed! He! Pfui! He was always like that!"

"You knew it?"

"You have only now begun to open your eyes."

"But you have understood, Lulú?"

Berta stopped crying, straightened up, looked at Lulú with astonishment.

"I understand what I have always understood: that which Papa has always thought about Pascual."

"What has he thought of him?"

"That he is a miserable ——; a low-down sort!"

"Lulú!"

"My poor sister!"

"Lulú, that's not so. Pascual has a fault—a fault that matters only to me, but he is a gentleman. Lulú don't go, don't leave me before I have finished saying what I have to say. Lulú, one moment, listen to me—"

The sound of Lulú's light feet descending the steps was her answer.

When Berta called out from the window of the vestibule to offer the use of her automobile, Lulú was already some distance away. She ran, flying, without feeling the sun which softened the asphalt and struck the encircling peaks, because another fire was burning her soul.

Like a sacred statue of grief, Berta watched her going farther away, getting smaller in the distance and finally disappearing. Then that abominable thought, like the last hope of salvation, rose up in her mind. She saw laid out before her the only and fatal road. Frightened at her own thoughts, she stepped backward; her breast heaved as if in the whole park there was not an atom of oxygen available. With the pupils of her eyes dilated, her face rigid, her legs trembling, having made an inexorable decision, she entered the wine cellar, took some bottles, and immediately returned to the dining room. She opened the door and cast an uncertain glance about the room, looking at each in turn. To the extreme surprise of them all, she took a seat by Don Ulpiano Pío and said with complete serenity,

"Pascual, serve me some wine."

VI

"When?" panted Don Ulpiano, his face now so close to Berta's that his greasy mustache touched her cheeks, bringing to them two red blotches of shame.

In a gesture of uncontrollable loathing, but not of fear, with one hand she upset a glass of sparkling wine while with the other she restrained the old man.

In her chaste ears buzzed coarse jokes and obscenities from the tavern. She became afraid. The plot of the play exceeded the limits she had planned for it.

"Mother of Perpetual Help, come to my aid! Lord of Penance, defend me! I'm suffering a just punishment. I've listened to the words of an evil enemy."

Suddenly Heaven was deaf. Don Ulpiano Pío seized her tightly in his stringy arms.

"Pascual," she moaned.

A strangled wail. She was afraid of Pascual and was even afraid of herself.

A bloody scene might end such an abominable farce! The innocent victims of a tragedy she had provoked! But Pascual, enveloped in the gray smoke of his cigar, his eyes closed, slept the sleep of the inebriated.

Like a snake curled around her waist, she felt the skinny, leathery arm that imprisoned her, that encircled her, getting tighter, pulling her closer and closer. Beside herself, she turned her eyes imploringly toward the General.

He returned her glance with a lascivious and shameless look. General Covarrubias, son of a respectable rich family of the Northern frontier, a revolutionary in order to defend his interests, was like his confrères, morally no different from any of the other rubbish thrown up by the revolution from the manure heaps of the Bolsa and Santa Julia districts. His psychology was like that of any other contemptible sneak thief who saw in the revolution a rich vein of ore which he could use for his own ends. Instead of landing in the Islas Marías[6] he received his merited crown in some one of the ministries, in the Senate, in some diplomatic post, or at least in the Chamber of Deputies. His name rang out more in the gambling casinos and brothels than on the field of battle: a name encrusted with the blood of helpless victims, but one celebrated enough to be brought to the knowing and foresighted eyes of the Citizen First Chief who knew how to recognize and reward such rich talents with the best posts in the government.

A cynical and sinister smile hovered on the General's lips. It all happened in a few seconds. Silks and chiffons, brilliant beads, and disarranged bronze hair floated through the air. A row of sharp, white false teeth bit into her pale, dry lips. She could hardly keep from crying out. Like a dragonfly snatched away by two owls, she disappeared from the dining room in the arms of the ruffians.

On discovering herself on her soft bed she escaped from the arms that restrained her like a spring which suddenly expands. The old man fell on his face on the carpet. On the General's fat cheeks, soft as those of a young shepherd, resounded a sharp blow. More than surprised when he proposed to take revenge on his own account, two sharp, shining points of steel restrained him, bringing him back to his right mind.

Standing in the center of the room erect, transfigured, Berta awaited the attack with her right hand extended and her fingers firmly grasping the handles of the open, flashing scissors.

It all happened in the most discreet silence. When Pascual awakened from his heavy sleep with a beatific smile on his lips, he exclaimed,

"It seems we bestowed on this little wine the honor it deserved, didn't we?"

Arousing himself he took out his watch, raised up, and exclaimed in surprise,

"Five o'clock! Gentlemen, pardon me, I have some very important matters at the Ministry to attend to."

Dejected as defeated cocks, the General and Don Ulpiano remained some distance from the table without opening their mouths.

"I also have something to do," the old man finally said, pulling his greasy felt hat down to his ears.

He left the room grunting. His legs trembled more than usual. When he crossed the garden, the General calling from a window made him turn around,

"Be careful about the one that is loose! Better tie her up!"

In her bedroom, on her knees before the image of *Nuestra Señora de los Remedios*, Berta heard the General's stentorian burst of laughter. Suddenly, a very strange feeling in her head and chest made her laugh too. At the same time an uncontrollable trembling shook her whole body. Her hollow laughter, at first unrestrained, increased in intensity until it ended in shrill bursts. A servant, much alarmed, inquired,

"What is the matter, Madam?"

Berta was unable to reply. Her lips trembled, her jaws were rigid in a painful contraction; her whole body struggled in convulsions and spasms, and her eyes were enormously dilated and full of tears.

The maid poured some mint-scented cologne in the palm of her hand and rubbed it over Berta's cold body, vigorously massaging her from feet to neck. Little by little Berta calmed down, the convulsions lessened, her face took on its normal appearance, her breathing was easier and, finally warm, she fell into a deep sleep.

The next morning when she opened her eyes, she felt as though lead weights were pressing down on her temples. Her throat burned and her lips were like cardboard. In the silence of the bedroom a lamp swayed rhythmically, projecting the shadow of its bell-shaped, violet-colored shade on the walls tapestried in gold and silver and on the golden reflections of the polished furniture.

"Where am I? What time is it?"

"Five o'clock."

Startled on hearing the fresh young voice from the foot of her bed, she raised up quickly.

"Who are you? What are you doing there?"

"I slept here on the rug, in case you might need me, Madam."

"Oh yes! Thank you."

"How ashamed I am," she thought, "that the servants have seen me like this! What mortal sin have I committed, dear Lord, that you punish me this way?"

"A glass of water," she asked without being aware of doing so but responding to a pressing physical need.

When the maid came with the water, she brought also a letter which she handed her.

"Your husband left this for you last night."

"A letter? Open a window at once."

The morning light entered in a bright, wide swath. Outside birds were singing, the rising sun cast a rose tint on the tips of the trees in the woods.

"Expect me at nightfall. We must have a very serious talk," read Berta, and her heart gave a leap.

"Wonderful!"

All her remorse, all her sorrows were erased instantly. "It worked! It worked!"

VII

Hardly able to contain herself on hearing Pascual's voice, she almost had a dizzy spell. She had been counting the minutes and seconds ever since the gold timepiece tightly clutched in her hand had indicated seven o'clock. Before she had time to calm down, the bell sounded and she heard Pascual's measured steps mounting the stairway. He entered with his arms hanging inert, his neck bent. Moments of infinite anguish. Pascual put his hat and cane on the rack, walked slowly toward her, and pulled a chair up to the divan where she was sitting.

Always so sure of himself, now he was hesitant and doubtful about how to proceed. Berta, on seeing that handsome forehead usually so serene, creased in perplexity, had mixed feelings of intense compassion and deep joy. Hers was a blessed folly which had returned her life to her, her very life: her husband.

"Berta," Pascual finally said.

In the silence of the bedroom, during an instant which seemed like a century, the buzzing of a mosquito could be heard.

"Berta," he said again, after swallowing, "I have observed that Don Ulpiano Pío—"

Berta had an impulse to laugh but it was necessary to carry the play to its end. She made a gesture of astonishment; then opened wide her light-colored eyes. Her proudly raised head trembled so that she almost lost her equilibrium.

"What are you saying?"

"I say that you have been very attentive to him—perhaps too much so."

The delight that Pascual's torture gave her was so keen that she felt her skin crawl in a wave of delicious chill. Gracefully stretched out on a quilt of crimson plush, wearing a magnificent kimono of palest silk, she looked like a lily, broken off at the stem, in a lake of blood.

"Answer me Berta. Why are you silent?"

If Pascual would cry a single tear, just one tear, she would forget forever the torrents of tears he had caused her to shed; she would feel entirely recompensed.

Like a vague lunar phantom she sat up in the uncertain light of the bedroom. Standing up, she said,

"How dare you to reprimand me for my conduct, you who have left me alone for whole weeks and months? What does it matter to you, then?"

Humiliated, Pascual lowered his eyes.

"Am I only one of your possessions? Are you the only one who has a right to live your own life?"

Pascual looked up in surprise. A flash of light illuminated them intensely.

Berta, whose energy had burned out, made a great effort to finish,

"You ask for an account of my acts when your dissipated life is today the scandal of Mexico City! What a mistake! Haven't you more sense than that? I also wish to live! In me exists a woman that you, poor you, have not even known how to awaken."

Pascual's eyes opened in astonishment. Horrified at herself, she hid her pale, thin face in her hands that were like dry stalks, and dropped down again. How could that disturbing phrase of that demon of a woman who had instigated this farce have presented itself to her mind in that instant?

Her head sank back in the cushion. The lines of her face grew sharper, her eyes disappeared in their leaden sockets. Her face was damp with a cold sweat. Pascual, without coming out of his stupor, stared at her penetratingly. When he came to himself, thinking he figured everything out, he remarked slowly and seriously,

"Berta, now we can speak frankly."

Berta opened her eyes; even yet not a tear shone in Pascual's. But why prolong his suffering now that she had been convinced of his innocence or at least of his absolute repentance? Impulsively she arose and threw herself at his feet, clasped his knees lovingly in her arms, kissed them and exclaimed,

"Pascual, forgive me!"

"Bah, foolish girl, get up! Come to my arms, for I'm the one who should beg for your pardon; I, who in the years I have lived with you, have never caught a glimpse of the woman who sleeps in you. What a wonderful lesson! Berta, I confess that I thought you to be of the inferior species of your family. What a joke! Berta, all I can say is that from now on we shall go forward together."

Without blinking her eyes, scarcely breathing, her heart stopped. Berta looked at him dumfounded. Pascual continued,

"You were the only obstacle to our actual, definitive triumph.

If that old Carranza has a single moment of bad humor we're out in the street. It is most necessary to secure, by whatever means, a position that does not depend on others. The previous owners of the luxuries which we now possess can recover them with no more than Don Venustiano's signature. But the venture which we are going to undertake is different. It's a simple business affair of a million and a half *pesos*. But in order to carry it out it is absolutely necessary to have the signature of someone not affiliated with the revolution. Do you understand? We have found the person we need in Don Ulpiano Pío. He is incredibly obstinate, but he has revealed his vulnerable spot and with that he is ours, do you understand? Your obstinacy made me think it hopeless! But now, come to my arms! Just one piece of advice, probably now superfluous, which you should always carry deeply engraved in your memory: we are allies now. In matters of this kind, Berta, one must only use his head, never the heart. But I'm being silly. What prompting do you need from me?"

Filled with satisfaction, without noticing the effect of his words, Pascual got up and, humming the tune of a fox-trot all the while, took his cane and hat, looked in the mirror and meticulously straightened the knot of his tie, and pushed back the unruly hair that danced over his forehead. Once outside he wheeled about quickly as if struck by remorse, and running on tiptoe, came up again to Berta and kissed her lightly on the nape of the neck.

When she was able to open her eyes, she moved her unsteady hands to search out the spot where the snake had bitten her. She stood up swaying on her feet, went over to the washstand, soaked a handkerchief in the cold water, and placed it on her burning neck. It was useless! The fang had sunk too deep. Now, not a sob, nor a tear; only a coldness, a frigidity that did not come from the quiet surroundings and melancholy of her room, but from some other source like a thrust of steel, penetrated to the depths of her soul.

VIII

In a stiff manner, a servant put five gold *hidalgos* in the Tabardillo woman's hand and said rudely,

"Don't come back here any more. The lady of the house has even forbidden us to announce you."

One morning as Berta was returning from the Mass of the Sacred Heart of Jesus, someone approached her as she stepped out of her automobile.

"Please pardon this discourteous approach but as you have such stupid and unmannerly servants, this is the only way I could get to talk to you."

Taking full advantage of Berta's surprise and weakness, *Señora* de Tabardillo crowded so close she entered the house with Berta.

"For the past three days I have asked to see you but the servants have always refused."

As they paused in the vestibule Berta asked, "Do I still owe you something?" as she raised from her pale and sunken eyes the fine veil sprinkled with minute black stitches of embroidery.

"More than with money, you have paid me in kindness and with such good will."

A challenging look was the response to the insolent remark of the intruder whose teeth showed cruelly when she smiled.

"In that case—"

"I'm out of place here, then, isn't that so?"

Like a butterfly that drops its wings to return to its chrysalis, Berta slipped out of her luxurious silk-lined fur coat and with unusual hautiness toward the Tabardillo woman raised her head.

"I find you're changed a lot, Berta dear. What sort of spider has bitten you?"

"That's enough. I won't allow you to talk to me like that. Understand we are not equals. You want money, always more money. Speak up, then, so that we don't waste any more time."

"I'll begin by reminding you of the recommendation which you promised me you would make in behalf of Payito."

"I never recommend people I don't know."

"Oh! Does that mean to say everything between us is over?"

"What?"

"Perhaps not, little one, if it doesn't suit me that way."

"There's the door!"

"Before I go I wish to say a few words that will make your heart soften or at least extinguish your ill temper."

"Get out of here."

"Just suppose I give an account of what took place here a few days ago between you and your husband's friends!"

"Hellcat! You're part of the same bunch!"

The Tabardillo woman repressed her impulse to laugh when Berta pressed a bell.

"Wait. Have you thoroughly considered what you're now doing?"

"I don't intend to put up with any familiarities from you. Get out of here."

"Understand that I can make some very revealing statements."

"What about? To whom? If you are all of the same ilk, if all are canaille—what do I care what you all say?"

"I have missed the mark," thought the Tabardillo woman to herself in some confusion.

With her hands covering her face, Berta held back the torrent of tears and sobs stored up during many days and months of desertion and loneliness. But she was unable to control herself any longer. She dropped down in a chair and began to sob.

With considerable effrontery, the old woman ordered a servant who appeared: "Bring her a cup of herb tea."

When Berta recovered somewhat, she straightened up, surprised to see the woman still in her presence, and exclaimed,

"What are you doing here? Are you waiting for me to call my servants to throw you out like a dog?"

"Oh, Madam, I didn't want to go without asking your pardon! I'm such an old wretch! I was not able to recognize an honest and pious wife. Everything I have done to you is criminal, I realize. Send me to prison—that's what I deserve or even worse. But for God's sake, before you do, pardon me, give me your blessing; for my greatest punishment would be to know that you hate me! I swear that your curse would be harder to bear than years in prison! Pardon! Pardon!"

"Get up. Leave me in peace."

Berta drew back, but the Tabardillo woman, dragging herself on her knees over the carpet followed her, embraced her legs, kissed the hem of her skirt, fervidly seized hold of her hands and kissed them frenziedly.

"Get up!"

"Pardon! Pardon!"

"Promise me that you will never return to my house."

"I swear it," cried the Tabardillo woman, standing erect with an impressive tragic gesture.

Like some remorseful nun with her head lowered and her hands tightly crossed over her chest, she departed, making low bows even to the gardener.

Many hours later, Berta became aware of the fact that the drawers of a little writing desk were open and that her jewels as well as the Tabardillo woman had disappeared forever.

IX

A shove flung the door open with rude abruptness. A figure stood silhouetted in the dim light unexpectedly admitted from the street.

"It's Pascual," cried Agustinita in a restrained voice. Didn't you say he would never come here, Lulú?"

"Pascual!" repeated Francisco José, trembling with joy.

Lulú did not open her lips; neither did Procopio. Both remained in the darkest corner of the room, reserved and motionless.

"Berta? What about Berta? Why didn't you bring her with you Pascual? Where is my daughter?" Overwhelmed with questions, immobile in the middle of the little room, his eyes dilated by the darkness, he pointed out the lack of proper illumination.

"We have grown accustomed to the dark," observed Procopio as he struck a match on the wall. He lit the stub of a candle which for months past had provided light for just the moment when each sought his corner and his blanket and threw himself down on the floor to sleep.

Pascual surveyed the room from the rotten wood of its floor to the walls from which the plaster had fallen, to the decayed ceiling, and to the miserable furniture, and even to their worn-out clothing.

The pitiful little flame of the tallow candle fluttering in the complaining wind from the garden added its lugubrious note.

"If by chance you do see a well-lighted house in this section of town," observed Procopio in a hoarse voice, "you can swear that it is the residence of a businessman or a *carrancista*. Only those fortunate mortals are now permitted luxuries of that sort."

Their miserable situation, Procopio's purposeful tone, their uneasiness all made Pascual very uncomfortable. His luxurious English suit, his Stetson hat, his massive gold chain and fob, his American shoes of patent leather were distinctly out of place.

"Berta will come tomorrow; she'll come tomorrow," he replied impatiently to Agustinita's avalanche of questions. Resolved to achieve his purpose, quickly, he said, "I bring bad news. Your family is on the list of Carranza's personal enemies. As you know, Carranza is incapable of pardoning anyone."

There was a brief silence of stupefaction.

"Who can prove that?" inquired Procopio.

"I know that it—"

"You know it is a lie."

"Unfortunately there are indisputable proofs."

"What proofs do they have?"

"A loan in silver money made by the Vásquez Prado family to Huerta's government."

"It's a lie!"

"The document has passed through my hands."

"Then you lie, too."

"I lie? You'd better be careful that—"

"That what?"

"That you'll be sorry for what you say. I can force you to retract your accusation."

"I am not the kind who ever repents. I repeat—you are a liar."

Pascual shrugged his shoulders, smiling with an air of commiseration.

"You are lying the way you always have lied; your life itself hasn't been anything but a lie. Proofs—not words."

"You want them?"

"I don't want them; I insist on them."

"I will give them to you when we are alone. I don't want you to have to blush with shame in front of anyone."

"I ask you to present them in the full light of day. If you don't give them to me—"

"What?"

"Then, you'll be the liar."

"Shut up, Pascual," interrupted Lulú, confronting him angrily.

"In this instance you'd better think before speaking," replied Pascual vigorously.

"He who leaves his house with only the clothes on his back," said Procopio taking a step toward Pascual, "and returns enriched—if he has no callouses on his hands, he must have very thick ones on his soul."

"Show me yours."

Something like the hiss of a snake escaped from Pascual's pursed lips.

"Thief!"

"Leech!"

The obscurity of the room was suitable for the unleashing of a mortal hate restrained with difficulty. In the full light of the sun the insults that flew back and forth would not have been let loose.

"You wouldn't repeat those words to me outside the house, you cheap——! Get out so I can spit in your face all I have said to you."

Procopio dashed toward the entrance with his fists clenched, while Pascual, very pale, with a sinister smile on his face, stayed where he was.

As Procopio, in his paroxysm of anger rushed at him resolutely, Agustinita intervened,

"That's enough! I have to tell the truth. What Pascual says is so. I alone am responsible."

"You?"

"Yes, I. I loaned 20,000 *pesos* to Huerta's government. Pascual spoke the truth. We are compromised."

Like a corraled animal, Procopio breathing hard let out a moan of pain, of rage, of frustration.

"I didn't tell you, Procopio, because you were an irreconcilable enemy of that government. I always had access to the strong-box, and took what I needed; there wasn't enough time for you to make an account of the assets before we left Zacatecas."

Only the sound of Procopio's broken, panting breathing could be heard.

"It would have been better if you never had put your foot in this place!" exclaimed Lulú confronting Pascual.

"I'm going, yes; but before I do, I'm going to clear up something that is of great interest to you. Agustinita, examine these papers."

"Our notes. I assure you that as soon as our properties are returned—"

"Remarkable hope! You must realize that in payment of this debt, I could, if I wished, take possession of all your holdings. But as I have never intended to do you any harm, as someone has dared to insinuate, watch carefully what I am going to do."

Stunned, Agustinita and Francisco José, with eyes staring, saw Pascual crumble the documents which Agustinita had given back to him. As he made a bundle of them which he held by his fingertips, he asked Francisco José for the candle. Big flames leapt up, gloomily illuminating the house. A red-tinged light made a path to the street. It cast a glow on Pascual's plump, clean-shaven face and on the others, some troubled, some inflamed with anger, some with eyes burning— all with most contrasting expressions.

When Pascual blew at it forcefully, the flame burned his fingers. His breath scattered the ashes and the crackling yellowish fragments of paper. In the darkness the little fluttering flame of the candle glowed again for an instant before it burned out.

Procopio was stunned. Lulú's face burned in a feverish excitement. Agustinita and Francisco José exercised great restraint in not throwing themselves at the feet of Pascual, their saviour.

"Now you don't owe one cent, to me or to anybody else. I have performed my duty and I am leaving."

"You aren't going with things this way. It is necessary that we talk before—I must make up for my error," said Procopio drawing near him uncertainly.

His muffled, trembling voice had the fugitive radiance of lightning.

"I have offended you," he added, "consequently I owe you an apology. I cannot let you leave this way. Above everything I am honorable. Forgive me, Pascual."

"No, Father," interrupted Lulú impulsively, "he is to blame for it all. Don't lose your head."

"Be quiet, Lulú," burst forth Agustinita.

"It is my duty, daughter. I have offended him. I feel that here within me there is still something that distresses me. I must have Pascual's forgiveness."

"You are acknowledging your present mistake, but you have always been mistaken about me."

"How rude you are! Don't speak that way to Papa!"

"Lulú, leave the room at once."

"I will not obey you, Mother, for all of you are taking advantage of him. I will not leave."

"I wish to point out to you," said Pascual with arrogant calm, "the only way in which you can save your holdings. That is all that is keeping me here."

"Speak up—go on, speak up," exclaimed Agustinita and Francisco José in one voice.

"It is necessary to draw up a fictitious bill of sale for all of your properties and date it before the revolution. I have a well-thought-out plan, but the way you have received me does not permit me—"

"For God's sake, my dear son, forget the insults that have been visited on you. For us! For Berta! Procopio, poor fellow, is extremely weak. Don't pay any attention to him. He will do everything you tell him to do."

"He will do it," repeated Francisco José with determination.

"Well then, it's all very simple. Here is a draft of the agreement. All you have to do is fill in the blank with the name of a person in whom you have absolute confidence in whose hands you will place all your holdings."

"Who could that be except you?" interrupted Agustinita, delirious with joy.

"After what has happened, the very idea of thinking about anyone else would simply add to the injury done to you," affirmed Francisco José authoritatively.

"The condition that I impose, however, is that neither you, Agustinita, nor Francisco José be the one to designate me, but only and exclusively Procopio."

"What a gesture!" exclaimed Francisco José, slapping himself on the forehead resoundingly.

"Procopio," said Agustinita jubilantly, "here is the opportunity for you to apologize in the best possible manner."

"No, Papa dear, not him—don't name him—" whispered Lulú in his ear.

Procopio turned his unfathomable eyes, first to Agustinita, then to Lulú. He had to repeat the words many times. His brain was like a stopped watch. When he approached the table and picked up the pen, his movements were like those of a person moving in his sleep.

"Write in those blanks the name of the fictitious buyer," said Pascual in a clear voice with complete serenity.

"Write 'Pascual,'" ordered Agustinita sharply.

"Pascual," repeated Francisco José eagerly.

Procopio wrote Pascual's name in all the blanks they pointed out to him.

Dancing and clapping her hands like an eight-year-old child, Agustinita showered her husband with caresses.

"At last the Lord God has had mercy upon us! Now we are going to be happy again!"

Francisco José called attention to his poem "Resurrexit," the initial portion of an epic which he was slowly elaborating. No more laments nor spells of weeping: have confidence in the fullness of life, which is good and beautiful, and sing to it in the manner of those in the New Ship.

Then they made Procopio and Pascual shake hands.

Lulú went out of the room in a turmoil of pain and frustration.

X

As soon as they closed the door after Pascual's departure, Lulú came out of the darkness and said in words like hammer blows,

"Pascual has robbed us!"

Agustinita, without paying any attention to her, threw herself into Procopio's arms, who was, however, quite insensitive to what was happening.

"Thank you, my dear, thank you because at last you have been just and have given back to us our peace and happiness. I have often thought: 'Procopio is not a mean man; he could not be one. Procopio has a very noble heart, but there are a great many things he doesn't really understand—it isn't his fault—it couldn't be!' Oh thank you, heart's dearest! Because of this most gracious act of your life, we forgive you for all that you have made us suffer and all the ills you have caused us to bear."

Procopio drew away like an automaton. Gropingly he sought the straw mattress where daily he lay down to sleep. He remained standing silent and motionless for a few instants. Suddenly, like a drunken person in a coma, he fell heavily to the wooden floor. At the sound of his fall Lulú went to him with a lighted candle in her hand.

Lying on his back, his eyes closed, his mouth half-open, Procopio was rigid. His chest moved with uneven and superficial breathing. The ravages of all the pain which that strong nature knew so well how to hide under a suave and ironic smile were now plainly revealed.

Deep hollows showed on each side of his straight nose and two vertical creases became deeper. Many silver threads shone in his thick, curly hair.

"Papa, dear! Papa, dear!"

Lulú held his head in her arms. Agustinita tried to help out by sprinkling his face with water. Procopio opened his eyes at the touch of the cold liquid. He took notice of the anxiety in the faces about him; he heard Lulú's sobs.

"What? What happened?"

"What's the matter with you, Papa dear?"

"No, I don't think it was anything much. Bah, I feel all right—go on to bed."

His customary kind smile reassured them more than his words. They all went to bed.

Procopio dreamed as he slept. It was the first time he had dreamed in a long time. It seemed as though he was in Zacatecas, attending to his business affairs, counting money—all the money in the strong-box. What a quantity of money! Gold, gold, heavy and shining. Gold in closely arranged piles: *hidalgos*, half-*hidalgos*, American gold pieces, all in an exact and orderly arrangement in such close order that there wasn't room for a pin between them. Actually rather than piles, they were heaps, hills that had crumbled. Meanwhile, faster than hands could diminish the contents of the strong-box, the amount increased and overflowed onto the floor in such a torrent that he could not find a crack in which he could put his hands. Opening them, he stopped that cataract of gold which had struck him in the chest and on the knees, which had piled up at his feet and mounted higher and higher until it had imprisoned him in his chair. Gold in a cascade reached his waist. Panic stricken, he turned his eyes in search of salvation.

Rivers of gold flowed in the windows. A torrent of gold poured down from the ceiling. He felt as though the gold had reached his chest, his mouth, that it was suffocating him, that he could not breathe, that it was choking him. He made a colossal effort—superhuman and definitive.

Wet with sweat, panting and gasping, anguished, with his hands pressing against his leaping heart, he got up from his wretched bed. Clearly and distinctly he heard the bells of the Ángeles Church. One— two—then complete silence.

Two hours of rest were sufficient to enable him to recover his mental acuity. He waked up again when the bells sounded four o'clock. Lulú's words recurred to him clearly, "Pascual has robbed us."

He got up, stealthily looked for his clothes, dressed in silence, and walking on tiptoe went out the entrance door.

"Yes, she understood it all!"

The silence was solemn. The central light in the Ángeles Garden diffused a warm, milky glow. Stars filled the sky. In the distance, toward the Santiago district, rumbled the deafening sounds of the first pulque wagons. Hurrying, he turned the corner of the house. One by one he collected the half-burned scraps of paper scattered over the sidewalk. He returned to the house without making a sound.

"Did you hear any noises last night?" asked Agustinita as they were having breakfast. "I think someone got up, or else I was dreaming. As I had stayed up late, I fell asleep immediately."

Instead of replying, Procopio asked,

"What evidence in writing was there of the loan which you made to Huerta's government?"

Agustinita's glance sought out Francisco José's face. They exchanged slight smiles. First she made a gesture of impatience and then one of resignation.

"It was a secret from everyone except Pascual who delivered the money, and the *Jefe de la plaza* of Zacatecas who received it."

"What that means is that only Pascual could have revealed the secret to Carranza, or else this whole business is a miserable lie."

"That is evident," affirmed Lulú.

Agustinita and Francisco José again exchanged smiles of infinite pity.

"I hope that you will always be able to smile that way."

"Dear, you ought to consult a doctor. It's natural that following such blows as we have suffered, your brain isn't up to par."

"How much better it would be if this were just a crazy notion of mine."

"Is it possible that you still have doubts about Pascual after what happened last night?"

"I did have my doubts; now I no longer doubt. Now I tell you that he has cynically fooled us all."

"For God's sake, Procopio."

"Pascual is canaille; Pascual is a thief."

"Procopio!"

"Here are the proofs."

He pulled out of his pocket some fragments of paper blackened and burned along the edges. In one corner, blistered by the heat, were some government stamps still intact.

Curious, everyone drew close to see them. Agustinita and Francisco José were struck with profound amazement.

"I see that you understand nothing. Look closely and you will see the stamps are dated this year—look at them. Do you know what that means? These documents are forgeries; they weren't signed in 1914; Pascual has arranged to deliver a master stroke against us. Do you understand now?"

"How dreadful!" exclaimed Lulú in a wary voice.

"And so, the darling of your heart, instead of being a great actor, is a great bandit."

Agustinita let out a disconcerting burst of laughter. Her eyes sparkled like those of a young she-wolf and her eye-teeth like those of a viper. She said,

"Well, I've more confidence in a bandit like Pascual than in my own husband—a good-for-nothing!"

"Mother," shouted Lulú, her fingers contracting convulsively.

Molten lead seemed to flow in Procopio's veins. His cheeks and lips were the color of lead. The buzzing induced by very high blood pressure sounded in his ears. He did not see nor even feel Lulú hanging about his neck trying with all her force to restrain him.

XI

He became aware of the distance he had traveled over only because of the jam of pedestrians, cars, and trolleys that impeded him at the Post Office corner. When the traffic started up, he accelerated his pace, lost in thought, with nothing or no one disturbing the silence and solitude of his soul. Just as moments before he absent-mindedly passed through the wide streets swollen with noisy, swarming crowds without taking any notice of the magnificent profusion of the many-colored lights, the tall government buildings, the luxurious clothes of the women, nor the exciting perfumes of the ones who frequently brushed against him; no more was he aware of the silence of the dark, deserted lanes of the Alameda when he entered it, nor of the insidious aromas of the night-blooming flowers. Without hesitation he crossed the Alameda to come out on the left of the Juárez Hemicircle. Its marble surfaces brilliantly reflected the glow from the clusters of street lamps nearby. He turned to go into the narrow entrance of Dolores Street and was quickly lost among the multitude of pedestrians. He stopped in front of the enormous door of a dirty and evil-smelling tenement house. Wiping off the sweat which was bathing his face, he waited a few moments and then, having made up his mind, went into a narrow, dark passageway just when a horde of young people ran and frolicked about yelling like cats on the tiles. Faint little lights flickered from some of the opened doors. In the middle of the patio a bunch of clacking gossips blocked his way. Beyond them some others were engaged in a violent quarrel.

"Beg pardon," he said courteously, but no one paid any attention to him or moved to let him by. He had to wait until the fight was over. From insults, the quarrelsome ones resorted to deeds. One woman was nude to the waist; her tattered clothes clung to her body. Another wore a fine astrakan coat, unbuttoned shoes with the flaps falling down, her tangled hair flying wildly.

Each seized hold of the other's matted hair as they rolled on the concrete, each buried her teeth in the other's flesh, all in the midst of a solemn, almost religious silence. Procopio repeated, "Beg pardon," and jumped over them hardly noticing what he was doing and without being noticed by anyone. Farther on, a net strung from wall to wall like a clothes line knocked off his felt hat which bounced against one of the wash basins lined up down the middle of the patio. Picking it up he carefully shook it. Continuing on his way with his hat in his hand, he came upon dank, worm-eaten planks with holes in them which served as crude toilets for the place. A small lantern diffused a miserable, waving light over the scene which made one feel even more keenly the squalor and filthiness of the people of a whole section brought together in one great tenement. He stopped in front of a miserable pigsty of a place, struck a match, looked at the number, and knocked lightly on the rickety door.

"He's not here," he said to himself after he had waited a few moments. He peered through the cracks in the door. In the tremulous light of a little oil lamp, he was able to see the form of a man stretched out on a bare cot. "It's he," he said to himself, his heart constricting within him. Then he knocked forcefully.

On seeing the shining barrel of a pistol the very moment Archibaldo opened the door, he stepped back.

"It's I, Archibaldo!"

"You here, Uncle Procopio?"

"I know that you are here incognito. You came here from the State of Morelos as a fugitive."

"How did you know?"

"Three nights ago I saw you on one of the streets of the Tacuba district. I followed you because I wanted to know what you were doing and where you were living. The rest is easy to figure out. But my object in coming here is something else. Lend me your pistol, Archibaldo."

"My pistol?" Archibaldo echoed, more surprised than ever.

"It's the first favor that I have ever asked of you. Are you going to refuse to grant it to me?"

"But what are you going to do?"

"Nothing. It's just that I've heard noises on the roof of the house and—I am afraid—"

"Of an assault?"

Archibaldo felt like laughing heartily; but in that very instant he noticed that water was dripping from Procopio's hat, that he had a strange look in his eyes, that the tone of his voice was unusual, and that his gestures and movements were vague. "Either he has committed a crime or is going to," he thought.

"Come on, man, don't stall. Lend me your pistol."

Archibaldo went over to his bed. "I am a blockhead. Poor old Uncle doesn't put on a very good act. He doesn't want me to know that he is so hard up that he doesn't even have money for breakfast tomorrow. My poor pistol will go to the *Monte de Piedad*.[7] Whatever God wills!"

He quickly took from under the pillow the last of his money. He turned back to Procopio to give him the pistol, at the same time furtively putting the money in a pocket of his coat.

As soon as Procopio felt the contact of the cold steel of the pistol, he smiled somberly. He left the room without taking leave; without any expression of gratitude.

That bothered Archibaldo. "Suppose he didn't want it for the reason I suspected? Suppose he is seeking a quick way out of his

misery?" The terrible suspicion having occurred to his alert imagination, he did not waste another second on speculation, but caught
up his hat, threw his coat over his shoulder, and left in a run.

At the risk of being run down by the automobiles which at that
hour passed in a constant stream in both directions, he went straight
across Juárez Avenue. At the entrance of the Alameda, he saw
Procopio's spare shadow appear and disappear as he passed through
the brilliant illumination of an arc light in the park. Like an arrow,
he set out to catch up with him. A policeman tried to stop him,
only to suffer a blow that laid him flat on the sod with the light
of his lantern shining up into the foliage of the trees high overhead.

"Now the responsibility falls directly on me." His feet hardly
touched the ground until finally he caught up with Procopio and put
his hand on his shoulder.

Procopio's sunken eyes stared blankly.

"Uncle Procopio, I have run after you to bring you the bullets.
That pistol isn't loaded."

"Well, well, man, I certainly do thank you. Give them to me."

His eyes shone with a melancholy light. The tone of his voice
was strange.

"Thanks, thanks. Now you can go along."

"Uncle Procopio, let me go with you to your house."

"Ah! I'm not going there. It's something else. Leave me, right
away."

"I will go where you go."

"Impossible; it is something confidential."

"I promise to be absolutely discreet."

"That's too much for you to do, dear Archibaldo. Thank you, but
do return to your house and leave me alone."

"I don't have anything to do and being in your company has always
been a pleasure."

"You're pestering me like a thousand devils, chatterbox. Leave me
alone. I don't want anyone to go with me."

"Uncle, you are going to fight someone and I want to be a witness."

"Dunce, I'm not going to fight with anyone; I'm no swordsman.
Go to hell."

"All right, Uncle, then I'll go where you go. It's useless for you
to get mad."

"Oh, I would never have believed that you are such a fool! Well then, let's go home."

"Sure, Uncle, let's go home."

For half an hour they went along without saying a word. In the vicinity of the Ángeles district, Archibaldo stopped briefly in the light of a street lamp to write a couple of lines on a paper torn out of a memo pad. Absent-minded, Procopio paid no attention.

On reaching the door of the house, he asked in a low voice,

"Do you want to go in, Archibaldo?"

"I'll just greet them and then go on, Uncle."

"Go in then."

Procopio, with a penetrating look at Archibaldo, opened the door and showed him in.

"Archibaldo here!" exclaimed Lulú.

"Archibaldo!" they all exclaimed in surprise.

No one had known that he was in the capital.

It was a short visit. On taking leave of Lulú, Archibaldo slipped the folded piece of paper in her hand.

Procopio accompanied him to the corner and said very quietly,

"I have seen it all, Archibaldo. Thanks. You can go away without having to worry."

Archibaldo turned about much surprised. His eyes caught Procopio's in a glance that said everything.

"Thank you, Uncle Procopio. For yourself and for—her."

In the meantime Lulú had gone to the dining room and had read, "Take care of your father. He came to get my pistol. Do not leave him alone for a moment."

Lulú's eyes grew wide. She paused to get hold of herself before returning to the living room.

"Aren't you going with us to church?" asked Agustinita.

"I'd rather go with Papa."

"Suit yourself."

Agustinita took Francisco José's arm and they went on their way. The division of the family was accomplished. It was no longer a secret even to them.

XII

"Good heavens, Papa dear, you have so many gray hairs now that it looks as though ashes had rained down on your head!"

"With the passage of years, the struggle is in vain."

"The years? Scarcely twenty-four hours ago your hair was black as mine."

"Those were hours that were as long as years."

"That is the truth."

The wavering light of the candle cast a shadowy, ruddy halo about the sorrowful pair. Procopio was seated on a broken-down chair. Lulú, in a colorless, plaited robe full of darns, stroked his head with its halo of silver about the temples and forehead.

"Just look at your face—so many wrinkles! And where is Papa's cheerful smile hidden?"

Her voice was breaking; her tears began to flow. She was scarcely able to utter the last few words. Deeply depressed, Procopio bent his head, closed his eyes, and let his limbs fall inert.

"Be quiet, my dear little girl!"

"Am I the little girl who has to give a lesson to her teacher? Why, Papa dearest, do you declare yourself defeated when we haven't even begun to fight?"

Procopio straightened up. In his eyes appeared a glint of astonishment. He looked into Lulú's tear-drowned eyes.

"Egoist! Don't you have a daughter who adores you? Ah, surely you're no longer my father!" Procopio raised his face. Lulú's countenance reddened with anger; her eyes flashed,

"No, you aren't my father. My father taught me that it is always good to smile. He always knew how to smile. You don't smile, but he told me many times, 'Lulú, it's necessary to look life in the face with a smile on one's lips.' Isn't it a fact that *that* Papa no longer exists? Papa never lied; he was not the kind who is nothing but words and more words."

"Hush, Lulú, hush!"

"Didn't you tell me one time, 'Lulú the secret of happiness is not to ask of life more than it can give?'"

Humiliated, crestfallen, humbled, he finally reacted,

"Lulú, you ought not to pass judgment on me in this way. You are unable to comprehend the extent of my torment. Who will help me bear the final blow?"

"Is it my father who talks to me like that now? And those robust arms? That practical brain? And are these, my hands?"

"Your hands!"

Procopio caught hold of them and raised them to his lips. He was so moved by his deep affection that a burning tear fell on the hands he was holding. Lulú dropped her head on her father's heaving breast. The two of them cried for a time that was immeasurable.

When Agustinita and Francisco José returned from saying their prayers at the Ángeles Church, Lulú, shaking with joy, was on her knees before a little religious picture fastened on the wall, giving thanks to God.

Procopio went to bed. The copious tears they had shed had proved a beneficial rain. Lulú's forceful words had just given him a glimpse of a new course to follow. That night Lulú slept with the serenity of a child. Procopio slept with the weariness of a lion clawed in a tremendous struggle, but triumphant in the end, always the victor.

He awakened at dawn. His head was clear; his heart was beating deliberately. He turned from one side to the other on his straw mattress. Not being able to go back to sleep, he dressed and started to leave immediately. He was just unlocking the door when Lulú appeared—kindly, smiling, spirited.

"You, daughter?"

"From now on, always with you."

Procopio smiled tenderly.

"Where shall we go?"

"Where were you going?"

"You know that I like to get up early and set out without any fixed destination."

"Let's go."

Daylight grew stronger. The dark panels of the doors and windows along the sidewalks formed parallel lines ahead of them. In the near distance, the sharp edges, the friezes, reliefs, and façades were lost in a dense fog that reached the heavens; a fog which smeared in dirty gray tones trees, houses, the air, and the clouds. In the distance shone the red lantern of a drugstore. Along another street flickered the insignificant, multi-colored lights of a small hotel. Two great shining eyes, sending out flashes of light, appeared at the end of a street, soon turned out of sight. In the vague sounds of the morning to which one awakened could be heard the distant hum of an automobile.

XIII

The sound of church bells vibrated in the fresh air. They struck five o'clock. Then the bells in the tower began to ring out the call to Mass.

"Shall we go?" she asked.

"I will go wherever you want," responded Procopio with complete serenity.

The two of them disappeared into the cold gloominess of a church whose heavy doors had just creaked open.

Procopio left the church quite transformed. His voice vibrated with vigor. The long-absent smile had returned to his lips. He was more at ease in his manners and gestures.

They returned in silence, but at such a pace that they reached the house out of breath. Procopio quickly drank a cup of water, asked for soap, water, and brushes, and went to his room. He had recovered command of himself so well that he was able to spend a couple of hours in sprucing up and in making his old, shiny clothes look presentable.

"Why are you so silent, Papa dear?" asked Lulú who was helping him.

"Hush, hush. Here within, I have something new. You'll know about it."

When he appeared, rejuvenated, he said in an unaccustomed tone,

"I absolutely forbid that anyone from this house ever put a foot in Pascual's!"

"What about Berta?" remarked Agustinita instantly.

"This is our house and Berta's too."

He took himself off.

"Is he finally going to look for someone who can bring him to his senses?" murmured Agustinita smiling but confused.

"He isn't the one who most needs that," responded Lulú.

"Have you ever been *my* daughter?"

Before the week was out Procopio put three heavy gold coins in his wife's hands, saying,

"For the week's expenses."

"Four *pesos* a day!"

They all looked at each other in astonishment. Who had ever seen as much as thirty *pesos* in hard money all at once in the last two years?

Procopio hid his happiness and joy. A look into the past aroused his astonishment not at the present but at the past. By what miracle had they not lacked for even a day at least a cup of lima bean soup and a plate of boiled potatoes and a dozen tortillas? Proceeds from the sale of the last of Lulú's jewels, the mysterious monthly allotment that came through the grocer at the little corner store—an allotment which ceased coincidentally with Archibaldo's desertion from the *zapatista* ranks.

As soon as they had finished eating, Lulú went with him to the entrance. Procopio kissed her on the forehead and took leave, remarking,

"It's time now, Lulú, to raise another structure."

Agustinita who took notice of Procopio's gestures and words called her daughter to her and asked,

"What did he tell you when he took leave of you?"

"No secret at all, Mama. His only words were, 'It's time now to raise another structure.' "

Agustinita, batting her eyes like a gorilla, tried to unravel the meaning of the phrase. In the meantime the *hidalgos* passed from hand to hand, jingling pleasantly.

"To raise another structure," she uttered mechanically as her gaze absent-mindedly made a circuit of the dining room.

Then the miracle of the gold began. Vague desires stirred in her turgid and confused soul. Her thoughts took form and made themselves evident. Suddenly the objects which surrounded her took on a clear significance. They surprised her, for it was as though she had seen them for the first time. She exclaimed in consternation,

"Dear God, what a loathsome house."

She ran to the store for soap, bleach, and small brushes. "To raise another structure," she kept muttering. She obtained a bucket of water and put in it battered metal dishes, chipped glasses, handleless cups, and old pieces of rusty flatware. She commenced to move about still muttering, "To raise another structure."

Her hands became red and swollen. She attacked the wretched table service furiously, applying bleach and brush, ashes and pumice stone until she had eradicated the rust which had collected from neglect rather than from the course of time. Little by little all achieved a state of shining cleanliness. By evening she had finished her task with all the articles arranged symmetrically on some rough pine shelves that served as a cupboard. In a somewhat melancholy mood, she stood off to gaze at them. A sigh escaped her in the precise moment when a light dawned in her mind. "Bah! Now I understand it all! Pascual has succeeded in getting our properties restored to us or at least a good amount of money. Where else could the money have come from? Procopio is too proud to admit his mistakes and he resorts to subterfuges like 'It is necessary to raise another structure.' I would have said instead, 'It is necessary to raise all the structures that the bandits have torn down.' Just wait until he falls of his own weight —a fish dies by means of its own mouth."

Two weeks later instead of thirty *pesos* there was a tight roll of five-*peso* gold pieces. In her delight Agustinita started to throw herself in Procopio's arms, but her husband's gruff, dry tone affected her like a dash of cold water.

"Beginning tomorrow have lunch promptly at one-thirty."

If his words were short and his gestures moderate, his imperative tone gave no occasion for a reply. Agustinita just bit her lips. That day as always, when Lulú accompanied her father to the entrance to bid him goodbye, he said to her as he kissed her on the forehead,

"Now, Lulú, we are saved."

Agustinita, wild with joy, went to tell Francisco José the good news.

"Procopio has said that we are saved. It's quite clear; either Procopio has managed to get our properties restored, or the Germans have won, or Don Félix Díaz, who is expecting just that, is coming to take the city."

Overflowing with enthusiasm, she added,

"After all, Procopio isn't a mean man. Isn't that so, Francisco José?"

Then she made a firm resolution to pardon courageously all her husband's faults even though all the family's hardships had been owing to his rock-like hard-headedness.

She made up her mind to break the block of ice which separated them even at the sacrifice of her own dignity. Why keep up her antagonism toward him when the source of her anxieties had disappeared? That night, however, when Procopio returned and had

scarcely anything to say except the routine greeting, she felt profoundly inhibited. The odious authoritarian tone which Procopio had
assumed not only killed her old, facile impulsiveness, but it deprived
her of all her freedom of action. Consequently, her planned appeal
for harmony was smothered in anxious and anguished silence.

Days and weeks passed with little change. As the money continued to come in regularly and in increasing amounts and street
clothes took the place of modest house dresses; as Francisco José,
in spite of his neo-romantic airs, developed full, red cheeks like Cal-
ifornia apples, as Bernabé herself made up for bad times by using
all her culinary skill to provide new dishes each day, Agustinita felt
her hardships so diminished that she could submit blindly to her
destiny. She thought, "We can't go to see Berta because we are
strictly forbidden; but Berta can come to see us. It's just a case
of letting her know. Why hasn't she come again? Is it possible
that Procopio's antagonism went as far as criminal action? But that
isn't right, and nobody is obliged to commit acts against his own
nature and the law of God. On the other hand, this is the occasion
for me to wear my silk dress for the first time."

"Francisco José put on your new suit and go with me to visit Berta."

All dressed up and at the door to the street, prey of a bursting
anxiety, Agustinita suddenly became fully aware of the fact that her
husband was no longer the disregarded one in that household. She
exclaimed, burning with anger,

"It is necessary now to talk seriously with Procopio."

They went back and took off their new clothes.

The fear that Procopio had aroused in Agustinita was, nevertheless,
founded on sheer supposition; for, actually, if he had assumed for the
first time the attitude of head of the house, he never uttered a single
discourteous word. He was only more moderate in his manner and
more abrupt in his speech. He no longer practiced the habits of an idler.
Promptly at six he had his breakfast, left the house and remained away
until one o'clock. He left again after eating. He had his supper at
eight o'clock and then went to his room. After locking the door he
worked on large account books until late at night.

"They must be the books of the hacienda," said Agustinita.
"Everything must be in a muddle. Pascual undoubtedly required an

exact statement of the account in order to require the government to pay for the losses and damages resulting from the revolution."

Francisco José proposed the idea of taking a look at those books but a chance to do so did not occur, for Procopio never left them at the house.

They continued to live with the mystery of Procopio's muteness and Berta's inaccessibility, hoping to figure it all out when a newspaper "extra" would at last announce the triumph of the Germans or the presence of "Don Félix" in the environs of Mexico City.

XIV

One Sunday as the last bells were sounding the call to nine o'clock Mass, a luxurious automobile stopped at the door of the very dirty and ancient parish church of the Ángeles. From it descended a veiled lady who appeared sick and feeble. Her bearing was distinguished and her clothing fashionable. She entered the church at the moment when the priest, robed in gold and purple, stood before the bright altar to begin the Mass. But as soon as she had dipped her fingers in the holy water, she crossed herself and returned to the street murmuring a prayer.

"Wait for me at that little door," she directed her chauffeur.

As she crossed the garden, her sallow forehead and cheeks gleamed spectrally behind the fine veil which obscured them as though to hide them from the gaze of the tender leaves of the trees. She crossed the street; she let fall the rough, rusty knocker at a run-down entrance way.

"Berta!"

"Papa!"

"How ill you look!"

"My mother—and my brother and sister? Where are they?"

"Your absence from the city has been on account of illness?"

"Stomach trouble which I thought was going to kill me, Papa. Afterwards, two interminable months in Tehuacán. Now I have returned, about the same as when I went away, for my illness is not exactly physical. I wrote ever so many letters to Mama without getting a single answer. No one visits me. Mama, the only one who could console me, has abandoned me, too. What harm have I done to you all?"

Procopio waited until the sobs ceased rising from her poor, thin chest, then said, "Don't blame your mother, she has known nothing about it."

"What?"

"I intercepted your letters."

"Oh!"

"It was necessary."

"Has it reached that point?"

"Don't ask me why. It was so necessary that not only did my honor depend on it but that of the whole family, even yours."

"But I should have known—"

"The same tone as your mother's!"

Procopio's smile was bitter; his eyes reflected an infinite sadness.

"Don't speak to me that way, Berta. Understand that if I am silent it is in order not to add to the pain you already suffer."

"What importance is another drop of water in the ocean?"

"He's hurt you, too? Scoundrel!"

"What do you mean—me too? What does that mean? Me, only me!"

"Then you have not suspected what happened between Pascual and us? He has told you nothing about it, then?"

"I don't understand!"

"Berta, I have forbidden anyone from this house to put a foot in your husband's."

"How wicked, how wicked you are! Ah! Now I understand—"

"In the house of a thief—"

Berta uttered a strident cry and, horrified, raised her hands as if in an effort to hold back her father's words.

"Yes, of the thief who has stolen everything from us."

"Oh, no! Oh, no! Hush, hush. You make me lose my respect for you. Pascual is not a thief; he is an abominable husband, but he is and always will be a perfect gentleman. I will stand up for him to you."

"You are defending your own assassin and the thief who is enriched with what was ours."

"My God, how shameful! Hush! We, he and I, have been enriched while you have been reduced to dying of hunger?"

"No, Berta, that isn't so. Hunger flew out the window of this house the very day that I discovered that he was the thief."

"Papa!"

"Does your husband inspire more confidence in you than your father? Do you doubt me?"

"I don't doubt, I deny it. Why didn't I find out about this before now? What a disgrace! Let me go!"

"I am not stopping you; you can stay here as long as you want, for this is and always will be your home, your true home. Wait to see your mother, your brother and sister."

"I don't want to see them. I would not have the courage to tell them that I have vowed never to come here again. I lack the courage to tell them that you—that you lie!"

She rushed out of the door precipitately. But she was so weak that she had to accept the support of her father's arms to get into the automobile.

The sound of the motor increased; the car abruptly swerved down the street. Procopio, absorbed in thought, did not come to himself until a soft hand touched his shoulder caressingly.

"We have come back from Mass, dear Papa. Didn't you go?"

"Yes—no—"

As the tone of his voice would betray him, he chose to remain silent.

Agustinita and Francisco José arrived later, swelled up with pride like peacocks.

No one found out about Berta's visit.

XV

From among the multitude of heads—effeminate, elaborately dressed dandies; fat-cheeked *carrancistas* perspiring from alcohol and lasciviousness; affected, clean-shaven comedians; chorus girls like artificial flowers of wire and crepe paper—a lean face raised up, its watchful eyes following closely a man walking among the crowd of pedestrians on the opposite sidewalk.

"My Uncle Procopio! A new suit, a brand-new linen collar, shining boots, and an even more shining joy flashing from his eyes, his mouth, and from every pore of his body. Something has happened! I've got to know it right about now."

Archibaldo made his way through the crowd of ticket speculators, actors, and idlers who crowded around the entrance to the Principal

Theatre at the time that rehearsals began.

"Good morning, Uncle Procopio."

"Hello, Archibaldo, you here?"

"Congratulations, Uncle; you have taken at least ten years off your age."

"And to think that you are my savior!"

"Now don't joke, Uncle!"

"I owe you two debts—the money which I shall repay very soon and the other—I shall never be able to repay."

Procopio, who at first had paused, caught hold of his arm and they moved on together.

"I have tried to find you, but no one could tell me anything about where you were living; neither have you shown up at our house."

Archibaldo reported the latest events which had taken place in his room on Dolores. Political difficulties had made it necessary for him to leave suddenly for Morelos. Within the last few days a happy turn of events had made it possible for him to obtain an amnesty and return with safety to Mexico City.

"I have only been here two weeks. How do you expect me to come to your house looking like this?"

"Very soon, perhaps this very week I can turn over one hundred *pesos* to you so that you can get some suitable clothes."

"Uncle Procopio, please don't offend me."

"But it is your money; it is the money that you have been sending from Cuernavaca during the time that was most difficult for me."

"That's why I became a soldier. Tomorrow I shall collect my first ten days' wages."

"Here? What kind of work do you do here?"

"At last I am working, Uncle Procopio; right there at the Principal Theatre."

"You a comedian? Ha, ha, ha! No man, that isn't suitable. Wait for me here at this very spot at one o'clock sharp." They had just stopped in front of the doors of the store, *La Gran Ciudad de Hamburgo*. "I can do something for you. I have to leave you because it is time to go to the office."

"What office?"

"I am the cashier here. I'll be with you at one o'clock sharp."

"I'll be on time, Uncle Procopio."

"Bah!" thought Archibaldo. "My uncle toiling like any ordinary, miserable employee. What does that mean? It's clear—that the wealth of the Vásquez Prados has played out. Damn! That's just as though I had won the lottery. What good fortune! I'm working as second prompter at the Principal. I'm making three *pesos* a day and I have a bright prospect for the future—or what amounts to that. I can now found a home with anyone whose resources are similar to mine. I can scarcely believe in such good fortune."

His eagerness made him punctual for the appointment. Procopio took him by the arm and the two walked along Santa María la Redonda Street.

"Now, you'll find out what happened, Archibaldo. After that night of torment when you saved my life, I had a change of heart—one of those profound and definitive changes the extent of which you can scarcely appreciate unless you have experienced something similar. Pride, dignity, fear, anguish—all of that is past. You can imagine the tremendous struggles which preceded my firm resolution. Confusion of ideas, hesitations without number, unprecedented torments just thinking about it. How difficult it is to strip oneself of the cursed pride that takes such deep roots in one who has been wealthy at one time!"

"It's been so many years since I was," interrupted Archibaldo as though in a dream, "that I have forgotten what it was like."

"Perhaps if it had not been such a tremendous crisis I had to go through, I never would have dared face it. Just such a tremendous blow was necessary to awaken me. To see friends and colleagues of old times turned suddenly into rude chiefs and bosses who scarcely deign to reply to one even with a harsh word or unintelligible mutter. To entreat destiny, foregoing the confession of pain, of humiliation of a family in misery, ruined—then to begin as a collector, a clerk, a watchman; to rise through the exacting scale of promotion. If by happy chance at the end of two months I found myself at the head of the cashier's office, the few days during which I discharged the duties of the most modest sort were for me unending years. How cruelly punished was that well-known dignity! But, on the other hand, what a great satisfaction it is to struggle hand to hand with an adverse destiny! To feel hostility in the swarm of human beings that buzz outside; hostility in the friends who avoid us; hostility in the very beings that we love most who withhold their confidence from us;

hostility in the greatest and most powerful of our enemies; in that frightened and cowardly *I* who refuses to light the fuse, as if the cannon would explode in his own hands: that rebellious *I* out of whom it is necessary to wrench without compassion the sublime and all-powerful words: *I will*, the words eternally victorious."

"You became resigned to work?"

"Bah! Resigned? No, I work and in that work I have found myself. Do you understand? Listen to me closely."

His look was lively, his gestures quick, he was talkative as a student now that he had got down to intimate confidences. He, whose voice six months before had become hoarse from lack of use, was now overflowing with words.

"I had lost everything; I had even lost myself. I had let the best years of my life slide by and I wasted my best energies in the unconsciousness of a merely passive role. In my own home my only meaning was that of useful endurance—nothing else. Later, events forced me down step by step to the point of becoming a second rate individual— a decorative figure; later, one without voice or vote. Finally, nothing."

Archibaldo, very nervous, listened to him, but his thoughts were engaged with other matters. He awaited the opportune moment in which to speak. But astonishingly the many times he did have a chance, he did not take it, for he felt tongue-tied and as though pasteboard were sticking to his palate.

"Because now," continued Procopio, with joyous pride, "I provide for the needs of my wife and children; because now I speak as head of the house should speak, when he wishes and what he wishes; because now I am the head of the house. Money! That cursed scarecrow eternally came between me and my wife, always keeping me at a distance, restrained, belittled, and often frustrated. The saddest part is that neither did I fully realize my sorry role. I found out what kind of yoke bore me down when I held the pieces of it in my hands. Yes, money robbed me of my happiness."

"What you are telling me," finally interrupted Archibaldo, "fills me with joy and happiness."

"What are you trying to say to me?"

"That money has been like a dike placed between— Uncle, for the third time, I ask you for Lulú's hand."

"Archibaldo, don't take advantage—"

"I swear to you by my mother's holy memory that I have thought and figured much about it before deciding to say anything to you. If you have lost your fortune, then why can't Lulú and I get married?"

"Money hasn't been the barrier, Archibaldo; you yourself have been—"

"I don't understand."

"I am very fond of you and you know it. But you have never been a serious man."

"Ah! And what does it take to be a serious man, Uncle Procopio? To be like Pascual, for example?"

"I understand you. Enough. Archibaldo, will you be capable of making Lulú happy, the one I love most in the world?"

"Bah! I cannot answer that question; it's one to which she must reply."

They fell silent. Their extended hands met in a quick clasp; a strange vibration passed through them, a deep, mysterious shudder. Perhaps those twin spirits who believed they were journeying through life by different paths had just understood that they were following parallel lines.

Mutely, they separated with the same smile and the same sigh dying out on their lips and in their breasts.

XVI

The fragrant atmosphere of Havana tobacco, mahogany, and Russian leather of his employer's elegant private office had not made any effect on Procopio's emotional convalescence. He could remain standing, unchanging, whole hours at a time like any other employee waiting for a decision or an opinion. In turn, the owners no longer interrupted their conversation in the presence of the cashier who was entirely formal and discreet.

Good humor prevailed that day and they drank champagne. From the babble of voices, some speaking German, some Spanish, some English, emerged clearly the principal motive of their rejoicing. A customs concession skillfully acquired from the government for the importation of silk and linen goods; a sure and quick profit of half a million *pesos*. All that in exchange for a banquet and two thousand *pesos* to Carranza's new minister.

Carrancismo in that period had been uncovered in all its shameless depravity. It was not the big scale robbery of the entire nation through paper money, nor the millions extracted from the banks; no, now the stealing was that of petty thieves: railroad car concessions, for example, for two hundred *pesos*. And all that filthy business authorized by the signature of the President of the Republic: the signature of Carranza, the great man who, in an impulse typical of his nature, conceded his signature as a precious gift—sublime symbol—to the soldiers of the revolution, the night of December 25, 1918. The soldiers' Christmas bonus.

"The intervention of the consul was very useful," said an enormous, red-bearded man who overflowed his chair.

"Undoubtedly," replied another, "but the minister made it certain with the assistance he gave us. He is a truly respectable person; he is well known in Zacatecan circles. At any rate, a gentleman."

"Well, it seems," said the Spaniard, "that old Carranza has finally decided in favor of the upper classes."

"And the minister is one of them, without any doubt."

Procopio took the brief case containing the documents for which he was waiting and left followed by his young clerk.

"All they say about the new minister is true," commented the employee. "He is very agreeable. He did not give me the position I asked for, but he received me personally and that's more than I ever got from the government when Villa or Zapata was in power. I am full of hope, naturally!"

And that young dandy, with a face like a quince, corroded by the mania of parasitism, the illness of all his kind, rubbed his hands and capered like a circus monkey.

The press also applauded the first acts of the new minister and congratulated Carranza for his judgment in the choice of a collaborator so capable and intelligent, at the same time taking advantage of the opportunity to attack the would-be soldiers and the stupid fools who made up the cabinet.

"He has become a minister and his rise has been a complete success," thought Procopio.

Thoughts and reflections rose to his mind in such a mad rush that he had to suspend his duties for some minutes. He saw projected in all its grandeur the figure of Pascual, Carranza's minister: a figure of the very material of which the great Machiavellians are formed. He was the born anarchist in reach of his desires—not, however, the Bohemian sort half-dead of hunger, an unfortunate fowl in the government henhouse at the mercy of the first servant of the imperial or republican kitchen who might know how to twist its neck at the opportune moment; but the other kind, the real kind of anarchist— the one who, though mocking society and its law with the most exquisite delicacy, would know how to use that society and its law as a means of arriving at the peak of power and from that height spit in contempt on those who had elevated him. With impunity he will rob, violate, kill. Society, enamored with its Man, from its habitation in the mire, will know how to render full homage to him and later will engrave his name in letters of gold in the most imbecile of its books, and will erect marble statues and bronze plaques that they may perpetuate the one who found out how to embody its sentiments, its ideas, its ambitions. And he will deserve them, at least for having had the courage to be conscious of those sentiments, those ideas, and those ambitions which a hypocritical society will never dare to confess to itself.

Without asking anyone's permission, he soon closed the cashier's office, took his hat, and went out to the street. He gave in to one of those unusual aberrations which greatly disconcerted not only his family, but all the respectable people among whom he enjoyed the reputation of being a man of great prudence.

"Drive down the Paseo de la Reforma."

Ten minutes later a Ford stopped in front of the impressive entrance of the minister's residence.

With a firm step, Procopio made his way up the steps, gave his name in a resonant voice, and entered the house.

"The lady of the house has gone to church; she always returns before one o'clock."

"And your master?"

"It seems that he does not like to talk to people except in his office."

Attentive and ceremonious, nevertheless, the servant conducted him to a luxurious small salon where Procopio took a seat, ready to wait all day if necessary. Wait? Wait for what? For whom? He would have remained there perplexed if it had occurred to him to formulate those questions. The unknown force that had driven him there inexorably did not arouse his curiosity. He was scarcely conscious of it.

The servant responded loquaciously to all his questions; soon he had no further need of him. The objects around him began to take on life and to speak to him with a precise and eloquent meaning. When the servant withdrew and the echo of his words, which like arrows had struck sonorously against the stucco and panels of the arched ceilings, had died away, the solemn and magnificent silence of the rugs, the tapestries, the porcelains, the marble and bronze statuary, all things which feigned life and truth, spoke to him. The cold atmosphere, which seemed crystalized in the sumptuous Venetian mirrors asleep in hopeless idleness, spoke to him. It was a coldness more cold than that of the tomb because above the grave grain quickens, buds burst forth, and little plants take root. This was another more intense cold; the coldness of a dead soul. The suicide of the ambitious and egotistical spirit effected in the precise moment of achieving its unique ideal. The cursed soul of the one who on arriving at the peak of his ambitions collapses forever in the emptiness of its satiety—of its atrophied and solitary *I*.

A sorrowful shadow behind him—the abandoned companion, innocent martyr who would follow without rest and without serving any other purpose than that of being a drop of bitterness in the overflowing glass of his mortal boredom.

As Procopio began to understand it all, the same sort of sudden passion which had made him abandon the desk in his office now drove him out of Pascual's house like someone demented.

Two sentiments clashed in him: submission to the mystery of justice always mocked and yet unfailingly victorious, and the cruel pain in the paternal breast wounded to the heart.

XVII

"You ought to follow him. I will not rest content until I know for certain where he goes every day."

"It's no matter, for he will look out for us," responded Lulú without raising her eyes from her work.

"If you were a good daughter, as you claim, you would obey me."

Tired of Agustinita's persistence, she got up abruptly, took her hat, and went out,

"Well, I'll go follow him."

Just a few minutes before, Procopio had left for work. In those streets where there were few people, Lulú had to take care that he did not see her taking refuge behind bulky bundles people carried or light posts. In the central district she could go along a short distance from him, losing herself easily among the numerous shapely, well-dressed young women employees who came in from all parts of Mexico City to the offices, businesses, and stores. She could almost have touched him with her hands when a voice made her turn aside.

"Lulú!"

"Archibaldo! You here! I am very angry."

"I'm not to blame. Let me explain to you—you will see—"

"Your lies as always. Why didn't you at least write to me? God help me! You distracted me and now I have lost sight of him. It has taken me half an hour to get here and I'm breathless."

"Whom are you looking for?"

"Who else could it be, man, except Papa?"

"Ah, then don't bother. I will tell you where you can find him. Is it urgent?"

"It is urgent that he doesn't see me. I only want to know where he goes."

"It's eight o'clock. He can only be in his office at this hour."

"In what office? You know then?"

"Three days ago exactly we ran into each other on this same street. We spoke seriously about something that pertained directly to you and me. Hasn't he told you?"

"Absolutely nothing. Oh, yes, I remember something now. Yes, I think I have noticed some uneasiness in him. As if he wished to speak to me, but hesitated to do so. I have wanted to question him, but I am afraid of my own indiscretions."

"His worthy daughter as he is your worthy father."

"Stop that flattery and tell me what you talked about."

"Something quite insignificant! I asked him for your hand."

"And he?"

"Well, since the money, which was the only thing that came between us, had disappeared—"

"You know that, too."

"He told me."

"Well, what did he reply to your question?"

" 'Archibaldo, you know I'm very fond of you. Are you capable of making Lulú happy—the one whom I love most in the world?' "

Lulú's eyes filled with tears. She held Archibaldo's hand tightly.

"I said to him, 'Uncle Procopio, she is the only one who can answer that question.' "

Tightly holding hands, they stood pretending to look at the show window of *La Palestina*. Lulú, in a daze for a few minutes, pulled her hand away and inquired of him seriously,

"Tell me, Archibaldo, are you working?"

Archibaldo hesitated momentarily and then answered firmly,

"I'm a prompter at the Principal."

"Horrors! Then you actually see the legs of all those, uh, bad women!"

"The same sort of women passing by that you and I see now—good ones and bad ones."

"Hush, your jokes don't please me. Give up that work at once; better still, don't put your foot in any theatre whatever."

"You would rather I be a soldier?"

"No, not that either. Listen, why does Papa stay so late at that office?"

"He does not leave until all the employees do."

"But he is not one of the employees."

"He is just the cashier."

"What are you saying? Papa the cashier of this business?"

"Of *La Gran Ciudad de Hamburgo*. Good heavens, now I have done something stupid! You didn't know anything about it and if he had kept it to himself, he had a good reason."

"He actually is the cashier of *La Gran Ciudad de Hamburgo*?"

"Bah, what a blunder I've made! Listen, at least don't let him know I've told you about it."

"Don't bother; what you've done is all right."

Then, thoughtful, but quickly changing the subject, she made Archibaldo tell her about his latest adventures. Archibaldo noticed that Lulú listened to him, her eyes very attentive, but with an empty look, entirely unaware of what he was saying.

"Lulú!"

"Go on; continue. That is very interesting."

"But you are not listening."

"I'm sorry; that's true. Listen, it's urgent that I speak to Papa right away. Leave me now."

"What are you going to do?"

"I don't know. But I believe that until I have obtained a good position—"

"Lulú!"

"No, don't stop me, man, I have a wonderful idea. Wait for me tomorrow night at eight o'clock—by the side window, understand? Good-bye."

Ecstatic, Archibaldo followed with his eyes the small gracious figure of his beloved until it disappeared through the great door of *La Gran Ciudad de Hamburgo*.

XVIII

Thoughts fluttered through Lulú's mind like butterflies. She entered casually and asked the porter,

"With whom does one speak about employment here?"

"The manager is just now on the way up. Second floor, down a small passage, and turn to the right."

Lulú caught up with him. On getting out of the elevator, she said,

"Sir, I am looking for employment."

Surprised, the tall man in charge turned around. Her unusual procedure was not the best recommendation; nevertheless, Lulú's graciousness and candor disarmed him. Only for a moment, however. He, who had begun by sweeping offices and had risen step by step until he was manager of the great mercantile business, had acquired more understanding than a whole library would provide. Conscious then of the importance of his position, he replied rudely,

"Haven't you read the placards?"

"Yes, in very large type they say that there are no vacancies, but obtaining a position is a matter of great urgency to me."

Below his rough, gray mustache a slight smile hovered. He looked at her penetratingly from his small eyes.

"Give me your name, young lady. I will keep it in mind for the first opportunity."

"Do you think my mother will let me come every day just to find out whether there's a position open?"

"Then?"

"It's very simple! First I get a job, then, whether she likes it or not, it's all settled."

The manager, his interest aroused, said,

"Well, what can you do? In what businesses have you worked? What recommendations have you brought or at least what references can you give me?"

"God help me, sir, what recommendations do you want me to give you if not just the fact that on account of the revolution we lost all our fortune, and now, just to keep the family going, my father works like a Negro."

The manager observed that certain gestures and the timbre of Lulú's voice reminded him of one of his employees, but without his being able to recall which one. Suddenly it came to his mind and he understood everything.

"The proper thing, miss, would be for your father to come and solicit the employment."

"You don't know my father. If I don't take him by storm, already committed before everyone, surely he would never permit me to enter the business. But doesn't it seem to you, in a house of a poor person one who does not work is stealing from his own family?"

"Do you know how to take shorthand?"

"No, sir, but I will learn."

"Do you know how to type?"

"Four years ago I helped my father with his correspondence."

The manager scratched his ear, smiled slyly; then taking up the telephone, he spoke with the cashier's department.

"Go up to the third floor."

Crazy with joy, Lulú grasped the sinewy hands of the manager. She left and in three jumps stood before the grill of the cashier's office.

"What do you want, miss?"

"The manager sent me here."

"Oh yes. Come in and wait, please."

Standing for an interminable half hour, Lulú kept waiting until the head cashier felt like raising his eyes from the papers on his desk.

"What, Lulú! You here! What does this mean?"

"I am your secretary, dear Papa."

"But—"

Lulú drew near to him and in a low voice explained the situation. Hiding their interest, the personnel of the office waited to see what would happen.

"Mama sent me to spy on you and to find out where you kept yourself. Being here the notion occurred to me that—and here I am."

"What a harebrained girl! How did you do it?"

"It's very simple. I spoke to the manager and succeeded in obtaining a position just as you did, who knows how long ago."

When Lulú returned at midday, she called out merrily,

"Good news, congratulations, we are working at *La Gran Ciudad de Hamburgo*! Papa is cashier and I am his secretary."

"What did you say?"

Agustinita and Francisco José looked at each other dumfounded.

"I said," answered Lulú as she took off her hat and arranged her hair, looking in her little hand mirror, "that anyone in the house of a poor man who does not work is stealing from his own family."

"Liar!" exclaimed Francisco José, enraged.

"Francisco José is writing a book," responded Agustinita with an angry gesture.

"I didn't mean to offend anyone."

There was not time to prolong the dispute because Procopio who had stopped by the corner grocery store to buy ham, eggs, cheese, and beer, appeared in the doorway.

XIX

Truth fleshless and in the full sun is neither truth nor anything for those who can see only at night. Consequently Agustinita and Francisco José, far from having their hopes and illusions broken by the sudden revelation of Procopio's mystery, became imbued with new encouragement, with growing vigor which soon produced action. Things might have taken their ordained and definitive course if the occurrences of the following day had not taken such a violent and unexpected turn. That morning one of the porters of *La Gran Ciudad de Hamburgo* dashed precipitately out of the cashier's office, distracted and pale. He said that the cashier was stretched out there on the second floor, lying in a pool of blood.

"Papa? Is he injured?"

"I'm afraid he is dead."

Lulú fainted. A doctor arrived and reported the matter to the police. While some of the people were lifting Procopio off the floor, others were caring for Lulú. When, after several deep sobs, she came to her senses, she found herself on a couch with the manager personally lavishing attention upon her.

"Do you feel better? Calm yourself! That stupid Zacharías! I have thrown him right out on his ear."

"My father, where is he?"

"It wasn't anything but a slight wound on the head."

"I want to see him."

It was useless to try to stop her. She got to her feet and did not stop until she found Procopio whom the doctor had just finished bandaging. It was an insignificant wound which would heal in a couple of weeks. Although Procopio was extremely pale and a shadow made his dark eyes appear sunken, his smile restored the habitual expression to his face.

"I'm quite all right," he said in a very weak voice, "I'll go now to the office. Wait there for me calmly, Lulú."

She did not, however, wish to leave him alone for a moment. They went up together. When they had once more settled down to their tasks, Lulú asked him how he had happened to fall. He could not explain it, because he was not sure whether he had stumbled or not.

Lulú remained disturbed and preoccupied, said to him as they left, "Let's have a doctor examine you."

"What for? Didn't the one who came say that it was a matter of no importance?"

"He didn't even examine you."

"What do you want me to tell him if I feel no pain; if I'm as well and sound as you?"

"You must say just the opposite—that you are ill, although you don't have any pain and don't know what's the matter."

Procopio burst out laughing; but Lulú insisted to such a degree, that he followed her into one of the most famous clinics.

"He is a good doctor, one of the best in Mexico according to what I have heard," whispered Lulú as they ascended the stairs.

"Then if he is a famous doctor he won't pay any attention to me as soon as he makes the diagnosis that my poor monthly salary under no pretext will pass whole from my pockets to his."

Procopio's light tone did not succeed in smoothing out Lulú's forehead nor deter her from her intention. She stayed right by his side until she saw him disappear into one of the examination rooms.

The examination was irritatingly thorough. Like all persons who have enjoyed good health, Procopio professed a profound disdain for doctors and their medicines. He found all their practices and diagnoses superfluous, stupid, and ridiculous. But his habitual civility made him submit to them without protesting. When he thought he was free of the intrusion in the course of which the physician had inquired, with what seemed to him effrontery, about his most intimate customs such as the most insignificant minutiae of his organic life, he found that he still had to undergo laboratory tests and then go into the X-ray room. His head was spinning and his stomach felt empty. He had to go into still another room. He attempted to distract his bad humor by reading the captions at the bottom of the large, anatomical engravings hanging on the walls; but those large, dark-purple blotches, those tangled skeins of white threads, those skeletons which grinned in macabre fashion soon bored him too. When he turned his eyes to the other side of the room, they encountered the sight of large narrow-mouthed jars containing human viscera, blackened and shriveled, floating in acid. "These pickled members," he thought, "at least take away my appetite."

Finally he entered again the eminent doctor's office. The latter handed him a paper and said to him disagreeably, "Absolute rest. Only water for twenty-four hours; water and milk for as many more. Then call me to come to your home. Here is a prescription for medicine to take every four hours."

Procopio took the prescription with obvious indifference.

"Is it, then, something serious?"

"It will be if you're not careful."

At the door of the clinic, Procopio paused in meditation. In his right hand the prescription fluttered as of its own accord; he twisted it into a little roll, then converted it into a ball; he kept on compressing it with his fingers until it almost disappeared. Suddenly he straightened up his shoulders and a smile appeared on his lips. He continued ahead and the little paper ball leaped out to disappear in the middle of the street, without force, without particular effort, simply by the automatic contraction of his hand.

As though awaking from a dream, he suddenly drew out his watch and, on noticing how late it was, he turned back and entered the first restaurant he came to. "Oyster soup is very nourishing, ragoût of beef is my favorite dish, also a fillet of red snapper and half a bottle of Chambertin," he thought as he looked over the menu. "For a weak man who has lost blood surely this is better than resorting to water, bed, and doctor."

Smiling in his most pleasant manner, he indicated to the waiter the food he had selected from the menu. He came out of the restaurant, signaling for a taxi. He arrived at home stiff as steel, unable to get his breath.

XX

Francisco José was a serious poet; consequently the parasitic spirit had settled down in his brain. When Lulú uttered those fatal words: "Papa and I are working," he was seized with consternation. When he discovered that all the magic of his current well-being was encompassed in the term "work," he was full of anger and indignation as Agustinita was: a spiritual tempest hurled him from his marble tower through the windows of life. It was an inner, healthful jolt, because life, viewed straight in the face, revealed to him what it had never made apparent before: his great practical abilities.

"Mama, dear," he cried out after many hours of concentration, "I have solved our problem. They have found their word of salvation: 'work.' I have found ours, 'Pascual.' We must go at once to look for Pascual."

"I had to take an oath that if we did, we should never again be able to set foot in your father's house," exclaimed Agustinita in a solemn and hoarse voice.

"Your complaints are just and your indignation righteous, Mother!"

"Who can still doubt that what Procopio has proposed is to the dishonor of our ancestors? The pure name of our house dragged into the mud!"

"He has descended to the level of a common laborer."

"He insists that his family follow him in his ignominious descent. I cannot, I cannot. Death before that! I hear the voices of the Generals Prado protesting from their cold tombs."

Sobs rose in Agustinita's robust chest and tears trickled down her cheeks like a shower on the skin of a bitter orange.

"Come on, Francisco José, let's go. Your advice is wise and good. I think Pascual knows who is the real and only culpable one among us, and that we, martyrs to duty, have only retreated before the ignominy of—before the impossible!"

"Although Pascual was born in humble circumstances, his heart is noble, and he will understand us."

"He will open his arms to you like a son, Mother."

"And will listen to our pleas."

"Not so much pleas—we ask only an act of strict justice."

"A decent shelter in his house—that is all."

"The shelter which a respectable family has a right to."

Francisco José went to change his clothes and became absorbed in profound meditation. Without grave offense to beautiful style or esthetics, he could well ask himself now that he had come out of his marble tower, "Dear God, you who never forsake the vilest worm, who have always provided an abundant head of hair for the lowly louse, skirts with long plaits for the restless flea, a warm mattress for the blood-sucking bedbug, and even sticky ears for each tick, why have you failed to provide a decent and decorous shelter for the Vásquez Prados from Zacatecas?"

Prey of cruel remorse for not having put his wonderful practical ability at the service of his family before now, he let go of his mother's arm. Wordless, they proceeded along Chapultepec Avenue.

Two hours of distressing and fatiguing walking. Overcome, they stopped at the foot of the statue of Cuauhtémoc to catch their breath. The afternoon was cloudy, threatening rain; the warm, fragrant air swirled in great puffs.

With gold and silver money in circulation, Mexico City had become galvanized. No longer were those eternal stupid fools with horror-producing faces and the corpulence of bandits in ambush the only ones who rode in automobiles. Sirens sounded in every direction. Fast, quiet automobiles flashed by with jet-black reflections. Sensual, elegant ladies, stretched out voluptuously in them, displayed clothes of the latest styles and fabrics (high-top American shoes and sleek, silk stockings more transparent than a spider's web).

"It's going to rain, Mother."

Francisco José pointed out a swelling black cloud which billowed up over a grove of trees.

"Yes, let's go, we have rested long enough."

Step by step they followed their route along the Paseo de la Reforma. The cloud dissipated and the sun shone brilliantly again, bathing the trees with its rays and accenting the outline of the elegant residences. Within the verdure of a grove of trees and in the midst of the most elegant chalets, the marquee of Pascual's ostentatious house appeared prominently like the silvery, scaly stomach of an enormous fish. Agustinita and Francisco José felt in their hearts, dried and embittered because of so many days of frustrated illusions and disenchantments, a new hope fluttering. With profound joy they drew near the white façade; their eyes delighted in the sight of the marble front steps, columns and balustrades; the dull luster of the window gratings; and the flash of the sun as it inflamed the leaded windows. Again mute, beside themselves, they drew near, hardly breathing. When Agustinita pressed the electric bell on the gate with her feverish hand, she felt as though her heart would bound out of her body.

A servant in a brand new black suit and very white vest inquired in a supercilious manner what they wanted.

"We are looking for the lady of the house," responded Agustinita in a hushed tremulous voice.

The lackey looked them over insolently from head to foot and inquired whom he might announce.

"The lady's brother and mother," Francisco José replied in an Olympian manner.

The servant then lowered his head humbly and condescended to come down and unfasten the gate. He bowed slightly and allowed them to come in.

"Please be so good as to wait here a moment. I will announce your arrival."

Such a change of attitude made Agustinita and Francisco José conclude that they could dispense with the usual formalities. They seated themselves in the large, silent, half-lit hallway. Their gaze wandered over the moldings, decorations and bas-reliefs, which adorned the walls and arches. At one side of the other end of the hall exotic plants in large pottery urns were placed, bringing to Agustinita memories of her house in Zacatecas.

"Fortunately we are going to get out of this horrible nightmare, once and for all."

"Out of a nightmare that we thought would never end."

"Free at last."

Francisco José stood up and walked nervously up and down the room.

"Berta has become very careless, Mother. Look how that porcelain vase that has a magnificent Rembrandt painted on it is turned toward the wall. It's hard to understand."

Agustinita got up, put the piece in its correct position and observed,

"Good Lord, they never sweep here. There are spider webs everywhere."

"Berta's servants are playing off on her."

On making a careful inspection, Agustinita remarked, "Undoubtedly, here, the servants do as they please. But I will know how to set things to rights."

"May I call to your attention a certain insolent servant who does not know how to distinguish one person from another."

"Don't trouble yourself; he will be the first to go to learn his trade in the street."

Agustinita returned to her chair. She was restless. She was unable to find an explanation for Berta's behavior. It was very bad manners to make her mother wait, because Agustinita was in her own home, inasmuch as it belong to Berta.

In spite of such sensible reflections, when Berta did not appear, in order to further the illusion that it was actually her home, Agustinita remarked in a loud voice,

"Good Lord, this beautiful palace is submerged in solitude and silence. Even the sounds of the street are muffled here. This is very sad. Berta has no children, the joy of a home, but she ought to have many birds. I will have brought from Zacatecas some song birds which can be easily trained. I will fill this place with canaries, clarines, and larks—with sounds and gaiety."

"I will suggest that Pascual get Berta an Angora cat and a fox-terrier. That is so chic; gives a place character."

Suddenly, in the glass partition at the end of the room, back of the glass screen made opaque with arabesques and etched designs, a silhouette faded away and a shadow passed by.

"Did I see something or did I imagine it? What could it have been? Francisco, a cold draught passed by my shoulder. Death seemed to brush by."

The door opened and Berta appeared, pale, emaciated, with a disturbed manner.

"Berta!"

They embraced each other tightly.

"Dear Lord, you're just a shadow of yourself, daughter of my soul."

Her full, floating dressing gown of green silk with large, gold-colored flowers accentuated the funereal tints in her sallow face. Her dry skin looked like the miserable tatters of the wings of a magnificent irridescent gold butterfly.

They were scarcely able to make out what she muttered in tones half-choked with tears and moans: "I am a most unfortunate person."

Francisco José frowned. Had Berta lost her mind? How could a young wife who walked on rich carpets, lived in the sacred atmosphere of old masters and of modern art, breathed exquisite perfumes, and moved in the illumination of clusters of lights call herself unfortunate?

"Speak up, daughter, tell me all about it. I am here to defend you against anyone who dares to hurt you! Who is to blame for your troubles?"

Berta restrained her distress in order to speak.

"When we were living modestly in Zacatecas with only the monthly allowance from Papa, I was happy, very happy. I had everything I wanted—I had him. Now we are millionaires and now I am nothing, I am nobody; he doesn't belong to me."

She continued talking, but no matter how many times she repeated or changed the words, it was the same old story, the same refrain, the same lament, one which charmed, captivated, disturbed, and attracted the attention of its listeners.

Francisco José, emotional to the point of tears, asked,

"Aren't you satisfied, sister, to be surrounded by so many comforts and so much luxury?"

"What nonsense! Comforts! Luxury! If only I were poor! Work would be my consolation; in work I would find alleviation for my pain; work would drain my scanty strength, and overcome with fatigue I could sleep long hours, interminable hours. What a joy! In work I could surely find the resignation which today no one, no one, is able to give me."

XXI

Work! Work! Work!

The word sounded like blows of a hammer, the lashes of a whip inflicted full in the face.

Agustinita's mind began to connive. Berta could speak of nothing but her inconsolable grief. And as though she had discovered something, she seemed fascinated with the idea of work, because in work she saw something which could fill up, in part at least, the emptiness of her life. Work would be a loyal companion, capable at least of making her forget for a few moments the uselessness and absurdity of her life. In her hellish idleness the hours passed like centuries. If she were working, they would go by like seconds. What happiness for one who has no more purpose in life than for her body to pass into the cold enclosure of a premature grave, to see time rush by headlong!

"If I did not believe in God, I would leave Pascual and in work I would surely find my salvation. Happy are those who work so that they can forget the pain of living."

Listening to that interminable lament, Agustinita saw clearly that she who had come seeking consolation and tranquillity was now the one who must provide them.

Berta continued talking until she was drained of energy, like a feverish person when the fever breaks and no longer sustains the nerves with heat and energy. Her face became the color of a candle; her feeble limbs, so splendidly covered with the green and gold silk dressing gown, could not hold her up. Convulsed, she fell unconscious on the carpet like a bird fatally wounded.

Agustinita went to her aid; she knelt on the carpet and put her smooth, muscular arm under Berta's head which fell back lifelessly.

"Berta!"

A torrent of kisses and tears fell on the pale, thin face of her daughter.

Francisco José called out, imploring help.

A flurry of excitement. Bells sounded, hinges squeaked, doors banged deafeningly, and the servants clustered about. Even the cook's large carving knife flashed as first one side and the other of his snowy white apron licked against it.

"Cologne for my daughter!"

They realized what had happened. Responding immediately, a maid produced a flask of eau de cologne. With sympathetic expressions on their faces the servants silently encircled her. As Agustinita massaged Berta's flaccid limbs she murmured,

"She is a skeleton!"

Suddenly, like a group of mannikins operated by a hidden spring, the servants were obsequiously arranged in a straight line, stiff and erect. In a half-opened door Pascual appeared in a thick bathrobe, water still trickling from his bare head. His flabby hands worried with the cord about his waist from which hung two tassels like balls of gold.

Forgetting his mother and sister, Francisco José, his arms wide open, jumped over them to run towards Pascual.

"Brother!"

Pascual, his hawk-like eyes fixed on the chattering group on the carpet, said in a clear, serene voice,

"She is neurotic. The doctor wants these scenes avoided. It would be preferable, then, that we continue as in the past. Consequently, no visiting."

Agustinita raised her rigid face. Her eyes dilated; the hardened arteries in her temples wriggled like snakes; her disarranged gray hair emphasized the wildness of her appearance.

"Brother!" implored Francisco José, insensitive to the situation, moving toward Pascual to embrace him.

Pascual turned on his heels and as he went out, closed the door with a bang.

Francisco José bent his head, frowning in concentration. Quickly he straightened up, his forehead smooth and untroubled, and pronounced seriously in a low voice,

"Everything is all right. I've been hasty and incorrect."

Agustinita, whose mind had undergone a sudden transformation, afflicted by the catastrophe, remained on the floor with Berta's head in her arms, staring idiotically into space.

Berta muttered some unintelligible sounds, some inarticulate words. Half-opening her eyes and letting a sigh escape, she said,

"Ah—my mother—my brother also! Where am I?"

"Do you feel better, daughter?"

When Berta had come to herself, Agustinita said to her,

"When you want to see us, you know you are welcome to come to our home. It is a modest house, a house that poor people live in, a house of people who earn their living with their own hands; but it is your father, mother, and brother's house. Your true home. There you will feel the warmth of home."

"The warmth of a home!" responded Berta like a far-off echo, choked up again with tears.

"Francisco José, let's go."

"Are we going? But the most important matter still remains, Mother. Don't get upset."

"Here is your hat."

"But, Mother!"

"Yes, Francisco José, it's best that we go. Pascual may come back and—it's better that he doesn't find us here. God gave me this cross; it is my cross only. I must discharge my duty."

The wind started to rise; thunder rumbled.

"I don't understand you, Mama dear. This is absurd!"

"Isn't it true that you have never understood us, Francisco José?"

"Unquestionably I was at fault. It was not the opportune moment to embrace him. He had a perfect right to act as he did. An explanation on my part would have set everything right. There is still time, Mother. I tell you we ought to go back. Besides, look how it has already started to rain."

For the first time Agustinita was in doubt about the lofty intellectual and moral endowments of the poet of their home.

"Good Lord, Mama, this is a real downpour! See how dark it is getting; it's impossible to distinguish anything in the distance. Moreover, my legs feel as though they would break."

"I feel as though my soul had broken irretrievably. What an injustice!"

"You're raving, Mama dear. What's the matter with you? Tell me, does your head hurt? Come, follow me, let's take refuge near the walls of that house. Now the rain is pouring off my hat."

"Is it possible, Francisco José, that the horrible truth is not apparent to you?"

"The only truth I know now is that I am sopping wet."

"What a horrible injustice! God punishes us for our sins!"

Struggling with her inner torment, Agustinita was oblivious to the outer storm. Francisco José kept tugging on her; breathless, they moved up close to the walls of a luxurious residence.

The shadowy mass fused together. The broad, straight avenue, a shiny sheet of steel, stretched out like a silver snake.

In the distance the massive, heavy Peace column jutted up into the sky so that the golden Lucifer thrust itself into a crevice in the rolling clouds which rested on its crown.

After half an hour the rain began to let up. In anguished silence, huddled together, protected by a honeysuckle which was now dripping mud, withered leaves, and flowerettes stiff from cold, they watched it grow dark. Vehicles rambled about like will-o'-the-wisps; the trolleys traced an intermittent line of red fire.

"Let's go," Agustinita said suddenly—as though she were coming out of a dream.

Francisco José, foolishly, was gazing at a house with silvery eaves from which cascades of light were pouring through its narrow, Gothic windows and its great central glass door like a mass of flowers; at the polished green marble stairs and the flowery garden; at the honeysuckle that climbed up to the silent, peaceful balcony.

"Let's go now," Agustinita repeated, shaking him by the shoulders.

When they came to the Ángeles Gardens, they could hear the bugles in the barracks near Santiago Tlaltelolco. Streaks of light which spilled out at intervals over the stone pavement guided them through the gloom.

A sigh as vast as the night.

Before stepping through the little doorway of their house, Agustinita stopped, took her son by the arm and said,

"We have to throw ourselves at his feet and ask his pardon."

"Of whom, Mother? You are still raving!"

"Lulú is the only one who has understood him."

"I don't understand anybody, and now, not even you."

Transformed, Agustinita held herself erect, seized Francisco José's hand. Her fingers contracted so tightly that her nails sank in his flesh causing him to cry out in pain. Then in a voice as sharp and penetrating as a fine steel blade, she practically stunned him. "Imbecile! Pascual has robbed us."

XXII

As soon as they entered Procopio's room, aghast, they cried out.

"It was dreadful," explained Lulú coming over to meet them. "An attack; when he arrived in a car he was scarcely breathing; I ran for a doctor."

"And?"

"How do I know! Maybe it's his heart; maybe his kidneys."

Their voices were hushed. Procopio did not awaken. His face was lost in the whiteness of the pillows and sheets.

Two days of mortal anguish passed; on the third day he began to show improvement. The doctor, however, interjected a sad note in the general rejoicing. "It is not necessary for the attack to be repeated for his illness to have an unfortunate outcome."

When Agustinita brought in his first nourishment of the day, Procopio, smiling like a child eager for a sweet, grasped the cup of milk in his hands and could not hold back a sigh of satisfaction. He felt the joys of the convalescent: a napkin spread over his knees, a band of sunlight falling through the door, the portion of sky appearing through the window, the warbling of the birds in the garden, all of that which in the daily routine is so trivial it passes unnoticed was for him reason for lively happiness.

As soon as he had finished his breakfast, he took hold of Agustinita's hand.

"I am glad that finally you have opened your eyes. Look, this is true happiness, the happiness of trivial daily joys, because the other, the Happiness which is written with a capital does not exist; it is a mirage, a mournful lie. We all have the same chance to achieve happiness. All depends on putting the inner and outer worlds in harmony."

He spoke eloquently, his eyes glowed brilliantly, and color rose into his cheeks.

"Don't talk, you will tire yourself," observed Agustinita.

A cold sweat dampened Procopio's forehead.

Surprised at the lucidity with which he now perceived ideas

formerly confused or subconscious, seized by a strange fire he continued,

"One who has grasped the meaning of life will understand me. You, Lulú, you understand. I know it only too well. Those who look for happiness outside themselves will be miserable failures. There is only one road that leads to the meaning of life—that is the one of pain. Suffering reveals to us the reality of our inmost personalities. Along with that revelation comes the supreme revelation—the meaning of life. The higher we ascend the scale of suffering the greater will be the number of our small joys."

"You are tiring yourself, Procopio," insisted Agustinita, almost importunate.

All saw something strange in him and they listened deeply concerned. His voice was eager and his cheeks shone with the brilliance of twilight.

But also something very solemn must have imbued his spirit so that he paid no attention to his physical state.

Francisco José came in to say that Archibaldo wanted to see him.

"Yes, let him come in. Now is the time I wish to see all my favorites."

A clasp of hands; a cordial smile. Just as always.

"We owe the fact that we did not go without funds for more than a year to the periodic remittances Archibaldo sent us during the time he was with the *zapatistas*."

Admiring eyes turned on Archibaldo. Usually talkative, he now stood silent. Who could tell what it was he had on his mind or what he had seen that caused him now to restrain himself with his lips closed tightly and his manner distraught?

"Lulú says, Archibaldo, that you and I are alike as two drops of water. And it is true, because you have always understood me, only you."

He smiled sweetly although his words implied a reproach.

"I, worn out, helpless, overwhelmed by this unfortunate, sudden occurrence that has overtaken me, in spite of everything, am happier than all of you. I feel joy for the whiteness of my sheets, for the softness of my bed, for the pillows that support me and even for those dull window panes that tone down the sunlight."

He was silent for a brief moment as he suppressed an expression of pain. Then he said,

"I can scarcely believe that this illness has caused me to be in this condition. It seems as though I have run many leagues without any food. Lulú, I want to lie down. Please cover my legs. I have hardly any feeling in them. Now go out and let me rest awhile."

They all obeyed.

"Don't you think it would be proper to call a priest?" asked the frightened Agustinita.

No one ventured to answer her.

Lulú, who could not stay still a minute, went back into the bedroom.

"Do you know what happened last night in the Chapultepec Restaurant?" inquired Archibaldo with manifest perturbation.

"In God's name, who wants to be bothered about such matters now," protested Agustinita.

"It is rather a serious matter and directly concerns the family."

"Us?"

"In a scuffle among some drunken *carrancistas* Pascual was seriously hurt."

"Pascual?"

"Mortal blow? Mama dear!"

"Archibaldo, tell us the truth! Is Pascual dead?"

"Yes," he answered dryly to the clashing and tragic exclamations of Agustinita and Francisco José.

"He is dead, Mother!"

"He is dead, Francisco José!"

They looked at each other with deep emotion.

"Let us go at once, Mother."

A heart-breaking cry made them dash toward the bedroom.

That ascetic face, thin and yellow, those eyes where an intense spiritual flame no longer burned, that head with a halo of gray sank down softly into the white, smooth pillow.

Archibaldo came close, reverently kissed Procopio's forehead, then raised his fallen jaw, and bound a handkerchief about his face to keep his mouth closed.

Then he observed, outlined on the lips of the deceased, that expression that had been habitual, and there shone for one instant more his kind and gently ironic smile.

When Archibaldo looked around, only Lulú was there. On her knees at the foot of the bed, she raised her eyes wide open toward the heavens: large eyes, very large, like the universe.

THE UNDERDOGS

"I tell you, that's no animal. Listen how Palomo's barking! Must be somebody."

The woman stared into the shadow cast by the mountain.

"What if they're Federals?" asked the man who was squatting down in a corner eating, a clay bowl of food in his right hand and a *taco* of three rolled tortillas in the other.

The woman did not answer him; her thoughts were far away from the hut.

The sounds of the horses hooves could be heard in the nearby rocky region. Palomo's barking became frenzied.

"Anyhow, it would be a good idea for you to hide, Demetrio."

Impassively, the man finished eating. Reaching over for the water jar, he raised it with both hands and drank in big gulps. Then he stood up.

"Your rifle's under that straw mat," she said in an undertone.

A burning wick floating in oil lighted the room. In one corner a yoke, a plow, a bamboo pole, and other farm tools were piled up. An old adobe mould, suspended from the roof by leather strips, served as a bed in which a little boy lay sleeping on ragged, discolored, rough cotton sheets.

Demetrio, fastening the cartridge belt around his waist, picked up the rifle. The tall, robust man with a ruddy, beardless face wore shirt and pants of rough white cloth, a wide straw hat, and *huaraches*. He left slowly, disappearing in the impenetrable darkness of the night.

Palomo, enraged, had jumped over the corral fence. Suddenly a shot rang out. The dog uttered a dull moan and barked no more.

Some men on horseback rode up shouting and swearing. Two of them dismounted while one stayed with the horses.

"Hey, you, woman—something to eat! Eggs, milk, frijoles, whatever you got. We're dying of hunger."

"Damn the mountains! Only the Devil could find his way there."

"Even he would lose his way, sergeant, if he was as drunk as you."

He had chevrons on his shoulders while the other had red stripes on his sleeves.

"Where are we, woman? What the hell! Is this the only house around here?"

"Well, then, that light? What about that little boy? Woman, we want something for supper and we want it in a hurry! Are you coming out or have we got to make you?"

"Cruel men, you've killed my dog. What harm did he ever do to you? My poor little Palomo!"

The woman came in dragging a fat, white dog, his blank eyes open, his body limp.

"Look at those beautiful cheeks, sergeant! Now, my dear, don't get mad. I swear, I'll make your house a dovecote. But for God's sake—" Then he started to sing:

> Don't look at me haughtily;
> Don't get mad at me;
> Look at me lovingly,
> Light of my eyes.

His whiskey-roughened voice faded out.

"Lady, what d'you call this little place?" asked the sergeant.

"Limón," the woman answered curtly, putting more wood on the fire and blowing on the coals.

"Limón! You don't say! The region of the famous Demetrio Macías! Hear that, lieutenant? We're in Limón."

"What, Limón? S'all right with me. Bah! If I got to go to hell, there's no better time than now, particularly since I have such a good mount! Look at my dark beauty's lovely cheeks! They are like ripe apples ready for one to bite into!"

"You're bound to know that bandit, lady. I was with him in Escobedo Penitentiary."

"Sergeant, bring me a bottle of tequila; I have decided to pass the night in the charming company of this little brunette. The colonel? Why say anything about him to me at this time? May he go to ——! And if he gets mad, I don't care. Bah! Get along, sergeant, tell the corporal to unsaddle the horses and throw out some feed to them. I'm going to stay here. Listen, honey, let my sergeant fry the eggs and heat the *gordas*, you come over here to me. Look here, this wallet full of bills is just for you. It's yours. I want you to have it. I come here a little drunk and that's why I'm sort of hoarse. I left half my palate in Guadalajara and spit out the other half along the way! And what does it matter? This is yours. Sergeant, my bottle, my bottle of tequila. Honey, you are too far away; come over here and have a drink. Why not? You're afraid of

your—er—your husband—or whatever he is? Well, if he's hiding
out in some hole, tell him to come out. As for me! Hell, I don't
let rats bother me."

A white form suddenly filled the dark opening of the door.

"Demetrio Macías," exclaimed the frightened sergeant, shrinking
back a couple of steps.

The lieutenant, struck dumb, got up, frozen and motionless as a
statue.

"Kill them," croaked the woman.

"Ah, excuse me, friend—I didn't know—but I respect truly brave
men."

Demetrio stood there looking at them. An insolent and disdainful smile creased his face.

"I not only respect them; I like them as well. Here is my hand
in friendship. That's all right, Demetrio Macías, if you don't want
to— It's because you don't really know me; it is because you see
me at this humiliating, damned job. What else can I do? I'm poor
and got a big family to look after! Sergeant, let's go. I sure respect
the home of a brave man, of an honest-to-goodness brave man."

When they had left, the woman tightly embraced Demetrio.

"Holy Virgin of Jalpa! What a scare! I was sure they'd shoot
you!"

"Go, quick, to my father's house," said Demetrio.

She wanted to stay with him, she begged, she cried; but he, gently
pushing her away, replied somberly,

"Something tells me the whole bunch will come here."

"Why didn't you kill them?"

"Their hour's not struck yet!"

They went out together, she with the child in her arms. At the
door they separated, going in opposite directions.

The moon cast shadows on the mountain. From each crag and at
each bush, Demetrio kept looking back at the drooping figure of the
sad woman carrying the child in her arms. When, after many hours
of climbing, he looked back into the depths of the canyon, he saw
giant flames leaping up near the river. His house was burning!

II

Everything was still shrouded in shadows when Demetrio Macías
started down into the ravine. His path was a narrow ledge along

a steep grade between giant rocks veined with deep, eroded cracks and a giant, sheer cliff which looked as though it had been cut with one clean stroke.

As he descended with speed and agility, he was thinking,

"It's dead sure that when the Federals find our trail, they'll track us down like dogs. It's lucky they don't know the paths, the ways in and out of here. They could find them only if someone from Moyahua came along as a guide, for the people of Limón, Santa Rosa, and other places in the sierra are loyal and would never betray us. There's a *cacique* in Moyahua who's been chasing me through the hills who sure'd like to see me hanging from a telegraph pole with my swollen tongue sticking out of my mouth."

By the time the early morning mist had cleared he was at the bottom of the canyon. He threw himself down among the rocks and went to sleep. The river flowed gently, singing in its diminutive cascades; little birds chirped, hidden in the pitahayos; and the monotonous tones of the locusts filled the solitude of the mountain with mystery.

Demetrio awakened with a start, waded the river, and climbed the slope on the opposite side of the canyon. Like an ant he crawled over the ledges, his hands clinging to rocks and roots, his bare feet gripping the pebbles of the path.

By the time he had reached the summit the sun was turning the upland into a lake of gold. Toward the gorge there were enormous slabs of rocks, bristling prominences like enormous African skulls, pitahayos like gnarled fingers of a giant, and trees bent toward the depth of the abyss. Among the arid rocks and dry branches, the fresh San Juan roses bloomed like white offerings to the heavens which had begun to unravel threads of gold from rock to rock.

Demetrio paused at the summit. With his right hand he reached for the horn which hung down his back, raised it to his thick lips and, inflating his cheeks, blew it three times. From the distant crest across the canyon three whistles answered the signal.

In the distance out of a cone-shaped shock of cane and rotten straw, came one after the other a number of men with chests and legs bare, dark and burnished like old bronze. They rushed to meet Demetrio.

"They burned my house!" he responded to their inquiring glances.

There were imprecations, threats, oaths. Demetrio let them vent their feelings, then he drew a bottle out of his shirt and took a drink.

After wiping the mouth of the bottle with the back of his hand he passed it to the man next to him. One round of the bottle from mouth to mouth emptied it. The men smacked their lips.

"God willing," said Demetrio, "tomorrow or this very night we'll come face to face with Federals again. What do you say, boys, are we going to let them find out about these trails?"

The half-naked men leaped in the air, yelling shrilly in joy. Their insults, curses, and threats increased in volume and violence.

"We don't know how many of them there may be," observed Demetrio, watching them closely.

"Julián Medina, in Hostotipaquillo, with a half dozen *pelados* with knives sharpened on a *metate*, faced up to all the policemen and Federals of the town, and finished them off. What did Medina's men have that we don't?" asked the one with a very black, bushy beard and eyebrows, and a soft, gentle appearance; a massive, robust man.

"I'm the one who can tell them," he added. "I swear that my name's not Anastasio Montañés if tomorrow I'm not owner of a Mauser, cartridge belt, pants, and shoes. Sure! Look, Cordoniz, you don't believe me? I carry half a dozen lead pellets in my body. You can ask my *compadre* Demetrio if I don't. But those bullets scare me as much as little lumps of caramel. Now don't you believe me?"

"Hurray for Anastasio Montañés!" cried Manteca.

"No," replied Anastasio, "hurray for Demetrio Macías, who is our chief, and glory to God in Heaven and to Holy Mary."

"Hurray for Demetrio Macías!" they all cried.

They built a fire of dry grass and wood and stretched strips of fresh meat over the coals. They squatted down around the flames, sniffing hungrily the odor of the meat as it twisted and sizzled over the red-hot coals. The golden hide of a steer lay in a heap near them on the blood-soaked earth. Strips of fresh beef drying in the sun and air dangled from a cord stretched between two huisache trees.

"Well," said Demetrio, "except for my thirty-thirty, we've got only twenty weapons. If they're only a few, we'll give it to them until not a one's left; if they're a whole lot, we'll at least give them a good scare."

He untied a sash about his waist and loosening a knot, offered to his companions what he had carried in it.

"Salt!" they exclaimed with delight, each one taking a few grains with his finger tips.

They ate ravenously. When they had satisfied their appetites, they fell to the ground with bellies to the sun and sang monotonous, sad songs, letting out strident *ranchero* shouts after each stanza.

III

The twenty followers of Demetrio Macías slept in the brush of the sierra until awakened by a signal from a cow-horn which Pancracio had sounded from the top of a rocky mountain cliff.

"This is it, boys, get set!" said Anastasio Montañés, examining the springs of his rifle.

An hour passed without a sound other than the song of the locusts in the bushes and the croak of the frogs in the mudholes. When the rays of the moon faded away in the pale, rosy band of dawn, the silhouette of the first of the soldiers was discernible on the edge of the highest trail. Behind him others, then ten, then a hundred; then suddenly all were lost in the darkness. As the sun began to shine brightly it revealed the precipice covered with people: diminutive men on miniature horses.

"Look how pretty they are," exclaimed Pancracio. "Let's go, boys; come on, let's play with them!"

Those moving figurines which from time to time were lost in the thickets of chaparral would intermittently show up darkly against the ocher colored boulders. Demetrio's men could distinctly hear the voices of the officers and men. Demetrio gave a signal. Triggers and springs of the guns clicked.

"Now!" ordered a muffled voice.

Twenty-one men fired simultaneously and as many Federals fell from their horses. The rest, surprised, stopped motionless like bas-reliefs in the rock. A new fusillade and another twenty-one men bounded from rock to rock with their heads split open.

"Come out of there, bandits! Starved dogs!"

"Death to the sissy thieves!"

"Death to the rebels!"

The Federals shouted at their enemies who, hidden, quiet, and silent, were satisfied to keep on glorying in their fame as marksmen.

"Look, Pancracio," said Meco, whose eyes and teeth were the only white things about him, "this is for him coming back of that pitayo! Son of a ——! There! Right in the bean! Saw it, didn't you?

Now for the one coming on that roan! Down with you, *pelón*!"

"I'll give a bath to that one going now by the edge of the trail. If you don't fall into the river, unhappy *mocho*, you won't miss it far. How's that? See that?"

"Man, Anastasio, don't be mean! Lend me your rifle. Come on, just one shot!"

Manteca, Cordoniz, and the rest who had no weapons begged him as if for a precious gift to let them have at least one shot.

"If you're real men, then show yourselves!"

"Stick out your heads, you lousy cowards."

The cries from mountain peak to mountain peak were as clear as ones from a sidewalk out front. Cordoniz appeared suddenly, naked, contemptuously holding his pants toward the Federals in the gesture of a toreador. Then began a rain of shots on Demetrio's men.

"Ho! Ho! It's like a swarm of flies about my head," said Anastasio Montañés, already stretched out among the rocks and not daring even to raise his eyes.

"Cordoniz, son of a ———! Now, go where I told you!" roared Demetrio.

Crawling, they took new positions.

The Federals had begun shouting with triumph and had ceased fire when a new round of bullets confounded them.

"More men have come!" yelled the soldiers.

Seized by panic, many boldly turned their horses about, others abandoned their mounts and, taking to their feet, sought refuge among the rocks. It was necessary for the officers to fire over the fugitives to restore order.

"Get them down there—the ones down there!" exclaimed Demetrio, aiming his thirty-thirty at the crystal thread of the river.

A Federal fell into that very stream; and without fail, every time a shot rang out another fell. But only Demetrio was shooting toward the river; and for each one he killed ten or twenty untouched ascended the opposite slope.

"Get them down there—get them down there—" he continued shouting angrily.

The men lent their companions their guns. As they aimed at their targets, they exchanged bets.

"My leather belt if I don't put one in the head of that fellow on the black horse. Lend me your rifle, Meco."

"Twenty shots of the Mauser and half a length of sausage if you let me knock down that one on the dark colored mare. Good. Now! See how he jumped? Like a deer!"

"Don't run, *mochos!* Come, get acquainted with your old man Demetrio Macías."

They screamed insults. Pancracio shouted, sticking out his beardless face, expressionless as rock; Manteca yelled, contracting the cords of his neck, stretching the lines of his face with its grim, murderous eyes. Demetrio continued firing and warning the others of the grave danger, but they paid no attention to the despair in his voice until they felt the impact of the bullets on one flank.

"Now they singed me!" cried Demetrio, gritting his teeth. "Sons of ——!"

Then straightway he let himself slide into a deep ravine.

IV

Two were missing: Serapio, the candy-seller, and Antonio who played the cymbals in the Juchipila Band.

"Maybe they'll join us further on," said Demetrio.

They returned dispirited, only Anastasio Montañés retained the soft, sweet expression in his sleepy eyes and on his bearded face, and Pancracio kept the invariable repulsiveness of his hard, prognathous profile.

The Federals had retreated and Demetrio recovered all his horses hidden in the sierra.

Suddenly Cordoniz who was marching ahead cried out. He had just seen their lost companions hanging from the branches of a mesquite. There were Serapio and Antonio. As they recognized them Anastasio Montañés muttered a prayer, his teeth clenched.

"Our Father who is in Heaven—"

"Amen," murmured the rest with heads bent and hats against their breasts.

Hurriedly they took the northern route through Juchipila canyon, traveling without stopping to rest until very late in the night. Cordoniz did not leave Anastasio even for a second. He could not erase from his memory the silhouettes of the hanged men—necks limp, arms dangling, legs stiff—swaying gently in the wind.

The next day Demetrio complained about his wound. He could not mount his horse. It was necessary to carry him in an improvised stretcher of oak branches and bundles of brush.

"It keeps on bleeding a lot, Demetrio," said Anastasio Montañés. Tearing off a sleeve of his shirt, he tied it tightly around the muscle above the wound.

"Good," said Venancio, "that stops the blood and eases the pain."

Venancio was a barber. In his town he pulled teeth and applied caustics and leeches. He enjoyed a certain prestige because he had read *The Wandering Jew* and *The May Sun*.[1] Men called him "Doc;" and he, very proud of his learning, was a man of few words.

Four at a time, they took turns carrying the stretcher over the bare, rocky plateaus and steep hills. At midday when the chalky dust smothered and blurred the view, along with the incessant sound of the locusts could be heard the monotonous and rhythmical moaning of the wounded man. At each little hut hidden among the steep rocks, they stopped and rested.

"Thanks be to God! We never fail to find a kind soul and a *gorda* piled high with *chile* and frijoles!" said Anastasio, belching heartily.

The mountain dwellers, after extending their calloused hands in welcome, exclaimed,

"God bless you! God help you and lead you along the right way! Now you go; tomorrow we'll run ourselves, fleeing from the conscription, pursued by the damn government' officials who have declared war to the death on all poor people; who rob us of our pigs, our hens, and even what little corn we have to eat; who burn our houses and carry off our women; and who, finally, when they come on one of us, they kill him right there as they would a mad dog."

Late in the afternoon when the flames of the sunset tinted the sky in vivid colors, a few shacks in a clearing appeared in the dusk among the blue mountains. Demetrio had the men carry him there. Some poor, thatched huts were scattered along the bank of the river among small cultivated plots of corn and beans just coming up. They put the stretcher on the ground. Demetrio, in a weak voice, asked for a drink of water.

In the shadowy openings of the cabins were women in drab *chomites*, with bony chests and matted hair. Behind them were discernible the brilliant eyes and fresh cheeks of the young ones. A chubby youngster with dark, shiny skin drew near to look at the man on the stretcher. Then came an old woman and next all the rest circled about him. A kind young girl brought a jar of fresh water. Demetrio seized the little vessel with his trembling hands and drank avidly.

"Want some more?"

He raised his eyes. The girl had a very common appearance but an extraordinarily sweet, gentle voice.

With the back of his hand he wiped the beads of sweat from his forehead, and turning on one side, said wearily,

"May God reward you!"

He began to shiver so violently that he shook the leaves and the framework of the stretcher. The fever made him lethargic.

"Dew is falling and that's bad for the fever," said Remigia, an old barefooted woman wearing a *chomite* and over her chest a piece of cotton cloth for a blouse.

She invited them to put Demetrio in her hut. Pancracio, Anastasio Montañés, and Cordoniz lay down at the foot of the stretcher like faithful dogs waiting the will of the master. The rest scattered to look for food. Remigia offered what she had: *chile* and tortillas.

"Just think, I had eggs, hens, and even a goat and a kid, but those damned Federals cleaned me out."

Then she drew near Anastasio and holding her hand over her mouth, said confidentially,

"Just think, they even took the Nieves' little girl."

V

Cordoniz, startled, opened his eyes and raised up.

"Montañés, did you hear something? A shot! Montañés, wake up!"

He shook him until it was evident that he moved and had stopped snoring.

"What the _____ ! You're all stewed up again! I tell you the dead don't come back," muttered Anastasio half-awake.

"A shot, Montañés!"

"Go to sleep, Cordoniz, or I'll sock you."

"No, Anastasio, I tell you it's no nightmare. I'm not thinking about the ones they hung. I heard it plain enough to know it really was a shot."

"You say a shot? Well, then, hand me my Mauser."

Anastasio Montañés rubbed his eyes, stretched his arms and legs very lazily, and stood up. They went outside the hut. The stars sparkled in the sky and the rising moon was like a sharp sickle. Sounds of confusion came from frightened women in the huts. Outside, among the men aroused from their sleep, the rattle of weapons sounded.

"Stupid! You've mashed my foot!"

The voice sounded close by clearly and distinctly.

"Who goes there?"

The shout echoed from peak to peak, along the crests, and into the depths until it was lost in the distance and silence of the night.

"Who goes there?" repeated Anastasio in an even louder voice, cocking the hammer of his Mauser.

"Demetrio Macías!" came the response from nearby.

"It's Pancracio!" said Cordoniz overjoyed. Now that there was no danger, he rested the butt of his rifle on the ground.

Pancracio brought with him a young fellow covered with dust from his American felt hat to his rough shoes. There was a spot of fresh blood on his pants near his foot.

"Who's this *curro*?" asked Anastasio.

"While I was on guard, I heard a noise in the bushes and I shouted: 'Who goes there?' 'Carranzo!' this fellow answered. 'Carranzo? I don't know that rooster.' And he got his Carranzo: I put a bullet in his hoof."

Smiling, Pancracio turned his beardless face, expecting applause. Then the stranger spoke.

"Who is the chief here?"

Anastasio raised his head arrogantly, looking him straight in the face. The young man lowered the tone of his voice somewhat.

"But I am a revolutionary also. The Federals seized me in the draft and put me in the ranks; but day before yesterday during the battle I managed to desert, and I have come, journeying on foot, looking for you."

"So, he's a Federal!" many cried out, looking at him in astonishment.

"Hah, he's a *mocho*!" said Anastacio Montañés. "Why didn't you put the bullet right where it'd do the most good?"

"Who knows what kind of a tale he brings! He wants to talk to Demetrio, says he's got a lot to tell him, who knows what! No matter, for it'll all come out in time if you don't rush things," replied Pancracio, readying his rifle.

"But what sort of brutes are you?" remarked the stranger.

He was unable to say more, because a backhanded blow from Anastasio knocked him about, his face bathed in blood.

"Shoot this *mocho*!"

"Hang him!"

"Burn him, he's a Federal!"

They yelled and shrieked in their excitement, howling as they made ready their rifles.

"Ssh—ssh—shut up! I think I hear Demetrio saying something," said Anastasio, quieting them down.

Actually, Demetrio wanted to know what had happened and made them bring the prisoner to him.

"This is shameful, my chief, look here, look here!" exclaimed Luis Cervantes, showing the spots of blood on his pants and his swollen mouth and nose.

"Well, now, what son of a gun are you?" Demetrio asked him.

"My name is Luis Cervantes, I am a student of medicine and a journalist. Because I said something favorable about the revolutionaries, they persecuted me, they seized me and threw me in a barrack."

The story of his adventures which he proceeded to detail in a declamatory tone greatly amused Pancracio and Manteca.

"I have endeavored to make myself understood, to convince you that I am truly a co-religionist."

"Co-re—what?" Demetrio asked, turning his ear.

"Co-religionist, my chief. That is to say, I pursue the same ideals and defend the same cause that you do."

Demetrio smiled.

"What cause do we defend?"

Luis Cervantes, disconcerted, did not know what to reply.

"See what a look he's got on his face! Why so much fooling around? How about shooting him now, Demetrio?" asked Pancracio anxiously.

Demetrio pushed back his long hair which covered one ear, scratched himself a long time, meditating; then, not having arrived at a solution, he said,

"Get out of here. My wound is hurting me again. Anastasio put out the wick. Pancracio and Manteca, lock that fellow up in the corral and keep your eyes on him. Tomorrow we'll see."

VI

Luis Cervantes could not make out the exact shape of objects in the vague shadows of the starry night. Searching for the best place to rest himself, he dropped his weary bones on a pile of damp manure at the foot of the blurred mass of a huisache tree. More through exhaustion than resignation, he stretched out his full length and resolutely closed his eyes, determined to sleep until his fierce guards should awaken him or the morning sun should burn his ears. Something like a vague warmth at his side, then the sound of heavy, tired panting made him shudder. Feeling about, his trembling hand touched the stiff bristles of a pig which grunted, surely annoyed by his neighbor.

All his efforts to woo sleep proved useless, not because of the pain of his wounded foot, nor of his maltreated flesh, but because of the immediate and clear realization of his failure. Yes, he had not appreciated at the proper time the distance there is between manipulating a scalpel and fulminating against the robber factions from the columns of a provincial newspaper and coming to look for them in their own lairs with a rifle in his hands. During the first day's journey as a volunteer lieutenant of the cavalry, he had suspected his error. A brutal journey of fourteen leagues had made his hips and knees seem to be in one piece, as if his bones were welded together. His full realization came eight days later in the first encounter with the rebels. He would swear, hand on a Holy Crucifix that, when the soldiers raised their Mausers to their faces to fire, someone in a stentorian voice had shouted at his back, "Those who can, save themselves!" It was so clear that even his noble and spirited horse itself, accustomed to combat as it was, had turned back and stampeded, not wanting to stop until it was beyond even the sound of bullets. It was just at sunset when vague, wavering shadows began to gather on the mountain and twilight ascended quickly from the depths. What more logical notion could occur to him than that of searching for shelter among the rocks to give rest to body and soul and get some sleep? But a soldier's logic is the logic of absurdity. Thus, for example, the following morning his colonel wakened him with rough kicks and ousted him from his

hiding place, his face swollen from being beaten. Worse yet, the
hilarity of the officers was aroused to such a degree that they laughed
until they cried, imploring in one voice pardon for the fugitive. The
colonel, instead of shooting him, gave him a stiff kick in the rump
and sent him to the rear as a cook's helper.

That humiliating insult bore poisonous fruit. Luis Cervantes
changed sides from that moment although only in his mind for the
time being. The pains and the miseries of the underpriviledged had
the effect of arousing his feelings of compassion. His cause became
the sublime cause of the subjugated people who claimed justice, only
justice. He knew well the conditions of the humble soldier, and what's
more, he was so tenderhearted that he shed tears of pity when a mule
making a tortuous journey died of fatigue.

From that time the soldiers in the ranks held Luis Cervantes in
high esteem. Some of them rashly confided in him. One, a very
sincere person, outstanding for being moderate and retiring, said to
him: "I am a carpenter. I lived with my mother who was a little
old lady who had been tied to her chair by rheumatism for ten years.
In the middle of the night three policemen pulled me out of bed;
by dawn I was in the barracks and by night a dozen leagues from
my town. A month later I passed through there with the company.
My mother had died and been buried! She was my only comfort
in this life. Now, I have no one. But, by my God who is in heaven,
these cartridges they load on me aren't going to be used on the enemy.
And if by some miracle (and the Holy Mother of Guadalupe can grant
it to me), I can join up with Villa, I swear by my mother's sacred
soul that I'll pay back those Federals."

Another, young and intelligent but an out-and-out rascal, a drunkard who smoked marijuana, called him to one side and looking him
straight in the face with his vague, glassy eyes, whispered in his ear:
"*Compadre*, the—the guys on the other side; you get it? The ones in
the North and in the interior that ride the finest strings of horses, with
all the trimmings on the saddles and bridles made of pure silver. Us,
huh! Weak nags good only for raising buckets out of a well. See
what I mean, *compadre*? The others get shiny, hard money; and us,
we get paper money from the Assassin's² factory. I mean to say—"

And thus, all of them, even a second sergeant who related candidly:
"I am a volunteer, but I've sure been left holding the bag. What in
peace times you can't make in a whole life of working like a mule,

now you can make in a few months of running up and down the sierra
with a gun on your back. But with this bunch, no siree, not with
these!"

Luis Cervantes, who shared with the troops a hidden, implacable,
mortal hatred of the upper classes and officials, felt that the last veil
had fallen from his eyes and that he could see clearly the final outcome
of the struggle.

But look where he was at that moment. No more had he arrived
among his fellow believers than they had thrown him in a pigsty
instead of receiving him with open arms.

The new day dawned: roosters crowed in the village; the hens
roosting in the branches of the huisache in the corral began to stir.
They stretched their wings and ruffled their feathers and all jumped
to the ground.

He looked at his guards stretched out on the manure pile, snoring.
In his imagination he reviewed the looks of the two men whom he
had seen the evening before. There was one, Pancracio, whose fair,
freckled, beardless face with a protruding chin, flat, receding forehead, and ears set close to his skull had altogether a brutal aspect.
The other, Manteca, little more than skin and bones, had deep-set
eyes, a sullen look, very straight hair falling to his neck and over
his forehead and ears, and scrofulous lips always hanging open.

Once more he felt his flesh crawl.

VII

Half asleep, Demetrio ran his hand over the thick, curly hair,
parted toward one ear, which covered his damp forehead and opened
his eyes. Clearly he heard the melodious feminine voice to which he
had been listening in his dreams and turned toward the door.

It was full day; the rays of the sun darted through the cracks
between the canes forming the hut. The same girl who the evening
before had offered him a vessel of refreshing cold water (his dreams
through the whole night), now, just as sweet and kind, entered with
a jar of milk brimming over with foam.

"It's goat's milk, but it's good. Come on, now give it a try."

Grateful, Demetrio smiled as he raised up. Taking the clay vessel, he began to sip the milk, without taking his eyes off of the girl. Feeling uneasy, she lowered her eyes.

"What's your name?"

"Camila."

"It's pretty, but the tone of your voice is prettier."

Camila blushed painfully and, frightened when he tried to catch hold of her wrist, picked up the empty vessel and quickly slipped away.

"No, *compadre* Demetrio," Anastasio Montañés observed gravely, "you got to tame 'em first. Hmm, what marks women have left on my carcass! I've been around plenty!"

"I feel good, *compadre*," said Demetrio, pretending he had not heard. "Seems I had a chill; I sweated a lot and waked up feeling refreshed. What's bothering me still is this damn wound. Call Venancio to come doctor me."

"What are we going to do with that *curro* I caught last night?" asked Pancracio.

"Hell, man, I hadn't thought about him again!"

Demetrio, as always, thought and hesitated considerably before making a decision.

"Well, now, Cordoniz, come here. Look, here's the plan. Find the way to the chapel which is about three leagues from here. Go and steal the priest's soutane."

"But what are you going to do, *compadre*?" asked Anastasio, surprised.

"If this *curro* came here to kill me, it'll be a cinch to get the truth out of him. I'll tell him I'll shoot him. Cordoniz, making out he's the priest, will go to see him to hear his confession. If he's a sinner, I'll blast him; if not, he'll go free."

"Huh, what a notion! I'd finish him off and be done with it," exclaimed Pancracio contemptuously.

That night Cordoniz returned with the priest's soutane. Demetrio had the prisoner brought to him. Effects of not having eaten or slept in two days showed in Luis Cervantes' haggard, shadowed face and his dry, discolored lips. He spoke slowly and heavily.

"Do what you want to with me. It's evident that I was mistaken about you."

There was a prolonged silence. Then,

"I think you should welcome one who comes to offer you help, poor as mine is, but of benefit only to you. What difference does it make to me whether the revolution triumphs or not?"

Little by little he became more animated, the weakness in his glance disappearing for brief instants.

"The revolution benefits the poor, the ignorant, all who have lived the lives of slaves, all the unhappy souls who don't even know that they are like that because the rich convert into gold the tears, the sweat, and the blood of the poor."

"Bah! What's all that about? Sermons don't suit me," interrupted Pancracio.

"I wanted to fight for the sacred cause of the suppressed. But you don't understand me; you repulse me. So then, do with me what you will!"

"Right now what I'm going to do is put a rope around your gullet. See how plump and white it is!"

"Yes, now I see why you came here," added Demetrio, calmly scratching his head. "I mean to shoot you, how about it?"

Then, turning to Anastasio, he said,

"Take him away. If he wants to confess, bring a priest to him."

Anastasio, impassive as ever, gently took hold of Cervantes' arm.

"Come here, *curro*."

When Cordoniz appeared a few minutes later dressed in the soutane, they all burst out laughing.

"Hmm, this *curro's* a real chatterbox!" he exclaimed. "It seems he even laughed at me when I began to ask him questions."

"But he didn't sing?"

"He didn't say a thing more than he did last night."

" I guess he didn't come here to do what you're afraid of *compadre*," remarked Anastasio.

"O. K., then give him something to eat and watch him."

VIII

Luis Cervantes was barely able to get up the following day. Dragging his wounded leg, he hobbled from hut to hut, looking for some alcohol, boiled water, and some rags. Camila, with her customary kindness, provided him with what he wanted. When he began to wash his leg, she sat down beside him to watch him dress the wound with the natural curiosity of the *serrana*.

"Listen, who taught you to doctor? Why'd you boil the water? Why'd you cook the rags? My, how careful you are about everything! Why'd you put that on your hands? Phew! It's really brandy? Come now, all this time I thought brandy was good only for colic! Ah! you plan to be a doctor? Ha, ha, ha! Enough to make a body die laughing! Wouldn't it do better mixed with cold water? What'd you say? Bugs in water if you don't boil it? Bosh! I don't see any!"

Camila kept on questioning him, soon speaking in the familiar form. Absorbed in his own thoughts, Luis Cervantes quit listening to her.

"Where are those wonderfully mounted and armed men who get their pay in hard money that Villa's been minting in Chihuahua? Bah! Twenty old, naked, lousy, men mounted on decrepid mares, mangy from withers to tail. Can it be true what the government press and he himself had affirmed, that these so-called revolutionaries are no more than bandits with a magnificent pretext but united really for the purpose of slaking their thirst for gold and blood? Is it possible then, that what the sympathizers with the revolution have been saying about them is a batch of lies? Even though the newspapers still run the gamut of tones in proclaiming triumphs and more triumphs for the Federation, a paymaster recently arrived from Guadalajara let escape the bit of news that Huerta's relatives and particular friends had left the capital and taken the route to the port, all the more suspect since he continued to growl, 'I will have peace no matter what it costs.' Therefore, revolutionaries, bandits, or whatever you may wish to call them, are going to pull down the government; tomorrow belongs to them; I should be on their side then, only with them. No, I don't think I'm mistaken this time," he said to himself, almost aloud.

"What're you saying?" asked Camila. "I thought the rats had got your tongue."

Luis Cervantes frowned and looked angrily at that species of *chomite*-clad, bronze-colored monkey with marble-white teeth and broad, stubby feet.

"Listen, *curro*, you know how to tell stories, don't you?"

Luis looked at her in disgust and left without answering.

She, amazed, followed him with her eyes until his shape disappeared down the path by the stream. She was so absorbed that she gave a startled jump at the sound of the voice of her neighbor, the one-eyed María Antonia, who had been spying on her, calling to her,

"Hey there, you! Give him some love powder. See if he won't fall for you!"

"Golly! That's what you'd do!"

"If I wanted to. But, phew, *curros* make me sick."

IX

"Remigia, lend me some eggs, my hen's broody this morning. Men're over there wanting breakfast."

As she entered, she opened her eyes widely on account of the change from the vivid sunlight to the gloom of the hut intensified by the dense smoke arising from the hearth. After a few seconds she began to distinguish the outlines of various objects and the cot of the wounded man with the head of it touching the shiny, sooty shed.

She squatted down beside Remigia and, darting furtive glances toward the sleeping Demetrio, asked in a low voice,

"How's the fellow getting along? Any better? That's good! Look, how young he is! He's sure pale yet. Remigia, don't you think we ought to do something?"

Remigia, naked above the waist, her thin sinewy arms stretched out, rolled the *mano* of the *metate* back and forth over the cooked corn.

"How d'you know they'd want you to?" she responded, breathing heavily as she kept on with her strenuous task. "They got their own doctor and for that—"

"Remigia," said another neighbor entering, bending her skinny back to get through the door, "you got any laurel leaves you can give me to make a potion for María Antonia? She waked up with the cramps."

To tell the truth, her visit was only a pretext for gossiping and satisfying her curiosity. She turned her eyes toward the corner where the sick man lay and, with a wink, asked about his health.

Remigia lowered her eyes to indicate that Demetrio was sleeping.

"So you're here too, Pachita. I didn't see you when I came in."

"May God grant you a good day, Fortunata. How're folks this morning?"

"Well, María Antonia's got the curse, and like always, cramping something fierce."

She squatted down alongside Pachita.

"I don't have any laurel leaves, honey," replied Remigia, pausing in her corn grinding for an instant to brush back from her sweating face the hair which fell over her eyes. Then plunging both hands into the wet mass she took out a big handful of the cooked corn from which dripped cloudy, yellowish water. "I don't have any, but you go see Dolores. She's never without some herbs."

"Dolores went to the meeting of the *cofradía* last night. Some say they came to get her to take care of Aunt Matías' girl."

"Come now, Pachita, don't tell me that!"

The three old women in an animated group, talking in a low tone, began to gossip with lively interest.

"Just as sure's God's in heaven!"

"Well, I was the first that said, 'Marcelina is fat, she sure is fat.' But nobody'd believe me."

"Poor thing. And suppose it turns out it's her Uncle Nazario's!"

"God protect her."

"No, it *couldn't* have been Uncle Nazario. Devil take those Federals."

"Pshaw! She's just another unhappy woman."

The chattering of the old women finally awakened Demetrio.

They fell silent for a moment. After a bit, Pachita, taking from the bosom of her dress a young pigeon which opened its beak gasping for breath, said,

"I came on purpose to bring this remedy for the gentleman, but since he's in the hands of a doctor—"

"That's no matter, Pachita; this is something that goes on the outside."

"Mister, I'm sorry that this is such a little gift. Here, I've brought you this present," said the old woman drawing near Demetrio, "for there's nothing like this remedy for bleeding."

Demetrio nervously gave his approval. They had already placed on his abdomen some pieces of bread soaked in brandy. In spite of the effects of the evaporation, he felt as though he still suffered from a high fever.

"Come on, you know very well how to do it, Remigia," exclaimed her neighbors.

Out of a reed sheath Remigia took the sort of long, curved knife used to cut fruit off cactus. Holding the pigeon with its breast turned up she cut it in two with a single stroke as skillfully as a surgeon.

"In the name of Jesus, Mary, and Joseph!" said Remigia chanting a benediction. While the two halves of the pigeon were still hot and gushing blood, she quickly placed them on Demetrio's abdomen.

"You'll see how much relief you're going to feel."

Obedient to Remigia's instructions, Demetrio lay motionless on one side with his knees drawn up.

Then Fortunata gave an account of her troubles. She had a feeling of good will toward the men of the revolution. Three months ago the Federals had stolen her only daughter. She was, therefore, inconsolable and beside herself with grief.

At the beginning of the account, Cordoniz and Anastasio Montañés, lying at the foot of the cot, raised their heads and listened openmouthed to the story. But Fortunata included such a wealth of detail that by the time she was half through, Cordoniz was bored. When she had concluded solemnly: "I hope to God and Holy Mary that you won't leave alive a one of those Federal soldiers from Hell," he went outside in the sun to scratch himself. With his face turned to the wall and feeling much relief from the remedies applied to his stomach, Demetrio went over in his mind a route for the penetration of Durango. Anastasio Montañés was snoring like a trombone.

X

"Why don't you call the *curro* to look at your wound," Anastasio Montañés said to the chief, who continued to suffer from severe chills and fever. "You ought to see how he cured himself and he walks as lively as before without even a limp."

But Venancio, who had ready tins of lard and compresses of dirty lint, protested,

"If any one puts a hand to him, I'll not be to blame for what happens."

"Listen, bud, you're not a doctor or anything else special. I'll bet you've even forgot why you joined up with us," said Cordoniz.

"Well sure, I remember, Cordoniz, that you came with us because you had stolen a watch and some diamond rings," replied the high and mighty Venancio.

Cordoniz let out a bellow of laughter.

"That's no matter. But you ran away from your town because you poisoned your sweetheart."

"You're a liar!"

"Yes you did; you gave the girl Spanish fly so that—"

Noisy shouts of laughter drowned out Venancio's vociferous protests. Demetrio, showing irritation, made them shut up; then he commenced to complain and said,

"Let's see about it. Bring that student here."

Luis Cervantes came, uncovered Demetrio's leg, carefully examined the wound and shook his head. The cloth ligature had made a deep furrow in the skin. The swollen leg looked as if it were about to burst. Each time he moved Demetrio choked back a groan. Luis Cervantes cut the bandage, freely washed the wound, and covered the muscle with big wet strips of cloth and tied it up again.

Demetrio was able to sleep the whole afternoon and the whole night. The next day he awoke quite happy.

"That *curro* sure's got a light hand," he said.

Venancio quickly observed,

"That's good, but it's known that *curros* are like moisture, they seep in every place. We've lost the fruits of the revolution on account of those city guys."

Demetrio, believing blindly in the barber's wisdom, said to Luis Cervantes when he came the next day to look after him,

"Listen, do a good job on me because when you get me fixed up good and healthy, you're free to go on off to your home or wherever it suits you."

Discreetly, Luis Cervantes said not a word.

A week passed, then two; the Federals gave no sign of life. On the small farms in the nearby region, however, beans and corn were abundant. The people hated the Federals so much that they gladly furnished aid to the rebels. Demetrio's men, then, waited patiently for their chief's recovery. For many days Luis Cervantes remained melancholy and silent.

"Seems to me you're in love, *curro*!" Demetrio said to him jokingly one day after his wound had been cared for. He had begun to grow fond of him.

Little by little Demetrio took an interest in Luis' accommodations. He asked whether the soldiers gave him his ration of meat and milk.

Luis Cervantes had to say that he was able to feed himself only on what the good women of the *rancho* wished to give him and that the people continued to look on him as a stranger and an intruder.

"They're all good boys, *curro*," replied Demetrio, "it's all in knowing the way to handle them. Beginning tomorrow, you'll lack nothing. You'll see."

As a matter of fact, things began to change that very afternoon. Stretched out on big rocks, looking at the sunset clouds that were like giant clots of blood, some of Macías' men listened to Venancio recounting some of the delightful episodes from the *The Wandering Jew.* Some of them, lulled by the barber's mellifluous voice, began to snore; but when he finished his discourse with various extraneous anti-clerical comments, Luis Cervantes who had been very attentive, said emphatically,

"Admirable! You have a remarkable talent!"

"I'm not so bad," said the self-assured Venancio, "but my parents died and I wasn't able to study for a career."

"That's no hindrance. After the triumph of our cause you'll be able to get a degree easily. Two or three weeks of assisting at a hospital, a good recommendation from our chief Macías, and you're a doctor. You have such an aptitude that it will be child's play."

After that night, Venancio differed from the rest, for he no longer called him "*curro*." It was "Luisito" here and "Luisito" there.

XI

"Listen, *curro*, I want to tell you something," said Camila one morning at the time that Luis Cervantes went to the hut to get boiled water to use in dressing his wounded foot.

The girl had been going around disturbed for several days past. Her affected ways and shyness had finally annoyed the young man. Suddenly interrupting what he was doing, he stood up and, looking at her face to face, said,

"Well then, what is it you want to tell me?"

Camila felt her tongue become as limp as a rag and she could not utter a sound. She blushed as red as a hot coal, shrugged her shoulders, and hung her head until it touched her naked chest. Then without moving, her eyes fixed on the wound with the obstinacy of an idiot, she uttered in a very weak voice,

"Look how pretty it's healing already! Looks like a bud of a rose of Castile."

Luis Cervantes frowned with obvious irritation and began anew to dress his wound without paying any more attention to her.

When he was through, Camila had disappeared.

For three days there was no sign of her. Agapita, her mother, was the one who took care of Luis Cervantes' needs; it was she who boiled the water and the bandages for him. He took good care not to ask any questions. But in three days, there Camila was again, more giddy and coy than before.

His inattention and indifference emboldened Camila, and finally she spoke,

"Listen, I want to tell you something. Listen, I want you to repeat to me "*La Adelita*"[3] because—don't you see why? Because I can sing it often when you're gone; when you're not here; when you've gone far from here; when you've forgotten me."

Her words had the effect on Luis Cervantes of a steel point drawn down the side of a flask.

Quite unaware, she continued as disingenuously as before.

"Come, *curro*, I've not told you anything yet. You ought to see how bad that old man is who's your leader. Here's what happened to me on account of him. You know how that Demetrio allows only Mama to cook for him and only me to take his food to him. Well, the other day, when I went in with the *champurrao*, what d'you think the stupid old fool did? He grabbed my hand and held on tight, tight; then he began to pinch my behind. Oh! But what a good sock I give him! 'Leave me be! Be quiet, you old goat, where're your manners? Let me go; let me go; you shameless old fool!' I pulled back, got loose, and got outside as fast as I could. What do you think of that, *curro*?"

Camila had never seen Luis Cervantes laugh with such enjoyment.

"But is what you have told me actually a fact?"

Profoundly disconcerted, Camila was unable to reply. He burst out laughing uproariously again and repeated his question. Feeling more uneasy and oppressed than ever, she answered in a broken voice,

"Yes, it's so. And that's what I wanted to tell you. Don't it make you mad, *curro*?"

Once more Camila looked adoringly at Luis Cervantes' ruddy and radiant countenance, his eyes with their soft expression, his fresh, rosy cheeks like those of a porcelain doll; at the smoothness of his

white, delicate skin which showed above the neck and below the sleeves
of a coarse woolen undershirt; at his soft, blond, slightly curly hair.

"But what in the devil did you expect, dunce?   If the chief wants
you, what more could you ask for?"

Camila felt something rise in her breast, something that came up
into her throat and formed a knot there.   She closed her eyelids
tightly to clear the tears from her eyes, wiped her cheeks with the
back of her hand, and then, as she had three days before, fled with
the speed of a young deer.

XII

Demetrio's wound had healed.   They began to discuss various plans
for going North where, it was said, the revolutionaries had defeated
the Federals along the whole front.   An incident brought matters to
a head.   On one occasion Luis Cervantes, seated on an outcropping
of the sierra enjoying the fresh afternoon air, was gazing off into
the distance and killing time.   At the foot of the narrow ledge, lying
like lizards among the thick bushes along the river's edge, Pancracio
and Manteca were playing cards.   Anastasio Montañés was looking
on indifferently.   He turned his black-bearded face toward Luis
Cervantes and, looking at him with his soft eyes, said,

"Why're you so sad, you city feller?   Why d'you think so much?
Come over here by me and let's talk a while."

Luis Cervantes did not move, but Anastasio went over and sat down
beside him in a friendly fashion.

"You miss the stir of your own town.   Bet you shine your shoes
every day and wear a shirt and tie.   Look, *curro*, you see me here all
dirty and ragged, but I'm not what I look like.   You don't believe me?
I don't have to be here; I'm the owner of ten yokes of oxen.   Sure
enough!   Just ask my *compadre* Demetrio.   You don't believe me?
Look, *curro*; I sure like to plague those Federals; that's why they've no
use for me.   The last time, eight months ago (just the time I had to
come here), I stuck a knife into a smart aleck little captain (God
watch over me) here, right in the stomach.   Matter of fact, I didn't
have to come; I came here on account of that and to give a hand to
my *compadre* Demetrio."

"Come on, lady luck!" shouted Manteca with enthusiasm over a
winning hand.   He put a silver twenty-*centavo* coin on the queen of
spades.

"Would you believe it, *curro*, I don't care a thing about gambling! Want to bet? Come on, look; this little leather snake still rattles," said Anastasio taking off his belt and shaking it so they could hear the sound of coins in it.

As Pancracio dealt the deck of cards, the queen of spades turned up and a quarrel ensued. It was a regular free-for-all with shouts, then insults. Pancracio thrust his stony countenance close to Manteca's face. Manteca, convulsed like an epileptic, looked at him with snaky eyes. Any moment they might start swinging. When they ran out of sufficiently pointed invectives, they resorted to insulting each other's progenitors with a wealth of indecencies.

But nothing happened; as soon as they had exhausted their stock of insults, quitting the game, they threw their arms about each other's shoulders and went off together to look for a drink of whisky.

"I don't like to fight with my tongue, either. It's not decent, d'you think, *curro?* Look here, it's a sure thing nobody's ever mentioned my family to me. I like for them to respect me. That's why you don't see me going round running off at the mouth. Listen, *curro*," continued Anastasio in a different tone of voice, shading his eyes with his hand, and standing up, "what's that cloud of dust raising up over there behind that little hill? ¡*Caramba*! Maybe it's those *mochos*! Here we're caught unawares! Come along, *curro* let's go warn the bunch."

It was an occasion for great jubilation.

"Let's find them," said Pancracio who spoke up first.

"Sure, let's go get them. We know all their tricks!"

But the enemy turned out to be a couple of Indians driving a herd of burros.

"Stop them. They're from the highlands and must have some news," said Demetrio.

What they had to tell was sensational. The Federals had fortified the hills El Grillo and La Bufa in Zacatecas. It was said to be Huerta's last stronghold and everybody predicted the city would fall. Many families had fled precipitately toward the south. Trains left jammed with people. Because there were insufficient carriages and coaches, many people, panic-stricken, went on foot along the main roads with their belongings on their backs. General Pánfilo Natera was gathering his forces in Fresnillo and the Federals were just about "caught with their pantaloons down."

"The fall of Zacatecas is Huerta's *Requiescat in pace*," Luis
Cervantes assured them with extraordinary vehemence. "We need
to get there before the attack to join General Natera's forces."

Noticing the amazement that his words evoked in Demetrio and
his companions, he realized that he was still Mr. Nobody there. On
the next day, however, when the men went to look for good horses
so that they might undertake their march again, Demetrio called Luis
and said to him,

"Do you really want to go with us? You're a different stripe,
and to tell the truth, I don't see how you can like this way of life.
Who believes that anyone'd go along just because he likes it? Sure,
who'd deny it? Some like the excitement but there's more to it.
Sit down, *curro*, sit down, so I can tell you. You know why I'm
a rebel? See here, before the revolution I had my land plowed
ready for sowing. If it hadn't been for the quarrel with Don Mónico,
the *cacique* of Moyahua, right now I'd be hurrying to get the yoke
of oxen ready for the sowing. Pancracio, take down two bottles of
beer, one for me and one for the *curro*. By the sign of the Holy
Cross! It won't do any harm, will it?"

XIII

"I'm a native of Limón, very near Moyahua, right in the canyon
of Juchipila. I had my house, my cows, and a piece of crop land;
you might say I had everything. Then, sir, us farmers had the
custom of going to the village once a week. A body'd go to Mass,
listen to the sermon, then go to the plaza, buy some onions, tomatoes,
and all that was needed. Then with his friends he'd make it about
eleven o'clock to Primitivo López's store. He takes a little drink. To
be sociable, he keeps bending his elbow, and the drink goes to his head.
It makes him feel good and he laughs, shouts, and sings if he feels
like it. Everything's all right, because he don't bother nobody. But
they commence to bother him. The police go back and forth, put
their ears to the door. The commissioner or the auxiliaries decide
to stop the fun. Sure thing, man! Blood's not milk and water; you've
got a soul in your body; you lose your temper; stand up tell them off!
If they understand, well and good; they leave in peace and things
stop there. But sometimes it suits them to talk loud and get rough
and a body's naturally sort of brave, and don't want to be ordered

around. Yes, sir; out comes the dagger, out comes the pistol—and soon you're running for the sierra until they forget about the little dead one!

"Well! What happened to Don Mónico? Stuffed shirt! Much less than to the others. He didn't know what was going on. He got spit in his face for meddling, and that's all there is to tell. Well, with that he had the whole government down on me. You must've heard the rumor about what was going on in Mexico City, where they killed *Señor* Madero and another, some Félix or Felipe Díaz, how do I know! Well then, the aforesaid Don Mónico went in person to Zacatecas to bring a guard to seize me. He said I was a *maderista* and that I was going to rebel. But I had plenty of friends who let me know in time when the Federals were coming to Limón, and I had already skinned out. Afterwards my *compadre*, Anastasio, who'd killed somebody, then Pancracio came, as well as Cordoniz, many friends, and people I knew. Afterwards some more joined us, and now you see, we get along as well as we can."

"My chief," said Luis Cervantes after some minutes of silent meditation, "you know that near here, in Juchipila, there are some of Natera's followers. It would be a good idea to join them before they take Zacatecas. We present ourselves to the General—"

"I'm not good at that. It don't suit me to be under anybody."

"But you, with only the few men here, will never be anything more than an unimportant chief. The revolution will undoubtedly win; then when it is over they will tell you, as Madero said to those who helped him, 'Many thanks, friends, now you can go back to your homes.'"

"That's all I want, just to be let alone in peace to return to my home."

"I have more to say; I haven't finished: 'Now that I have succeeded in achieving my objective, you who raised me to the Presidency of the Republic, risking your lives with the imminent danger of leaving your widows and orphans in misery may take up your hoes and your shovels again; you may go back to your miserable life, always hungry and half-clothed, just as you were before, while we, the top dogs, make our millions of *pesos*.'"

Smiling, Demetrio nodded his head and scratched himself.

"Luisito speaks as true as a church!" the barber Venancio exclaimed enthusiastically.

"As I was saying," continued Luis Cervantes, "once the revolution is over, it's all over. What a pity so many lives were cut off, so many made widows and orphans, so much blood spilled! And all for what? In order that a few rascals may enrich themselves and every-thing remains just as bad or even worse than before. You are turned loose and you say 'I have no ambition but to return to my land.' But is it justice to deprive your wives and your children of the fortune that Divine Providence has put in your hands now? Is is right to abandon our country in these solemn moments in which she needs all the sacrifices of her humble sons to save her in order that she not be left to fall again into the hands of her eternal oppressors and tormentors, the *caciques*? That which is the most sacred in the world to a man must not be forgotten: family and country!"

Macías smiled and his eyes shone.

"Will it be a good thing, then, to fight with Natera, *curro*?"

"Not only good," remarked Venancio insinuatingly, "but necessary, Demetrio."

"My chief," continued Cervantes, "I have liked you ever since I met you, and I like you more all the time, because I know your worth. Let me speak to you frankly. You do not yet realize your true, high, and noble mission. You, a modest man without ambitions, are unaware of the important role you play in the revolution. It's an error to say that you came here just on account of Don Mónico, the *cacique*; you have raised the standard against the *caciquismo* that plagues the whole nation. We are elements of a great social move-ment which must end with the glorification of our country. We are instruments of destiny for reclaiming the sacred rights of the people. We do not struggle to overthrow one miserable assassin but against tyranny itself. That is what it means to fight for principles, for ideals. Villa, Natera, Carranza fight for them just as we do."

"Yes, yes, that's exactly what I have thought," said Venancio enthusiastically.

"Pancracio, take down a couple more beers."

XIV

"If you could've heard how well the *curro* explained it, *compadre* Anastasio," said Demetrio, pondering on what he had been able to figure out that morning from Luis Cervantes' words.

"I was listening too," replied Anastasio Montañés. "It's the truth that folks who know how to read and write understand such things. But what don't get through to me is how're you're going to offer your services to Natera with such a small bunch as us."

"Hmm, that's no matter. From today we're going do things different. I've heard that Crispín Robles goes in all the towns seizing what weapons and horses he finds; lets the prisoners out of the jails, and in a jiffy he's got more'n enough men. That's a fact. You know, Anastasio, it's a fact we've been plenty dumb. It seems mixed up that this tenderfoot has come here to show how to get things done."

"How wonderful to know how to read n' write!" Both sighed sadly.

Luis Cervantes and a number of others came in to find out when they would depart.

"We go tomorrow, for sure," said Demetrio without hesitation.

Cordoniz then proposed that they get some musicians from the nearby village and have a farewell dance. The idea was received with reckless enthusiasm.

"Course we're going," exclaimed Pancracio, letting out a whoop of approval, "but I'm not going by myself. I've got me a sweetheart and I'm going to take her with me."

Demetrio said that it would suit him to take along a girl he had set his eyes on, but that he did not want anyone to leave behind any sad remembrances as the Federals had done.

"You don't have to wait long; on your return it will all be arranged," Luis Cervantes whispered to him.

"How's that!" said Demetrio. "I heard that you and Camila—?"

"Certainly not, my chief, it's you she likes, but she is afraid of you."

"You sure, *curro*?"

"Yes, but it seems to me that what you said to your men sure hits the mark; there should be no bad impressions left behind. When we return in triumph, all will be different; so much so that they will all thank you."

"Ah, *curro*, you're sure smart!" answered Demetrio, smiling and clapping him on the back.

At the close of the day, as usual, Camila went down to the river for water. She met Luis Cervantes coming down the same path.

Camila felt as though her heart would jump out of her breast. Without taking the slightest notice of her, Luis Cervantes disappeared suddenly in a sharp turn among the large boulders.

At that hour as usual the twilight threw a common dull shade over the limestone rocks, the sun-parched foliage, and the dry weeds. A soft wind sighed gently, swaying the lancelike leaves of the young corn. Everything was the same; but in the rocks, the dry branches, the fragrant air, and the dry leaves, Camila now found something very strange: as if all these things had an aura of sadness about them.

She went around a gigantic, rough boulder and suddenly encountered Luis Cervantes perched on a rock, his legs dangling, his head bare.

"*Curro*, at least come tell me good-bye."

Luis Cervantes was agreeable. He got down and went over to her.

"You're a proud one. Have I waited on you so poorly that you won't even talk to me?"

"Why do you say that to me, Camila? You have been very good to me, better than a friend; you have taken care of me like a sister. I am grateful to you and I will always remember how you helped me."

"Liar!" said Camila transfigured with happiness. "And if I hadn't called to you?"

"I was going to thank you tonight at the dance."

"What dance? If there is a dance, I'm not going to go."

"Why not?"

"Because I can't stand to look at that man—that Demetrio."

"How foolish! Look, he likes you very much; don't lose this chance which won't ever come to you again. Silly, Demetrio is going to be a general and very rich. Many horses, many jewels, very rich clothes, elegant houses and much money to spend. Imagine what it would be like if you were at his side then!"

So that he could not see her eyes, Camila raised them toward the sky. A dry leaf falling from the heights of the cliff floated in the air slowly, drifted like a dead butterfly to the ground at their feet. She bent over and took it in her fingers. Then without looking him in the face, she murmured,

"Ay, if you only could realize how dreadful I feel on account of your talking like that! But it's you I love, nobody else, only you. Go, go away, for I don't know why I'm so ashamed. Go, go away!"

She threw away the leaf her anguished fingers had crumbled and covered her face with the corner of her apron. When she opened her eyes again, Luis Cervantes had disappeared.

She followed the path along the arroyo. The water seemed covered with a fine red dust; in its waves rippled the reflections of the colors of the sky and of the crags, half in the light and half in the shadow. Specks of light from myriads of luminous insects twinkled in a stagnant pool. The picture of her yellow blouse with green ribbons, her unstarched white skirt, her tightly combed hair, just as she had adorned herself to please Luis, was reproduced against the background of gravel over which the water flowed.

She burst into tears. Among the reeds, the frogs intoned the implacable melancholy of the hour. Swaying on a dry branch, a wild dove mourned also.

XV

The dance was very gay and the mescal flowed freely.

"I miss Camila," Demetrio announced loudly.

Everyone looked about for Camila.

"She's sick, got a bad headache," responded Agapita with asperity, uneasy because of the suspicious looks turned toward her.

When the dance was over Demetrio, staggering a bit, thanked the good neighbors who had received them so kindly and promised that he would remember all of them when the revolution had triumphed, for "in bed and in jail one learns who one's friends are."

"May God lead you with His holy hand," said an old woman.

"God bless you and show you the right road," said others.

María Antonia, very drunk, called out,

"Hope you come back soon, real soon!"

María Antonia, a person of such bad reputation that in spite of her pock-marked face and clouded eye it was generally asserted that there wasn't a man she hadn't known among the reeds by the river, cried out the next day to Camila,

"Hey, you. What's all this? What're you doing in the corner with a *rebozo* tied round your head? Huh? Crying! Look at those eyes! You look like a hag! Come now, don't take on so. No sorrow that afflicts the soul lasts more'n three days."

Agapita, frowning, muttered who knows what to herself.

Certainly the women felt very uneasy on account of the departure of the men. In spite of their insults and offensive chatter, the women regretted the fact that there would be no one to supply the *ranchito* with goats and calves so that they might have meat to eat every day. What a pleasure to spend one's life eating and drinking, sleeping stretched out in the shade of the rocks, while the clouds form in the sky and then dissolve!

"Look at them again! There they go," cried María Antonia, "they look like toys lined up on a corner shelf!"

In the distance where the broken rocks and chaparral fused into a smooth, velvety blue line, the silhouettes of Macías' men riding their thin nags along the edge of a cliff showed up sharply against the clear, sapphire sky. A gust of the hot air brought to the huts vague and broken sounds of "*La Adelita.*"

Camila, who had come out at María Antonia's call to see them for the last time, could not control herself and turned back choking with sobs. María Antonia laughed heartily and went on off.

"They've cast the evil eye on my daughter," said the perplexed Agapita. She considered the matter for some time, and when she had thought it over, she came to a decision: from a peg nailed to a pole in the hut, between the pictures of Christ and of the Virgin of Jalpa, she took down a crude leather thong which her husband used in yoking the oxen, and doubling it, she administered a sound thrashing to Camila to drive out all the evil.

Riding his chestnut horse, Demetrio felt rejuvenated. His eyes recovered their peculiar metallic brilliance. The hot, red blood in his coppery cheeks that revealed his purely indigenous origin pulsed with renewed force.

All the men expanded their chests to breathe in the fresh air scented with the aroma of the sierras in response to the effect of the distant horizons, the immensity of the sky, and the blue of the mountains. They made their horses gallop as though in that unrestrained speed they pretended that all the earth was theirs. Who among them now remembered the stern commandant of police, the cranky policeman, the proud *cacique*? Who thought of the miserable hut where he lived like a slave, always under the vigilant supervision of the master or the bad-humored and mean-tempered foreman, or of the hard necessity of getting up before dawn to go to work with shovel and basket

or plow and bamboo poles in order to earn the daily bowl of porridge
and plate of frijoles?

Drunk with the sun, the air, with life, they sang, laughed, and
shouted. Meco, prancing along, joked and clowned, his white teeth
gleaming.

"Listen, Pancracio," he remarked solemnly, "in a letter from my
wife she told me I'd got another son. How's that? I've not seen her
since Madero's time!"

"That's no matter. You left her with eggs to hatch."

All laughed uproariously. Only Meco very gravely and indifferently sang in a horrible falsetto:

> I gave her a penny
> She refused that amount
> I gave her half
> She said, "That doesn't count."
> She kept on begging me for more—
> until she got two bits from me.
> Ay! how ungrateful women are.

The merriment ceased when the heat of the sun stupefied them.
All day they journeyed through the canyon, up and down rounded hills
in endless succession, as bold and dirty as so many scabby heads. As
the afternoon wore on, several small stone towers far away in the midst
of a series of hills came in sight; then a highway with spirals of dust
rising up from it and gray telegraph poles along it.

They went on toward the main highway where in the distance
they made out the figure of a man squatting down by the side of the
road. They drew near him. He was an ill-featured old man, dressed
in rags, laboriously mending his *huarache* with a dull knife. A burro
loaded with hay grazed nearby.

Demetrio asked him,

"What are you doing here, grandpa?"

"I'm on my way to the village with alfalfa for my cow."

"How many Federals around here?"

"Yes, there're some; maybe no more'n a dozen."

The old man's tongue loosened up. He said that there were many
rumors of important happenings: that Obregón was beseiging Guadalajara; Carrera Torres was the master of San Luis Potosí and Pánfilo
Natera of Fresnillo.

"Good," said Demetrio, "you can go on to your village; but take care you don't say a word about what you've seen, or I'll shoot you dead. I'd get you even if I had to look for you in the middle of the earth."

"What d'you say, boys," asked Demetrio as the old man went off.

"Let's get at 'em! Don't leave a single *mocho* alive!" they all yelled as one.

They counted their cartridges and the hand grenades that Tecolote had made out of fragments of iron pipe and brass knobs.

"Not many," observed Anastasio, "but we're going to trade them for carbines."

Anxiously they hurried forward, driving their spurs into the thin flanks of their exhausted mounts. Halted by Demetrio's commanding voice, they camped on the slope of a hill where a dense thicket of huisache protected them. Without unsaddling the horses, each man sought a stone for a head rest.

XVI

At midnight Demetrio Macías gave the order to march with the intention of making a surprise attack at dawn on the Federals in the town which was one or two leagues away. In the cloudy sky, stars shone here and there. From time to time reddish flashes of lightning vividly illuminated the distant horizon.

Luis Cervantes asked Demetrio if the attack would not be more likely to succeed if they had a guide or at least obtained information about the topography of the town and the precise location of the barracks.

"No, *curro*," Demetrio responded with a smile and a scornful gesture, "we're going to fall on them when they least expect it, and that's that. We've done it this away many times. Did you ever see how squirrels stick out their heads when you fill their holes with water? That's just how stunned these unhappy *mochos* will be as soon as they hear the first shots. No more'n they come out than they'll be targets for us."

"And what if the old man we talked to yesterday lied to us? Suppose instead of twenty men, there prove to be fifty? What if he was a spy posted by the Federals?"

"This *curro's* afraid!" said Anastasio Montañés.

"Handling a rifle's hardly the same as putting on bandages and giving enemas!" observed Pancracio.

"Hmm!" observed Meco. "You chatter too much. Nothing to a dozen scared rats."

"It won't be long now before our mothers know whether they bore real men or whatever," added Manteca.

When they arrived at the outskirts of the town, Venancio rode forward and knocked at the door of a hut.

"Where're the barracks?" he asked the man who came out, barefooted and wearing a ragged poncho covering his bare chest.

"A little beyond the plaza, master," he replied.

As no one knew exactly where that was, Venancio forced him to go along at the head of the column and show them the way. Trembling with fear, the poor devil exclaimed that what they were doing to him was barbarous.

"I'm a poor day-laborer, mister. I've got a wife and a bunch of little ones."

"D'you think the ones I got are dogs?" replied Demetrio.

Then he ordered,

"Be very quiet. Go single file in the loose dirt in the middle of the street."

Looming up before them was the broad, rectangular cupola of the church which dominated the settlement about it.

"Look, sirs, the plaza's in front of the church; go only a little further on, then right there are the barracks."

Then he knelt down, begging them to let him return; but Pancracio, without replying, struck him across the chest with his rifle and made him go on.

"How many soldiers are there?" inquired Luis Cervantes.

"Master, I wouldn't lie. Fact is, the real fact, there's a whole bunch."

Luis Cervantes turned toward Demetrio who pretended he did not hear. Soon they entered a small plaza. A thunderous discharge of rifles deafened them. Demetrio's chestnut horse staggered, reared up, then its legs gave way and it fell down, kicking. Tecolote gave a piercing cry and tumbled off his horse which dashed off toward the center of the plaza.

Another volley, and the man who guided them threw up his arms and fell on his back without uttering a sound. Anastasio Montañés quickly raised Demetrio up to the rump of his horse. The rest had drawn back and were seeking protection behind the walls of the houses.

"Listen, men," said a townsman, poking his head out of a big door, "take yourselves around back of the chapel; they're all there. Turn back along this same street, turn to the left, then you'll come to a little alley, and go again straight so's to get right up to the back of the chapel."

Just at that moment a heavy rain of pistol fire from the nearby roofs began to fall on them.

"Huh!" said the man, "those aren't spiders that bite! They're city fellers. Get yourselves in here until they go away. They're scared of their own shadows."

"How many mochos are they?" asked Demetrio.

"There weren't more'n a dozen; but they got plenty scared last night and sent a telegram to those a little distance ahead. Who knows how many they might be now? No matter if there're a lot of them. Most are conscripts, ready to turn tail and leave the commanders a-lone. They conscripted my brother and brought him here. I'll go with you, give him a signal and you'll see how they'll all come over to our side. Then we'll finish off just the officers. If the gentlemen would just give me a little weapon."

"No more rifles, brother; but here's something you can use," said Anastasio Montañés giving the man two hand grenades.

The commanding officer of the Federals was a very conceited young man with fair hair and waxed mustache. As long as he was unsure about the number of his assailants, he had remained extremely prudent and quiet; but now that they had been thrown back so successfully that they had not even had time to return a shot, he boasted of his valor and unprecedented boldness. When the soldiers scarcely dared stick their heads up from behind the battlements of the portico, he conspicuously exhibited in the clear pale light of the dawn his slender silhouette wrapped in a flowing cape which billowed out in the breeze from time to time.

"Ah, I remember our insurrection!"

As his military career consisted of only one adventure which he had experienced as a student in the Military School when the treason against President Madero took place, he always brought up the subject of the feat at the Ciudadela[4] when a propitious occasion arose.

"Lt. Campos," he ordered emphatically, "go down there with ten men to wipe out those bandits who are hiding. Rabble! They are brave only at eating meat and stealing chickens."

A countryman appeared in the small doorway leading to the spiral stairs. He brought the news that the assailants were in the corral where it would be easy to seize them quickly. Prominent townsmen, stationed on the roof tops and ready to keep the enemy from escaping, sent the news.

"I will go myself to finish them off," the officer said impetuously. Quickly he changed his mind and turned back from that same stairway door.

"It is possible that they expect reinforcements, and it will not be prudent for me to forsake my post. Lt. Campos, you go and seize them all alive so that they can be shot today at noon, at the hour when the people are coming out after the principal Mass. Then those bandits will see what kind of an example we set! If that isn't possible, Lt. Campos, finish them off. Don't leave one of them alive. You understand me?"

Satisfied, he began to pace back and forth, meditating on the wording of the official report which he would make. "His Excellency, the Minister of War, General Aureliano Blanquet. —Mexico. —I have the honor, my General, of making known to you that in the early hours of the day a party of five hundred men under the command of the ringleader H————— launched an attack on this town. With the vigor that the situation demanded, I fortified myself on the highest spot of the town. The attack commenced at dawn; heavy firing lasted for more than two hours. In spite of the numerical superiority of the enemy, I succeeded in punishing them severely, inflicting a complete defeat. They suffered twenty killed and more than that wounded, judging from the bloody footprints they left in their precipitous flight. In our ranks we had the good fortune of not having a single one fallen. —I have the honor of congratulating you, Mr. Minister, upon the victory of the Government's forces. ¡*Viva* General Victoriano Huerta! ¡*Viva* Mexico!"

"And then," his thoughts ran on, "my promotion to the rank of major is certain."

And he clasped his hands with pleasure just at the moment a burst of gunfire left his ears buzzing.

XVII

"So if we go through this corral, we ought to come out right at the alley?" asked Demetrio.

"Yes, only beyond the corral there's a house, then another corral, and a store on beyond," responded the native.

Demetrio thoughtfully scratched his head but made his decision quickly.

"Can you get hold of a big iron bar, a pick, something like that so we can make a hole in the wall?"

"Sure, there's everything here—but—"

"But what? Where are they?"

"It's all here among the supplies, but all those things belong to the boss, and—"

Demetrio without listening any further, started toward the room which the man had pointed out as the tool shed.

It all happened in a few minutes. As soon as they were in the alley they ran in single file close to the walls to get back of the church. They first had to climb over a massive mud fence, then the rear wall of the chapel.

"God's with us," thought Demetrio, the first to scale the fence.

Like monkeys, one following the other, they reached the top with their hands covered with dirt and blood. The rest was easier; steps hollowed out in the masonry permitted them readily to clear the chapel wall; then the cupola itself which hid them from the soldiers' sight.

"Wait a bit," said the townsman, "I want to go see where my brother is. I'll signal you, then it'll be all over with the top dogs, how about it?" Only no one at that moment paid any attention to him.

For a moment Demetrio contemplated the capes which appeared darkly in the distance along the length of the parapet; at the towers packed with people behind the iron railings. He smiled with satisfaction. Turning toward his men, he called out,

"Now!"

Twenty bombs exploded at one time in the midst of the Federals who started up with their eyes staring with fright. But before they could exactly figure out the dangerous situation, another twenty bombs burst with a crash, leaving dead and wounded strewn about.

"Not yet—not yet—I haven't seen my brother yet," the villager implored with anguish.

In vain an old sergeant harangued and cursed the soldiers with the hope of rallying them to save the situation. They were dashing about like rats in a trap. Some, attempting to get through the little door to the spiral staircase, fell pierced by Demetrio's shots; others threw themselves at the feet of that score of specters with heads and chests dark as iron, clad in long, ragged white pants that hung down to their *huaraches*. In the belfry some struggled to get out from among the dead who had fallen on them.

"My chief," exclaimed Luis Cervantes in great alarm, "we've used all the bombs and the rifles are in the corral! What a blunder!"

Demetrio smiled, drew out a dagger with a long, shining blade. Immediately steel blades flashed in the hands of his twenty soldiers; some long and pointed, others broad as the palm of one's hand, and others as heavy as a machete.

"The spy," cried Luis Cervantes with the sound of triumph. "Didn't I tell you!"

"Don't kill me, master!" implored the old sergeant at the feet of Demetrio who had his knife raised high. The old man raised his head with hair unmarked with gray, revealing the wrinkled face of a man of the indigenous race. Demetrio recognized the one who had deceived them the evening before. In a gesture of terror Luis Cervantes suddenly averted his head. The blade of steel encountered ribs with a snapping sound, and the old man fell on his back with his arms flung wide and his eyes open in a dreadful stare.

"My brother, no! Don't kill him, he's my brother!" cried the old villager crazy with terror as he saw Pancracio hurling himself at a Federal.

It was too late, Pancracio with one blow had sliced through his neck and two streams of scarlet spurted forth as from a fountain.

"Kill the Federals! Death to the *mochos!*"

Pancracio and Manteca were foremost in the carnage, even finishing off the wounded. Worn out, Montañés let his hand fall. The soft look of his face persisted; the ingeniousness of a child and the amorality of a jackal shone on his countenance.

"Here's one still alive," cried Cordoniz.

Pancracio ran toward him. It was the blond captain with the Burgundy-styled mustache who was white as wax. He had sought shelter in a corner near the spiral stairway where he had remained for lack of strength to go down.

Pancracio shoved him to the edge of the parapet. A shove of the knee against his buttocks, and over he went, somewhat like a sack of stones, falling from a height of more than sixty feet upon the courtyard of the church.

"What a dope you are!" exclaimed Cordoniz. "If I'd suspected what you were going to do, I wouldn't have told you. Such good shoes he had that I was going to get!"

The men, now stooping over, devoted themselves to stripping those who wore the best clothes. They dressed themselves in their spoils, laughing and joking in their enjoyment.

Demetrio, brushing aside the heavy locks of hair that had fallen over his sweaty forehead, covering his eyes, said,

"Now, get those city slickers!"

XVIII

Demetrio arrived at Fresnillo with a hundred men the same day Pánfilo Natera initiated the attack of his forces upon Zacatecas. The Zacatecan chief received him cordially.

"I know who you are and what excellent men you bring. I have had news about the hiding you have given the Federals from Tepic to Durango!"

Natera shook hands with Macías effusively, while Luis Cervantes began to declaim,

"With men like my General Natera and my Colonel Macías, our country well be covered with glory."

Demetrio understood Cervantes' intention when he heard "my colonel" repeated several times to Natera.

Wine and beer flowed freely. Demetrio drank many glasses with Natera. Luis Cervantes proposed a toast "to the victory of our cause which will be the triumph of Justice; because soon we may see realized the redemption of our suffering and noble people. May the very men who have watered the earth with their blood be those who reap the fruit that is legitimately theirs."

Natera briefly turned his stern face toward the speaker; then with his back to him, he began to talk to Demetrio.

One of Natera's officers, with his gaze fixed intently on Luis Cervantes, had drawn near him little by little. He was a young man with a candid air and open countenance.

"Luis Cervantes?"

"Solís?"

"Ever since you entered, I have thought that I recognized you. And would you believe it, now that I see you, it still seems that· it can hardly be the case!"

"And isn't it—?"

"And so? Let's go have a drink, come on."

"Ho!" continued Solís offering Luis Cervantes a seat. "Since when have you turned revolutionary?"

"Two months ago."

"Ah! That explains your still speaking with that enthusiasm and that faith which we all started out with."

"You've lost all yours?"

"Look here, friend, don't be astonished at these sudden confidences. I long to talk to someone around here with common interests so that when I run into such a fellow, I seize him with the same eagerness with which I would a jar of cold water after walking with parched throat hour after hour under the burning sun. But, frankly, I need above all to have you explain to me—I don't understand how one who was the correspondent of *El País*[5] during Madero's time, one who wrote heated articles in *El Regional*,[6] one who so freely designated us bandits now is fighting in our ranks."

"Truth is truth. They have convinced me!" replied Cervantes emphatically.

"Convinced?"

Solís let a sigh escape; he filled the glasses and they drank.

"Have you, then, become tired of the revolution?" asked Luis Cervantes in a reserved manner.

"Tired? I am twenty-five years old and, as you see, in abundant good health. Disillusioned? Could be."

"You must have your reasons."

" 'I dreamed of a flowery meadow at the end of the road; I found a swamp.' My friend, there are deeds and there are men which are nothing but pure bitterness. And that bitterness falls drop by drop on the soul; it embitters everything; it poisons everything. Enthusiasm, hopes, ideals, happiness—nothing! Soon nothing remains: either you turn into a bandit like the rest, or you withdraw, hiding yourself behind the walls of an impenetrable and ferocious selfishness."

The conversation disturbed Luis Cervantes; the remarks seemed to him to be unsuitable to time and place. In order to avoid taking an active part in the conversation, he requested Solís to give a circumstantial account of the events that had brought him to such a state of disenchantment.

"Events? Insignificant matters, things of no moment which went unnoticed by most people; a fleeting expression, flashing eyes, lips pressed together; the fugitive meaning of a casual remark. But events, gestures, and expressions, grouped in their logical and natural expression make up the frightful and grotesque mask of a race—of an unredeemed race."

He drained another glass of wine, then continued after a long pause.

"You will ask me why I stay on in the revolution. The revolution is a hurricane. The man who is swept up in it is no longer a man; he is a wretched dry leaf snatched away by the gale."

The presence of Demetrio Macías who appeared just then interrupted Solís.

"Let's go, *curro*."

Alberto Solís, expressing himself fluently and with accents of profound sincerity, congratulated him effusively for his military deeds, for his adventures which had made him so famous that he was known even by the men of the powerful Northern Division themselves. Demetrio, delighted, listened to the tale of his deeds, composed and embellished in such fashion that he himself did not recognize them. All that sounded so pleasant in his ears, furthermore, that he ended up telling them later in the same manner so that he even came to believe that it had happened that way.

"What an agreeable and admirable person General Natera is!" observed Luis Cervantes when they had returned to the inn. "On the other hand, that insignificant Captain Solís; what an annoyance he is!"

Demetrio Macías, in good humor, paid no attention to what he said but seized his arm and whispered to him,

"Now I'm a real colonel. And you, you're my secretary."

Macías' men made many new friends that night, and "for the pleasure of having known them," drank quantities of mescal and *aguardiente.* As not everybody is always congenial and at times alcohol is a bad counselor, naturally there were disputes; but everything was settled in a friendly manner outside the cantina, the inn, or the brothel, without bothering their new friends.

On the following morning some were dead: an old prostitute with a bullet in her stomach and two of Colonel Macías' recruits with their skulls broken.

Anastasio Montañés gave an account of it to his chief, and he shrugged his shoulders, saying,

"Psch! Might as well as bury them."

XIX

"The 'tall-hats' are coming," shouted the people of Fresnillo uneasily when they learned that the revolutionary assault on Zacatecas had failed.

The reckless mob of men returned, sunburned, filthy and almost naked, heads covered with straw sombreros with high, conical crowns and immense brims which half hid their faces.

Those whom they called "tall-hats" returned as happily as they had marched out a few days before the fight, sacking each town, each hacienda, each village, and even the most miserable hut they encountered on their way.

"Who'll buy this machine from me?" asked one, overheated and fatigued from carrying his loot.

It was a new typewriter which fascinated all of them with the dazzling gleam of the nickel trimming. In the course of only one morning, the Oliver had had five owners. Its price had begun at ten *pesos* and had depreciated by one or two *pesos* with each change of hands. As a matter of fact it was excessively heavy and no one could carry it more than half an hour.

"I'll give you a *peseta* for it," offered Cordoniz.

"It's yours," responded the owner, giving it to him promptly, evidently fearful that he would change his mind.

For twenty-five *centavos* Cordoniz had the pleasure of taking it in his hands and then dashing it against the stones where it broke up with a great clatter.

It was like a signal: all of those who carried heavy burdensome objects began to get rid of them, dashing them against the rocks. Pieces of crystal and porcelain, heavy mirrors, brass candelabra, fine statuettes, china jars, and all the accumulation of the looting during the expedition flew through the air and then lay in fragments by the road.

Demetrio, who took no part in that outbreak of high spirits, oblivious of all except the outcome of the military operation, called Montañés and Pancracio apart and said to them,

"They've got no guts. It's not such a big job to take a town. Look, first you spread out like this, then you turn in close together— closer together—until, wow! That's all there is to it."

He opened his powerful, sinewy arms in a sweeping gesture; then he brought them together little by little, accompanying his words with his gesture until his arms hugged his chest.

Anastasio and Pancracio found his explanation so simple and clear that they replied, convinced,

"That's true's you're born. They've got no guts."

Demetrio's following camped in a corral.

"Do you remember Camila, *compadre* Anastasio?" said Demetrio, sighing as he threw himself flat on his back on the manure where all had bedded down, yawning sleepily.

"Who is that Camila."

"The one who fixed my food there back at the *ranchito*."

Anastasio made a gesture as if to say: "All this business about women doesn't interest me."

"I can't forget her," continued Demetrio, a cigarette in his mouth. "I was feeling awful when I got there. I had just finished drinking a jar of very fresh water. 'Don't you want some more?' the little dark girl asked me. Well, because I was worn out by the fever, I kept on seeing a jar of fresh water and hearing her sweet voice saying, 'Don't you want some more?' It was a voice which sounded in my ears like a little silver organ. Pancracio, what d'you say? How about going to the village?"

"Look here, *compadre* Demetrio, you believe me don't you? I've had a lot of experience on that score. Women! Just for a little while! But what a time it is! How they have scarred and scratched my hide! Bad luck to them! They're bad enemies. That's so, *compadre*, don't you believe me? That's why you'll see that— But I've had a lot of experience along that line."

"What day can we go to the *ranchito*, Pancracio?" insisted Demetrio, blowing gray smoke rings in the air.

"Just say when. You know I left my sweetheart there."

"Yours, and not—" said the drowsy Cordoniz.

"Yours, and mine, too. Sure, it's a good thing that you're so kind and will go to bring her to us," murmured Manteca.

"Man, you bet, Pancracio; bring one-eyed María Antonia, for it gets plenty cold here," cried Meco from a distance.

Many of them burst into roars of laughter while Manteca and Pancracio began a contest in shouting insults and obscenities.

XX

"Villa's coming!"

The news spread with the speed of lightning.

Ah, Villa, the magic word! The great man, the idol; the invincible warrior who even from a distance exercises the fascination of a boa constrictor.

"Our Mexican Napoleon!" exclaimed Luis Cervantes.

"Yes, 'the Aztec eagle, who has thrust his steel beak in the head of the viper Victoriano Huerta!' So I said in a speech in Ciudad Juárez," said Alberto Solís, Natera's staff officer, in a somewhat ironic tone.

Seated at the bar of a cantina, each drained a glass of beer.

And the "tall-hats," wearing bandanas about their necks and heavy leather shoes on their feet and with the calloused hands of the cowboy, were eating and drinking endlessly, talking only of Villa and his troops. Natera's men made Macías' followers gape with admiration.

Ah, Villa! The battles of Juárez, Tierra Blanca, Chihuahua, Torreón! Clear and vivid experience was not enough. It was necessary to hear the story of his extraordinary prowess with a deed of brutal cruelty following an instance of surprising magnanimity. Villa was the indomitable master of the sierra, the eternal victim of all governments who pursued him as though he were a wild beast. Villa was the reincarnation of the old legend: the bandit-benefactor who goes through the world with the lighted torch of an ideal: rob the rich to enrich the poor! And the poor created a legend which time embellished so that it lived from generation to generation.

"But I know what I'm talking about, Montañés," said one of Natera's men, "that if Villa takes a shine to you, he'll give you an hacienda; but if you rub him the wrong way, you get shot!"

Ah, Villa's troops! All men of the North, well dressed, who wear Texas hats, new khaki uniforms and shoes from the United States that cost four dollars a pair.

While Natera's men talked in this manner, they looked at each other disconsolately, fully aware of their own straw hats rotted by sun and dampness and of their ragged pants and shirts which barely covered their dirty, lousy bodies.

"They don't go hungry there. Their box cars are packed full with loads of oxen, sheep, cows. Freight cars full of clothes, entire train loads of ammunition and guns; and enough food to fill everybody's stomach."

Directly they began talking about Villa's airplanes.

"Airplanes! On the ground, close up, you don't know what they are. Look like canoes, like *chalupas*. But, when they begin to go up, wow, it makes such a noise it deafens you. It's something like an auto going real fast. It makes you think of a big bird, very big, that suddenly doesn't even seem to flap its wings. Now here's the best part: inside this bird, a gringo's got thousands of grenades. Think what that means! Then comes the time to fight; and, like someone scattering corn to chickens, there goes one fistful of lead after the other on the enemy. And that place turns into a cemetery; dead ones here, dead ones there, dead everywhere!"

When Anastasio Montañés asked the speaker whether Natera's men had fought with Villa's it turned out that all he had recounted with such enthusiasm was only hearsay since none of them had ever set eyes on Villa.

"Hmm, it seems to me that one man's pretty much like another! It's my notion that one is just about as much of a man as another. To fight, all you got to have is a little bit of self-pride. Me, well I wasn't meant to be a soldier or anything else for that matter! But, listen, even if you see me so ragged— You don't believe me? But, for sure, I don't have to—"

"I got my ten yokes of oxen! Don't you believe that?" said Cordoniz at Anastasio's back, mocking him and laughing uproariously.

XXI

The din of firing diminished and seemed farther away. Luis Cervantes screwed up his courage enough to stick his head out of his hiding place in the middle of the ruins of some fortifications on the highest part of the hill.

It was difficult to figure out how he had got up there. He did not know when Demetrio and his men had disappeared from beside him. Suddenly he found himself alone. Then an avalanche of infantry overwhelmed him, knocked him from his horse, and trampled over him. When he managed to get up again, someone on horseback pulled him up on the horse's rump. But in a few moments the horse and the two men on it fell to the ground. Without knowing what happened to his rifle or his revolver or anything, he found himself in the middle of a white cloud of smoke with bullets whistling about him. That hole and that pile of adobe ruins had offered him a safe shelter.

"Solís!"

"Cervantes!"

"The horse threw me; they fell on top of me; they thought I was dead and stripped me of my weapons. What could I do?" Luis Cervantes said ashamedly.

"Nobody threw me off. I'm here out of simple precaution. Understand?"

Alberto Solís' light hearted tone made Luis Cervantes blush.

"¡Caramba!" Solís exclaimed. "What a man your chief is! What daring and what assurance. He not only amazed me, but he left many much more experienced with their big mouths hanging open."

Luis Cervantes, confused, did not know what to say.

"Hah! You weren't there? Bravo! You looked for a secure place at the right time. Look, my friend, let me give you an account of it all. Let's go over there back of that big rock. Notice that from that little slope at the foot of the hill there isn't any way up here except the one in front of us? At the right it's so steep that

any maneuver on that side is impossible; the left side's even worse
—the ascent is so dangerous that to take a false step is to tumble
down and be dashed into pieces on the sharp edges of the rocks.
Good; we, one part of Moya's brigade, were stretched out flat on
our stomachs on the slope, our breasts to the earth, intending to advance on the Federals' first trench. Bullets buzzed over our heads;
the fighting became general; there was a moment when they quit
firing at us. We supposed that they were being attacked vigorously
in the rear. Then we hurled ourselves in the trench! Brother,
imagine! Half the slope below became a veritable tapestry of corpses.
The machine guns did it all; they literally mowed us down; only a
few were able to escape. The generals were white as sheets and
hesitated to order a new charge with the reinforcements which had
joined us. That's when Demetrio Macías, without waiting or asking
for orders from anybody, shouted,

" 'Let's go, boys!'

" 'That's crazy!' I cried in amazement.

"The officers, surprised, said not a word. Macías' horse sped
over the rocks as though it had the claws of an eagle instead of hooves.
'Let's go! Let's go!' cried his men following him over the rocks
like deer, each man and his horse moving as one. Only one fellow
lost his step and rolled into the abyss. In a few brief moments
the others appeared at the crest, storming the trenches and knifing
the soldiers. Demetrio lassoed the machine guns, pulling them out
as if they were brave bulls. That couldn't last long. Their numerical
superiority would have made it possible for them to annihilate
Demetrio's men in less time than it took for them to get there. But
we took advantage of their momentary confusion and with dizzying
rapidity, threw ourselves on their positions and cleared them out
easily. What a wonderful soldier your chief is!"

Visible from the height of the hill was one side of La Bufa with
its crest like the haughty feathered head of an Aztec king. Dead men,
their hair matted, their clothes and the earth splotched with blood,
covered the slope for a thousand feet. Like ravenous coyotes, ragged
women moved about among the still-warm bodies, looking for spoils.

In the midst of the white cloud of smoke from the firing and
the black puffs from the burning building, massive doors and many
windows, all closed, reflected the bright sunlight. A confusion of

streets, twisting and turning through the picturesque rocky region, climbed the surrounding hills. Above the pleasant cluster of buildings rose the many arches of the slender columns of farmhouses and the towers and cupolas of the churches.

"How beautiful is the Revolution, even in its very barbarity," said Solís with emotion. Then in a low voice and with a vague melancholy, he said,

"What a pity that what remains to be done is not equally beautiful. It is necessary to wait a while. Until there are no more men fighting, until there is no longer the sound of shooting except from the mob engaged in the congenial task of looting; until the psychology of our race glitters transparently like a drop of water, condensed in two words: rob, kill! What a mockery, my friend, if we who come to offer our whole enthusiasm, our very lives to crush one miserable assassin turn out to be the builders of an enormous pedestal on which a hundred or two hundred thousand monsters of the same species may be raised up! People without ideals, all tyrants! Blood shed in vain!"

Many Federals fled up the hill away from the soldiers wearing big straw hats and wide white pants. A bullet whistled by. Alberto Solís, who, with his arms crossed, had remained absorbed after his last words, quickly jumped back and said,

"Friend, damned if I like the way these buzzing mosquitoes get after me! Do you want to move a little farther away from here?"

Luis Cervantes' smile was so scornful that Solís, annoyed, sat down quietly on a rock. Smiling again, his attention followed the spirals of smoke from the rifles and the dust from each house as it was destroyed and from each roof as it fell in. He believed he had discovered a symbol of the revolution in those clouds of smoke and those clouds of dust which in brotherly fashion rose arm in arm, intermingled, then faded away.

"Ah," he exclaimed suddenly, "right now!"

His outstretched hand pointed toward the railroad station. Trains puffed furiously, sending up dense columns of smoke, their coaches crowded with people who were escaping as quickly as possible. He felt a sharp little blow in the stomach. As if his legs had turned to cloth, he slid from the rock. Then his ears buzzed. Afterwards, darkness and eternal silence.

Part II

I

Demetrio Macías preferred the clear tequila of Jalisco to champagne in which bubbles boiled up and burst, refracting the light from the lamps. Men filthy with dirt, smoke, and sweat were grouped around the tables of a restaurant. They were a rough-looking lot, covered in dirty rags, with tousled hair and curly beards.

"I killed two colonels," exclaimed one in a gutteral, harsh voice. He was a short, fat fellow wearing a decorated sombrero, a chamois skin jacket, and around his neck, a purple silk handkerchief. "Their bellies were so big they couldn't run, they stumbled over the rocks and when they tried to climb the hill, they got as red as tomatoes, and their swollen tongues hung out. 'Don't run so hard, *mochitos*,' I yelled at 'em. 'Stop, I don't like scared chickens. Stop, Federal wretches, I'm not going to do anything to you. You've lost!' Ha! Ha! Ha! They fell for it! One for each of them—then they could rest sure enough."

"One of the big brass got away from me," said a very dark-faced soldier who sat in a corner of the saloon between the wall and the bar with his rifle between his stretched out legs. "How much gold braid that damn rascal wore! And what a sight all that gold braid on the epaullettes and the cape was! And me? Like a donkey I let him get away. He took out his handkerchief and gave me the countersign, and I just stayed there with my mouth open. But hardly had I lit out to get around the corner when there was shot after shot! I got away just as he finished a round of ammunition. Now it's my turn! Holy Mother of Jalpa, don't let me miss this son of—a bad word! He escaped! He had a dandy horse! He passed by my eyes like a streak of lightning. Another poor devil who came up the same street got it instead of him. What a flip he turned!"

While words flew and they referred enthusiastically to their adventures, olive-skinned women with bright eyes and teeth like ivory, wearing revolvers at their waists, cartridge belts crossed over their breasts, and great huge straw sombreros on their heads, came and went among the groups like stray dogs.

One girl with rouged cheeks, dark brown neck and arms, and a coarse appearance, in one jump landed on the cantina bar near Demetrio's table. He turned his head toward her, meeting a glance from lascivious eyes under a small forehead between two hanks of coarse hair.

The door opened wide. In came Anastasio Montañés, Pancracio, Cordoniz, and Meco, one after the other, open-mouthed and dazzled. Anastasio gave a cry of surprise and went over to greet the small, fat *charro* wearing the decorated sombrero and purple silk handkerchief. They were old friends who now recognized each other and embraced with such vigor that their faces turned dark.

"*Compadre* Demetrio, I have the pleasure of presenting to you my friend Margarito. An honest-to-goodness friend! How I do like this feller! You'll agree when you get to know him. He's a real he-man! Remember, the Escobedo penitentiary, there in Jalisco? A year together!"

Demetrio, who had remained silent and withdrawn in the middle of the general uproar, murmured without taking the cigar from his lips as he extended his hand,

"Glad to meet you."

"So you're Demetrio Macías?" broke in the girl seated on the bar swinging her legs and touching Demetrio's shoulder with her kidskin shoes.

"Yes, I am," he answered her, scarcely turning his face.

Indifferently she continued to swing her uncovered legs, ostentatiously revealing her blue silk stockings.

"Hi, Pintada, you here? Come, get down and have a drink," the blond Margarito said to her.

With ready acceptance, she boldly made a place for herself opposite Demetrio.

"So you're the famous Demetrio who made such a big name for himself at Zacatecas?" asked Pintada.

Demetrio nodded his head in assent, at which the blond Margarito burst out laughing and said,

"What a devilishly clever girl you are, Pintada! Now you want to take on a general!"

Without comprehending the situation, Demetrio turned toward her. They looked at each other face to face like two strange dogs sniffing at each other with distrust. Unable to meet her intensely provocative gaze, Demetrio lowered his eyes.

From their places, Natera's men began to make obscene jokes at Pintada's expense. Without taking the slightest notice, she said,

"General Natera is going to give you your little eagle. Come on, let's shake on that!"

Stretching out her hand to seize Demetrio's she shook it with the strength of a man.

Demetrio, filled with pride by the congratulations which rained upon him, ordered that champagne be served.

"No, I don't want any wine now. I feel punk," said the blond Margarito to the waiter, "just bring me some ice water."

"I want something to eat; just anything you got except *chile* or frijoles," said Pancracio.

Officers kept coming in and little by little the restaurant filled up. Stars and bars appeared repetitiously on sombreros of every form and shape. The men wore great silk bandanas around their necks, rings set with showy diamonds on their fingers, and heavy gold chains across their chests.

"Listen, waiter," cried the blond Margarito, "I asked you for some ice water. Understand I'm not asking for a hand-out. See this bundle of bills: I can buy you and—your mother as well, you understand? It makes me no difference if there's none nor why there isn't. You'll have to figure out where to get it for me. Look here, I'm very ill-tempered! I tell you, I don't want any excuses, I want ice water. Are you going to bring it or not? No? Then take this—"

He knocked the waiter down with a resounding blow.

"That's the sort I am, General Macías, You see there's no beard on my chin. Do you know why? Because I'm so hot-headed that when I don't have somebody to take it out on, I pull out the hairs to relieve my anger. My word of honor, general, if I hadn't done it, I'd died of fury."

"It's bad to let your anger eat you up," seriously affirmed one of the men wearing a straw sombrero like the roof of a hut. "When I was in Torreón, I killed an old woman who didn't want to sell me a plate of enchiladas. There was a fight. I didn't get what I wanted, but anyhow I was satisfied."

"I killed a storekeeper in Parral because there were two Huerta bills in the change he gave me," said one who wore a star on his hat and flashing jewels on his calloused black fingers.

"I killed a fellow in Chihuahua because I met up with him always at the same table at the same hour when I went to get lunch. He rubbed me the wrong way. Well, what d'you think happened?"

"Huh, I killed—"

The theme was inexhaustible.

By early morning, when the restaurant was full of merriment and the floor foul with spit, when heavily made-up young women from the suburbs of the city mingled freely with the ashy-faced dark women of the North, Demetrio took out his gold repeating watch, heavily encrusted with jewels, and asked Anastasio Montañés the time.

Anastasio glanced at the face of the watch, then stuck his head out the window, and, looking at the starry sky, said,

"The Pleiades are still hanging in the sky, *compadre;* it'll soon be daybreak."

Outside the restaurant the cries, the shouts of laughter, and the songs of drunken men did not let up. Soldiers passed by at break-neck speed fooling around. In every part of the city sounded rifle and pistol shots. Arm in arm, Demetrio and Pintada staggered down the middle of the road toward the hotel.

II

"What idiots you are!" exclaimed Pintada shouting with laughter. "Where on earth did you come from? It's not the style for soldiers to stay at hotels any more. Where do you come from? When somebody comes to some place, all he's got to do is pick out any house he wants and take it without asking. Who's the revolution for? For city folks? Now we are going to be real city folks. Look, Pancracio, lend me your machete. Rich people—those! They've got to lock everything up with seven keys."

She sank the steel point into the crack of a drawer, and, pressing down on the hilt, broke the lock and raised the splintered top of the desk. Anastasio Montañés, Pancracio, and Pintada sank their hands in the piles of letters, religious pictures, photographs, and papers which they scattered over the rug. When he found nothing he wanted, Pancracio vented his anger by kicking into the air with the point of his *huarache* a framed picture which broke against the candelabra in the center of the room. Cursing, they withdrew their hands empty from searching among the papers.

The indefatigable Pintada continued taking locks off one drawer after the other, searching every spot. She did not notice a small, gray velvet-covered box which rolled silently over the floor, coming to a stop at Luis Cervantes' feet. He, who had looked on with an air of profound indifference, drew the little box closer with the toe of his foot, and leaning over to scratch his ankle, deftly picked it up. Demetrio was stretched out on the rug apparently asleep. They were dazzling: two first-water diamonds in a filigree mounting. Quickly he hid it in his pocket.

When Demetrio awakened, Luis Cervantes said to him,

"General, look at what devilishness those fellows have been up to. Don't you think it would be a good idea to forbid them to do this sort of thing?"

"No. Poor fellows! It is the only pleasure left to them after sticking out their bellies as targets for the enemies' bullets."

"Yes, General, but they don't have to do it here. You see, this lowers our prestige; what's worse, it lowers the prestige of our cause."

Demetrio fastened his eagle eyes on Luis Cervantes. He tapped his fingernails against his teeth and said,

"Don't get so red. Look here, don't talk like that to me! We know that what is yours is yours, and what is mine is mine. You took the little box, O. K.; I took my repeater watch."

Understanding each other, the two displayed their plunder. In the meanwhile, Pintada and her companions rummaged through the rest of the house.

Cordoniz entered the living room with a twelve-year-old girl already marked with coppery splotches on her forehead and arms. Astonished, the two of them stood there speechless, staring at the piles of books on the carpet, tables, and chairs; the broken mirrors taken off the walls; huge framed prints and pictures shattered; furniture and bibelots smashed to pieces. With avid eyes, holding his breath, Cordoniz searched for booty for himself.

Outside, in an angle of the patio, Manteca cooked corn-on-the-cob in the suffocating smoke. He fed the coals with books and papers, making the fire blaze up in a lively fashion.

"Hey," Cordoniz soon shouted, "look what I found! What good sweat blankets for my mare!"

With a hard jerk he pulled down a plush curtain, rod and all, which fell across the finely carved back of a sofa.

"Look, you ——— how many naked old women!" exclaimed Cordoniz's little one, vastly amused by the engravings in a de luxe edition of the *Divine Comedy*. "This is what I want. I'm going to take it."

She commenced to tear out the engravings which most attracted her attention.

Demetrio got up and sat down by Luis Cervantes. He asked for some beer, offered a bottle to his secretary, and downed his in one draft. Then, heavy with sleep, he closed his eyes and dozed off again.

"Listen," said a man to Pancracio out in the passageway, "at what time can I talk to the general?"

"He can't talk at any time; he got up with a hangover," responded Pancracio. "What d'you want?"

"I want to buy some of those books they are burning."

"I can sell them to you myself."

"For how much?"

Pancracio, perplexed, knit his brows,

"Well, if they got pictures, five *centavos*, and the other—you can have them for *pilón* if you'll buy them all."

The prospective buyer returned for the books with a large basket.

"Demetrio, man, Demetrio, get up!" cried Pintada. "Don't sleep any longer like a fat pig. Look who's here! The blond Margarito. You don't know how much this blond soldier's worth!"

"I esteem you highly, General Macías, and I come to tell you that I bear you good will and that your ways suit me. Thus, if you don't object, I will join your brigade."

"What is your rank?" inquired Demetrio.

"Captain, sir."

"Well, then, from now on you're a major."

The blond Margarito was a chubby little fellow with waxed mustaches and malignant blue eyes which were lost between his forehead and cheeks when he smiled. The ex-waiter of Delmónico's of Chihuahua now sported three yellow brass bars, the insignia of his rank in the Northern Division.

Margarito's fulsome praise of Demetrio and his men was sufficient occasion for bringing out a case of beer which was emptied by the time one could say "Amen."

Just then Pintada appeared in the middle of the living room, displaying a splendid silk dress trimmed with rich lace.

"You've forgotten your stockings," exclaimed the blond Margarito shaking with laughter.

Cordoniz's girl also burst out laughing. Pintada paid no attention; she made a face indicating her indifference, threw herself down on the rug, kicked off the small white shoes into which she had squeezed her feet, wiggled with pleasure her freed toes which were numb from their confinement, and said,

"Hey, Pancracio, go get my blue stockings there with my loot."

The living room became filled with both new and old friends of the campaign. Demetrio, becoming animated, recounted in great detail some of his most notable deeds of arms.

"What's that noise?" asked Demetrio, surprised by the sound of string and brass instruments tuning up in the patio of the house.

"General," said Luis Cervantes solemnly, "your old friends and companions have arranged a banquet to commemorate the celebrated action at Zacatecas and your merited promotion to the rank of general."

III

"General Macías, I wish to present my future wife to you," Luis Cervantes announced impressively as he led a rarely beautiful girl into the room.

She opened her large blue eyes in wonder as they all turned to look at her. She was scarcely fourteen years old. Her skin was as fresh and soft as a rose petal and her hair blond. Much childish fear and a bit of malicious curiosity shone from her eyes. Luis Cervantes felt satisfied when he observed that Demetrio stared at her with eyes of a bird of prey. They made a place for her to sit down between the blond Margarito and Luis Cervantes just in front of Demetrio.

Numerous bottles of tequila stood among the crystal glasses, porcelain dishes, and pottery vases of flowers. Sweating and cursing, Meco came in with a case of beer on his shoulder.

"You still don't get the low-down on this here blond rascal," said Pintada, noticing that he did not take his eyes off Luis Cervantes' betrothed. "He's got a lot on the ball. I've never seen anybody in the world sharper'n he is." She cast a lewd glance at him and added,

"That's why I can't stand to look at him, even in a picture."

The orchestra broke out with a loud march of the sort played at bull fights. The soldiers were wild with merriment.

"What good tripe, General! I swear I've never tasted better stew in my life," said the blond Margarito as he began to reminisce about Delmónico's in Chihuahua.

"Do you really like it, Margarito?" asked Demetrio. "Tell them to bring you some more. Eat till you're full."

"That's what I like," confirmed Anastasio Montañés. "That's excellent. If I like a stew, I eat and eat until I belch."

The noise of gobbling of food and gulping of drinks continued. Liquor flowed freely. At the end, Luis Cervantes took a glass of champagne and rose to his feet.

"Honored General—"

"Huh," interrupted Pintada, "now they're starting speech-making and that's something that bores me plenty. There's no more to eat, so I'm going out to the corral."

Luis Cervantes accompanied his presentation of the small brass eagle resting on a black velvet medallion with a toast which no one understood but which they all applauded enthusiastically. Demetrio took the insignia of his new rank in his hands. Very flushed, his eyes flashing, his teeth shining, he said with much simplicity,

"What am I going to do with this buzzard?"

"*Compadre*," said Anastasio Montañés in a tremulous voice as he stood up, "I don't have to tell you—"

Whole minutes elapsed; Anastasio Montañés was unable to summon a single word. His dirt-encrusted face reddened; his forehead broke out in beads of sweat. Finally, he decided to finish his toast,

"Well, I don't have to tell you except that you know I'm your *compadre*."

As they all had applauded Luis Cervantes, Anastasio himself on concluding clapped his hands very gravely. Everything went along smoothly and his awkwardness served as a stimulus. Manteca and Cordoniz offered toasts.

Just as Meco's turn came, Pintada broke in shouting jubilantly. Clicking her tongue, she attempted to coax into the dining room a very beautiful jet black mare.

"My booty! My booty!" she shouted as she patted the arched neck of the superb animal.

The mare resisted entering the door, but a jerk on the rope and a lash on her haunch made her prance in briskly and noisily. The drunken soldiers observed her rich prize with slightly concealed envy.

"I don't see what that she-devil Pintada's got that makes her get all the best loot!" shouted the blond Margarito. "That's the way it's been since she joined up with us in Tierra Blanca."

"Hey, you, Pancracio, go along and bring me a bale of alfalfa for my mare," Pintada ordered airily.

Then she threw the lead rope to a soldier. Once again the men filled their glasses. Some began to drowse with head dropped and eyes half-closed. Most of them, however, continued to shout and laugh. Among them Luis Cervantes' girl, who had knocked over the wine on a handkerchief, looked from one to another with her great blue eyes full of bewilderment.

"Boys," cried the blond Margarito standing up, dominating the clatter of voices with his sharp, gutteral tones, "I'm tired of living and I've got a notion to kill myself right now. I've had enough of Pintada and this heavenly little cherub doesn't even cast a glance at me."

Luis Cervantes noticed that the last words were directed at his betrothed. With considerable surprise he realized that the foot he had felt between those of the girl was not Demetrio's but the blond Margarito's. Indignation boiled in his breast.

"Look closely, boys," continued Margarito, holding his revolver up high, "I'm going to put a bullet smack in my forehead!!"

He aimed at the great mirror on the other side of the room which reflected his whole body.

"Don't move, Pintada."

The mirror shattered into large, jagged fragments. The bullet in passing singed the hair of Pintada who didn't even blink an eye.

IV

Luis Cervantes wakened late in the afternoon, rubbed his eyes, and sat up. He found himself on the hard ground among the flower-pots of a garden. Soundly asleep and snoring noisily, Anastasio Montañés, Pancracio, and Cordoniz lay nearby.

Luis' lips felt swollen and his nose stiff and dry. He noticed blood on his hands and his shirt. Instantly he recalled what had happened. At once he stood up quickly and went toward a bedroom. Shoving at the door several times without succeeding in opening it, he stood hesitating a few moments.

It all had really happened; he was sure it was not a dream. He and his companion had left the dining room table and he had conducted her to the bedroom. But before he could close the door, Demetrio, staggering with drunkenness, had hurled himself after them. Then Pintada followed Demetrio and they commenced to scuffle. Demetrio, with eyes like burning coals and froth from pulque on his thick lips, searched avidly for the girl. Shoving him with all her strength, Pintada forced him back.

"Hey, you, what d'you think you're doing?" the irritated Demetrio cried out.

Pintada put her leg between his and using it as a lever, caused him to fall full length outside the room. He got up furiously angry.

"Help! Help! He'll kill me!"

Vigorously seizing Demetrio's wrist, Pintada turned aside the pistol barrel. The bullet embedded itself in the bricks. Pintada kept on bellowing. Anastasio Montañés came up back of Demetrio and disarmed him. Like a bull in the middle of the ring, he turned his bulging eyes to look at Luis Cervantes, Anastasio, Manteca, and many others who encircled him.

"Dirty dogs! You've disarmed me! As if I needed guns to deal with you!"

Flailing about him, he knocked flat on the brick floor all who came near him. And after that? Luis Cervantes could remember no more. Certainly they must have remained there asleep and exhausted. Surely his betrothed in fear of such a brute had had sense enough to lock herself in.

"Maybe that bedroom has an entrance into the living room and I can get in that way," he thought.

The sound of his steps awakened Pintada who was sleeping near Demetrio on the rug at the foot of a love seat filled with alfalfa and corn for the black mare.

"Who're you looking for?" the girl asked. "Oh, yes, I know who you want! Scoundrel! Look, I locked your sweetheart up because I couldn't control this damned Demetrio. Get the key; it's there on the table."

Vainly Luis Cervantes looked in every hiding place in the house.

"Look, *curro*, tell me how it was with that girl."

Luis Cervantes, very nervous, continued looking for the key.

"Don't be so anxious, man, I'll get it for you. But tell me—such things give me a kick. This little city gal is your kind; her feet aren't calloused like ours."

"I have nothing to tell. She is my betrothed and that's it."

"Ha! Ha! Ha! Your betrothed and not—! Look, man, where you go, I've already been. I've cut my eyeteeth. Manteca and Meco snatched that poor little thing out of her house. I know that, but you made a trade with them for her: some plated cuff links, a little miraculous picture of the Christ of the village. Am I lying? They are fools, we know it. Now we've got to find them. That so?"

Pintada got up to give him the key, but was much surprised at not being able to find it. She was thoughtful for a good bit of time. Suddenly she rushed over to the door of the bedroom, put her eye to the keyhole and stayed still until her sight was adjusted to the darkness of the room. Quickly, without taking her eye away, she murmured,

"Aha, you blond devil! Son of a ——! Come take a peep, *curro!*"

She drew back, letting out a loud laugh.

"Didn't I tell you that he's the sharpest rascal I ever saw in my life?"

The following morning, Pintada watched for the moment when Margarito would leave the bedroom to go feed his horse.

"You poor little thing! Come along and go on home! These wretches around here could kill you without batting an eye. Get along, run on home!"

She threw Manteca's ragged, lousy blanket around the young girl with the great blue eyes and virginal appearance who stood there dressed only in chemise and stockings. She took her by the hand and led her out to the street.

"God be blessed!" Pintada exclaimed. "Now it's my turn. How I want that blond one!"

V

Demetrio's men galloped through the mountain country like colts
that neigh and frolic in the first May rains.

"To Moyahua, boys!"

"To Demetrio Macías' country."

"To the country of Don Mónico, the *cacique*."

The landscape grew clear; the sun rose in a scarlet band over the
transparent sky. The mountains stood out like great stretched-out
monsters with angular backbones. There were hills which looked like
the heads of colossal Aztec idols with gigantic frightening faces and
grotesque grimaces which now made one smile, then aroused a vague
fear—a sort of mysterious foreboding.

Demetrio Macías rode at the head of the troop with his staff:
Colonel Anastasio Montañés, Lieutenant Colonel Pancracio, and Majors
Luis Cervantes and the blond Margarito. In the second line rode
Pintada and Venancio who courted her with many fine compliments
and recited to her the despairing verses of the poet Antonio Plaza.

When the sun's rays touched the edges of the eaves of the houses,
four abreast and to the sound of trumpets, they made their entrance
into Moyahua. The roosters crowed deafeningly, dogs barked with
alarm, but the people gave no sign of life.

Pintada spurred her black mare and with one jump, drew up
alongside Demetrio. Very gay, she was brightly dressed in silk and
wore massive gold rings dangling from her ears. The pale blue
of the bodice accentuated the olive tint of her face and the coppery
blotches which were damaging evidence of her past. Riding astride,
she pulled up her skirts to her knees, revealing dirty stockings full
of holes. She wore a revolver on her breast. A cartridge belt lay
across the head of the saddle.

Demetrio was also elegantly dressed in embroidered sombrero,
suede trousers adorned with silver buttons, and a jacket embroidered
with gold thread.

The sound of doors being forced open could be heard. The soldiers, already scattered through the town, were collecting ammunition
and mounts through the whole neighborhood.

"We're going to have our before-breakfast drink at Don Mónico's
house," announced Demetrio gravely, dismounting and tossing the

reins of his horse to a soldier. "Let's have breakfast with Don
Mónico, a friend who likes me a lot."

His staff smiled in a sinister fashion. Noisily dragging their spurs
along the sidewalk, they went toward a large, pretentious house which
could be none other than the residence of a *cacique*.

"It's locked up tighter'n a drum," said Anastasio Montañés pushing
against the door with all his might.

"I know how to open it," replied Pancracio quickly aiming his
rifle at the latch.

"No, no," said Demetrio, "knock first."

Three blows, with the butt of the rifle; three more, but no one
responded. Pancracio, paying no further attention to orders, took
things in his own hands. He fired, knocking off the metal plate,
and the door opened. They could see the hems of skirts, the legs
of children, all rushing away toward the interior of the house.

"I want wine! Bring wine here!" demanded Demetrio in an imperious voice, pounding heavily on the table.

"Sit down, *compañeros*."

A lady appeared, then others, and between the black skirts showed
the frightened faces of children. One of the women, trembling, went
to a closet and took out glasses and bottles and served wine.

"What weapons have you got?" inquired Demetrio severely.

"Weapons?" replied the lady, her tongue limp as a rag. "What
arms do you expect that some respectable women living all alone
would have?"

"Oh, alone! What about Don Mónico?"

"He's not here, gentlemen. We only rent the house. We only
know Don Mónico by name."

Demetrio commanded his men to make a search to see what they
could find.

"No, please, gentlemen! We ourselves will bring you what we
have; but, for love of God, don't fail to pay us proper respect. We
are respectable maiden ladies!"

"And the kids?" inquired Pancracio brutally. "Did they come
out of the ground?"

The ladies disappeared precipitately and returned a few moments
later with a broken rifle covered with dust and cobwebs, and a
pistol with a rusted, broken spring.

Demetrio smiled.

"Good. Now let's see how much money you've got."

"Money? What money do you think some poor maiden ladies would have?"

They turned their eyes in supplication toward the soldiers nearest to them; then they squeezed them shut in horror: they had seen the executioner who crucified Christ in the representation of the Calvary in the parish! They had seen Pancracio!

Demetrio ordered a search. All at once the ladies disappeared and quickly returned with a moth-eaten wallet with some bills of Huerta's issue in it.

Demetrio smiled and without further delay ordered his men into the house. Like hungry dogs smelling their prey, the mob burst in, trampling the women who tried to defend the entrance with their own bodies. Some fell fainting, others fled. The children screamed.

Pancracio got set to break the lock of a huge wardrobe when the doors opened and a man with a gun in his hands jumped out of it.

"Don Mónico!" they exclaimed in surprise.

"Demetrio, man! Don't do anything to me! Don't harm me! I am your friend, Don Demetrio!"

Demetrio Macías smiled craftily and asked if one received friends with gun in hand. Don Mónico, confused, dazed, threw himself down at Demetrio's feet embraced his knees, kissed his feet,

"My wife! My children! Friend Don Demetrio!"

Demetrio, with trembling hand, put his revolver back in its holster. The vision of a sad figure passed through his memory. A woman with her son in her arms, trudging over the rocks of the mountain country in the middle of the night by the light of the moon. A house in flames.

"Get out! Everybody!" he shouted somberly.

His staff obeyed; Don Mónico and the ladies kissed his hands and cried with gratitude. Joking and laughing, the throng waited happily in the street for the general's permission to sack the *cacique's* house.

"I'm sure I know where they've hid the money, but I'm not telling," announced a youngster with a basket under his arm.

"Oh, I know that!" reported an old woman who carried a sack in which to carry away 'that which God would provide.' "It's up very high; where there's a lot of furniture and odds and ends. Among all that stuff there's a little leather-covered case with shell ornaments. That's exactly where the valuables are."

"That's not for sure," said a man. "They're not such dunces as to leave their silver there. The way I see it, they've hung it all down a well in a leather bag."

The crowd was restless. Some had ropes to tie up bundles, others had hampers. The women stretched out their aprons or their *rebozos*, estimating how much they would hold. Giving thanks to his Divine Majesty, they waited for their fair share of the loot.

When Demetrio announced that he would not allow any looting and ordered all of them away, the people of the town disconsolately obeyed him and soon scattered. But among the soldiers there was a muffled undertone of disapproval and not one moved from his place. Irritated, Demetrio again ordered them to leave. One of the recent recruits, a young fellow whose liquor had gone to his head, laughed and advanced boldly toward the door. Before he could reach the threshold, a sudden shot brought him to the ground like a bull pierced by the dagger. Motionless with his smoking pistol in his hands, Demetrio waited for the soldiers to withdraw.

"Set the house on fire," he ordered Luis Cervantes when they got to the barracks.

Luis Cervantes, with curious eagerness, did not transmit the order but carried it out himself. Two hours later when the plaza was black with smoke and enormous tongues of flame rose from Don Mónico's house, no one understood the General's strange conduct.

VI

They found quarters in a big, gloomy house which belonged to that same *cacique* of Moyahua. Their predecessors had left powerful evidence of their presence in the patio, converted into a dung heap; on the walls with the stucco peeled off in places showing the rough adobe; on the floors of the house torn up by animals' hooves; in the orchard where withered leaves and dry branches covered the ground. On entering the house, one stumbled over legs of pieces of furniture, over seats and backs of chairs, all filthy with dirt and refuse.

At ten o'clock in the evening Luis Cervantes, quite bored, yawned and said goodbye to the blond Margarito and Pintada who were seated

on a bench in the plaza downing one drink after the other. He went
to the barracks. The only furnished room was the living room. As
he entered, Demetrio, who was stretched out on the floor with his
eyes wide open looking at the ceiling, left off counting the beams
and turned his head.

"That you, *curro*? What d'you know? Come on, come on, sit
down."

First Luis Cervantes went over to trim the candle, then drew up
a backless chair with a piece of rough burlap serving in the place
of the wicker seat. The legs of the chair squeaked, and Pintada's
black mare snorted and moved about in the shadows, tracing a graceful curve with its smooth, rounded hindquarters.

Luis Cervantes sank down on the seat and said,

"General, I have come to give an account of the commission. Here
you have—"

"Man, as if I'd want anything like that! Moyahua is almost like
my own country. They'll say that's what I came for!" replied Demetrio
looking at the sack stuffed full of money which Luis offered him.

Luis rose and went over to kneel beside Demetrio. He stretched
a *serape* out on the floor and emptied out the bag of ten-*peso* gold
pieces shining like embers.

"In the first place, General, only you and I know about this money.
On the other hand, you know that when the sun shines brightly, it's
necessary to open the window. Today it's shining in our faces, but
tomorrow? It is always necessary to look ahead. A bullet, the sudden
leap of a horse, even a ridiculous head cold, and a widow and orphans
in misery! The Government! Ha! Ha! Ha! Go to Carranza, to
Villa, or to any other of the highest chiefs and tell them about your
family. If they respond with a kick—you know where—then you
submit abjectly. They're right, my General, for we have not taken
up arms in order that some Carranza or some Villa might become
president of the Republic; we are struggling in defense of the sacred
rights of the people trampled on by the evil *cacique*. Just as Villa
nor Carranza nor any other has come to ask our consent for what
they have paid themselves for the services that they have given to the
country, neither do we have to ask permission of anybody."

Demetrio half raised up, took a bottle that stood nearby, tilted
it, then blowing out his cheeks, forcefully spat out a mouthful of the
beer.

"My, you talk big!"

Luis felt dizzy. The spat-out beer seemed to intensify the stench of the rotten garbage on which they were lying—a tapestry of orange and banana peels, fleshlike slices of watermelon, fibrous kernels of mangoes, chewed-up pieces of sugar cane mixed up with shucks from enchiladas and tamales and the whole mess damp with human excrement.

Demetrio's calloused fingers passed back and forth over the shining money, counting and recounting it.

Having recovered from his dizziness, Luis took out a small tin baby food box full of lockets, rings, earrings, and many other valuable pieces of jewelry.

"Look here, General, if, as it seems, this upheaval is going to keep on, if the Revolution isn't going to stop, we've got enough here to make it possible for us to leave Mexico and live abroad luxuriously for a while."

Demetrio shook his head.

"You wouldn't do that? What's the use staying on? What would we be fighting for then?"

"It's something I can't explain, but I sort of feel it wouldn't be acting like a real man."

"Pick out what you want, General," said Luis Cervantes indicating the jewelry laid out in a row.

"Keep it all yourself. Really— If you could only see that I don't have any love for money! You want me to tell you the truth? Well, then, long's I got something to drink and a cute little girl I like, I'm the happiest man in the world."

"Ha! Ha! Ha! What a man my General is! Well then, why do you put up with that snake of a Pintada?"

"Man, *curro*, I've had enough of her, but I'm that way; I just can't get up the nerve myself to send her to— That's the way I am; that's my nature. You see, when I like a woman, I'm so backward that if she don't start something, I just do nothing." He sighed. "Take for example, Camila, the one at the *ranchito*. She's sure an ugly girl, but if you would just guess how she fills my eye—"

"Any day you say, we'll go get her for you, General."

Demetrio winked maliciously.

"I swear that I really would, General."

"For sure, *curro*?   Look here, if you do me that great favor, you can have the gold watch and chain you want so bad."

Luis Cervantes' eyes glittered.   He took the tin box, now filled to the top, rose to his feet, and smiling, said,

"Until tomorrow, General.   Sleep well tonight."

VII

"What d'I know?   Just what you do.   The General says to me: 'Cordoniz saddle your horse and my black mare.   You're going with the *curro* to attend to something.'   Well that was the way it happened.   We left here at noon and by evening we got to the *ranchito*. One-eyed María Antonia put us up.   She asked about you, Pancracio. In the morning the *curro* waked me up: 'Cordoniz, Cordoniz, saddle the horses.   Leave my horse and go on back with the General's mare to Moyahua.   I'll catch up with you in a little while.'   The sun was high when he came up with Camila in the saddle.   She got down and we put her up on the mare."

"Well, and her—how'd she take it?"   asked one of the men.

"Huh, she was so happy her tongue kept running off."

"And the *curro*?"

"Say-nothing as always; same as he usually is."

"I believe," Venancio gravely remarked, "that if Camila wakes up in the morning in Demetrio's bed, it will only be by mistake. We drank a lot.   Remember!   The drinks went to our heads and none of us knew what we were doing."

"Wasn't the drinking or anything of the sort!   It was something cooked up by the *curro* and the General."

"Sure!   T'my way of thinking that *curro's* nothing but a—"

"I don't like to talk about friends behind their backs," said the blond Margarito, "but I can tell you this that of two sweethearts that he's had, one has been for me and the other for the General."

They shouted with laughter.

As soon as Pintada found out about all that had happened, she went to console Camila with a great show of affection.

"Poor little thing, tell me all about it!"

Camila's eyes were swollen from crying.

"He lied to me, he lied to me!   He came to the village and said to me, 'Camila, I've come just for you.   Will you go with me?' Huh, you bet I wanted to go with him. As for loving him, I love him, I love him something fierce. Look how thin I've got just thinking about him! I never felt like working when I would get up in the morning. When my mama called me to eat, the *gorda* would stick like a rag in my mouth. What a terrible time! What a terrible time!"

She commenced to cry again, and to keep anybody from hearing her sobs, she covered her mouth and nose with the end of her *rebozo*.

"See here, I'll get you out of this trouble. Don't be silly; stop crying. Don't you know what he is? That's the truth. I tell you that is the only reason the General has him along! How silly you are! Well, do you want to go back to your home?"

"May the Virgin of Jalpa protect me! Mama would beat me to death!"

"Oh, no she won't. Come on, let's make a plan. The troop will leave any minute. When Demetrio tells you to get ready to go, you tell him you hurt all over, like you'd been beaten. First stretch yourself out and yawn. Then put your hand to your forehead and say, 'I'm burning up with fever.' Then I'll tell Demetrio to leave both of us; that I'll stay and take care of you and soon's you're able, we'll catch up with them. Instead, I'll deliver you safe and sound in your own house."

VIII

The sun had set and the village was wrapped in the gray melancholy of its old streets and in the terrified silence of its people who had sought shelter very early in the evening. Luis Cervantes arrived at Primitivo López's store to interrupt a spree which had promised to be a champion one. Demetrio had got drunk with old friends. The bar could not accommodate another person. Demetrio, Pintada, and the blond Margarito had left their horses outside, but the rest of the officers had rudely pushed themselves in, all on horseback. The decorated sombreros with great turned-up brims were in constant motion. The horses curvetted and pranced, their fine heads with great black eyes, flaring nostrils, and small ears were in constant motion. Along with the infernal racket of the drunken men could be heard the snorting of the horses, the stamp of their hooves on the tiled floor, and, from time to time, a quick, nervous neigh.

When Luis Cervantes arrived, they were discussing a trivial incident. A native of the village was stretched out in the middle of the road with a small, blackish hole in his forehead. At first there was a division of opinion, but now there was agreement as a consequence of the blond Margarito's sound explanation. The poor devil lying there quite dead was the sexton of the church. The fool, he was to blame himself. Sir, who would think of dressing up like a dude from the city with pants, jacket, and a beret? Pancracio cannot stand to come face to face with a *catrín*.

At Luis Cervantes' command, the eight musicians who had been performing valiantly on their wind instruments since dawn, their faces round and red as suns, their eyes bulging, ceased playing.

"My General," he said as he made his way among the mounted men, "a special messenger has just arrived. They order you to leave immediately to pursue Orozco's men."

In a moment somber, gloomy faces brightened with joy.

"To Jalisco, boys!" cried the blond Margarito, striking the bar a sharp blow.

"Get ready, Jalisco charmers, here I come!" cried Cordoniz, cocking up his hat in front.

All was merriment and enthusiasm. Demetrio's friends, in their drunken excitement, offered to join his ranks. Demetrio's exhiliration left him speechless. To set out to whip Orozco's forces! To find themselves at last facing real fighters! No longer would they be killing Federals which was as easy as killing hares or turkeys!

"If I could get hold of Pascual Orozoco alive," said the blond Margarito, "I'd rip off the soles of his feet and make him walk twenty-four hours across the mountains."

"Was he the one who killed Madero?" asked Meco.

"No," replied Margarito solemnly, "but he socked me once when I was a waiter at Delmónico's in Chihuahua."

"The black mare for Camila," Demetrio ordered Pancracio who was saddling the horses.

"Camila can't go," said Pintada quickly.

"Who asked your opinion?" replied Demetrio sharply.

"Camila, didn't you get up this morning aching all over and now you've got a high fever?"

"Well, I—well, I—just whatever Don Demetrio says."

"Bah, what a dunce! Say you're not going; say so," Pintada whispered, much disturbed.

"Seems I'm getting sort of willing—would you believe it?" Camila replied, also whispering.

Pintada flushed darkly, her cheeks inflamed; but she said nothing as she mounted her mare which the blond Margarito had saddled.

IX

The whirling dust which stretched out for a long way down the road suddenly broke into turbulent and diffused masses revealing the horses with inflated chests, tangled manes, quivering nostrils, violent staring eyes, and stiff legs drawn up as at the beginning of a race. The bronze-faced men with ivory-white teeth and flashing eyes brandished their rifles in the air or carried them across the pommels of their saddles.

Riding together, Demetrio and Camila caught up with the rear-guard. She was still trembling, her lips white and dry; he was in a bad humor because of their fruitless endeavor. Not one of Orozco's men; not a fight. Some scattered Federals, a poor devil of a curate with a hundred deluded followers joined under the antiquated banner of "Religion and Rights." The curate was left dangling there from a mesquite and on the ground a scattering of dead who bore on their breasts an insignia of red cloth carrying the words: "Halt! The Sacred Heart of Jesus sustains me!"

"The truth is that I more than paid myself all my back salary," said Cordoniz showing the gold watches and rings he had taken from the rectory.

"That's why it's so much fun fighting," Manteca exclaimed, inserting insults after each of his phrases. "Now you know why you risk your hide!"

In the same hand with which he held the reins, he clutched a bright ornament he had torn from the Divine Prisoner in the church. When Cordoniz, the expert in such matters, covetously examined Manteca's loot, he let out an imposing shout of laughter,

"Your treasure is tin plate!"

"Why are you weighing yourself down with that no-good fellow?" Pancracio asked Margarito who came from the rear with a prisoner.

"You know why? Because I never saw up close a human face when a rope tightens round its neck."

The very fat prisoner breathed heavily with fatigue; his face was red as fire, his eyes bloodshot, his forehead wet with sweat. They were leading him on foot, his wrists tied together.

"Anastasio lend me your rope; this rooster's busted my halter. But no, I've got a better idea. My Federal friend, I'm going to kill you right now; you are in too much agony. Look, the mesquite trees are still a long way off and not even a telegraph pole 'round here to hang you on."

The blond Margarito took out his pistol, put the barrel against the prisoner's left breast and little by little drew back the trigger. The Federal became as pale as a corpse, his face dropped, his glassy eyes rolled. His chest heaved tumultuously and his whole body shook as though he had been seized with a hard chill. The blond Margarito held his pistol for seconds which seemed an eternity. His eyes shone in a strange manner, and his chubby face, his bulging cheeks burned with a sensation of extreme sensuality.

"No, my Federal friend!" he said, slowly withdrawing the weapon and returning it to its holster, "I don't want to kill you yet. You're going to be my orderly. You'll see I'm not so bad-hearted."

He winked malignantly at those nearby. The prisoner was stupefied; he could only gulp; his mouth and throat were dry.

Camila who had been staying back spurred her mare and drew alongside Demetrio,

"What a mean man that Margarito is! If you'd seen what he's been doing to a prisoner!"

She recounted what she had just witnessed. Demetrio frowned but did not answer.

Pintada called to Camila from a distance.

"Listen here, what gossip are you telling Demetrio? That blond Margarito is my real love; I want you to understand that! Now you know. Whatever you got against him, you got against me. Now I've warned you!"

A very frightened Camila hurried to catch up with Demetrio.

X

The troop camped in a field near three small houses standing in a solitary row silhouetted against the purple band of the horizon. Demetrio and Camila rode toward them. A man in white shirt and pants, puffing greedily on a long cigarette of shucks, stood inside the corral. Seated near him on a small, flat rock, another was shelling corn, rubbing the ears between his hands. To scare the chickens away, he constantly shook his thin, twisted, crippled leg with its foot like a goat's hoof.

"Hurry up, Pifanio," said the one standing up, "the sun's gone down and you haven't watered the animals yet."

When a horse outside neighed, the men raised their heads in bewilderment. The figures of Demetrio and Camila loomed up over the wall of the corral.

"I just want a place for me and my woman to stay," Demetrio said reassuringly.

When he explained to them that he was the chief of a troop of soldiers which was going to pass the night nearby, the man standing, who was the owner, begged them to enter. He ran to get a tub of water and a broom. Quickly he swept and sprinkled down the best corner of the granary in order to prepare a decent lodging place for such distinguished guests.

"Move, Pifanio; unsaddle the horses for these folks."

The man who was shelling corn rose with great effort. He wore a ragged shirt and vest, a threadbare pair of pants which spread out like two wings with the ends hanging down from his waist. His gait marked a grotesque measure.

"But, friend, are you able to work?" Demetrio asked, not allowing him to unsaddle the horses.

"Poor fellow," shouted the owner from the interior of the granary, "he's not very strong! But you ought to see how he can earn his pay! He begins working when God wakes up! The sun's already set, but look at him, he's still at it!"

Demetrio and Camila went out to take a walk around the encampment. Stripped clean of vegetation, the golden earth of the plain ploughed ready for sowing spread out in an immense desolation. The three great ash trees standing in front of the little houses seemed veritable miracles with their rounded, dark green, waving crests and their dense foliage drooping down until it almost kissed the earth.

"I can't make out what there is round here that makes me feel so sad."

"Yes," replied Camila, "I feel the same way."

At the bank of a little stream, Pifanio was strenuously pulling on the rope of a windlass. An enormous jug turned over on a pile of freshly cut hay and the streaming crystal water glistened in the last rays of the sun as it flowed into the trough. A thin cow, a burro, and a decrepit horse noisily drank the water.

Demetrio recognized the crippled peon and asked him,

"How much do you make a day, friend?"

"Sixteen *centavos*, master."

He was a blue-eyed, fair, small, scrofulous man with straight hair. He complained about the boss, about the place, and about his bad luck.

"You really work for your salt, son," Demetrio interrupted him kindly. "You gripe and gripe, but you work and then work some more."

Turning to Camila he said,

"There are plenty fools more stupid than us from the sierra."

"Yes," answered Camila.

They kept on walking. The valley was lost in the darkness and stars were hidden. Demetrio amorously put his arm around Camila's waist and whispered in her ear as he drew her close.

"Yes," answered Camila.

Because now she was gathering up her willingness.

Demetrio slept badly. He got up very early and left the house.

"Something is going to happen to me," he thought.

It was a silent and subtly joyous morning. A thrush chirped timidly in the ash tree; the animals in the corral trampled the refuse from the stubble; the pig grunted sleepily. The sun rose orange-colored, and the last little star flickered out. Demetrio walked slowly to the encampment. He thought about his yoke of young, black oxen which he had worked for scarcely two years and of his two measures of very fertile land. The features of his young wife appeared clearly in his memory: sweet and infinitely gentle toward her husband; forceful and proud toward a stranger. But when he made the effort to recall the image of his son, it was in vain; he had forgotten how he looked.

He arrived at the encampment. The soldiers were sleeping stretched out among the furrows. The horses were scattered among them, their heads drooping, their eyes closed.

"The string of horses is worn out, Anastasio; it'd be a good idea for us to stay here to rest at least for a day."

"Yeah, *compadre* Demetrio! Wish we were in the sierra! If I could see—don't you believe me? Nothing here strikes me right. Sad and blue! Who knows what it is that I miss?"

"How many hours to get to Limón?"

"It's not just a matter of hours: it's a hard, three-day journey, *compadre* Demetrio."

"If I could only see— I sure want to see my woman!"

Pintada did not lose any time looking for Camila.

"Oh, my goodness! Just for that reason Demetrio is going to leave you. To me, myself, he said so. He's going to get his real woman. She's real pretty, very white. Such pink cheeks! But if you don't want to go, they can give you something to do. They've got a baby and you can take care of it."

When Demetrio returned, Camila, crying, told him what she had heard.

"Don't pay any attention to that crazy loon. Just lies, nothing but lies."

As Demetrio did not go to Limón nor spend any more time thinking about his wife, Camila was quite content. Pintada became a veritable scorpion in her anger.

XI

Before dawn they set out for Tepatitlán. Scattered along the main road and the field, their silhouettes wavered vaguely with the monotonous and rhythmical gait of the horses and disappeared in the pearly light of the waning moon which bathed the whole valley.

They heard the distant barking of dogs.

"By noon today, we'll get to Tepatitlán, tomorrow to Cuquío, and then—to the sierra," said Demetrio.

"Wouldn't it be well, General," whispered Luis Cervantes, "to go first to Aguascalientes?"

"What'd we go there for?"

"Our funds are getting low."

"What! Forty thousand *pesos* in eight days?"

"In this week alone we have recruited nearly five hundred men, and all of it's gone in advances and gratuities," replied Luis Cervantes in a low tone.

"No; we're going straight to the sierra; then we'll see—"

"Yes, to the sierra!" many shouted.

"To the sierra! To the sierra! There's nothing like the sierra."

The plains oppressed them; they talked of the sierra with enthusiasm and wild excitement. They thought of it as a cherished loved one not seen for a long time.

The day brightened. Then a cloud of red dust rose toward the east in an immense curtain of fiery purple.

Luis Cervantes reined in his horse and waited for Cordoniz.

"Well, how do we stand now, Cordoniz?"

"I told you, *curro*: two hundred *pesos* just for the watch."

"No, I want to buy the whole lot from you: watches, rings, all the jewelry. How much?"

Cordoniz hesitated, became very pale; then said impetuously, "Two thousand bills for all of it."

But Luis Cervantes gave himself away; his eyes shone with evident greed so that Cordoniz changed his mind and quickly exclaimed,

"No, I was joking. I don't mean to sell the whole lot. Just the watch, and that because I owe two hundred *pesos* to Pancracio who won from me last time."

Luis Cervantes took out four brand new bills of "two faces"[7] and put them in Cordoniz's hands.

"Come on, now" he said to him, "I'm interested in the lot. Nobody will give you any more than I will."

When they began to feel the heat of the sun, Manteca suddenly shouted,

"Margarito, your orderly's about to die. Says he can't walk no more."

The prisoner had fallen from exhaustion in the middle of the road.

"Shut up!" shouted Margarito, turning back. "So you're all tired out, my fine friend? Poor old thing! I'm going to buy a glass corner closet for my house to keep you in like the Child Jesus. But first we got to get to my town, so I'll give you some help."

Taking out his sword, he struck the unfortunate prisoner repeatedly.

"Let's see your *reata*, Pancracio," he said, his bulging eyes shining brilliantly.

Cordoniz, who noticed, however, that the Federal no longer moved either hand or foot, let out a raucous laugh and said,

"What an idiot I am! I had just taught him how to do without food."

"This is it, we're just about to Guadalajara," said Venancio as he noticed the agreeable prospect of the houses of Tepatitlán nestled snugly against the hillside. They entered the village in high spirits. Rosy cheeks and beautiful dark eyes appeared at the windows.

The men converted the schools into barracks. Demetrio found lodging in the chapel of an abandoned church. Then the soldiers scattered about as usual looking for loot under the pretext of collecting arms and horses.

In the afternoon some of Demetrio's men lay stretched out in the courtyard of the church taking their ease and scratching their bellies. Venancio, his chest and shoulders bare, was intently occupied in killing the lice on his shirt.

A man who came to the wall of the church asked permission to speak to the leader. The soldiers raised their heads, but no one answered him.

"I'm a widower, gentlemen, I've got nine children and nothing but what I work for. Don't be so hard on poor people."

"You don't have to worry about getting another woman, uncle," said Meco who was greasing the soles of his feet with a tallow candle. "We brought Pintada with us and we'll turn her over to you for cost."

The man smiled bitterly.

"She's got only one fault," observed Pancracio who was lying on his back looking at the blue sky. "Just as soon as she sees a man, right away she gets ready."

They laughed loudly, but Venancio gravely pointed out the door of the village church. The man timidly entered and registered his complaint with Demetrio. The soldiers had just cleaned him out. They had not left a single grain of corn.

"Why should they leave any?" responded Demetrio indolently.

The man persisted with weeping and lamentation. Luis Cervantes prepared to throw him out forthwith, but Camila intervened.

"Come now, Don Demetrio, don't you be so hard-hearted, too; give him an order for the return of his grain."

Luis Cervantes had to obey; he wrote out a few lines at the bottom of which Demetrio made an illegible scrawl.

"May God repay you, child! May God give you the joy of seeing His glory. Ten measures of corn; just barely enough food for the year," cried the man with gratitude. He took the paper and kissed the hands of all of them.

XII

They had almost reached Cuquío when Anastasio Montañés rode up to Demetrio and said,

"Listen, *compadre*, I didn't tell you what a real tricky rascal that blond Margarito is! Do you know what he did yesterday to that bird that came here to complain that we had taken all his corn for our horses? Well, with the order you gave him he went to the barracks. 'Yes, friend,' that Margarito said to him, 'come this way; it is quite just to return what is yours. Come in, come in. How many measures did we steal from you? Ten? Are you sure it wasn't more? Yes, that's it; about fifteen, a little more or less: Could it be twenty? Be sure you remember. You are very poor. You have many children to take care of. Yes, it's just as I say, about twenty; that's what it must've been. Come this way; I'm not going to give you fifteen nor twenty. All you have to do is count. One, two, three. And then as soon as you've had enough, tell me,' Margarito then struck him with the flat of his sword so hard that he begged for mercy."

Pintada broke out laughing.

Camila, unable to restrain herself, said,

"That damned old skunk, how mean-hearted! No wonder I hate the sight of him!"

Pintada's expression changed instantly.

"And what's that to you?"

Frightened, Camila spurred her mare on ahead. Pintada sent hers headlong and, crying insults as she slammed into Camila, seized her by the head and pulled loose her braids. The heavy blow on Camila's mare caused it to rear. Having let go the reins to brush the hair from her face, Camila hesitated, lost her balance, and fell from the horse, cutting her forehead on the stony ground.

Laughing immoderately, Pintada galloped up to the unruly mare, catching it very skillfully.

"Come along, *curro*, there's work for you," said Pancracio when he saw Camila riding double with Demetrio, her face wet with blood.

Luis Cervantes officiously hurried up with his medical supplies. Camila, however, choking down her sobs, wiped her eyes and said in a muffled voice,

"From you? Not even if I was dying! Not even a drop of water!"

In Cuquío Demetrio received a special messenger.

"We must return to Tepatitlán, General," said Luis Cervantes, running his eyes quickly over the official document. "You will have to leave the men there and take the train at Lagos to Aguascalientes."

There were heated protests. Along with groans, complaints, and mutterings, some of the mountain men swore they would not continue with the column.

Camila cried all night. On the next morning she asked Demetrio permission to return home.

"If you don't like me!" answered Demetrio sullenly.

"It's not that, Don Demetrio; I like you all right, very much, but don't you see what's going on? That woman!"

"Don't fret, I'll send her off today. I've already been thinking about it."

Camila ceased crying.

All the horses had been saddled. Demetrio went over to Pintada and said in a very low voice,

"You're not going with us."

"What did you say?" she inquired without taking in his meaning.

"You've got to stay here or go where you want to, but not with us."

"What are you saying?" she cried in astonishment. "Do you mean you're running me off? Ha! Ha! Ha! What then—what kind of a fool are you to believe all the gossip of that——."

With energy and originality Pintada cursed Camila, Demetrio, Luis Cervantes, and all the others who came to her mind. The troop heard curses and insults new even in their extensive experience.

Demetrio waited with patience for a considerable period of time, but as she did not give any evidence of stopping, he said very calmly to a soldier,

"Throw that drunken woman out."

"Margarito, Margarito, love of my life! Defend me from these ——! Come, dear one of my heart! Come, show them you're a real man and that they they are nothing more than sons of ——!"

She gesticulated, kicked, and shouted.

Margarito appeared. He had just awakened and his blue eyes were lost under swollen lids. His voice was hoarse. They told him what had occurred. Going over to Pintada he said to her in a very serious voice,

"Yes, it seems to me that you should take yourself far away to— we've all had enough of you."

Pintada's face became as rigid as granite. She wanted to speak, but her muscles were stiff.

The highly diverted soldiers laughed. Desperately frightened, Camila held her breath. Pintada's gaze passed in turn over those around her. Then it happened in the blink of an eye. She bent over, drew a shining dagger from her stocking, and hurled herself at Camila. A strident cry and a body fell to the ground with the blood gushing from it.

"Kill her," cried Demetrio, beside himself.

Two soldiers rushed to seize Pintada. Brandishing the dagger in her fist, she fended them off.

"No, not you, miserable trash! You, Demetrio, you kill me," she said as she stepped forward, surrendering her dagger and thrusting out her chest as her arms dropped to her sides.

Demetrio held high the dagger, red with blood. His eyes clouded over, he hesitated, then stepped back.

Then in a low, hoarse voice, he said,

"Clear out! I mean right now!"

No one dared restrain her. She went on her way slowly, mute and somber.

Margarito's harsh and gutteral voice broke the silence.

"That's good! At last I'm rid of that bed-bug!"

XIII

A dagger pierced the middle
of my body.
Without knowing why,
Nor did I know why.
He knew why,
But not I.
Much blood flowed from
that mortal wound,
Without knowing why,
Nor did I know why.
He knew why,
But not I.

Head lowered, hands crossed over the pommel of his saddle, Demetrio sang in a melancholy tone the tune which obsessed him. Then he fell silent. For a long time he remained silent and sorrowful.

"You'll see that when we arrive at Lagos this depression will leave you, General. There are plenty of pretty girls there to provide us pleasure," said the blond Margarito.

"All I feel like doing now is getting dead drunk," Demetrio replied.

Once more he drew apart from the others, spurring his horse as though he wished to give himself up entirely to his sadness.

After many hours on the way, he callel Luis Cervantes to him,

"Listen, I've been thinking; what bells am I going to ring in Aguascalientes?"

"You're going to cast your vote, General, for the Provisional President of the Republic."

"Provisional President? Well, then, what—what about Carranza? The truth is I don't know a thing about this business of politics."

They arrived at Lagos. Margarito bet that he could make Demetrio laugh out loud that very night.

Dragging his spurs, his leather pants sagging below his waist, Demetrio entered *El Cosmopolita* with Luis Cervantes, Margarito, and his orderlies.

"Why do you rush off, you city slickers? We don't eat people!" exclaimed Margarito.

The townspeople, surprised at the very moment they had attempted to escape, remained where they were. Some, concealing their fright, returned to their tables and continued with their drinking and chattering; others after hesitating a bit, went up to pay their respects to the rebel leaders.

"General! Delighted! Major!"

"That's it! That's the kind of friends I like, refined and respectable," said Margarito.

"Let's go, boys," he added as he carelessly drew his pistol, "there goes a firecracker at your feet to make you prance."

A bullet ricocheted on the concrete floor among the legs of the tables and of the men who jumped up as startled as a lady who found a mouse under her skirt.

Pale, they smiled dutifully for the entertainment of the major.

Demetrio hardly moved his lips although his followers were convulsed with laughter.

"Margarito," observed Cordoniz, "the one who's leaving must have got stung; see how he's limping."

Margarito, without paying any attention or even turning his head toward the wounded man, announced enthusiastically that from a distance of thirty paces and without taking aim he could hit a straight, slender glass of tequila.

"All right, friend, stand there," he said to the waiter in the cantina. Then taking him by the hand he led him to the principal part of the hotel patio and put the glass of tequila on his head. The poor devil, frightened and wishing to escape, resisted, but Margarito held out his pistol and took aim.

"At your place you piece of jerked beef! Or for sure I'll put a hot little one in you."

Margarito turned to the opposite wall, raised his weapon, took aim, and hit the mark. The glass flew in pieces; tequila bathed the boy's face which was the color of death.

"Now the real thing!" he exclaimed, running into the cantina for another glass of tequila which he placed on the young fellow's head. Returning to his place, he spun around on his feet, and without aiming, fired. Only this time he had got an ear instead of the glass.

Laughing so heartily that he had to hold his stomach, he said to the boy,

"Take these bills, son. That's not bad! It'll stop hurting with a little arnica and brandy."

After he had drunk much whisky and beer, Demetrio said,

"Pay the bill, Margarito. I'm leaving."

"I didn't bring any money, General; but don't bother about it. How much is coming to you, friend?"

"A hundred and eighty *pesos*, chief," replied the bartender amiably. Promptly Margarito jumped up on the bar, and with two sweeps of his hands, knocked down all the flasks, bottles, and glassware.

"You can send the bill to your papa Villa, understand?"

He left laughing uproariously.

"Listen, friend, where'll we find some girls?" he asked as he reeled up drunkenly to a small, well-dressed individual who was closing the door of a tailor shop. The man he questioned carefully stepped off the sidewalk to leave the way open.

Margarito detained him and looked at him impertinently and inquisitively.

"Listen, friend, how little and graceful you are! How's that, you aren't? Then I'm a liar? Good, that suits me. You know how dwarfs dance? You don't know? Think again! I saw you in a circus! I swear you know how and plenty good, too! Now you'll see!"

Margarito took out his pistol and began to shoot at the feet of the short, fat tailor who gave a little jump with each shot.

"Don't you see, you do know how the dwarfs dance?"

Throwing his arms around his friends' shoulders, he made them lead him to the district of the ladies of joy, marking his passage with shots at the lights at the street corners, at the doors, and in the houses along the way. Demetrio left him and returned to the hotel, humming to himself,

> A dagger pierced the middle
>   of my body,
> Without knowing why,
> Nor did I know why.

XIV

Cigar smoke, the penetrating odor of sweaty clothes, alcoholic vapors, the breathing of a multitude of people; an accumulation of smells worse than a carload of pigs. Men wearing Texas-style hats with braided bands and khaki outfits were predominant.

"Gentleman, a well-dressed man stole my suitcase in the railroad station at Silao. My entire life's savings. I've nothing left to buy food with for my little boy."

It was the shrill voice of a whiner and professional mourner, but it carried only a short distance in the clamor of that packed railroad coach.

"What's that old woman saying?" asked the blond Margarito as he entered the coach looking for a seat.

"Something about a suitcase—about a respectable boy," replied Pancracio who had already found the knees of some villagers to sit on.

Demetrio and the others elbowed their way in. As the two persons Pancracio was sitting on preferred to give up their seats to continue their journey standing, Demetrio and Luis Cervantes gladly appropriated the places.

A lady who had been standing holding a child in her arms all the way from Irapuato fell in a faint. A villager quickly took the child in his arms. Others paid not the least attention. The women camp followers each occupied two or three seats traveling with suitcases, dogs, cats, and small parrots. The fellows wearing Texas-style hats, however, laughed uproariously at the sight of the plump flesh and limp breasts of the woman who had fainted.

"Gentleman, a well-dressed man stole my suitcase in the railroad station at Silao. My entire life's savings, I've nothing left to buy food with for my little boy."

The old woman spoke rapidly and mechanically with sighs and sobs. Her sharp eyes darted from one side of the coach to the other. Here she collected a bill, farther on another. They rained down on her in abundance. She finished the collection and moved on a few seats.

"Gentlemen, a well-dressed man stole my suitcase in the station at Silao."

The words produced an immediate and sure effect.

A well-dressed man! A well-dressed man who stole a suitcase! That's unpardonable! It awakened a feeling of general indignation. What a pity that the well-dressed man was not at hand so that each one of the generals there could take a shot at him!

"There's nothing makes me hotter than a mean city slicker thief," said one, bursting with noble sentiment.

"Stealing from a poor lady!"

"Stealing from an unfortunate woman who cannot defend herself!"

All manifested the compassion in their hearts by word and deed; insults for the thief and a Villa-issue five-*peso* bill for the victim.

"To tell the truth, I don't think it's wrong to kill because when one kills he does it always when he's angry; but to steal—" exclaimed Margarito.

All seemed to agree with such profound reasoning; but after a brief silence and a moment's reflection, a colonel ventured his opinion,

"Truth is, everything's got its 'thus and so.' But after all, the truth's the truth. The actual fact is, I have robbed; and if I say that everybody we see here has done the same, I guess I'm not lying."

"Huh, the sewing machines I stole in Mexico City!" exclaimed a major, "I accumulated more than five hundred *pesos* even though I sold them for only fifty *centavos* a piece."

"In Zacatecas I stole some horses so fine that I said to myself: 'This piece of business will make your fortune, Pascual Mata; you won't have a thing to worry about the rest of your days,'" said a gray-haired captain who was almost toothless. "The worst of it was, General Limón took a shine to my horses and stole them from me."

"Well, there's no use denying it! I've stolen, too," confessed Margarito, "but you can ask any of my companions here how much I've got left. Yes, it's my pleasure to spend it all with my friends. It suits me better to get drunk with all my friends than to send a *centavo* to the women back home."

The theme of "I stole," although apparently inexhaustible, was about to run out when on each seat a deck of cards appeared, attracting the officers as a light draws mosquitoes.

The shifts in fortune in the gambling soon absorbed them all and the atmosphere became hotter and hotter with exhalations of the barracks, the jail, the brothel, and even the pigsty.

Dominating the babble, there could be heard from the next coach, "Gentlemen, a well-dressed man stole my suitcase—"

The streets in Aguascalientes had become no more than garbage dumps. Like bees at the mouth of a hive, men in khaki hung around the doors of the restaurants, low-class inns, small hotels, at the tables put out in the open air and piled with a hodgepodge of foods including trays of rancid pig cracklings and piles of dirty cheeses.

The smell of fried food made Demetrio and his men realize they were hungry. Pushing and shoving they forced their way into an inn where a disheveled, filthy old woman served them in pottery bowls some pork bones cooked with *chile* swimming in a clear soup along with three leathery, burned tortillas for which each of them paid two *pesos*. On leaving, Pancracio asserted that he was hungrier than before he had gone in.

"Now," said Demetrio, "let's go consult with General Natera."

They followed a street toward the house occupied by the Northern general. An unruly and excited group of people stopped them at a street crossing. A man lost in the multitude muttered in a sing-song unctuous voice something that seemed to be a prayer. They drew near enough to see him clearly. The man, dressed in shirt and pants of coarse white cloth, was repeating: "All good Catholics who pray with devotion this prayer to the Crucified Christ will be spared from tempests, pestilences, wars, and famines."

"He hit the nail on the head," said Demetrio, smiling.

The man waved a fist-full of papers in the air and said,

"Fifty *centavos* for the prayer of Christ Crucified, fifty *centavos*."

Then he would disappear for an instant to come up again with a snake's fang, a starfish, or the skeleton of a fish. With the same pious tone he praised the medicinal qualities and rare virtues of each article.

Cordoniz, who did not put any faith in Venancio, asked the vendor to extract a molar; Margarito bought the black kernel of a certain fruit which had the property of freeing its possessor from lightning as well as from any other "catastrophe;" and Anastasio Montañés, a prayer to the Christ Crucified which he carefully folded and with great piety placed next to his breast.

"As sure as God exists, *compañero*, this upheaval will keep on. Now it's Villa against Carranza!" said Natera.

Demetrio stared at him without replying and asked for further explanation.

"It means," persisted Natera, "that the Convention[8] does not recognize Carranza as First Chief and is going to elect a Provisional President of the Republic. Do you understand, *compañero*?"

Demetrio nodded his head in assent.

"What do you say to that, *compañero*?" inquired Natera.

Demetrio shrugged his shoulders.

"It seems to me that we keep on fighting. Good, then let's do it. You know, General, that on my side there's no way out."

"All right, but whose side are you going to support?"

In great perplexity, Demetrio raised his hands and scratched his head for a few moments.

"Look, don't ask me any questions. I had no schooling. You gave me the little eagle that I've got on my sombrero. Well, then, now you know all you got to do is tell me, 'Demetrio, do this and this'— and that's all there is to it!"

Part III

I

El Paso, Texas, May 16, 1915

My dear Venancio:

I have not been able before now to answer your letter of January this year because my professional duties take up all my time. As you already know, I was graduated last December. I was sorry to hear about the fate of Pancracio and Manteca, but it did not surprise me that they stabbed one another on account of a game of cards. It is a pity; they were men of courage. I am grieved not to be able to communicate with Margarito in order to express my fervent congratulations upon the most noble and admirable act of his life—that of committing suicide!

I think it would be difficult, my dear friend Venancio, for you to obtain here in the United States the medical degree to which you aspire even though you have accumulated sufficient gold and silver to pay for it. I esteem you highly, Venancio, and I believe you are worthy of a better fate. Now then, an idea occurs to me that would benefit our mutual interests and the proper ambition you have to improve your social position. In partnership you and I could have a very nice business. It is true that for the moment I have no cash reserve, for I used it all up in pursuing my studies and setting up my office; but I can count on something much more valuable than money: my exceptional knowledge of this city, of its needs and of the sorts of businesses that would surely succeed here. We could open a genuine Mexican restaurant with you appearing as the proprietor and with the two of us dividing the profits at the end of each month. And there is something of much interest to us both: your social advancement. I remember that you play the guitar very well, and I think it would be easy through my recommendations and your musical knowledge to get you admitted to membership in the Salvation Army, a very respectable society which would give you much prestige.

Don't hesitate, my dear Venancio; come at once and bring your funds and we will make ourselves rich in a very short time. Please convey my affectionate regards to the General, to Anastasio, and my other friends.

Your affectionate friend,
Luis Cervantes

Venancio had just finished reading the letter for the hundredth time, and, sighing, he repeated his comment,

"That *curro* really knows his way around."

"What I can't get through my head," observed Anastasio Montañés, "is why we have to keep on fighting. Haven't we finished that business with the Federation?"

Neither the General nor Venancio answered; but those words continued to beat on their dull minds like a hammer on an anvil.

The long strides of the mules carried the men up the hill. They rode pensively, their heads drooping. Stubborn and restless, Anastasio made this same comment to another group of soldiers who laughed at his simplicity. If one carried a gun in his hands and cartridges in his belt, surely they were for fighting. Against whom? For whom? That never made any difference to anyone!

The interminable column of dust floating in the air stretched in both directions along the trail over an ant-like procession of straw hats, old dirty khakis, drab blankets, and the dark mass of the moving horses.

They were burning with thirst. Not a puddle, not a well, not a little stream of water along the entire way. Heat waves rose up from the white uncultivated fields of the valley, and quivered over the curly tops of the huisache trees and the clumps of pale-green prickly-pear. Like a mockery, the cactus flowers were newly opened, some fleshy and bright as fire, others pointed and diaphanous.

At noon they came across a hut clinging to a crag of the mountain, then three more strung along the sandbank of a river; but all were abandoned and silent. As the troops had drawn near, the people had hurried to hide in the gorges.

Demetrio became angry.

"Anybody you find hiding or running away, grab them and bring them to me," he ordered the soldiers in a harsh voice.

"What? What did you say?" exclaimed Valderrama, surprised. "Men of the sierra? Brave men who have not imitated the chickens who are making their nests in Zacatecas and Aguascalientes? Our own brothers, who have braved the storms to cling to these rocks like moss? I protest, I protest!"

Spurring his miserable nag in the flanks, he rode forward to catch up with the General.

"The men of the sierra," he said emphatically and solemnly, "are flesh of our flesh and bone of our bone. *'Os ex osibus meis et caro de carne mea:'*[9] The men of the sierra are made of the same timber we are. It's the stout timber that heroes are made of."

And with a self-confidence that was as impetuous as it was spirited, he punched the General in the chest with his closed fist. The General smiled indulgently.

Did Valderrama, the tramp, crazy and bit of a poet, know what he was saying?

When the soldiers reached a little settlement, they eddied about the empty houses and huts despondently without finding even a hard tortilla or a rotten *chile*, or even a few grains of salt to rub on the fresh meat they were so tired of. Watching from their hiding places were countrymen who had not gone out to fight, some with the stony impassivity of Aztec idols, others more human with enigmatic smiles on their oily, beardless lips. They saw how those fierce men, who a month before had violently attacked their scattered, miserable homes, now depressed and humiliated, came out of their huts where the ovens were cold and the water tanks were dry—their heads hanging like those of dogs kicked out of their own houses.

The general would not countermand his order and some soldiers brought to him four tightly bound fugitives.

II

"Why are you hiding?" Demetrio asked the prisoners.

"We're not hiding; we're just following our trail."

"Where?"

"To our country—Nombre de Dios, Durango."

"Is this the road to Durango?"

"Peaceful people can't go by main roads now. You know that, chief."

"You're not really ones who aren't fighting; you're deserters. Where do you come from?" persisted Demetrio watching them sharply.

The prisoners became disturbed; they looked at each other in perplexity without finding a ready reply.

"They're *carrancistas*!" one of the soldiers observed.

The prisoners instantly recovered their fortitude. The terrible enigma posed for them from the first by the unknown troops no longer existed.

"Us *carrancistas*!" replied one of them haughtily. "We'd rather be pigs!"

"It's the truth, we're deserters," said another. "We got cut off from General Villa this side of Celaya, after the skinning they gave us."

"General Villa defeated? Ha! Ha! Ha!"

The soldiers laughed uproariously. Demetrio, however, frowned as though a black cloud had passed before his eyes.

"The son of a — isn't born yet who can defeat General Villa!" proudly exclaimed a coppery faced veteran with a scar from his forehead to his chin.

Without altering his expression, one of the deserters stared fixedly, saying,

"I know who you are. When we took Torreón, you were with General Urbina. In Zacatecas you came with Natera and there you joined the troops from Jalisco. So?"

The effect was abrupt and conclusive. The prisoners were able to give a detailed account of the tremendous defeat of Villa in Celaya.

They listened, silent and stupefied.

Before resuming their march, they built fires to roast some meat. Anastasio Montañés, who looked for firewood among the huisache trees, saw some distance away among the rocks the cropped mane of Valderrama's little horse.

"Come here, you loon, we haven't massacred anybody yet," he began to call out.

Valderrama, that romantic poet, always disappeared for the whole day when there was any talk of shooting. He heard Anastasio's voice and must have been convinced that the prisoners had been set free, for in a few minutes he appeared near Venancio and Demetrio.

"You heard the news?" Venancio said to him very seriously.

"I don't know a thing."

"Very bad! A disaster! Villa defeated in Celaya by Obregón. Carranza's winning everywhere. We're all washed up!"

Valderrama's gesture was as disdainful and as solemn as an emperor's,

"Villa? Obregón? Carranza? X, Y, Z! What difference does it make to me? I love the Revolution the way I love an erupting volcano!

The volcano because it is a volcano; the Revolution because it is the Revolution! But the stones left above or below after the cataclysm, what do they matter to me?"

There shone on his forehead the reflection from a white bottle of tequila as bright as the noonday sun. With rejoicing in his heart, he turned his horse around abruptly toward the bearer of such marvelous news.

"I sort of like that loon," said Demetrio smiling, "because he sometimes says things that make you stop and think."

As they resumed their march their uneasiness was translated into a gloomy silence. The other catastrophe was silently but inevitably dawning on them: a defeated Villa was a fallen god. Fallen gods are no longer gods; they are nothing.

Cordoniz expressed the feelings of all of them,

"Well, that's it boys—each spider to its own web."

III

The people of one of the little towns they came upon, like those of other settlements, *ranchos*, and villages, had left to go to Zacatecas and Aguascalientes. Consequently, the discovery of a barrel of tequila assumed the proportions of a miracle. Profound secrecy and much mystery surrounded the plan for the troop to assemble early the next morning at a command of Anastasio Montañés and Venancio. When Demetrio awakened at the sound of music, his staff, now composed for the most part of young ex-Federals, informed him of the discovery. Cordoniz, interpreting the thoughts of his colleagues, said laconically,

"Times are bad and we got to take advantage of what turns up, because 'some days the duck's got enough water to swim in, but some days he lacks enough to drink.' "

The string musicians played all day and paid solemn respect to the barrel. Demetrio, however, remained very sad, "Without knowing why, nor do I know why," and kept muttering the refrain under his breath.

In the afternoon there were cockfights. Demetrio and his chief officers sat under the shed over the little door to the municipal building which fronted on an immense weed-covered plaza, an antiquated and dilapidated kiosk, and some isolated adobe houses.

"Valderrama!" cried Demetrio, wearily turning his eyes from the ring, "come sing 'The Gravedigger' to me."

Valderrama did not hear him, for instead of watching the cock-fighting, he was standing watching the sun setting behind the hills, reciting a dramatic monologue with emphatic voice and solemn gestures,

"Lord! Lord! how good it is for us to be here! I will raise three tents—one for Thee, one for Moses, and the other for Elijah."

"Valderrama!" Demetrio cried again. "Come sing 'The Grave-digger' to me."

"Loony, the General's calling you," one of the officers closest to him shouted.

With his eternal complacent smile on his lips, giving in to the request, he asked one of the musicians for a guitar.

"Be quiet!" shouted the gamblers.

Valderrama finished tuning his guitar. Cordoniz and Meco let loose in the arena a pair of cocks armed with long, exceedingly sharp blades. One cock was almost black with the beautiful iridescence of obsidian; the other, the golden one, had feathers like scales of copper, glowing with a fiery sheen.

The fight, over in a few moments, had the ferocity of men duel-ing. Moving as though on springs, the roosters hurled themselves into the contest. With their necks rigidly curved, eyes coral red, combs erect, feet contracted, for an instant they were suspended in the air with feathers, beaks, claws in one confused mass. The dark one gave way and hurled back with its feet beyond the bounds of the arena. Its leathery eyelids, as they slowly closed, extinguished the vermillion of its eyes. Its ruffled plumage vibrated convulsively in a puddle of blood.

After a gesture of violent indignation which he could not sup-press, Valderrama began to play. His anger dissipated with the first solemn notes. His eyes glittered like eyes in which the gleam of mad-ness shines. Glancing over the wide plaza, the tumbled-down kiosk, the huddle of old houses with the mountains in the background, and the flaming sky like a roof overhead, he began to sing.

He knew how to put so much feeling in his voice and to evoke so much expression from the strings of his guitar that when he finished Demetrio had to turn his head so that no one could see his eyes.

Valderrama threw himself into Demetrio's arms and embraced him vigorously. With that unexpected boldness with which he knew how to address everyone at the appropriate moment, he whispered in his ear,

"Drink those tears! They are beautiful!"

Demetrio asked for the bottle and passed it to Valderrama.

In almost one gulp Valderrama greedily drank half its contents. Turning to his listeners, his eyes staring, he announced with dramatic stance and declamatory voice,

"I have here all the great pleasures of the Revolution summed up in one tear!"

He continued in an irrational vein about everything, about the dusty weeds, the broken-down kiosk, the dirty gray houses, the lofty hill, and the immeasurable sky in the background.

IV

White and bathed in sunlight, Juchipila rose up in the distance from the midst of foliage at the base of a high and imposing hill folded like a turban.

As they saw the little church towers of Juchipila, some of the soldiers sighed with sadness. Their march through the canyons was now the march of blind ones without a guide; now they felt the bitterness of their leaving.

"Is that village Juchipila?" asked Valderrama.

Valderrama, in the beginning of the first drunken spree of the day, had been counting crosses scattered along the roads and trails, in the hollows among the rocks, on the rough edges of the arroyos, and the banks of the river. Crosses of black wood newly varnished, crosses formed of two pieces of firewood, crosses of piled-up rocks, crosses painted with lime on ruined walls, humble crosses traced with charcoal on the faces of boulders. Tokens of the spilled blood of the first revolutionaries of 1910, of those treacherously killed by the government. On catching sight of Juchipila, Valderrama threw himself on the ground, bowed, then kneeled and gravely kissed the earth. The soldiers passed by without stopping. Some laughed at the crack-brain, others made some slighting remarks.

Valderrama, deaf to everyone, prayed his solemn prayer,

"Juchipila, cradle of the Revolution of 1910, blessed earth, earth sprinkled with the blood of martyrs, with the blood of dreamers—of the only good ones!"

"Only because they didn't have time to be bad," an ex-Federal officer who was passing, rudely completed his sentence.

On being interrupted, Valderrama reflected, frowned, burst into sonorous laughter that echoed among the rocks, galloped up to the officer and asked for a swig of tequila.

One-armed soldiers, cripples, rheumatics, and consumptives spoke bitterly of Demetrio. Upstart townsmen had brass bars on their hats before they even knew how to hold a gun, while veteran riflemen of a hundred battles, now unfit for work, who had begun as privates were still privates.

The few officers who remained of Macías' old comrades were angry because many on his staff were wealthy young men, perfumed and exquisitely dressed.

"But worst of all," said Venancio, "is that we're overrun with ex-Federals."

Anastasio himself, who usually thought highly of everything his *compadre* Demetrio did but was now making common cause with the discontented, exclaimed,

"Look here, fellows, I'm real plain-spoken. I'll tell my *compadre* that if we're always going to have these Federals around, we're in a bad way. That's right! Don't you believe me? I'm not afraid to speak up, for the life of the mother who bore me, that's what I'll tell Demetrio."

And he did tell him. Demetrio listened to him indulgently, then when he finished speaking, replied,

"What you say is right. We're in a bad way. The soldiers gripe about the officers, officers about the officials, and officials about us. And we are all about ready to send Villa and Carranza to — and may they amuse themselves there. But I guess that it's the same way with us as it was with that peon of Tepatitlán. Remember him, Anastasio? He never stopped grumbling about his boss but he never stopped working either. It's the same with us: we gripe and gripe some more, and kill and kill some more. But that has nothing to do with it, *compadre*."

"Why, Demetrio?"

"I don't exactly know why. Because we—do you understand me now? What ought to be done is to get the people aroused. I got orders to return and stop a band of men coming through Cuquío. Within a few days we're sure to have a run-in with the *carrancistas*, and now we've got to give them a beating."

Valderrama, the vagabond of the highways who had joined Demetrio's troop one day without anybody's knowing exactly when or where he came from, fished up an idea from Demetrio's words. Since no madman eats fire, Valderrama that very day disappeared the same way he had arrived.

V

They entered the streets of Juchipila as the church bells rang merrily, loudly, and with that peculiar timbre which shook all the people of the sierra with emotion.

"I like to imagine that we are back in the days when the revolution had just begun, when we'd come to some little settlement the people would welcome us with music, flags, many cheers, and even with fireworks," said Anastasio Montañés.

"Now, they don't care anything about us," answered Demetrio.

"Yes, since we come back all beat up!" observed Cordoniz.

"That's not it. They don't want to see the others either, not even if their faces were on religious pictures."

"Why should they like us, *compadre?*"

Nothing more was said. They entered the plaza in front of a rustic, massive octagonal church which was a relic of colonial times. The plaza probably had been a garden, judging by the miserable, diseased orange trees planted among the remains of iron and wood benches.

He listened again to the sonorous and rejoicing peal of the bells. Just then with melancholy solemnity there poured from the church the mellifluous voices of a woman's chorus. The young ladies of the village were singing the "Mysteries" to the accompaniment of a guitar.

"What is the fiesta today, lady?" Venancio asked an old woman who was running as hard as she could toward the church.

"The Sacred Heart of Jesus!" answered the pious old woman in a half-choked voice.

They recalled that it was just one year ago they had taken
Zacatecas. They all became sadder than ever.

Just like all the other towns they had come through from Tepic by
way of Jalisco, Aguascalientes, and Zacatecas, Juchipila was in ruins.
Black traces of fire could be seen in the unroofed houses, in the burned
parapets. Houses shut up, yet here and there a store was open for
business as if to show in bitter irony its empty shelves which called to
mind the white skeletons of horses scattered along the roads. The
dreadful grimace of hunger was on the dirty faces of the people; in
their eyes a luminous flame which burned with the fire of malediction
when it fell on a soldier.

The soldiers scoured the streets in vain in search of food and they
bit their tongues in their burning rage. One little lunch room was open
but was closed immediately. There were no beans, no tortillas, only
chopped *chile* and coarse salt. In vain the chiefs offered their pockets
full of bills or became threatening.

"Paper money, yes! That's what you have brought us! Well then,
eat it!" said the innkeeper, a big, old insolent woman with an enormous
scar on her face who told them, "I've already slept on the straw
mat of the dead and nothing else can scare me."

In the sadness and desolation of the town, while the women sang
in the church, linnets in the dry branches of the orange trees chirped
ceaselessly.

VI

Demetrio Macías' wife, delirious with joy, went out to meet him
on the mountain trail, the little boy going along holding her hand.

An absence of almost two years!

They stood mute in a warm embrace; sobs and tears overcame
her. Demetrio was stunned to see how his wife had aged—as though
ten or twenty years instead of two had passed. The little boy looked
at him with bewilderment in his eyes. Demetrio's heart leaped when
he observed the reproduction of the steely lines of his own countenance and the flaming brilliance of his eyes. He wanted to draw
the child to himself and embrace him, but the little one was very
frightened and turned his face against his mother.

"He's your father, son! He's your father!"

The child, still shy, hid his head in the folds of his mother's skirt.

Demetrio, who had turned his horse over to his orderly, walked slowly along the steep mountain trail with his wife and son.

"Now that you're actually here, thank God you have come! You'll never leave us, will you? You will stay with us, won't you?"

Demetrio's face grew somber. The two of them were silent and anguished. A black cloud rose back of the mountain and thunder roared deafeningly. Demetrio repressed a sigh. His memory was a bee-hive of recollections.

Big drops of rain began to fall and they took refuge in a small cave in the rocks. Accompanied by thunder, the heavy shower scattered the white petals of the San Juan roses which were like clusters of stars in the trees, on the rocks, among the low bushes, in the pitahayos, and all over the mountain country.

In the bottom of the canyon and through the gauze of the rain they could see the tall, waving, palm-like trees with their angular heads swaying and their leaves opening like fans in the gusts of wind. The whole prospect was mountainous: one long row of hills beyond another, more hills bound by mountains and enclosed by a wall of peaks so high that the blueness of their summits was lost in the sapphire sky.

"Demetrio, for God's sake! Don't go away! My heart tells me that if you do something will happen!"

She began to shake again with sobs. The frightened child began to cry loudly. She had to control her great grief in order to quiet him.

The rain slackened. A swallow with a silvery breast and pointed wings slanted through the crystal strands of rain which were suddenly illuminated by the afternoon sun.

"What are they fighting for now, Demetrio?"

Demetrio, frowning, picked up a stone absent-mindedly and cast it into the depths of the canyon. Pensively he gazed into the defile and said, "See how that rock keeps on falling—falling."

VII

Truly it was a morning made for a wedding. It had rained from the evening before all through the night. The morning sky dawned with puffs of white clouds across its face. Along the mountain ridges wild young colts trotted, their manes flying and tails streaming, proud with the pride of the peaks that raised their heads high enough to kiss the clouds.

The soldiers journeyed along the steep rocky way infected by the splendor of the morning. No one thought about the treacherous bullet that might be waiting for him farther ahead. The great joy of the game rests entirely in the unforeseen. Consequently, the soldiers sang, laughed, and chattered wildly. In their souls stirred the souls of the old, nomadic tribes. It was not necessary to know where they were going or where they came from. All that mattered was to keep on going, always going, never stopping; to be masters of the valley, of the plains, of the mountains, of all the eye could embrace.

The trees, cacti, and ferns looked as though they had just been washed. Large drops of water dripped from the rocks, which were streaked with ocher like old armor with rust.

Demetrio's men fell silent for a moment. They thought they heard a familiar sound: a burst of firing in the distance. But several minutes passed and there was no repetition of the sound.

"In this very mountain range," said Demetrio, "I, along with twenty men, downed more than five hundred Federals."

When Demetrio began to talk about that famous engagement the men began to realize the grave danger they were facing. What if the enemy instead of being two days' journey distant turned out to be hidden in the underbrush of that formidable narrow ravine into whose depth they had ventured? But who could afford to show his fear? When had Demetrio's men said: "We won't go this way!"

When firing began in the distance engaging the vanguard, no one was in the least surprised. The recruits turned about in unrestrained flight seeking the way out of the canyon.

A curse escaped Demetrio's dry throat.

"Fire! Shoot anyone running away!"

"Drive out the ones on the heights!" he roared later like a wild beast.

But the thousands of the hidden enemy opened fire with their machine guns and Demetrio's men fell like wheat before the scythe.

Demetrio shed tears of rage and pain when Anastasio slipped slowly from his horse and fell stretched out on the ground without uttering a sound. Venancio fell by his side with his breast horribly riddled by machine gun bullets. Meco fell over the precipice and rolled into the depth of the abyss. Suddenly Demetrio found himself alone. Bullets zoomed by his ears like hail. He dismounted, crawled over the rocks until he found a natural parapet, placed a rock to protect his head, and, lying with his chest to the ground, began to fire.

The enemy scattered to pursue the few fugitives remaining hidden in the bushes.

Demetrio fired without wasting a single shot. Ssst! Ssst! Ssst! His famous marksmanship filled him with joy. Where he directed his eyes, his bullet followed. He finished that round, reloaded his gun and took aim.

The smoke of the firing was still hanging in the air. Locusts sounded their imperturbable and mysterious song; from crannies in the rocks doves sang lyrically; cows placidly grazed.

The mountain range displayed its fairest aspect. Over its inaccessible peaks the brilliantly white clouds fell like a snowy veil over the head of a bride.

At the foot of a great hollow as impressive as the portico of an old cathedral, Demetrio Macías, with his eyes forever fixed, continued to aim the barrel of his rifle.

THE TRIALS OF A RESPECTABLE FAMILY

The Book of Bitter Hours

[1]A title which the Mexican government officially bestowed on Benito Juárez.

[2]A low expression of various figurative meanings, such as "fate," "luck," "pride." The expression could mean: "You are being led by the nose." As used here possible meaning too vulgar for translation.

[3]For making a sort of tea.

[4]A newspaper published in México, D. F., which supported Carranza.

[5]A tribe of Indians of the state of Sonora who were followers of Villa.

[6]There is an humble shrine near México, D. F., dedicated to the *Virgen de los Remedios.*

[7]Psalms 25:6.

[8]A periodical published in México, D. F., favorable to Carranza.

[9]Job 5:26.

[10]Carranza. He was born at Cuatro Ciénegas.

[11]Name of a socially prominent family in the Díaz regime.

[12]Carranza.

Procopio's Victory

[1]A newspaper published in México, D. F., favorable to Carranza.

[2]A newspaper published in México, D. F., which until 1913 favored Huerta.

[3]Félix Díaz and Bernardo Reyes.

[4]The Arsenal in México, D. F., where the uprising against Madero, February 13, 1913, began.

[5]The revolution of the Plan of Tuxtepec of Porfirio Díaz, 1876.

[6]Mexico's penal islands.

[7]Government pawnshop.

THE UNDERDOGS

[1]The first is a novel by Marie Joseph Sué (Eugène), French novelist of nineteenth century; the second, a novel by Juan Antonio Mateos, Mexican novelist of the same era.

[2]Huerta.

[3]*"La Adelita"*—a song popular with the revolutionaries.

[4]See note 4, "Procopio's Victory."

[5]A conservative newspaper published in México, D. F.

[6]A conservative newspaper published in Guadalajara, Jalisco.

[7]Bills printed with the representation of the face of Abram González on one side and Madero on the other.

[8]Convention at Aguascalientes, October, 1914, under control of Villa.

[9]Genesis 2:23.

GLOSSARY

aguardiente—brandy, whisky.

cacique—a local boss or chief.

caciquismo—system of subjugation of the people of a locality to the *cacique*.

cajeta—a confection of milk and sugar.

cantina—bar.

caramba—expletive.

carrancismo—system pertaining to Carranza.

catrín—a dressed-up dandy.

centavos—one-hundreth part of a *peso*.

científicos—a particular group of intellectuals and businessmen who supported Porfirio Díaz.

cofradía—a religious organization.

compadre—associate, companion, partner.

compañeros—companions, buddies.

Constitutionalist—follower of Carranza, Villa, Zapata, or Obregón.

curro—a derogatory term used by the countryman to express his contempt for the "city slicker." A *curro*, according to a saying in Mexico, would do without a beefsteak to buy a cravat. A dude, a well-dressed person.

chalupa—small launch; two-man canoe.

champurrao—localism for *champurrado*, a chocolate-flavored porridge.

charamuscas—candy twisted in the shape of a corkscrew.

charro—young man wearing elegant, elaborately decorated apparel.

chile—pepper. There are numerous varieties of edible peppers in Mexico.

chomite—a type of homespun skirt worn by Indian women of the sierra.

Federals—followers of Victoriano Huerta.

gorda—a thick sort of tortilla.

hacendado—ranch owner.

hidalgo—equivalent to a ten-dollar gold piece.

huaraches—sandals; footwear of the poor.

Jefe de la plaza—chief official in the town government.

mano—stone roller used to crush, by hand, corn, etc., on the *metate*.

metate—slightly concave stone resting on three short legs (*tenamastres*). Used for crushing corn, etc.

mescal (mezcal)—alcoholic liquor made from the maguey plant.

mocho, mochito—a term of derision applied by country people to townsmen; a term that had been applied to reactionaries in the War of the Reform (1857-1860); applied to followers of Huerta.

pelado—peon, used disparagingly.

pelón—Federal soldiers who were distinguished by short hair cuts. The term is derogatory.

peseta—twenty-five *centavos*.

peso—coin worth (1915) about twenty-seven cents; equal to a hundred *centavos*.

pilón—something extra; lagniappe.

pitahayo (*pitayo*)—a species of cactus (*Cereus variablis.*)

pulque—a liquor made from the maguey of lesser alcholic content than mescal.

rancho, ranchito—small group of humble dwellings out in the country.

ranchero—belonging to or pertaining to the *rancho.*

reata—rope for tying a horse or mule.

reboso—a long scarf.

rose of Castille—a wild red rose (*Lippis callicarpaefolia.*)

rose of San Juan—a wild white rose (*Bouvardia longiflora.*)

serape—a gaily colored rectangle of woolen cloth used as a covering.

serrana—woman of the mountain country.

Spanish fly—a preparation made from an insect believed to be an aphrodisiac.

tequila—an alcoholic liquor made from various species of the agave.

tenamastres—the short supports on which the *metate* rests.

Barrón, Medina—a general of Huerta's forces.

Blanquet, Aureliano—a general who served under Díaz, Madero, and Huerta. Involved in the plot to overthrow and assassinate Madero. Minister of War in Huerta's government.

Cabrera, Luis—writer, publicist, supporter of Carranza.

Carranza, Venustiano—leader of forces against Huerta. President of Mexico, 1917-1920.

Carranzo—A mistake in pronunciation by which Pancracio reveals his ignorance of the revolution of which he is a part.

Carrera Torres, Francisco S.—a general in the forces opposing Huerta.

Díaz, Félix—nephew of Porfirio Díaz. Plotted against Madero. Later participated in overthrow of Huerta.

Díaz, Porfirio—President of Mexico, 1880-1884; 1887-1911.

Díaz Mirón, Salvador—eminent poet of the state of Veracruz.

González, Abram—organizer of supporters of Madero in state of Chihuahua; later governor of that state.

González, Pablo—general who was a follower of Carranza.

Huerta, Victoriano—leader of forces which overthrew Madero; President of Mexico, 1913-1914.

Limantour, José Yves—Minister of Finance during regime of Porfirio Díaz.

Madero, Francisco I.—initiator of the Revolution; President of Mexico, 1911-1913; known in Mexican history as *El Redentor.*

Medina, Julián—a general in Villa's forces.

Natera, Pánfilo—a general in Villa's forces.

Noriega, Íñigo—an intimate friend of Porfirio Díaz.

Obregón, Álvaro—a general in Carranza's forces; President of Mexico, 1920-1924.

Orozco, Pascual—a general in Huerta's forces.

Ortiz de Domínquez, Doña Josefa—"*La Corregidora,*" a heroine of the War of Independence.

Plaza, Antonio—a popular Mexican poet of the nineteenth century.

Reyes, Bernardo—an officer in Porfirio Díaz's forces.

Robles, Crispín—a leader of forces opposed to Huerta.

Urbina, Tomás R.—an officer in Villa's forces.

Vicario, Doña Leona—heroine of the era of the War of Independence; wife of Quintana Roo, champion of independence.

Villa, Francisco (Pancho)—pseudonym of Doroteo Arango; first a follower of Carranza; later his bitter enemy.

266

PLACE NAMES

Aguascalientes—capital city of the state of Aguascalientes. Location of the Revolutionary Convention of October, 1914, dominated by Villa.

Bufa, La—mountain near city of Zacatecas.

Celaya—town in the state of Guanajuato near which Obregón defeated Villa, April 15, 1915.

Ciudad Juárez—city in state of Chihuahua opposite El Paso, Texas.

Cuernavaca—capital city of the state of Morelos.

Cuquío—a town in the state of Jalisco.

Chihuahua—capital city of the state of Chihuahua.

Delmónico—restaurant in Chihuahua City.

Durango—a state in the northwest part of the Republic of Mexico.

Fresnillo—a city in the state of Zacatecas.

Grillo, El—mountain near the city of Zacatecas.

Guadalajara—capital city of Jalisco.

Guadalupe—suburb of México, D. F., which is the location of the shrine to the Virgin of Guadalupe.

Hill of Bells—place near Querétaro where Maximilian was executed.

Hostotipaquillo—a village in the state of Jalisco.

Irapuato—a city in the state of Guanajuato.

Jalisco—a state in the central part of the Republic of Mexico.

Jalpa—a town in the state of Zacatecas.

Juchipila—a small town in the state of Zacatecas; site of first conflict in revolt against Porfirio Díaz.

Lagos—a city in the state of Jalisco.

Limón—country village near Juchipila, Zacatecas.

Moyahua—a small town in the state of Zacatecas.

Nombre de Dios—a small town in the state of Durango.

Orizaba—a town in the state of Veracruz.

Parral—a city in the state of Chihuahua.

Salamanca—a town in the state of Guanajuato.

San Juan del Río—a town in the state of Querétaro.

San Luis Potosí—the capital city of the state of San Luis Potosí.

Santa Rosa—a village in the state of Zacatecas.

Silao—a city in the state of Guanajuato.

Tehuacán—a spa in the state of Puebla.

Tepatitlán—a town in the state of Jalisco.

Tepic—capital city of the state of Nayarit.

Tierra Blanca—a town in the state of Chihuahua.

Tlaxcala—capital city of the state of Tlaxcala.

Torreón—a city in the state of Chihuahua.

Zacatecas—the capital city of the state of Zacatecas.